A Child in the Storm

Emily Gunnis is the internationally bestselling author of five novels. Her novels have sold in twenty languages. Emily previously worked in TV drama and lives in South Wales with her family. She is one of the four daughters of the bestselling author Penny Vincenzi.

Also by Emily Gunnis

THE GIRL IN THE LETTER
THE MISSING DAUGHTER
THE MIDWIFE'S SECRET
THE GIRLS LEFT BEHIND
A CHILD IN THE STORM

A Child in the Storm

EMILY GUNNIS

REVIEW

The right of Emily Gunnis to be identified as the Author of the Work has been asserted by her in accordance with the Copyright, Designs and Patents Act 1988.

First published in 2025 by Headline Publishing Group Limited

1

Disclaimer: The author has made every effort to credit the owners of material quoted in this book. If your material has been used without the correct credit please contact us and we will update for the next edition.

Cataloguing in Publication Data is available from the British Library

Paperback ISBN 978 1 0354 1681 3

Typeset in 12.5/14.75pt Adobe Garamond Pro
by Six Red Marbles UK, Thetford, Norfolk

Printed and bound in Great Britain by Clays Ltd, Elcograf S.p.A.

MIX
Paper | Supporting
responsible forestry
FSC® C104740

Headline's policy is to use papers that are natural, renewable and recyclable products and made from wood grown in well-managed forests and other controlled sources. The logging and manufacturing processes are expected to conform to the environmental regulations of the country of origin.

Headline Publishing Group Limited
An Hachette UK Company
Carmelite House
50 Victoria Embankment
London EC4Y 0DZ

The authorised representative in the EEA is Hachette Ireland,
8 Castlecourt Centre, Dublin 15, D15 XTP3, Ireland (email: info@hbgi.ie)

www.headline.co.uk
www.hachette.co.uk

This book is dedicated to my sisters, Polly Harding, Sophie Cornish and Claudia Vincenzi.

'I could never love anyone as I love my sisters'
From Little Women *by Louisa May Alcott*

A woman in Russia is the same as myself, the same emotions, leading the same sort of life. In no way will I be part of anything that will murder her.

Sarah, Greenham Peace Camp,
'The Greenham Factor', Rebecca Johnson

Prologue
Rachel

2 April 1983

As dawn broke after the most testing night shift of her career, WPC Rachel Rees slammed the door of the police van on the twelve women handcuffed inside and let out an exhausted sigh.

Slowly she turned away and began walking wearily to the driver's side, her neck, shoulders and back aching from a night of dragging dozens of women across the frozen concrete, out of the path of the transportation trucks loaded with cruise missiles arriving at their final destination: the military base at Greenham Common, in the heart of the English countryside.

Rachel reached out to open the police van driver's door, then stopped and looked back at the scene that she had found hard to comprehend when she'd arrived twelve hours earlier. Fifty thousand women holding hands, completely surrounding the nine-mile perimeter fence of Greenham Common. Each of them using mirrors to reflect the base, and those guarding it, back on itself. Singing to keep up their spirits, as they had done throughout the entire bitterly cold April night, each one forming a link in a human chain and encircling the military base that was soon to become home to eighty of Ronald Reagan's cruise missiles.

Rachel ran her eyes along the human chain; their mirrors,

lighters and torches twinkling in the misty morning glow, while flags and banners, as far as her eye could see, fluttered in the icy wind: 'Peace on Earth', 'Greenham Common Peace Camp', 'Nuclear Free', 'CND'. Large barrels every hundred yards with the words 'rice', 'pasta' and 'beans' painted on them in white. An oil drum in the distance, a stubborn fire struggling to stay alight in the cold dawn after a night of rain. Handmade tapestries, adorned with pictures of doves, hearts and peace symbols woven into the wire fence, alongside poems, ribbons, photos and flowers. One woman had even tied her wedding dress to the fence, many others, their children's baby grows and photographs, each a constant reminder of what they were fighting for.

Rachel had spent an increasing amount of time at the camp over the months, as the presence of the women at Greenham Common became more and more of a problem for her male superiors: her sergeant, her chief inspector, her chief superintendent, the commander and commissioner of Thames Valley Police – all the way up to Michael Heseltine, the Secretary of State for Defence. It hadn't been easy witnessing the women suffering the horrendous conditions, visibly shaking from the cold in the terrible weather and huddled together as any supplies, tents, sleeping bags or blankets were confiscated almost daily by West Berkshire Council. The locals had banned the women from using their pubs, cafés or facilities, shouting abuse and hurling all manner of disgusting concoctions at them, including pig's blood and cow slurry. In summer it was easier, but in winter it was spirit crushing. There would be large pieces of plastic sheeting, tied with string and propped up with branches, under which the protestors would shelter,

2

often in the rain, sleet or snow, just managing to survive until morning.

Over the past year Rachel had arrested hundreds of women for obstruction of the highway and criminal damage. They would lie for hours on the freezing cold roads, making a human blockade so that the trucks couldn't enter the site. As she had done several times already that night, she would put twelve women inside the individual cells in her van, to stop them going straight back to lie down on the road again or, worse, to climb on top of the lorries. Now the nuclear weapons were actually being shipped in, tensions had increased. Her superiors were frantic: 'These are nuclear missiles. You can't have them being stopped in the middle of the road so those women can clamber on the lorries.'

Arresting them all was a long-drawn-out, expensive process, which, with fifty thousand women, felt insurmountable: unloading them one by one at the station – or at Newbury Racecourse where they had set up marquees to cope with the pressure – each one having her photograph and finger-prints taken, the custody sergeant recording what she'd done, her name, address and medical history. Then each would be checked in and put in a cell, sometimes waiting on her solicitor before she could be interviewed, charged and given her bail sheet to be processed at the magistrates' court.

Some of the women Rachel had arrested had gone to prison for refusing to pay the fines they had been given at court or for cutting through the fences and causing criminal damage. They found the only way to get press coverage was to make a mockery of Michael Heseltine's claim that the base was secure by gaining access to the control tower or the nuclear weapons themselves.

For the first year Rachel and her colleagues had worked hard at their relationship with the women. But press coverage was making the government look powerless to remove them and the police had changed tack. There was a large police presence now, police whom Rachel didn't know, who had been trained to use violence to deal with the miners' strikes.

The atmosphere between the police and the women was growing increasingly strained.

'Think next time you want to make a nuisance of yourself, you stupid bitch.' Rachel pushed back the memories of daybreak, when she had been forced to intervene. A male colleague had decided to drag one young girl by her ears, which had made her scream out in pain. Rachel had winced in horror, and rushed over.

'Graham!' she had called out. 'Graham! I'll take this one. I've got one more slot in my van.' Rachel had prised the girl away from him, until eventually he had released his grip.

'She's a fucking slag, this one – scratched my face. Don't let her get away,' he said, glaring at her.

'I won't,' Rachel said firmly.

'Please let me go,' the girl with green eyes had pleaded with her. 'I need to help my friend. Please! She has a baby – she needs me. Please let me go!' She had screamed at Rachel, thrashing and twisting to get away.

'Calm down!' Rachel had forced the girl to the ground, handcuffing her to try to protect herself before loading the girl into a cell in her van.

Whilst most of her colleagues tried to treat the women with care and respect, some had resorted to causing pain, kicking hard at their bodies as they lay on the ground and using force matched only by the strength of the women's resolve. The police had started to feel outnumbered and pressure was intense to keep the highway clear for the vehicles coming in.

It had been raining relentlessly all night: freezing rain that Rachel thought was determined to break her. It had finally stopped at dawn, and a pink sky had flooded the horizon, marking an end to her night of hell. Handcuffed, the green-eyed girl had gone limp, so that for Rachel it was like dragging a corpse into the van as her back screamed at her to stop.

Rachel climbed into the driver's seat and a grey-haired lady in a yellow shawl, sitting on the frozen ground next to her police van, caught her eye. She looked as weary as Rachel felt, and Rachel's eyes fell to a muddied sheet of paper on the ground, advertising the time and place of the event. It was still staggering what the women had achieved. She had overheard them talking at the start of her shift. 'Five women phoned five women, and those women phoned five women. We had no idea how many were going to turn up until the coaches started arriving this morning.' The elderly woman sat completely still, clutching a wooden board embossed with a printed poem. Rachel started the engine and read the unsettling words.

In the event of a nuclear war
There will be no chances
There will be no survivors

All will be obliterated
Nuclear devastation is not science fiction
The world now stands on the brink of the final abyss
Let us all resolve
To take all possible practical steps
To ensure that we do not, through our
Own folly, go over the edge.

Lord Mountbatten

Rachel had managed to stay composed during every long night shift and back-breaking arrest, until the event that finally broke her: the day the previous month when the trucks carrying the USA's medium-range missiles first arrived at Greenham. For the first time, the women had fallen silent – no chants, no songs, the only sound the roar of the trucks as the enormous weapons of mass destruction thundered past. She choked back tears as the women sobbed, expressing their profound grief for the two wasted years they had spent camped out in the bitter cold, leaving their children and husbands at home, living with little or no sleep, trying to keep their spirits up with campfires and singing, cold to the bone, no hope of hot showers, their bellies empty.

As Rachel turned the police van round and pulled out onto the main road, the women in the cells in the back began to sing, as they always did, in perfect harmony with one another.

Well, have you seen pictures of bodies all burnt
Imagine it's you and your family so hurt

We can stop the madness but we must do it now
So come down to Greenham
Take a fence down at Greenham
We won't move from Greenham
For time's running out.

Rachel let out a heavy sigh. It was undeniable that the Greenham women made her life harder, but they had her empathy. There was no doubt in her mind that the government's handling of the crisis had scared people. She and every home in the country had received the now infamous leaflet, giving instructions on what to do in the event of a nuclear attack. It had been swiftly followed by a government broadcast on the radio. Four minutes, they were told; four minutes to gather their loved ones, prop suitcases against the walls, stuffed with clothes or anything to help absorb the radiation, and hide as best they could under the stairs. Four minutes to say goodbye to their loved ones. One woman she had spoken to at Greenham had told her she would be unable to get to her children in time, a thought that had kept her awake at night and spurred her on to join other women, ones who thought that they were only good for nurturing and home-making, but who were now changing the world.

'Do whatever it takes to get those women out of there. They are making us look incompetent and we need to get them under control,' Rachel's superintendent had barked at her.

Rachel rolled her head around in a circle and let out a heavy sigh. Her back screamed in pain from dragging women away from the road, but there had been so many of them this time, too many to be able to cope with. Rachel and her colleagues were starting to suffer. They couldn't arrest fifty thousand women and they had started to discuss putting the women in cells for the night, but not charging them.

The atmosphere felt electric that night, in a way that it hadn't before, echoing the storm she had battled against for the entire shift. The balance of power had tipped. The women were starting to make up ground, take the upper hand, and it felt to Rachel as if the police were now on the back foot. A helicopter had thudded away overhead as her colleagues battled to prevent women breaking through the fences with bolt cutters, using ladders to scale the barbed-wire fences and run into the base to dance on top of the missile silos.

Rachel pulled up in front of Newbury police station, and looked around for anyone who might be able to help her escort all the women to the back of the station. Their singing always escalated in volume when they arrived there, as if to summon increased strength and resolve. Rachel reached for her radio and requested help, shouting to be heard over the women's voices.

We are women, we are women
We are strong, we are strong,
We say no, we say no
To the bomb, to the bomb.

Over and over they began to repeat the words as Rachel raised her voice above the cacophony.

'Requesting back up,' Rachel said. 'Need assistance escorting twelve females into Newbury station.'

She was instructed to wait, but the women were becoming stressed and they began banging on their cell doors. Nobody was available, everyone was stretched to the limit, she would just have to stay calm and take one at a time round to the back of the station, sign them in and get them into holding cells as quickly as she could. She took a deep breath and opened the van door. Her legs felt like lead, her body throbbed from exhaustion. As she walked round to the rear door and opened it, the increased volume of song from the women caused her headache to splinter.

'Come on, you first,' she said, as the green-eyed girl, barely out of her teens, looked up and, for a moment, their eyes met. She was caked from head to toe in mud, the tracks of her tears visible on her filthy face, the whites of her eyes sparkling as she shivered in the bitter cold. Rachel pulled her out of the police van cell, locked it again, and clung on to her tightly.

'Can you take the handcuffs off me, please? They are really hurting me,' the girl said.

'Excuse me . . .' The voice, a man's, behind her was faint, and it barely registered over the women singing.

Rachel ignored it, hoping the person wasn't talking to her, took the green-eyed girl by the arm and began walking her towards the station. It was bitterly cold, the coldest night of the year, she had been told, and she could barely feel her hands.

'Please, I won't try anything. They are cutting into me.' Rachel stared at the girl, who had a thick Welsh accent, trying to assess whether she could trust her, then slowly reached into her pocket, retrieved the key, and slid it into the small lock. *Click.*

'Excuse me!' The male voice, in a thick Welsh accent, called out, louder now. Rachel spun round and stopped in her tracks. A tall man – in his late thirties, she guessed – wearing a checked shirt, a thick cord jacket and a black woollen scarf was walking slowly towards her, carrying a large cardboard box.

'Yes?' She found herself snapping out of sheer exhaustion. 'Can I help you, sir?'

'I've found a baby abandoned this morning on St Phillip's church steps,' he said calmly.

Rachel froze, unable to take in what he was saying. At that moment, she felt the weight of the world on her shoulders. She had been up all night, she was soaked through, every inch of her body ached, she needed to process twelve Greenham women hammering on the side of her van, nobody was available to help her, and now she was being told there was a baby in a cardboard box requiring her urgent attention.

'I'm sorry – what?' she said, loosening her grip slightly on the girl with the green eyes, who in that split second took her opportunity. She violently yanked her arm away and before Rachel could even react, began running at full pelt towards the main road. Rachel watched her go, her legs heavy with weariness, her brain too exhausted to react.

She turned back to the man, taking a moment to transfer her focus onto him, before her eyes travelled down to the box he was carrying in his arms. Slowly she walked over and peered inside it. There, in a pink hand-knitted cardigan, matching mittens, and wrapped in a soft blanket, was the most beautiful baby she had ever seen. It had a flush of fair hair, a button nose and porcelain skin. It was breathing softly, its little belly rising and falling as it slept. She couldn't believe that the noise of the women singing and carrying on hadn't woken it, and that immediately worried her. They needed to get this baby out of the cold and to hospital, quickly.

'What is your name, sir?' Rachel asked, her eyes darting around for anyone who may be able to help her. Thankfully she spotted her colleague Constable Bill Bailey, who had been working at Greenham with her all night, walking into the station. She called out to him but the traffic noise meant he didn't hear her. She now had an emergency on her hands, as well as a van full of fractious, cold and hungry women kicking off.

'Howell, Howell Jenkins,' the man answered. He was tall and slim, with a warm smile and blue eyes that crinkled at the edges like Mr Mischief.

'Come with me, please. We need to get this baby into the warm and call an ambulance.'

Rachel led Howell inside. She walked past the queue at reception and spotted Bill, now behind the counter.

'Call an ambulance, Bill, quickly. We've got a foundling. Then I need your help checking a van full of women into custody.'

The young constable's eyes widened as he nodded and immediately picked up the phone.

Rachel turned back to Howell. 'Can I ask you a few questions about where you found the baby, sir?'

By now, Howell was sitting in reception with the box on his knee, clutching it tightly. He had a kind, wind-beaten face, and his hands were flushed from being exposed to the cold. Rachel crouched down next to him, went back to her notebook and began scribbling.

'The first I knew of it was a car starting up outside my window at around six. It woke me. I'm the caretaker at the church, so I live in the annexe next door. It's very quiet in the mornings; nobody is usually around until after eight.'

'This is St Phillip's? In Newbury?'

'Yes, that's right.'

'Did you get the registration?' Rachel enquired.

Howell shook his head. 'I was still not fully awake, but it sounded to me like a classic car of some sort. It had a guttural roar and whoever it was took off at quite a pace.' Rachel saw his hands were trembling. 'I did actually take a look, and I could see him pulling away. The car was bottle green, I think, possibly a Jaguar E-Type.'

'Him?'

'Yes, I'm pretty sure it was a man. He was wearing a shooting cap. Did you see there was an envelope in the box, with quite a large amount of money,' Howell said, handing it to her. Rachel looked down at the thick cream parchment paper, the word 'Emma' in slanted handwriting on the front in black ink.

She handed the money to Bill at reception. 'Can you bag this up, put it in the book and store it as evidence? I'll need a photo of the front of it, too. Someone might recognise the handwriting.'

'Will do,' he said, pulling a bag from behind the desk and putting it in, as Rachel dashed back to Howell.

'So she's called Emma,' Rachel said quietly to him.

Howell frowned and bit his lip. 'What will happen to

the baby? Poor bach,' he said in his Welsh lilt, glancing down at the tiny person. 'Why would anyone do this?'

'We will take her to the hospital to get her checked over,' Rachel said, making a note of what Howell had shared about the car. 'Then we will try and find her mother. She is well dressed, and obviously loved, so hopefully someone is missing her and will come forward.'

'I thought it was kittens at first. I went to open up the church as usual and saw the box on the top of the steps. I heard a faint squeaking sound and I thought somebody had dumped a litter. I couldn't believe it when I looked inside. She was so calm, not crying, just gurgling to herself, looking at the sky.'

'Ambulance is on its way,' Bill Bailey called out from behind the counter. 'Shall I start unloading the van?'

'Yes, please, Bill,' said Rachel, walking over to him and handing over her keys.

'How will they try and find the mother?' Howell asked, clutching the baby's makeshift crib tighter.

'They'll send CID – that's the criminal investigation department – to the hospital, take photos of her, make a note of all her clothing, and the box she's in. They'll speak to you again, no doubt. Then they'll contact the press to share the photos and all the information they have, to see if any member of the public knows anyone who was due to have a baby but doesn't have one now.'

'Oh, here, there was a tiepin in the box, a silver one, looks expensive,' Howell added, pleased with his detective work. He lifted it out and gave it to Rachel, who looked carefully at it. The initials EJM were engraved in slanted letters.

13

'Thank you, I'll make sure that gets passed on.'

Rachel could hear the ambulance sirens already. They always responded fast to calls about babies.

'Wait here, please,' she told Howell.

She watched Bill coming back in with the first of the Greenham women she had arrested that night. The green-eyed girl would probably be long gone, trying to hitch a lift back to camp by now. There was no point Rachel beating herself up: the women were on an endless conveyor belt and no doubt their paths would cross again.

The ambulance sirens were louder now, filling reception, as Rachel pulled her weary body up, and headed for the door to open it for the paramedics.

Within seconds there was a rush of activity. Cold air blasted through the door as two paramedics dashed in with a trolley and their bags. Rachel watched as they gently lifted the baby girl from her handmade crib and began tending to her, checking her vitals, and wrapping her up carefully in a foil blanket.

'Does she have a name?' one of the paramedics asked.

Rachel looked at Howell, who nodded his encouragement.

'Emma,' Rachel said as, at last, the tiny girl began to cry.

Chapter One

Adele

'Adele?'

'Yes?' said Adele, looking up at her boss, Simon, as he swept past her desk.

'Have you got a minute?' he asked, continuing into his office at the small estate agency at the entrance to the picturesque town of Thatcham in Berkshire.

'Sure,' Adele lied, jumping to her feet. The phones hadn't stopped all day, she had three offer letters still to type up, four property details to upload to Rightmove and she was meant to have left ten minutes ago.

She took a breath as her phone burst into life again, ignoring it in favour of Simon, the head of the family-run agency where she worked five days a week from ten until three.

'Take a seat.' He smiled warmly and sat down at his desk. Simon was a family man, with two sons he doted on, and a 'work hard, play hard' attitude. His wife, Gemma, was also an estate agent and worked in the office part-time, helping out during busier periods. But Gemma's first priority was home. Simon respected his wife immensely and spoke often about how amazing she was at keeping them all organised. Adele watched with envy the way Simon treated her, offering to help her at home when he could, encouraging the boys to be polite to her when they came in. They were a team and Adele knew Gemma had encouraged Simon to let Adele go part-time when she'd originally made the request the year before.

Adele felt her heart race as Simon pulled his chair up to his desk and immediately started to panic that he was about to let her go – or ask her to increase her hours again. She had worked at Thatcham Estates since Sophia had started primary school six years ago but, by and large, it had not been the experience she had hoped for. She knew a lot of mothers went back to work when their children started school, but it had been almost impossible to manage her ever-increasing workload with Sophia's occasional sick days, the cancelling of before- and after-school clubs and other mothers letting her down when it was their turn to do play dates. The cost of a nanny would have wiped out her salary entirely and she couldn't face the thought of a homesick teenage au pair in their house, making a mess and coming and going at all hours, particularly when they were trying to sell.

A lot of the working mums at school had help in the form of grandparents, but sadly that wasn't an option for her and Sophia. Alex's parents had been killed in a car accident when he was a teenager and Adele's father, to whom she was very close, had recently passed away. The only remaining grandparent, therefore, was her mother, who had never been forthcoming with offers of help – or anything else.

It had taken a year to get her boss to agree to let her go part-time to fit around Sophia's school day. Although she went above and beyond to get her tasks completed, often working late or in the evenings, it was obvious Simon was irritated when she had to miss work if Sophia was ill or had an inset day. Even though she took the missed days as holiday, it was short notice if Sophia was poorly and that ended up causing problems for her colleagues. Gemma's help in the office was a bonus – she could easily not come in if one of their boys were ill – whereas Adele, as Simon pointed out, was paid to be part of the team and any absences she took had a real impact.

'I know you're supposed to leave early tomorrow, but we've had a request for a viewing on Greenham Gardens and she's a cash buyer. Nobody else is available, and it's a stone's throw from your house – could you squeeze it in on your way home? We really need to get Greenham sold.'

Adele's heart plummeted as she forced a smile. The way he phrased his request made her bristle. She wasn't leaving early, she was leaving at the end of her working day, which was 3 p.m., and she had pressing things to do, but she swallowed her pride and dug deep. She knew there were a hundred mothers looking for part-time roles and she couldn't really afford to turn down her boss's requests.

'Obviously I'd love to help but I need to take the dog to the vet and collect my daughter from school. What time is the viewing?' she asked.

'Three,' he said, in a way that conveyed it was non-negotiable.

Adele's brain began to race. Sophia was having a hard time with friendships. Ruby, her BFF since primary, had recently started walking home with another girl, leaving Sophia to walk alone. She had sobbed to Adele at bedtime the night before and Adele had promised her she would do her best to finish on time on Tuesday and walk home with her at three thirty, when school finished. She had also cancelled the vet's appointment twice, for Leia to have her jabs, and without them the kennels wouldn't take her for their up-coming holiday. Both meant finishing work on time for once.

'I'm sorry to ask you to take one for the team, Adele. I think your daughter is at the same school as my son, isn't she? He walks with his friends and he's fine. I think you mums worry too much. I know Gemma does,' he said, smiling and then standing as if to signal the conversation was over.

'No problem,' Adele said, forcing a smile as she thought of Alex, at work without a single fleeting thought about his home life. No doubt he would have a very similar suggestion to her conundrum. Cancel the vet; let Sophia walk home alone. Anything that required zero effort from him. As long as the client turned up on time she should be able to meet Sophia still. School was only five minutes' drive from the house-viewing. But she would have to warn Sophia that she might be held up and to start the walk home without her. Then they could race to the vet afterwards. If she made up some bullshit excuse they would hopefully fit them in. It wasn't ideal. She was letting Sophia down again, and having to deal with another heap of guilt and stress, but what else could she do? Even if Alex was working from home, he would no doubt be on an 'important' call, and tell her that Sophia would be fine on her own.

'Is the key for Greenham Gardens in the key box?' she asked, standing to leave.

'Not sure. Check with Issy – she's across everything,' he said, implying Adele wasn't and referring to his favourite staff member, the twenty-something, child-free, single girl of the office, who worked crazy hours, hit all her sales targets, and was able to get pissed with clients every Friday night.

'Oh, one other thing,' Simon said, walking over to his printer. 'We've just had a bit of bad news regarding your house sale. I know you were hoping to exchange this week, but the buyer just emailed to say he's pulling out, due to the issue with the planning.'

Adele felt the blood rush to her face as she stared at Simon in disbelief. 'But, but . . . they've had the survey done and the mortgage offer, they even came to measure up for their sofa last week,' she said, struggling to keep the tears back. 'We gave them fifty grand off to exchange by Friday.'

'I know. They love the house, Adele, but they got a second opinion this week, and they are just too nervous the council will ask them to pull the extension down.'

Adele swallowed her tears; there was no point arguing with Simon about it. 'OK, I understand. So back to the drawing board?'

'I think we need to get that planning issue sorted before we go to market again,' Simon said bluntly, returning to his desk.

'We've got planning,' Adele said quietly.

'Well, your neighbour is disputing that the build is not what was agreed. So while that is under investigation, I think we need to hold off going back to market,' Simon said. 'Sorry, I know it's not the news you were hoping for, but I'm sure we'll get there.'

He handed her a copy of the email and she stared at it

wide eyed as panic flooded through her. She knew Simon was irritated with her for wasting his time by breaching the planning permission. He had worked hard on an impressive open house to get their home under offer, and it had worked, but soon after, the neighbour had lodged a complaint with the council about Adele and Alex's extension. Adele had denied it to her boss, but Alex had indeed told the builder to go slightly wider with the floor, although she had pleaded with him not to. It had taken a year to get planning, and Alex was beyond irritated that what he was allowed to build had shrunk to almost half of the square footage of the original plans. Not one to accept rules and regulations, his solution, as usual, had been to push the boundaries in every way.

'OK, thank you. Alex and I will have a chat and work out what to do,' Adele said, knowing that Simon didn't really care about her house sale or home life any more. He was tired of all the problems and time-wasting her house had caused.

'I'll let the buyer know you will meet her at Greenham Gardens at three. Thanks, Adele,' he said.

Sitting back at her desk, she tried to calm her breathing. Her husband wouldn't take any responsibility for the sale falling through and would instead spend the evening ranting about how it was Simon's fault the house hadn't sold, that her boss had let it drag on, and should have pushed the sale through quicker before the neighbour had a chance to lodge a complaint with the council. Their solicitors would also be to blame; that they hadn't chased the buyer enough. Or possibly the neighbour for reporting the breach of planning regs. Anyone's fault but his. She had warned him they would be found out, and they had. Added to which they had forked out nearly five grand in deposits and fees on a two-bedroom flat that they were due to live in until their finances settled down.

Adele sat back down at her desk, a desire to get home to Sophia gnawing at her. She sometimes felt that Sophia was her only real friend in the world. Sophia's baby and toddler years had been tough and she felt teenage hormones descending already, but right now Sophia was just twelve and couldn't be lovelier, sticking up for her when Alex was being difficult, helping her around the house, making dinner with her, giving her compliments and much-needed moral support and confidence. Adele sometimes felt guilty that she was in danger of using her daughter to fill the void in her marriage, but Sophia struggled with friendships, just as Adele had done all her life. They just felt at ease with one another and loved hanging out; chatting, cooking, shopping, taking long walks with Leia and binge-watching Netflix. All while Alex worked late or locked himself away in his study and largely ignored them both.

It was a strange feeling, being so close to Sophia, and one Adele had never expected, having always had a very difficult relationship with her own mother. She had actually cried at her twenty-week scan when they had told her it was a girl, thinking that history was bound to repeat itself, and she would feel no love or affection towards her daughter. But as soon as she was born, Sophia had brought the love with her, and Adele had been flooded with relief. She had resolved to have no other children in case she jinxed it.

Adele looked back down at Simon's email from their buyers

21

declaring that they had 'regretfully decided to pull out due to the issues with planning', then dragged herself back to the tasks she needed to get done before going home. In less than half an hour she managed to rattle off three offer letters and upload four new property details to Rightmove, before jumping into her Mini, grabbing dinner ingredients from Tesco on the way home and pulling up outside the house just as Sophia was walking down the road towards her.

'Hi, sweetheart,' she said, relieved to see that Alex's car wasn't in the driveway. She needed time to compose her thoughts and work out what to say about their house sale falling through. Despite the fact that the problem with planning permission was his fault, she knew in his own way he was trying to help their situation. He had pushed the extension boundaries to make the house more impressive and it had backfired. She also knew he was trying to hide money worries due to a lack of projects at work and a crippling business loan he had been forced to take out for cash flow. They desperately needed to sell the house and she knew that he would completely lose his rag over this news. The fact was, at times, she was scared of him, but she knew so much of his temper was due to losing his parents in such a horrific way at an early age. She had suggested counselling, but he would never agree to it and so she continued trying to be understanding and brushing his behaviour under the carpet.

As the house news began to sink in, she started to consider that it might be better not to say anything to Alex until she'd found a solution to soften the news. Maybe she could get on to the council tomorrow, and see if she could make some headway with their decision, something that would mean their buyer might decide to proceed after all.

'Hi, Mum, said Sophia, smiling warmly at her mother, despite her weary walk.

'Hi, honey. How was your day?' Adele asked, knowing already from Sophia's demeanour that it hadn't been good.

'OK. I'm glad it's Tuesday tomorrow – no maths. Are you still meeting me from school?' Sophia asked, her dark hair falling in front of her face as she put her heavy school bag down.

'I will do my best,' Adele said, trying to sound cheerful. 'I may be a little held up.'

Sophia's blue eyes flashed with alarm, due to her mother having to cancel several of their plans recently. 'I thought we were going to walk home together with Leia?'

'I'm sorry, sweetie, work have asked me to do a viewing at three, but I will meet you after that – either on your walk home or here – and we will take Leia for a lovely walk on the common once she's had her jabs at the vet, I promise,' said Adele, making a mental note to call the vet first thing. 'And we can go to Frank's for an ice cream as a treat.'

Sophia nodded and scrunched her nose, as she did when she was upset.

Adele knew her daughter was struggling to keep it together and that the smallest hiccup could send her over the edge. Sophia was a tough kid who could cope with a lot, as long as plans didn't change, which was something Adele found herself doing a lot lately. She had spoken tentatively to Alex about finding another job, but he had pushed her to continue, citing that they really needed the money. She longed to take some time out; she felt that she was failing as a mother and an employee. Sophia was lonely at the enormous comprehensive school, which she had just started, because Ruby, her best friend through primary, had essentially dumped her. She needed extra support with maths and English, and she wasn't eating properly. She needed her mother.

'How was Ruby today?' asked Adele, opening the front door.

'OK. She just kind of ignored me, which is better than her being mean, I guess.'

'I'm sorry.'

Adele looked at her lovely daughter. Sophia was gentle, honest and thoughtful, nothing like Alex personality-wise, although she looked the spitting image of him. Adele was blonde, blue-eyed and fair-skinned, and although Sophia had Adele's blue eyes, everything else – her Mediterranean look, with dark hair and skin – she had inherited from Alex. She was tall and willowy, with recently fitted braces, which made her feel self-conscious, but Adele knew that it wouldn't be long before she grew into herself and emerged from her cocoon as a beautiful, confident young lady.

'I just miss my best friend. Even though she's standing right there, it's like she's died and a different person has taken her place. She says we're not into the same things any more. She's bought a vape, Mum.' Sophia's voice wobbled, as Adele opened the front door and their lurcher came bounding down the hallway and launched herself at them.

Adele's heart ached for her daughter. Her primary school had been a bubble of happiness, kind teachers and an

24

endless supply of friends, play dates and birthday parties. In the short space of a year, she had started in the local comprehensive with fifteen hundred kids, and all her friends had gone from playing at each other's houses, trampolining, baking, swimming and gymnastics clubs, to hanging out in town, vaping, and chasing boys. Sophia was a July baby, young for her age and had only recently turned twelve. Everyone in Year Seven had suddenly matured in too short a time for her, and Sophia had found herself completely unable to keep up.

Sophia lay down in the hallway and started to giggle, as Leia climbed all over her. Adele felt a surge of love for the stupid, lanky dog, who was Sophia's constant companion.

'I'm making spag bol for tea,' said Adele.

'Yay! Can I help?' Sophia said, smiling up at her as Leia continued to eat her own foot.

'Absolutely. You can chop while I supervise – and sample the wine, of course.'

'Deal.' Sophia held out her hand to shake her mother's.

From the kitchen, Adele heard the phone ring and she scrambled to get past Leia and Sophia, who was unpacking the bolognese ingredients. She knew it was silly, but she couldn't help hoping it was some good news; that the buyers had changed their minds or that the council had decided to drop the enquiry. The fact that both of those outcomes meant it was more likely they would call on her mobile didn't cross her frazzled mind, as she ran through the kitchen and lifted the receiver.

'Hello,' she said, catching her breath.

Silence. Adele pressed the receiver to her ear. 'Hello?' It

sounded to her as though the caller was outside: there was road noise, and a police siren in the distance.

'Adele speaking. Can you hear me?' she said, before the caller finally hung up.

Adele returned the phone to its cradle. Although she knew it was probably nothing – a call that hadn't connected, or a wrong number – something in her guts stirred. Her mind darted back to the week before when she had found a small silver hoop earring under Sophia's bed.

She had known instantly it wasn't her daughter's, or hers, and her mind raced as she tried to decipher who it belonged to. Ruby perhaps, or another friend of Sophia's, or maybe someone who had viewed the house. But Ruby hadn't been over for weeks and as far as she knew neither had any of Sophia's other friends. And how would someone viewing the house manage to lose one earring under the bed? It also didn't look like a teenager's earring; it had small diamond studs and a Tiffany & Co stamp. It had unsettled her, particularly as it was in her precious daughter's room, and she had buried it deep in her own sock drawer in an effort to forget.

'Mum, do I put the garlic and onions in first?' Sophia said, smiling.

'Yes,' Adele said distractedly, staring at the phone.

'I saw this video on TikTok that showed a girl wearing swimming goggles to cut onions. It stops you crying – I might try it,' said Sophia cheerfully, dashing out, thudding upstairs to her bedroom, before reappearing wearing her goggles.

Adele dragged her attention from the phone call back to her daughter, as she squeezed the garlic from the press, and watched it sizzle and spit in the pan. Sophia then began to chop an onion on the board. 'It works!' she announced.

Adele smiled, as her daughter giggled up at her. She was a sight for sore eyes, and Adele felt her body relax. She was worrying too much about everything as usual.

'Alexa, play Olivia Rodrigo,' Sophia said, throwing onion in the pan and dancing round the kitchen in her swimming goggles. Adele joined in, and Leia jumped up at them excitedly. Sophia grabbed Leia's front paws and the three of them danced in a circle laughing and singing along to 'get him back!'

For a moment, all was well in their world. It was lovely for Adele to see Sophia smiling after so many tears over Ruby, and the anxious butterflies that had become a permanent fixture in Adele's tummy lately began to ebb away. She looked around. They had worked so hard to make their new open-plan kitchen beautiful, with months of builders and rubble and plaster dust. She would do anything to stay. Maybe it was fate the buyers had pulled out; maybe things would turn round at Alex's work and they would be able to afford to keep this house after all.

'You two look happy,' Alex called out. 'I guess you haven't heard the news then?' Adele turned to see Alex at the kitchen door scowling at her with his dark eyes. He must have finished work early and the music had drowned out the crackle of his car on the gravel driveway, which usually warned her he was home.

Adele felt her tummy drop. He had heard about the house sale falling through already. There was no way of softening the blow now.

'Alexa, turn off,' she said.

'I'm going upstairs to do my homework,' Sophia said quietly, walking past her father, goggles in hand.

Adele could smell alcohol on her husband's breath as he walked over to her and leaned on the kitchen counter. In less than a minute, the atmosphere in the kitchen had gone from light and happy to heavy and unsettling. She focused on finishing off the bolognese, stirring in the bloodied mince and adding the chopped tomatoes and purée.

'Please tell me you didn't sign the tenancy agreement for that flat?' Alex added, looking through the post.

'I signed a month ago, like you told me to,' said Adele.

'Great, that's five grand down the drain. Presumably you called them to say we don't want it?' he snapped.

'No, not yet. I wanted to talk to you first,' she said as calmly as she could.

'What about?' Alex barked.

'I don't know. Maybe you want us to live in the flat and rent this out to save money,' she said.

Alex frowned at her. 'Obviously we can't sell this house if we are renting it. So, what is Simon's plan then?'

Adele stirred the dinner, trying not to make eye contact. She was tempted to lie to avert an argument, but she knew it would be futile. 'His advice is for us to get the planning issues resolved before we go back to market.'

'So he doesn't have a plan? Great. Did he let the buyers know we are giving them fifty grand off?'

'Yes, Alex, he did, but they are worried they will have to pull the extension down.'

'There's no way it will come to that. How ridiculous,' he said, pouring himself a beer from the fridge.

'It's not actually ridiculous. We've breached the planning

permission. It would be very expensive to put right, a lot more than fifty grand.' Adele was careful to use the word 'we' and not 'you'.

'Well, if you've been saying that to Simon, it's no wonder they've pulled out.'

'Alex, that isn't fair. I haven't said anything, but he's not an idiot,' Adele sighed.

'I think the problem is you don't want to move. You don't seem to realise how important this is. We can't make the mortgage payments. We are going to be repossessed if we don't sell the house now.' Alex was raising his voice.

'My salary will cover the mortgage payments for now,' she reasoned. 'They can put us on interest-only for six months, which will help. We just need to cut back on everything, and call round all the utilities and they will have to give us some breathing space.' Adele reached out and put her hand over Alex's, but he swiftly pulled it away.

'You live in a fantasy world, you really do. You have no idea the pressure I'm under. A few phone calls isn't going to magically make all this go away,' he hissed.

'Alex, it's not my fault you hide things from me. How am I supposed to know the pressure you're under if you don't tell me?' Adele tried to keep her voice down for Sophia's sake.

'You aren't interested in anything other than Sophia. You don't care about me, how worried I am, how bad things are.'

Adele let out another sigh. 'That's not true and you know it. I'm doing everything I can.'

'Are you? Well then, maybe you can prove it by doing your job and getting this fucking house sold,' he said, stomping off to the study and slamming the door.

Adele poured a large glass of wine to stop her guts churning, and then went upstairs to Sophia, who was sitting at her desk.

'I'm sorry, sweetie, Dad's stressed that the house sale fell through today.'

Sophia nodded. 'Poor Mum,' she said, looking up from her homework. 'Dad's such an asshole sometimes.'

'He really isn't good at handling stress, but he is doing his best,' Adele said, ashamed of herself for making excuses for him. If Sophia's husband behaved like Alex, she'd be telling her to get out of the marriage.

'You always make excuses for him, because of what happened to his parents,' Sophia said.

'Yes, I know. But he was only a couple of years older than you when they were killed. He lost everything.'

'But that doesn't mean he can bully you,' Sophia said quietly. 'Wanna watch a movie after dinner?' she added, searching her mother's face for a smile.

'Thanks, sweetheart. What would I do without you?' Adele said, knowing it irritated Alex how often she fell asleep in Sophia's room, not wanting him to touch her lately. 'I think I'm going to have a shower and get into my PJs.'

Adele turned the shower on as the landline trilled into life again. She let it ring and eventually she heard Alex pick up in the kitchen. She tiptoed out onto the landing to listen.

'How did you get this number?' he snapped, quietly. 'I can't talk now. I'll call you later.'

She had no idea who was calling the house, but in her heart she felt a line had been crossed. In fact she was glad they couldn't pull out of the flat rental. It would give her and Sophia an option, an escape, which was something she had been thinking about a lot lately.

As long as she had Sophia she would have the strength to survive. She walked back into the bathroom, locked the door, turned the shower on as hot as she could stand it and climbed in.

Chapter Two

Felicity

Wednesday, 1 December 1982

Seventeen-year-old Felicity Mills lifted the handset in the phone box in the middle of the chocolate box village of Kingsclere, in the heart of the English countryside, and swallowed the vomit that had been threatening to come up all morning.

Slowly she looked down at the scrawled telephone number on the crumpled piece of paper in her hand – which was shaking from the bitter cold of the winter's morning – and pressed the fifty-pence piece into the slot.

'Yes?' came the greeting, after six or seven rings. It was a woman's voice, sharp. Felicity hesitated before she spoke.

'I've been given your number,' she said, her eyes darting around the village, hoping none of her parents' friends were loitering, ever ready to report back on her. 'I'm pregnant, you see, and I—'

'What was the date of your last period?' the woman interrupted.

Fliss gathered her racing thoughts and then told her.

'I'm sorry, but I can't help you,' the woman said abruptly.

Fliss's heart began to race. Anthony had given her the number and said the woman would help her. She hadn't expected to be dismissed just like that. It didn't make sense.

'But my friend said you might be able to do something.'

32

'You sound young – how old are you?'

Felicity hesitated. Her instinct was to lie, but maybe the woman would be more willing to help if she knew how desperate she was. 'I'm seventeen.'

'Did you have sexual relations before you turned sixteen?'

Felicity stayed silent as her heart pounded in her ears.

'Your partner could get into a lot of trouble for that,' the woman continued. 'Was he aware that it's viewed as child sexual abuse and statutory rape in the eyes of the law?'

Felicity's head spun. Child abuse? They had been sleeping together for over a year, since just before her sixteenth birthday, but could a married colleague of her father's, to whom she had lost her virginity in his car and slept with countless times, be described as a rapist? A man three times her age, who she lied to her friends and family about, who she had fallen for completely, a man she couldn't resist seeing, who she obsessed over, and whose wife and children she sometimes followed and watched, knowing he would never leave them for her. Anthony Hislop, a local counsellor and pillar of the community, who now refused to see or even speak to her, other than to give her the crumpled piece of paper she now held in her hand.

'He's not my partner.' Felicity heard her voice waver. 'Please can you see me? Examine me, at least? I don't have anywhere else to go—'

'No, you are too far gone for any intervention. I don't know who gave you my number, but I really can't do anything for you. It would be much too dangerous, too likely to involve complications, and if something went wrong and you had to go to hospital—'

'I wouldn't care! Anything would be better than this. My mother will throw me out on the street when she finds out.'

'You might not care, but I would. There is the potential issue of sexual abuse, so the next thing would be that the police would become involved. Where would that leave me?'

'Please!' Felicity was crying now, as an elderly woman with an umbrella walked up to the telephone box and started tapping at it impatiently. 'You must be able to do something,' Felicity pleaded.

'I can't, I'm so sorry. I just can't.'

Fliss continued to beg the woman, before she realised she'd hung up on her.

'About time too,' huffed the woman as Fliss opened the door of the telephone box and stood in the ice-covered high street. The village was a scene awash with Christmas merriment: a busker played, families bustled past her, clutching one another, laden with shopping. She spotted a friend of her mother's emerging from a coffee shop with her young daughter, and Fliss turned on her heel before she caught the woman's eye. She couldn't speak to her, not when she'd been crying. The woman would know instantly and call home before Fliss had even arrived back there: *I saw Fliss in town, is she all right? She looked rather upset. She was coming out of the phone box. Boy trouble, perhaps?* And her mother would grill her about it, follow her to her room, refuse to let it lie, push and push until eventually Fliss would cave and tell her the truth. She would watch her mother's face fall, a look of disbelief and horror, before she backed out of the room and closed the door. Then it would be Fliss following her, begging her to talk to her. Her mother's concern only stretched so far: superficial problems, period pains or teasing at school. Anything more than that, anything that might affect what her precious friends thought, and Fliss would be stonewalled.

It was suffocating, their picturesque village, her mother's nosy, snooty friends. Cities she had visited, like London and Paris, were noisy and thronging with people, bustling about, too occupied to mind anyone's business but their own. But in the quiet countryside, nothing was private. 'I saw your light was on late last night,' they would say in the post office queue. 'Is everything all right?' They would frown intensely, hoping for a morsel of gossip. She knew everyone in this village, and everyone knew her – and her parents – yet there was nobody for her to turn to now. No one.

As Felicity made her way to the other end of the high street, towards the main road which led to her house, she could hear the sound of a Tannoy in the distance. 'Greenham Common women, out out out! Newbury has had enough!' The female voice echoed through the winter's scene as the villagers turned to see what must be a hundred people marching towards them, alongside a Mini Cooper, with two large loudspeakers fastened to its roof, and Union flags billowing from its wing mirrors. Her heart lurched. She had forgotten: today was the day her mother, Camilla Mills, was marching with RAGE, the Ratepayers Against Greenham Encampments.

Camilla, and all her tweed-clad friends, were furious about the scores of women who had set up camp at Greenham Common, women whom they described as disgusting, awful, dirty-looking things who lived like pigs and spoiled the quiet, rural atmosphere of the rest of the common. Never mind – Felicity thought, but never dared to say – that they were trying to stop government leaders from blowing us all up, and that there wouldn't be a common left – or anything, for that matter – if it weren't for the likes of them. But that wasn't important to her mother. What was important was appearances, and these women needed to go home to their husbands and children. Felicity thought that the way Camilla and some of her friends behaved towards the poor women, stuck out in freezing conditions, trying to survive on the side of the road, was a lot more shameful than anything they had done. She knew from working in the pub that some of the local farmers would throw things at them – pig faeces, maggots and pig's blood – and that at night the young farmers would hurl fire crackers to make the poor women think they were being shot at.

Felicity hid behind a post box as she spotted her mother climbing up the steps of the war memorial. Despite being in her late forties now, she was still stunning, tall and willowy with long blonde hair tied back from her blunt fringe. Everybody commented on her beauty. She moved elegantly, and talked slowly, always watching and observing everyone around her, like a bird of prey. Not least Fliss's eating habits. In her mother's world, being fat was worse than being a lesbian. Even the slightly overweight were labelled 'vast', and ever conscious of her mother's critical eyes on her, Fliss would pick at her dinner, then drive to the garage and down sausage rolls and Mars bars by the bucket load. Her mother's dull, glossy friends clearly viewed Fliss's looks and lack of charm as something of a disappointment and it wasn't hard to see that Fliss had taken after her father. Frumpy and awkward, she had her father's fair skin tone, auburn hair and chunky build. She, along with everyone else, rather suspected her mother had married the politician and not the man.

Fliss watched one of the women lift the Tannoy to her lips. 'Their behaviour is a disgrace to womanhood,' she belted out. 'They are very anxious to be considered martyrs, but they will never be martyrs in a thousand years.' Her mother's hair was blow-dried especially for the occasion; she wore dark red lipstick, her favourite Houndstooth jacket and a black fur hat.

Felicity watched as the crowd cheered, their ruddy farmers' cheeks glowing in the wind. 'But I'll tell you who are the martyrs, and that is the children they have left behind.' At that moment her mother scanned the crowd and seemed to look directly at Felicity, as if she knew all along exactly where she was hiding. She paused for a moment, then continued, her eyes still on her daughter. Felicity could no longer listen. She put her coat hood up, and began walking at speed towards the main road, the sounds of cheers and applause slowly fading into the distance. Their house was only a mile outside the village, but she walked at a snail's pace along the winding country lane, aching for a miracle, willing one of the cars that whizzed past to strike her so she would be knocked down and lose the baby. Wake up in hospital, bleeding, with no one any the wiser and free from this abject terror she felt inside her. Why hadn't she acted sooner, why had she left it so late? Now there was nothing she or anyone could do to stop this runaway train she was clinging to for dear life.

As she reached the iron gates leading to the drive of Maberley Manor, the Georgian house her mother had inherited from her father, also a local Conservative MP, she pressed the fob on her keyring and slowly they began to open. She walked through, the frozen gravel crunching under her feet, and glanced over to the lodge by the entrance. There was smoke coming from the chimney but no sign of Mr and Mrs Owen, the gardener and housekeeper, who lived there. She liked Mr Owen. Sometimes she would stop and talk to him as he clipped the hedges or pruned the rose bushes, his tall frame, warm smile and calm nature often soothing her fiery personality. He was most unlike his wife, who was rotund and brisk, and never stopped to talk to anyone unless it was to bark instructions. Mrs Owen could only ever be spotted passing through the house at lightning speed, caught by the rustle of her skirt or the clacking heel of her black boots as she darted from room to room, leaving just the scent of lavender in her wake.

As she made her way down the driveway, Felicity's feet felt heavier with each step. The woods flanking either side of their garden looked dark and foreboding, and the roots of the elms that lined the drive felt like claws reaching out for her. Only an hour earlier she had marched towards the village, clutching the piece of paper Anthony had given her with hope and purpose; now there was none. In the distance she heard her father's familiar laughter. His corporate laugh, she called it, saved for the people he wanted to charm. He was probably seeing someone off who had come for a working brunch, a press adviser or his trusted accountant, perhaps. But as she reached the top of the driveway, her heart lurched as she saw it was neither of those people. It was Anthony, laughing as he shook her father's hand. Felicity watched as if in a trance – she had obsessed about seeing him again so often, his handsome face occupied her every waking thought – and the world slowed down as if she were dreaming. He wasn't especially tall, maybe five foot ten, but he was solidly built, powerful. He looked like he could take care of himself, and she had often fantasised about him taking care of her and their baby. He ran his fingers through his floppy dark fringe, then walked down the steps towards his black Mercedes – in which they had spent many hours together – climbed into the driver's seat and started the engine. She had tried so many times to reach him by telephone at his office. She had even resorted to writing him a letter and posting it, all of which he had ignored. And now he was here, at her home. Had he come to see her? She had never known him to come to Maberley before, and had only ever set eyes on him at her father's office, or at The Crown in Kingsclere, where he had dined one evening when she was waitressing.

Fliss watched him, transfixed. Her stomach lurched with obsession. She had spent the last two months crying in her bedroom, pining desperately for him, barely leaving the house to go to college or to see her friends, and the one hour she actually went out, he came here.

Fliss's mind raced. If he stopped as he drove by she might be able to talk to him, convince him to come and see her at The Crown, like he used to. She just needed to let him know how desperate she felt. Maybe he had just been giving them both space; maybe he assumed she had called the number he had given her two months ago, and it was all dealt with. It wasn't his fault she was still in denial. Why had she left it so long to call? She was stupid, so stupid.

As his car began to roll towards her, she held her breath. Fliss glanced up at her father, still waiting on the steps, waving at Anthony, smiling, oblivious. Anthony stopped and wound down his window slightly, as if not quite committing to the gesture.

'Morning, kiddo, how are you?' he said, barely pulling to a stop.

'That woman couldn't help me,' Fliss blurted out.

'I don't know what you're talking about. What woman?' he said, starting to pull away too soon.

'The number you gave me. I'm still pregnant. I need your help.' Fliss looked up again at her father, who was still smiling on the steps.

'Well, you need to get that boyfriend of yours to take responsibility,' he said, referring to a young lad she was friends with at the restaurant.

Fliss reeled at his words, and felt her face burning. 'He's not my boyfriend. I've never slept with anyone but you. You know it's your baby, Tony.'

'No, I really don't. And it's your word against mine,' he said, revving the engine of the car that had taken her to so many secluded spots around the English countryside. She ached for him to want her again, to feel desired and in control, a wise woman of the world. Not the stupid child that she was, who had got pregnant and become a burden and a bore.

'Take care, Felicity.'

She watched helplessly as he drove away in a cloud of fumes that made her retch. She stood still, not wanting to walk away from their last moment together, before she was entirely alone in the world. Fliss looked up at her father, who was standing at the entrance to the house, chatting to Mrs Owen now. As she approached them, the strong smells of lunch being prepared made her gag as she fought back the tears.

'I'm terribly sorry, Mrs Owen, I really wouldn't know about timings. Camilla will be home soon, I'm sure,' he said, before turning to his daughter. 'Are you all right, darling? You look a little pale. You didn't see your mother in the village, did you?' he asked as she smiled weakly at him and followed him wearily into the hallway.

Felicity gagged at the smell of onions, chicken and garlic cooking in the kitchen. She felt faint and collapsed into the armchair in the hall as a taxi pulled up outside the house and her mother climbed out.

'Ahh, here she is. How was the demonstration, darling?' her father asked, taking Camilla's bags from her.

'Jolly cold, but a good turnout, despite my own daughter running away from me,' Camilla said. 'Word is, the women's peace camp is dying out. Morale is low, and they are losing numbers. The council are doing a wonderful job with the evictions, they have no supplies left, and it's due to snow next week. With any luck the wretched vagrants will be gone by the weekend. What's the champagne situation, darling? Is it in the fridge already?'

'I believe so. Mrs Owen just asked me what time everyone is arriving,' said Felicity's father as he watched his wife take off her coat and hat. 'Fliss looks very pale, don't you think?'

'She always looks pale, lately. A bit of blush wouldn't

41

hurt. Heaven knows, I wouldn't have been seen dead at her age without my make-up on. How she ever expects to catch a husband is beyond me.'

Both of them stared at Felicity expectantly, wanting some kind of explanation. She stared back, feeling as if she were holding a hand grenade. Sitting in the entrance hall of Maberley Manor, it was slowly dawning on her that she was having this baby, and for the first time she felt something resembling relief.

She had been so convinced that she had to have a termination – that it was the only way to hide her pregnancy from her parents – that she hadn't even stopped to think if it was what she really wanted.

Her heart thudded in her ears as she felt her baby kick deep inside her tummy, giving her courage.

Fliss closed her eyes. 'I'm pregnant,' she said quietly, then held her breath and waited.

Chapter Three

Emma

Wednesday, 7 February 2024

'Blake! Solicitor's here to see you.'

Emma looked up from the steel vat of semolina bubbling on the large stove in the kitchen of Heathfield Prison.

'Kathy will take you down,' said the screw who had appeared at the doorway.

Emma nodded and followed the guard, wiping the sweat off her forehead with her apron. The guard was quite a bit smaller than Emma, but she commanded authority, with a stern manner and fierce frown that never left her brow. However, like most of the screws, Kathy was perfectly civil once she knew Emma wasn't going to be any trouble. In her five years at Heathfield, Emma had made it her business never to fall out with anyone. Only once had she ever picked a fight – on the third day of her sentence, after being brought up from the psychiatric wing, where she had spent her first two nights under observation.

After the humiliation of being strip-searched for drugs after her arrival straight from court in the police van, those two nights had been the longest of her life, with a ten-year jail sentence for manslaughter stretching ahead of her. She had spent the nights locked in her tiny cell, trying to block out the sight of the stains covering the lino floor, the stench of vomit mixed with bleach coming from the toilet in the corner, and the scratch marks in the plaster on the yellow walls. A metal army bed, stained mattress, coarse blanket and flimsy pillow had been her only comfort.

She had walked into the dining room that first evening and, after being given two greasy sausages swimming in gravy and watery mash, she had sat down at a table on her own, trying not to catch anyone's eye. After only a few forkfuls, a pale, scrawny girl with slicked-back hair had snatched her plate and began wolfing Emma's food down.

Every instinct in Emma's body had told her to walk away, but she knew it was a test, and that if she let this girl walk all over her, other inmates would see her as an easy target and her sentence would be a hundred times harder.

Her hands were shaking under the table as she stood up and walked over to the girl, who didn't look up from shovelling Emma's dinner into her mouth. Before she could change her mind, Emma had picked up her plate and tipped it into the girl's lap. It had clattered onto the floor and silence had fallen in the dining room, as everyone turned to stare at the unfolding events.

Emma had stood over her and said as loudly as her trembling voice would allow, 'Don't ever steal my food, unless you want to wear it.'

The girl had shot to her feet and faced Emma, so that their noses nearly touched, and for what felt to Emma like forever, there was a stand-off. The woman's breath smelled of cigarettes and as Emma held hers, the other prisoners began laughing and chanting for a fight. Emma hadn't flinched, her heart thudding in her chest, with no idea how she would handle a physical altercation if it happened, until finally, to her overwhelming relief, the girl had stormed off.

Following that, Emma had, mostly, been left alone. She couldn't understand prisoners arguing with the screws or fighting amongst themselves, not when the punishment could be having time added to your sentence. But then, for some of the women, she learned, prison was a safe haven, somewhere their pimps and dealers couldn't get to them. It had surprised Emma that she was far from alone in having nobody looking out for her, no one sending her supplies to keep her going, or visiting her. Most of the women had grown up in care, then been preyed upon and forced into prostitution. They had no family support outside, no one waiting for them except the men who had got them into drugs and prostitution, landing them in Heathfield in the first place.

After a couple of weeks of being locked in her cell for eighteen hours a day, she was told that because she had no previous criminal convictions and been 'no trouble so far', she would be allowed to work in the kitchen and clean the communal areas as long as she continued to behave. She was overwhelmingly relieved that she would be out of her cell and busy most of the day, and she found that being in some control of the food – and able to give larger portions to those who could keep the bullies at bay – was a gift. Reports in the *Daily Mail* of prison food being up to Jamie Oliver's standards were laughable. Everything was barely edible, which didn't matter much as she had found it almost impossible to eat.

A curvy girl, with mousy-blonde hair and blue eyes, Emma had always battled with her weight and comfort-eating had been a way of life for as long as she could remember. But since arriving at Heathfield her anxiety had gone through the roof, she lived on adrenaline and she had been barely able to touch her food. Her weight had fallen off at such an alarming rate that she had started to panic that she was dying. She barely recognised herself in the mirror. Her cheeks were sunken, her skin flaking and her face covered in spots. But over time, things had settled, and while she remained three clothes sizes smaller than she had been her whole adult life, she had managed to put on some of the weight she lost when she first arrived.

She would rise at six and, after eating her breakfast of white bread with two streaks of fatty bacon, she set about her tasks: sweeping and scrubbing floors, then dusting and cleaning everywhere except for the individual cells. She would eat lunch, then help serve it to the other inmates before going back to her cell, by which time she was tired enough to sleep the afternoon away. Ten years had seemed insurmountable, but as the shock and depression subsided, she had managed to establish a routine that got her through the days. She had always felt safest in her own company, and eternally grateful that she had her own cell on a fairly quiet row, to which she could escape at night with her books and her radio.

Emma followed Kathy down to the rooms used for appointments with inmates' legal teams. They were tiny, with bare walls, a flimsy table, two chairs and a red panic button. She had walked across the peeling lino floor to this room many times over the years. The hours sitting with her solicitor had resembled the various stages of grief over the five years she had served of her sentence so far; shock and denial, pain and guilt, anger and bargaining, depression and, finally, acceptance.

Emma's solicitor, Michael Vincent, was sitting patiently at the table, clutching a bottle of water and looking flustered, with red cheeks, sweat patches under his shirt sleeves and his black suit jacket on the back of his chair.

'Hello, Emma, how are you?' he said, panting like an overweight Labrador in the heat.

'I'm OK, thanks. You look a bit hot,' she said as he gulped his water.

'It's very hot in these places, don't you find?' he said, using a few sheets of his paperwork to fan his flushed cheeks.

'You should try working in the kitchen. I've heard they turn the heat up to make us sleepy and keep us out of trouble. You get used to it,' said Emma matter-of-factly. 'Like everything, I guess.'

There was a moment's silence between them. Emma didn't want to ask about the appeal. She had received so many disappointments and knock-backs over the years, she had stopped fantasising about justice and escape. She watched Michael doing a dance with his pile of papers, pulling them in and out of his bag, examining them and frowning, clearing his throat. It was obvious he was putting off what he had to say.

'It's OK,' she said. 'I understand.'

'Understand what?' Michael frowned and pushed his glasses up his nose.

'About the appeal. I know you did your best. I'm kind of resigned to doing the full seven years now. I was unlucky with the judge and sentence I got, but not as unlucky as my dad,' Emma said quietly. 'At least I'm alive.'

'Sorry? No! Emma, the appeal was successful. You've had two years taken off your sentence.'

'What?' Emma stared at her solicitor, unable to take in the news. 'How?'

'Well, because you were let down by your barrister. And by the duty solicitor assigned to you at the time. And because you had a judge who gave you an unreasonably harsh sentence. I was able to argue a good case.'

Emma stared at Michael. 'Two years,' she repeated. 'I can't believe it.'

'Your solicitor at the time didn't do his job, Emma. He failed to do any background research on you. He just let the prosecution go to town with the report from social services detailing your troubled teenage years and brushes with the police. If they had spoken to your actual social worker, they would have known you are not a criminal. The fire wasn't arson, it was an accident.'

Emma nodded, her mind darting back to the horrific day when she woke up in hospital, an oxygen monitor clipped to her finger, a cannula in the back of her hand and her right arm burning as if it were still on fire. She had cried out in pain as she lurched back into consciousness, memories of the flames burning her skin as her shirt set alight. It could only have been seconds but it felt like forever as the material melted onto her skin. To this day, she could still hear the shouts of the fire brigade as they rushed past her towards the house, feel the sprays of water catching her as she was being lifted onto a trolley by the paramedics, recall the sense of panic as she cried out for her mother and father still trapped inside the house.

A policeman, Detective Inspector Thomas Price, had been at her bedside when she woke. 'Your mother, Sally Blake, is being treated for smoke inhalation but is due to be released soon. However, I'm sorry to tell you that your father, Jim

Blake, is in intensive care and fighting for his life. Can you tell us anything about how the fire started, Emma?'

She had taken to sleeping on an old armchair in the garage of her parents' house, she told him, to avoid having to talk to them when she came home from her shift at the pub every night. But the weather had got so cold that in her spliff-induced daze, she had thought it a good idea to light the portable fire pit that was stored there.

'It was an accident. I fell asleep. I didn't start that fire on purpose, if that's what you're thinking,' Emma had pleaded, starting to cry. 'My mother knows that.'

'I'm afraid Sally Blake wants to press charges, Emma. And if your father's condition continues to deteriorate, I'm sorry to say that we could be looking at manslaughter.'

Emma felt tears sting her eyes at the memory, and blinked them away before Michael saw.

'You were suffering a major depressive episode at the time,' Michael continued, 'and were on anti-depressants, which should have warranted a psychiatric report.' He pulled out a pad and began flicking through the endless pages of scribbled notes. 'Also your social worker was off sick for the trial; the one person – other than your mother – who knew your history, the fact that you were adopted and had suffered with your mental health for years.'

Emma's relationship with her mother, Sally, had always felt, to her, like swimming upstream. They had both tried to get along, but the chemistry between them was simply off, and Emma's whole childhood felt like trying to make polite conversation at a social event. Sally was a very private person, who always kept the world – and her daughter – at arm's length and was visibly uncomfortable about any conversation that went deeper than superficial platitudes.

Whereas Emma had been born with her heart on her sleeve and for most of her life felt like a fish, writhing and gasping for air on the riverbank, desperate for someone to push her back into the water. So discovering, at the age of fifteen, that she was adopted had been simultaneously unsurprising and had blown her world apart. Keeping a lid on her emotions was no longer possible and everything had very quickly unravelled. She had got in with the wrong crowd at school and started smoking dope in the park, something that calmed her brain down, but then made her extremely paranoid and volatile. Three school expulsions later and a social worker was assigned and anti-depressants prescribed.

Emma could no longer keep up the façade of a relationship with her parents and, after dropping out of college, had moved in with a very unsuitable boy who, after ten years of bleeding her dry financially and emotionally, left her all alone and with no option but to go home with her tail between her legs. What once had been a somewhat stilted relationship with her parents now broke down completely, culminating in a chain of events that had led to where she sat today, opposite her solicitor in Heathfield Prison, halfway through a ten-year sentence for manslaughter.

'Not wanting to be insensitive, but usually when a number of things slip through the net like this, a client's family steps in to push their legal team, fill in the gaps, encourage them to focus on all the parts of the jigsaw so the judge has the full picture. But in your case, that didn't happen . . .' Michael's voice faded away. 'Sorry, probably not a helpful comment.'

Emma picked at the skin around her fingernails. 'That's OK, I understand. It didn't help my case that I have no one vouching for me. Does my mother know about this development?'

'Not yet. She wasn't at the appeal hearing, but I'm happy to contact her for you. I take it you haven't heard anything?'

Emma shook her head. She had not seen or spoken to her adoptive mother since the day her father died. Sally Blake had applied for a restraining order, forbidding Emma from contacting her or going within a hundred yards of her, which the judge had granted. It was the opposite of a character reference and perhaps the final nail in the coffin for Emma.

'I still write to my mother sometimes. She hasn't replied, but she hasn't lodged a complaint with the police for me contacting her, which is something, I guess. I don't want to hurt her, I want to respect her desire not to see me, but it's helping me a lot to try and unpick my childhood. I'm actually having better conversations with her than we've ever had, which is kind of strange as she never writes back. I just want her to know that I'm sorry.'

Emma felt her voice tremble. 'Anyway, so where does this leave us now? I mean, presumably I'm still guilty of manslaughter?'

'Yes, there wasn't really a defence, and you were right to plead guilty. But there are mitigating circumstances, which should have been taken into consideration during sentencing. You were not in your right mind, you were under extreme stress due to a relationship breakdown. You have suffered considerable setbacks in your young life and potentially have a personality disorder that is treatable.'

'It seemed like the judge had it in for me from the start.'

Michael smiled. 'Well, you shouldn't take it personally. It was most likely laziness. When he set a date for sentencing he should have ordered a variety of reports: a welfare report from the social services, as well as a psychiatrist report. And he should have completely dismissed the prosecution's argument that you made no attempt to call an ambulance or the fire service. You were in and out of consciousness from smoke inhalation and had third-degree burns on your arm, which we have medical reports to confirm.'

'I vaguely remember the judge did mention a psychiatric report . . . or a welfare report . . . I'm not sure,' Emma said.

'And what did the barrister say?'

'That it wasn't necessary, I think – there were no grounds for one, or something like that.'

Michael sighed and shook his head. 'You just got really unlucky, Emma, with Judge Bastard and the Green Barrister. I'm really sorry. In the circumstances, no reasonable judge would have sentenced you to that length. Ten years was outside the grey area, and too high. But you wouldn't have got less than eight years, which is what you have now, following the appeal, but you've had the pain of this long sentence hanging over you all this time, which is rough. But the fact is that, as of now, you won't have to serve it.'

'Thank you, Michael, really.'

Emma started to feel the familiar waves of anxiety returning. She had refused to hope the appeal might work and had no idea what this development meant. Knowing how every day looked had kept her sane, and the thought of launching into the unknown was hard to take in.

'So, eight years, with automatic remission of a third, takes it down to five and a half, so you'll be out in six months. Which definitely means that you should no longer be at Heathfield,' Michael said, beaming at her.

The room began to swim, as Emma tried to focus. Her chest felt tight as she gripped the edge of the table. 'What do you mean? Where will I go?'

'You'll be moved to an open prison, somewhere nicer than this place, possibly Westwood Park near Bristol, to begin the process of going home,' Michael said cheerfully.

'What, hang on! What are you talking about? Bristol?' she said, panicked.

Michael frowned at her. 'It sounds like you don't want to leave. I've never heard of anyone wanting to stay in a high-security prison before.'

'But I've got my own cell, my routine. If I go to another prison, I don't know what to expect. They might make me share.' Emma's words were tumbling over one another, and her face flushed.

'Well, it will only be for six months. You need to be integrated back into the community, Emma. You can have visitors, who are allowed to take you out and you can get a job in the local town during the day – start building a new life for yourself. This is what we've been working towards.'

Emma pulled again at the skin around her fingernails. She hadn't been expecting this. She felt the hot room closing in. 'What visitors? I've never had any visitors – you know that. Where will I go when I get out?' she asked quietly. 'I don't have anyone.'

Michael nodded. 'I know. I'm hoping that offender management will help you sort a hostel until you can get a job and back on your feet.'

For as long as she could remember, Emma had learned to bottle her emotions and get through the day. Routine, hard work, books and the radio were her constant companions, along with knowing exactly what each day held. She knew every inch of her cell, recognised who made every cough, scream and holler and could set her watch by every meal and yard break. Talk of a new prison, a new cell, going back out into the world where she had no one, no home, nothing to look forward to, was making it hard to breathe.

'Look, I have to shoot. Nothing will happen imminently. You'll have time to get used to the idea, and a lot of support, including from me, going back out into the world. This is a good thing, Emma.'

She looked at him as tears stung her eyes. She so desperately wanted to be happy, to look forward to having the simple freedoms back that had been ripped from her so violently: making a cup of tea, running a bath, walking barefoot in the grass, feeling sand between her toes.

But it was hard to look forward to any of those things when she knew no one was going to be waiting for her outside the gates of Heathfield Prison.

Chapter Four

Rachel

Rachel walked into Thames Valley police station, in St Aldates, Oxford, up the stairs to the first floor, through the double doors and into the Criminal Investigations Department. As always, by eight thirty in the morning the open-plan office was buzzing with activity: phones trilling, colleagues chatting and Rachel's boss, Detective Inspector Bill Bailey, shouting for someone to get him a coffee.

As she made her way to her desk through the organised chaos created by the twelve detective constables, four detective sergeants and one detective inspector in her unit – acknowledging her colleagues with a smile – she overheard the familiar snippets of conversations about interviews, court dates, arrests, photographs and DNA profiles. While she mostly liked the camaraderie of an open-plan office and having the option to yell across the room when she needed a hand, since coming back from a five-year career break caring for her husband, she sometimes found the distractions and noise levels made it impossible for her to concentrate.

In her former life, when she was happily oblivious to the day-to-day suffering her husband would have to endure – the pain, the sedation, the progressive weakness and loss of appetite, the fluctuating levels of consciousness, the diapers and catheters, and the shallow, laboured breathing – she had found no issue with all the bureaucracy and paper-work, the long shifts, the decision-making, the complaints and aggression from members of the public. In fact, she had thrived on them, such was her love for the job she had done since leaving school at sixteen.

Now, however, six months back into the routine, she found herself rather changed. She spent her days darting from interview to arrest to evidence-gathering, her nerves a little frayed, her attention span a little shortened and her skin constantly irritated, as if she were wearing a woolly jumper on a hot summer's day.

Rachel sat down at her desk and fired up her laptop for the day ahead. As much as she tried to give the impression of feeling happy to be back, joining her colleagues for lunches, post-shift drinks and charity fundraisers, privately she questioned her decision to return to work several times a day. In the end, however, she'd had little choice. She had felt as if she was going mad with too much time on her hands, walking in and out of the rooms in which she had cared for her husband for six long years after he had been given his terminal cancer diagnosis. According to an article she had read during one long night by his bedside, seventy-five per cent of cancer sufferers wanted to die at home, surrounded by loved ones. But as the Macmillan nurses, who had been a lifeline for her, pointed out, a loved one dying at home can been a very haunting experience once they are gone.

So Rachel had decided it was for the best to return to the job she loved – detective constable in CID – and for the most part it was. She gave her all and it was the distraction she needed, but deep down she knew David had taken a piece of her with him. And so she walked around with a hole in her soul, scared that at any moment the façade, the one layer of flimsy skin covering her missing insides, would fall away for all the world to see.

'Rachel, can I borrow you for a minute, please?' Detective Inspector Bill Bailey called out from his office, before she had a chance to log in to her computer to check her emails.

Bill and Rachel went way back, they had been police constables together when Rachel had first joined the force in 1982. He was a tall, gentle man, with an ability to find humour in the most trying circumstances, and they had been through a lot together. As he had risen through the ranks, he had become more assertive, but he had stayed a good friend to her, particularly when she had to take prolonged absences due to her husband's illness, and for the last twenty or so years he had been her boss. She knew him well, and from the tone in his voice that morning, she could tell he was stressed. Rachel caught the eye of a colleague, who smiled sympathetically and mouthed 'good luck' as she passed his work station.

Bill was leaning forward at his desk, telephone in one hand, coffee in the other.

'Yup, yes, I understand,' he said, gesturing her in.

Rachel waited while he finished his call. She looked around briefly, catching sight of herself in the mirror on the wall in which Bill checked himself before press conferences. Despite it being mid-July, she looked pale and drawn against her chestnut hair and blunt fringe. Her grey roots were showing and she made a mental note to pick up some hair dye in the supermarket on her way home. In the past months she had really started to look her fifty-eight years. She had always taken pride in the fact that she was naturally attractive and didn't need to bother much with make-up or frequent visits to the hairdresser, but she had aged twenty years in the past five, and the cream and blue clothes she had relied on in the past no longer suited her.

Her appetite had failed her since David's death and her navy suit and crisp white shirt now looked slightly baggy. She needed a makeover, some colour on her face and in her wardrobe, but she didn't have a clue where to start. She knew a holiday would help, to get some sun and put on a few pounds, but she hadn't been away without David since they'd met forty years before, and she couldn't face going on her own – or with a friend with whom she would have to be constantly cheerful.

'OK, I'll send our FLO, Rachel, over now . . . yup, got it,' said Bill, as Rachel let out an internal sigh of relief.

Surprisingly, the one thing that had saved her, and where she felt her old self creeping back in, was in her work as a family liaison officer. Sensing her need to be out of the office more when she first returned to work, Bill had kindly suggested she do the five-day FLO training course. Since then she had worked with several families whose loved ones had been the victims of crime, usually a road fatality or a homicide, visiting their homes, offering them support in their most vulnerable moments and providing them with as much information as she could to help them get justice for their child or parent.

In her fragile emotional state, she found a strange comfort in people feeling as desperate as she did. Cheerful people, with no sense of how cruel the world could be, were far more tiring to her than a mother who had lost her child. She was more empathetic and understanding towards the victims' families – perhaps in ways she hadn't been in the past. Having this added compassion, alongside all the time in the world and no desire to go home, helped her get a better picture of the victim and their life. Then, like a jigsaw puzzle, she could listen and watch, gathering all the little pieces together to help the team find that invaluable break in the case.

'Rachel, have a seat,' said Bill, having finished his call. 'Sorry to keep you.'

'No problem.' She opened her notebook and took a pen from her pocket.

'So, we have a missing child, Sophia Norton, age twelve, female, parents Alex and Adele Norton, married. Family live in a nice semi-detached house in Sandleford, which backs onto Greenham Common. She goes to the local comp and walks home from school, twenty minutes to her house. Her mum, Adele, is an estate agent and was due to meet her on her walk home yesterday after a viewing but was held up. When Adele got home Sophia wasn't there.'

'So do we know the last time she was seen?'

'She walks home alone so it's hard to tell when she set off, but we've checked CCTV. She showed up on camera, walking past the shops on the main road, but there's no sighting of her after that. Strangely, their dog is also missing, which they initially thought was the reason – that Sophia had maybe come home, grabbed the dog and gone straight out to walk it on Greenham Common. But there's no CCTV record of her on the way to the common, so we don't know if perhaps someone took the dog from the house to lure her into their car. In which case it would possibly be an individual who knows the family and the dog. She's now been missing all night. Which she never has been before.'

'Where was Dad?' Rachel asked.

'On a work call. He came downstairs at four p.m. and noticed Sophia and the dog weren't there, and presumed they were out together,' Bill said.

'Who is at the parents' house at the moment?' Rachel asked.

'Sally. She's been with them most of the night, but her shift finishes soon. I was hoping you could go over there now.' Bill stood up and pulled his jacket from the back of his chair.

'Sure. Presumably the parents have rung round all her friends?' Rachel said.

'Yes, and Sally's searched the home to double-check she's not hiding anywhere, and been through all her things to make sure she hasn't packed a bag or any clothes. We've checked the railway stations' and bus stations' CCTV, put out an amber alert to the taxi companies, and filed a missing person report. She hasn't used her bank card today or yesterday. This is out of character, apparently. She doesn't skive off school and has a good relationship with her parents. That's the story, anyway. Obviously that's where you come in.'

Rachel nodded. 'That's weird about the dog. It does sound like she's maybe taken the dog out and something's happened to them. Or she's popped in to see a boyfriend or friend they don't know about.'

'Yes, except the dog lead isn't missing. And both parents

are sure that she didn't come home because her school bag isn't there.'

'Could a boyfriend have picked her up and the dog jumped in the car?'

'Who knows? As usual in these cases, the parents are adamant there's no boyfriend, she's a saint, never been in trouble before, totally out of character, etc. But you'll need to work out if all that's true. Even the nicest of girls can be naughty, as we both know.'

'Well, she's only twelve, young for a boyfriend,' Rachel reflected.

'Still, not unheard of,' Bill added.

'Phone?' Rachel asked

'Switched off.' Bill replied. 'Last signal was in a cul-de-sac she has to walk down, before she takes a twitten through to her road.'

'OK, if she hasn't been home all night, the press are going to get hold of this,' Rachel added.

'I'm already getting calls. Middle-class white girl, vanishes without a trace – it's going to make the lunchtime news. I've put Ben James on as the senior investigating officer. We'll release an appeal at nine a.m. Here's a copy – can you show the parents?' Bill said, handing it to her. 'I think if she hasn't turned up by midday we'll have to do a press conference, so you'll need to manage that with the family. Ben will meet you at the Norton's house. He's currently coordinating the search and press conference, tracking down CCTV and doorbell cameras of her route home, and interviews of Sophia's friends and school staff.'

Rachel scribbled in her notebook as Bill continued, 'So it's number fourteen Greenham Park Road. We'll seize their computer, have a rummage there, take a look at their finances. Tell them it's standard, obviously.'

'OK, shall I head over straight away?' Rachel asked.

'Yup, I suspect there will be some journalists outside by now. I'll tell Sally to expect you.'

Dismissed, Rachel nodded and left, picking up her coffee from her desk without speaking to any of her colleagues. She hadn't worked on a missing child case as an FLO yet, but she felt the familiar sensation of her chest tightening. Outside and heading to her car, she felt her head rushing with thoughts, not wanting anyone to speak to her as she climbed in and tried to calm her breathing. Media attention was something she hadn't dealt with at all since coming back to work after David's death, and if the missing child, Sophia, still hadn't turned up by lunchtime the press would grow into a monster by that evening. Rachel held on to the steering wheel and breathed in deeply through her nose, trying to calm the heat that was creeping up her face and chest. It was a compliment, she supposed, that Bill hadn't hesitated to send her into a potential shit storm. They'd known each other for forty years and he obviously felt she could handle it. Ben James, however, was another matter.

He had arrived at Thames Valley Police and risen up the ranks fast to senior investigating officer whilst Rachel had been on her career break. He hadn't seen the old Rachel, the assertive, confident woman who turned up, did her job, handled difficult situations and people with ease and then went home and slept through the night. All Ben James knew was the current Rachel, who hesitated, questioned herself and let others take the lead – and she knew he had noticed. Ben was a results-driven man, and, at only twenty-nine years of age, would have little patience with her anxieties. Ben James would no doubt want her to hit the ground running and grill the family with endless questions about their daughter in order to find Sophia before the press interest escalated out of control. But with their twelve-year-old child missing, Rachel knew the parents would want answers, not questions.

Rachel put Greenham Park Road into her sat nav and started the engine. The house backed onto Greenham Common. She knew the area well, particularly from her days as a young WPC arresting hundreds of women at the protests in the early eighties. Whenever she returned it brought back a lot of mixed feelings about how the force had treated the women. It had been a highly stressful time, with her superiors under an enormous amount of pressure to remove the women from the common. In the end, the women's resolve had been so strong that even physically dragging them away, arresting them, seizing all their belongings, and imprisoning them hadn't been enough. After ten long years of protests, the government had been forced to back down and return Greenham Common to the people.

Rachel turned on to the main road, and opened the window. It was a warm summer's day, and as she stepped on the accelerator the breeze began to calm her nerves. By the time she had pulled on to the A34 towards Newbury, she had managed to talk herself down from her panic.

'You know this, you can do this,' she mumbled to herself, going over the procedure for a missing child in her head. It was her job, as Ben would no doubt remind her, to be his ears and eyes in the house and find out as much as she could about Sophia and her family. The age-old adage, that a family member was normally involved, usually rang true.

As she settled into her journey, Rachel began to mentally checklist the questions in her head. Did Sophia usually walk home alone or was she normally with a friend? If so, which friend? If her parents were willing, Rachel would be keen to walk the route Sophia usually took from school to home, find the CCTV blind spots where she could have got into a car without anyone noticing. Bill had told her that the girl's mobile was switched off and that the last signal had been from a cul-de-sac she had to walk down, before she took a twitten through to her road. Could they pinpoint the exact moment it had been switched off and see if there were any taxis or delivery drivers on that road at that time who possibly had dash-cam footage?

Had any residents of that cul-de-sac spotted anyone sitting in a car outside their house in the past few days? If someone had taken Sophia, why? Who would benefit from taking her?

Her mind occupied with questions, it wasn't long before Rachel was driving through Newbury, into Greenham. She slowed down as she approached the common. She felt it was significant that the dog was also missing. Presumably they walked the dog on Greenham Common. Maybe she could walk with one of the parents a route they took with the dog. It was unlikely to throw up anything, but walking side by side was always better for getting information than face to face. It was less confrontational; it relaxed people and sometimes jogged their memories.

Greenham Park Road appeared ahead of her, a wide

tree-lined road, wall to wall with smart bungalows and terraced houses. She scanned the house numbers, immediately saw a squad car up ahead, and slowed down until she reached number fourteen and pulled up outside. It was a large semi-detached Victorian house, with a paved driveway on which were parked a Volvo estate and a Mini. The wall running the perimeter of the driveway was lined with beautifully manicured shrubs and the house looked recently painted in a crisp white, with a pale blue front door and roman blinds in all the windows. Notably there was a 'For Sale' sign outside, and Rachel made a mental note to ask about it.

She turned off the engine, and what she presumed were two members of the press turned to look at her. She took several deep breaths, then climbed out, locked her car door and began to walk down the path to number fourteen.

'Helen Kelly, *South West News*. Do you have any idea where Sophia is yet?' asked an attractive blonde girl in a very tight black suit as Rachel walked past. 'Are there any plans for a press conference?'

Rachel ignored her and pressed on to the front door, ringing the bell as the journalists glared at her back.

Experience told her that it was likely that the parents would be very distressed and on the defensive, saying, as Bill had suggested, that this behaviour was out of character, that Sophia never skived off school, didn't have a boyfriend, and was never late home. It would take some time to get to the truth, and Rachel hoped Sophia would appear before she needed to.

The fact was that ninety-nine per cent of missing teen cases – and Sophia was nearly a teen – resulted in the child turning up safe after staying at a friend's house following a family row. Rachel knew she needed to stay calm and go through the procedures methodically. The key would be Sophia's friends, who were being interviewed now and who would probably be more honest about whether she was in a strop or upset about anything to do with her parents than Alex and Adele would – and whether there was a boy on the scene. For now, she just needed to be present, to watch and to observe.

Rachel took a deep breath, just as the door opened.

Chapter Five

Adele

Wednesday, 17 July 2024

Adele's heart jolted as the front doorbell rang, and she watched Sally, the police constable who had been sitting with her and Alex most of the night, spring from her chair and walk down the hallway as the doorbell rang a second time.

She knew it wouldn't be Sophia, but she couldn't help glaring at the front door and praying to a god she didn't believe in as it opened, revealing a woman in a suit, with dark hair and a blunt fringe, standing on the doorstep.

She envied Sally. She had arrived with gusto, full of cheeriness and positivity that Sophia would turn up before dark. Now, after a long night, most of which Adele and Alex had spent searching Greenham Common, she looked exhausted. Adele glanced up at the clock, which told her it was nine a.m. She had been awake all night, her eyes stung and her head throbbed. She had put in a call to her boss an hour before, following two texts from him asking how the viewing the previous afternoon had gone. Simon had picked up immediately and she'd had to explain that the viewing had been a no-show and that she wouldn't be in work as her daughter was missing. He had feigned sympathy, but was clearly irritated as they were already a man down in the office and it was obvious he thought Sophia was probably with a friend – and that Adele was being neurotic involving the police.

Adele watched Sally let her colleague in. She could tell from the speed at which Sally had dashed to the front door, that the tension and strain in the house was getting to her. Now, though, she got to leave, go back to her home, to her family; all was well in Sally's world. It was the end of her shift, but it seemed that Adele and Alex's nightmare was only just beginning and now it was this new police-woman's turn to take over.

'Rachel, hi. Thanks for coming so quickly,' Adele heard Sally say quietly, as Adele's heart plummeted again. She felt sick, but her stomach was empty. She couldn't remember the last time she had eaten anything, but the thought of food repulsed her.

'No problem. Any updates?' Rachel asked, looking up and catching Adele's eye as she took off her jacket and hung it on the stairs. Adele felt a flutter of irritation. She didn't want these people in her house, dumping their stuff every-where, treading their shoes all over her floors, leaving their bags and coats scattered in the hallway. She wanted to scream at them to get out, but of course she didn't. She couldn't; she needed them. So she just sat and tried to focus on not throwing up.

Adele watched as the two women approached the kit-chen where she sat helplessly, not knowing what to do with her jittery body. She could hear Alex upstairs on the phone, speaking to one of the dozens of friends who kept calling, offering their sympathies and help with the search for Sophia. 'No, nothing yet,' he said over and over. 'Yes, of course I'll let you know if I hear anything.'

She wished everyone would stop calling. There was only one person in the world she wanted to hear from, and every time the phone rang and it wasn't Sophia, her pain doubled.

She could tell Alex was feeling guilty. Her house-viewing the night before had been a no-show, but she knew her boss would have wanted her to hang on, so she had asked Alex to meet Sophia on her walk home instead. Alex had told her he was caught on a work call, but it was more likely he couldn't be bothered and because of his laziness her greatest fear had become reality.

Although they only lived a twenty-minute walk from school, most of it on a main road, because of the rift with her best friend, Ruby, her daughter was having to walk on her own, which always worried her. Sophia was petite, like Adele, and she looked so vulnerable. She would have no hope of fighting anyone off who tried to hurt her. But Alex and Sophia assured Adele that she would be fine; Sophia because she knew her mother was overworked and stressed, Alex because he felt that Adele needed to stop mollycoddling their daughter. Adele had nodded her agreement at the time, but her guts had still fluttered with concern. Now, although she knew it was probably unreasonable, she felt fury towards her husband for not being kind – just for once – and going to meet Sophia because she was missing her friend.

She heard the hurried thud of Alex's footsteps on the stairs, obviously rushing to see who had arrived at their front door. Now she was missing, Sophia finally had her father's undivided attention. The two policewomen had reached the entrance to the kitchen, and Adele gripped her cold cup of coffee as Alex walked in, stood next to her chair and put his hand on her shoulder, making her shudder. Her whole body felt like an exposed nerve.

'Hello,' said Alex.

Adele knew that Alex would also hate these people taking over their house. It was strange to have the police entering your sacred space. They were nice and friendly enough on the surface, but the undercurrent, the tone they set from the very first call, was that you did things their way and you did what you were told or you would be viewed as uncooperative and it would work against you. She felt she had lost control in her own home. The people in charge were friendly and warm enough, but the tingling feeling from her head to her toes told her that she was at their mercy.

'Adele, Alex, this is Rachel Rees, the family liaison officer I was telling you about. She is going to be taking over from me.' The woman with the dark auburn hair smiled warmly. She was older than Sally – about her mother's age, Adele guessed – and quite slim and pale, nothing like Sally, who was ruddy-cheeked, with an enormous bosom and personality to match.

'Hello, nice to meet you,' said Rachel.

Alex stepped forward, holding out his hand. 'Hi, Rachel, I'm Alex, and this is my wife, Adele.'

'Hello,' said Rachel, shaking Alex's hand, and smiling gently down at Adele. Adele knew she should say something, but she felt as if she were on a fairground ride she couldn't get off and that if she opened her mouth she might vomit. Although it was a warm July day, she shivered, her jaw chattering constantly.

'I'm so sorry to hear that Sophia is missing. I'm a family liaison officer at Thames Valley Police and I'm here to work with you to get your daughter home safely and as quickly as possible.'

'Thank you,' said Alex. 'Perhaps you can help me with getting a search party organised. We've been driving around the neighbourhood and searching the common all night, and we have countless friends wanting to help, but we've been told to wait, as apparently it needs to be coordinated.' As Alex moved around the room, gathering cups from the endless caffeine being consumed, Adele clocked Rachel looking at the large map of the local area open on the kitchen table, covered in various coloured dots and Post-it notes.

'It does, yes,' Rachel said. 'We need to plan it so that lots of people aren't searching the same areas repeatedly, and also, members of the public would need to be briefed on how not to contaminate any items that could be required as evidence at a later date.'

'Evidence for what?' Adele said, glaring up at her.

'If we find something of Sophia's it could have DNA on it, which might help us in our search. I can certainly speak with Ben James, the senior investigating officer, about letting you know the plan when he arrives. I know that as Sophia didn't turn up last night, they will definitely be planning to start searching soon,' Rachel added.

'We've wasted a whole night already – when is this Ben James coming here?' Alex asked, curtly.

'I'm hoping in the next hour,' said Sally, wearily.

'The next hour? I'm sorry, but there just seems no sense of urgency. I get the impression you lot think she's run

71

away, and I don't know how to get through to you that she isn't like that. Something has happened to her,' Alex barked.

Adele flashed him a look. She didn't need his temper flaring up now, and diverting the police's attention away from Sophia and onto themselves.

Adele clocked Sally shooting Rachel a look before she replied. 'Ben definitely senses the urgency, Alex. I understand he's been going through local CCTV most of the night, and also speaking to the school and Sophia's friends.'

'Yes, Sophia's friends could be key here,' Rachel added.

'We've already been over this. Sophia doesn't have any friends she hangs out with outside school,' Alex said. 'She's a quiet child who has one best friend, Ruby, who didn't walk home with her and has no idea where she is. Adele and I have been through Sophia's bedroom twice and nothing is missing. If she has run away, surely she would have taken something with her?'

'Maybe we can sit down and discuss if there is anywhere you feel we should look for starters,' Rachel offered.

Adele felt a rush of blood to her head. She couldn't stand all these words, talking, talking, talking . . . Why were these people standing around in her house, doing nothing?

'I'm sorry, but isn't that your job?' Adele said. 'To tell us where we should look, I mean? I can't believe nobody has done a thorough search of the common yet. We've been out all night, on our own, stumbling around in the dark, looking for our baby . . .' Adele stopped herself, then stood up and went over to the window. 'There are journalists out there, ringing on our front door constantly, desperate for a comment, and I am getting very tempted to tell them that so far the police have done nothing except sit in our house, drink tea, and tell us not to worry.'

Rachel went to stand beside Adele. 'I understand, but we would really appreciate you not talking to the press as it could jeopardise the investigation. We will be asking all the reporters to go through our press office at Thames Valley, and they have just released an appeal so the journalists will be busy with that.'

Adele sat back down. 'What sort of an appeal?' she asked.

'A police appeal, to the press. Asking members of the public to come forward with any information. We'll be using the picture of Sophia in her school uniform that you gave Sally, as presumably that was what she was wearing when she went missing.' Rachel looked enquiringly at Sally.

'Yes, none of Sophia's other clothes are gone,' Sally confirmed.

'We will be going from door to door in the area where she went missing, to see if any residents have doorbell camera footage of her. If we can get the exact time she vanished from any CCTV, it would help hugely with a reconstruction, so we can try and trace any vehicles with a dash cam that do the same route every day and may have captured Sophia's movements.' Rachel glanced at Sally. 'It's also standard to invite the missing person to get in touch with us, and say that we are here to support them and not judge. Then we send it out in a press release,' Rachel said, handing a copy to Adele.

Adele read the short statement and felt bile burning her stomach. 'But this makes it sound like you're trying to persuade Sophia to come home. You're putting the onus on Sophia because you think she has run away. No one is listening. Something has happened to her. Something needs to be done as a matter of urgency. Please.' Adele heard the whoosh of blood in her ears.

'This type of incident normally ends happily with the child returned safely – and rather embarrassed about all the fuss,' Sally added.

Adele put her head in her hands, and let out an internal scream. Rachel sat down next to her and put her hand over Adele's. 'The reason I asked if you have anywhere you feel we should look is that you know Sophia better than anyone,' she said. 'We don't have all the answers. We are going to need a lot of help getting to know Sophia – and both of you – and from that try and work out where she is.'

Adele pulled her hand away and Rachel looked over at Alex.

Adele was exhausted. They had been up all night on the common with torches, calling out Sophia's name over and over until they were hoarse. Now, despite the warm morning, her whole body was shaking and her teeth chattering from the shock and she couldn't calm down.

'Honey, why don't you go and lie down, just for five minutes? You haven't slept all night.'

Adele looked at her husband. His dark eyes, fixed on her, were like Sophia's. Adele had a flashing thought that she would never be able to look at him again if anything had happened to Sophia. Every time, she would see her baby's eyes in his. She wanted to scream that she didn't want to lie down, that none of them should even think about resting until Sophia was home, but instead she nodded feebly, got up and walked towards the stairs.

She had lost Sophia once before, years ago, in Sainsbury's for about four minutes, during which time Adele had stopped breathing as she rushed from aisle to aisle, looking for her three-year-old. Every scenario had rushed through her head. She had pictured a stranger taking her little girl by the hand and walking from the store, putting her in their car, driving her away. She saw herself calling the police, telling them what Sophia was wearing that day, explaining that she only looked away for a second. By the time she found her at the pick-and-mix, she had convinced herself that she would never see her daughter again and that her body would be found somewhere, by a river or on some disused parkland. And once they were reunited, it still took her the next two hours for the adrenaline to stop pumping.

She had felt that same panic when she had got home and asked where Sophia and Leia were because neither of them were in the house. She had tried to stay calm, racking her brains for an explanation; had Sophia taken the dog out on her own without saying anything to Alex? Alex hadn't seemed particularly worried, but when he'd told her Sophia's school bag wasn't there, she'd tracked Sophia's phone. She had strummed her nails on the kitchen table, waiting an eternity for it to update. That was when she discovered Sophia's phone had been turned off. Her stomach had suddenly plummeted as if she had fallen off a skyscraper, and even now she still hadn't hit the ground.

Adele stood by the bedroom window and stared out at the two journalists at the end of her driveway.

'I'd appreciate your help in coordinating a search.' She

had left the bedroom door open and heard Alex talking from the kitchen. 'Friends keep calling and offering their help, and I feel so helpless having to turn them down,' he added.

'Of course. I am confident that will be a priority today, once the appeal goes out,' Rachel said, as Adele heard footsteps in the hallway.

'Right, I think I'll leave you to it, if that's OK,' she heard Sally say.

Adele moved to her bedroom door to listen as the policewomen spoke in hushed tones below.

'Of course,' said Rachel, who had followed Sally down the hall. 'Are you due to come back later?'

'No, I don't think so. But let me know if you need me to do anything. You've got my number,' Sally added.

'Thanks, Sally,' said Rachel as she closed the door and stood in the hall for a moment.

Adele watched Rachel taking in the array of prints and family photographs of holidays, sunsets and beach walks in bobble hats and wellies – Leia, their white lurcher, running at full pelt across the sand. Rachel leaned in, gazing at the pictures of Adele's family.

Adele could already feel Rachel judging her and Alex. No doubt it was her job to size up the family, the house, and decide if they had anything to do with Sophia's disappearance. It was all moving at a glacial pace. The police had decided Sophia had run away, and until they realised she hadn't, her and Alex's hands were tied, as precious minutes and hours ticked by.

Adele heard Alex's mobile ring again, and then his voice: 'No, nothing yet, no, she's just vanished . . . We are utterly baffled. Adele is beside herself. I just don't know what to say or do . . . I'm going out looking again in a minute . . . Thanks, I'll let you know when there's a search plan.'

Adele looked over at a photograph of her daughter and Alex in a frame on her chest of drawers. She picked up the photograph and stared at Sophia. 'Where are you?' she said, tears sliding down her cheeks. It made no sense. Sophia was shy, cautious, she didn't speak to strangers, and took a while to trust anyone. She wouldn't have walked off with someone she didn't know, or gone into their house. It would be completely against her nature. She would have kicked off in the street if anyone had tried to drag her away, and if she was with Leia on Greenham Common, Leia would have been distressed and run home if anything had happened to Sophia. Someone would have seen or heard something. She couldn't have just vanished.

'I'm going to head out again,' said Alex to Rachel. 'I can't stand just sitting here. Can you call me when this Ben James arrives and I'll come straight back?'

'Of course. I've been asked to take any family laptops, iPads and computers, yours, your wife's and Sophia's,' Rachel said.

Alex paused. 'Right, but there is a lot of confidential information on my laptop, regarding clients.'

'I understand your concern. There's nothing to worry about. It's completely routine,' said Rachel. 'And I should also let you know that, as a matter of procedure, sniffer dogs will probably come to the house later today. They will need items of Sophia's so the dogs can get her scent. Can you and Adele please make sure that no one interferes with

Sophia's bedding as this is usually the best place,' Rachel added.

'So you're searching the house before you search outside?' Alex snapped.

'It's to assist with the search outside. If Sophia hasn't been found by lunchtime, we will also schedule a press conference for this afternoon so you and Adele can personally appeal for help.'

Adele stared out of the window at the female journalist who had begged her for a quote. She was standing in front of a man with a camera on his shoulder labelled 'BBC News', and talking into a microphone. Adele walked over to the remote, and switched on the television. The woman at the end of their driveway was now on BBC *Breakfast* news.

'A twelve-year-old girl has gone missing from Newbury on her walk home from school. Sophia Norton left school yesterday afternoon at three thirty and never arrived at her house in Greenham Park Road, which is normally a twenty-minute walk. Police are appealing for any witnesses who may have seen Sophia walking down Newton Road, Deadman's Lane or Greenham Park Road between three thirty and four thirty yesterday afternoon.'

Adele closed her eyes as the enormity of the situation started to sink in. The minutiae of their life was about to be ripped apart and forensically examined by the police and the media: every aspect of Alex's work, their financial situation, that they were selling the house to pay off their debts, possibly even the fact that Adele had been sleeping in Sophia's room. Within moments her phone started to beep: mothers of Sophia's school friends who had upset Sophia, Adele's work colleagues, her boss, now sending a gushing message for her to take all the time she needed. The news was out.

As she turned off the television and glared down at the journalist wrapping up her piece, her mother's car pulled up. Felicity Stanton climbed out, dressed in a denim jacket and white jeans. She navigated the journalists without talking to them, before walking up the path and ringing on the front door.

Adele guessed that most women would be desperate to see their mothers in a situation such as this, but she didn't hold out much hope of her mother saying anything to make her feel better. They didn't have a close relationship, and although she presumed her mother would be distraught at Sophia's disappearance, Adele knew Felicity would struggle to express her emotions, and Adele didn't have it in her to be patient with her.

In fact, before she had even reached the front door, Adele found herself wishing that Felicity would just turn round and leave.

Chapter Six

Felicity

Wednesday, 1 December 1982

Silence fell. Felicity forced herself to open her eyes as her mother's hand flew to her mouth and time seemed to stop. For one minute she allowed herself to dream she had a different mother, one that would rush over and hold her, and tell her everything was going to be all right.

'Dear God,' Camilla said. 'Jesus, Lord, preserve us. Oh, Fliss, what have you done?'

Since the question was rhetorical, Felicity didn't answer it. She couldn't meet the glares of her parents either. She could just see her father's face, out of the corner of her eye, and it was all that was needed to gauge his complete horror. Her mother and father simultaneously sank side by side onto the bench in the hallway, and said nothing, staring like judge and jury as Mrs Owen scuttled off, out of the line of fire. Eventually her father turned to her mother, who was still shaking her head in disbelief.

'I think I'll leave you girls to it. I'll be in my study,' he said, as Fliss watched him walk away.

'Who is the father?' Camilla asked.

'I don't want to say,' Felicity said.

'Is he going to marry you?'

Fliss felt her face burn again. 'No, he's already married,' she said finally.

'What have you done?' Camilla said again. She clasped her hands together, as if in prayer. 'Dear God,' she gasped. 'What have I done to deserve this? Oh, Felicity, how on earth am I going to deal with this? Oh, this is a nightmare. Oh, Felicity . . .' She got up and paced back and forth like one of their hens in the barn. 'What are we going to do?'

Felicity felt her racing heart slow as a strange sense of calm engulfed her; her secret was finally out.

'We will have to go to Dr Hartley. He can have it seen to.'

'It's too late. I'm nearly six months pregnant already. I'm going to have to have it,' Felicity said quietly.

'Six months! If you weren't carrying so much extra weight, I'd have noticed before.' Camilla raised a finger and jabbed it at her daughter. 'Well, you can't stay here; we will have to send you away. What if the press get wind of this? Your father would never recover. You'll have to find a place to stay.'

'What do you mean? Where will I go?' Felicity gasped.

Camilla exhaled heavily. 'You might have thought of that when you were carrying on with a married man! This really is the most extraordinarily bad timing. I just can't think about it now.' Camilla flapped her hands as if batting a fly away. 'I have a house full of people coming today. Your timing is impeccable, as always,' she barked, before stalking off into the kitchen and slamming the door behind her.

Felicity sat in the silence of the hall, then slowly stood up and began climbing the stairs, her head throbbing. In her bedroom, she pulled out her hold-all from under her bed and began stuffing underwear and jumpers into it, not knowing what to pack for her and the baby. She pulled her

81

wallet from the drawer, and examined its pitiful contents. Her eyes then fell on the pregnancy test she had hidden in there, weeks before, pushed into the back of the drawer. She pulled it out and stared at it. She had barely slept since the circle in the bottom of the tube had confirmed her worst fears. Since then she had lived with the news alone, for four weeks, until she plucked up the courage to tell Anthony. He had swiftly produced a telephone number and told her to 'have it seen to' immediately, as if it were an ingrowing toenail. Terrified that her secret would come out and her world would end, her diary, which she also retrieved from her drawer, had been her only friend. She pushed it all into her holdall, zipped it up, took one last look at her pink childhood bedroom and walked out.

When she returned to the hall nobody was there and it was as if she had dreamed the conversation with her mother. Her father had probably locked himself in his study as he always did when there was an argument or an issue he didn't want to deal with, and her mother had no doubt retreated into a deep bath. Felicity picked her coat off the coat stand in the hall, then pulled open the drawer and plucked out a hat, gloves and scarf. She picked up her car keys, and without looking back, she walked out of the front door.

Felicity made her way along the gravelled drive, the ice crunching under her feet, towards her red Mini parked under the car port at the end of the driveway. She had spent two years saving up her wages from the pub to buy it, and her father had paid for her driving lessons when she passed all her O levels. She had aced her test first time, and never felt happier than when she was bumping along the country lanes, the windows down, Eurythmics blasting from the tinny speakers.

Fliss looked around the car port and grabbed a sleeping bag, two thick blankets and some pillows from when she had slept in the barn in the summer, and threw them into the boot. She climbed into the car, turned over the engine and backed onto the drive. She paused for a moment, looking in the rear-view mirror, waiting for some reaction to her departure, but there was none. As she pressed down on the accelerator, Maberley Manor disappeared into the distance like a doll's house. The radio crackled into life as Mr Owen watched her drive through the gates as they slowly closed behind her on the life she was leaving behind.

'Mr Heseltine, you caused quite a stir today in the House of Commons with your comments about shooting Greenham Common peace protesters,' the interviewer suggested, as Fliss stared out of the window at the December rain.

'No, I said that "intruders" run the risk of being shot. You know you cannot have weapons of this sophistication falling into the hands of people who don't know what they are doing.'

'Indeed, but these are peace protestors. It is not their intention to use them, quite the opposite.'

'I rather feel that the CND have hijacked the words "peace movement",' he continued. 'The peace movement is the people upon whom peace depends. The men and women in our armed service. The politicians who make the decisions. They are the people that keep the peace.'

'But is being armed to the teeth a guarantee of preserving the peace? Do you not think it makes it rather easy for someone to press the red button, so to speak,' argued the interviewer.

'We have preserved the peace. Whereas the CND want to take a gamble. They want to risk our not being armed, which would put us in an extremely vulnerable position.'

Felicity let out a sigh as the world rushed by outside. Soon she was heading out of Newbury, along the edge of Greenham Common. She could see the women camping out by the side of the road, tarpaulin and string the only things separating them from the harsh elements. Her eyes danced over the signs: 'Girls Say No – To The Bombs'. She pulled to a stop at the lights, beside a beautifully hand-made tapestry, which read: 'Women's struggle won the vote. Use it for disarmament'. She could see the women in their raincoats, huddled together, laughing and smiling. She wound down the window to let in some air, and could hear someone singing. Other women began to join in, their words soothing Felicity's anxiety.

You can't kill the spirit,
She is like a mountain.
Old and strong, she goes on and on and on . . .

'Well, their resolve isn't wavering,' the radio interviewer continued. 'They have been there for over a year and it seems these women are here to stay.'

'We will see about that. I wouldn't say they have a great deal of support. Certainly not from the press or from the locals, and as they are a security risk we will continue to evict these protestors. Most people see our need for nuclear weapons. They feel the very real threat which exists today.'

Felicity suddenly felt her heart ache to be a part of it. Seeing all the women in the flesh brought it home to her how real their fight was. They were cold to the bone, suffering terribly to try to get their voices heard. Being a public nuisance wasn't their intention. It was a cry for help.

As the traffic light turned green, Felicity felt a flutter in her stomach. Was that a first kick? She had felt so wretched, keeping her secret for so long, but now her secret was out, and as she had feared, her mother had told her to leave. But she was still breathing. The world hadn't ended. She still had hope and she had her baby. She felt a rush of empathy for these women. Without them there may not be a world for her baby to inherit.

On the spur of the moment, she indicated and pulled into the car park next to a large banner saying 'Green Gate'.

She would just take a look, she told herself. There was no harm in that. Talk to some of the women, perhaps, offer her support. Then she would go.

Felicity turned off the engine, took a deep breath, and climbed out of her car.

Chapter Seven

Emma

Wednesday, 7 February 2024

'Blake, pack your stuff up. Kathy is taking you down to reception.' Emma had not even reached her cell, after returning from her meeting with her solicitor, when one of the screws came marching towards her, smiling uncharacteristically broadly.

'Why?' she asked, still in a daze from the news that her sentence had just been reduced by two years and she would soon be leaving.

'Governor's orders. They've reduced your sentence, so you shouldn't be in a Cat A prison. You're going to West-wood Park today.'

'What? But I can't go today. I'm not ready,' Emma stammered.

'Why not? It will take you all of five minutes to pack. Chop chop, the sweat box is waiting,' said the screw, refer-ring to the prison van, which would be taking her to the open prison near Bristol. The screw handed her a black bin bag. 'You can use this.'

Back in her cell, clutching the plastic bag, Emma looked around in a daze. She knew every inch of the yellow walls, every scratch and chip in the floor. She had hung some thin net curtains that one of the screws had given her over the small window, and stuck magazine pictures of sunsets on the wall. It wasn't much, but it was home. She had very few belongings: toothbrush, toothpaste, three pairs of trousers, T-shirts, jumpers, two nighties, a radio and her writing pad and pen, all of which she carefully pressed into the bin bag. It was all she had in the world.

Emma hugged the girls in the kitchen and the screws who had been kind to her and made her way to reception, where a guard was waiting to snap handcuffs onto her. It was only the two of them in the back of the prison van as they pulled out of the gates of Heathfield, away from the high walls, steel bars and razor wire. Emma stared out of the blackened windows, transfixed at the people bustling by and the world carrying on, as it had done for the past five years.

'You'll find Westwood Park quite different from Heathfield, Emma,' said Kathy, smiling warmly. 'It operates mainly on trust. They let you come and go a lot more, and they want to help you get your independence back.'

Emma nodded, an overload of new smells, sights and feelings stunning her into silence. She had woken up that morning in Heathfield, thinking she had at least another year there, and suddenly she was on her way to an open prison, being talked to about independence and trust.

The journey out of Surrey, around the M25 and along the M4 towards Bristol, was a long one. She stared through the bars of the police van window as the world sped past, going over and over the meeting with her solicitor in her mind.

'Your solicitor at the time didn't do his job, Emma. He let you down. If they had spoken to your actual social worker, they would have known you are not a criminal. The fire wasn't arson, it was an accident.'

It was an accident. She had always known it was an

accident, but did that mean she wasn't guilty? No. She was in the garage, smoking a spliff her parents didn't want her to smoke. She had lit the fire, which had set the house alight and killed her father. Her mother had never forgiven her, and she didn't blame her. She would never forgive herself.

As they finally pulled in through the gate, Emma could see a beautiful Elizabethan mansion, surrounded by acres of grounds. Women were working everywhere, tending to the gardens, digging up vegetables, pruning shrubs. After removing her handcuffs and wishing her all the best, Kathy left her in the vast, high-ceilinged reception. Emma then sat waiting on her own in a small room with a bench and a window with bars over it. In contrast to Heathfield it was very clean with no cigarette butts or discarded bits of food littering the floor.

'Emma? Hi, I'm Sam, the governor here.' A middle-aged woman with long wavy hair and chestnut eyes smiled warmly and shook Emma's hand. 'Let's go to your wing. It's a lot calmer here than at Heathfield,' Sam said, before charging off down the corridor. Emma scuttled to catch up with her.

She immediately noticed how much lighter the atmosphere felt. The prisoners she passed appeared relaxed and unafraid to make eye contact. Their body language was very different from that in the corridors of Heathfield. People nodded and smiled at her and there was a sense of freedom; all the windows of the prison looked out over open fields.

'Everyone's at work now so it's very quiet. There's only two wings here, north and south, so it's much smaller than you're used to. As long as you stick to the curfews and rules, you'll be fine.'

'Aren't you going to strip-search me?' Emma said.

'No, we don't do that here. We operate on trust. If you want to run away you might as well do it now. But you'll be straight back to Heathfield so I wouldn't recommend it. Most of the girls are happier here, I think. We focus a lot on the garden; being outside in the fresh air is extremely healing and growing things can be very rewarding.'

Emma nodded, feeling somewhat steamrollered by the unfolding events. 'Where do the prisoners work?' she asked, already worrying about what she would be expected to do.

'Horticulture is a huge part of our lives here, we produce some of the best fruit and veg for miles,' Sam said, smiling. 'If you don't fancy gardening, you can work on the farm or in the community shop. Or you can study. There are courses in animal care, horticulture, vehicle repair, brick-laying and catering. At any one time about twenty of the women are working outside the prison in either voluntary work in the community or paid work with local compan-ies. Let's take a left down here and I'll take you to your cell.'

'Am I sharing?' Emma asked, butterflies fluttering in her stomach.

'Yes, but don't worry, Amanda is very friendly,' Sam said cheerfully. 'She's been here for a while, so she can show you the showers and the dining room, and help you get settled. Here we are.'

Emma held her breath as Sam stopped at the entrance to a cell and smiled at the person inside.

'Amanda, your new cell mate is here.'

'Great!' Emma heard a voice that sounded friendly enough as she forced a smile and edged forward.

In the small pale blue room was a set of bunk beds. A woman with two blonde plaits and wearing dungarees was sitting on the top bunk, sucking on a lollipop, swinging her legs and smiling. She had sparkling blue eyes, a childlike round face and was beaming at Emma.

'Hey, I'm Amanda,' she said, jumping down and holding out her free hand.

Emma caught her breath. Amanda couldn't have been less than thirty but acted more like a schoolgirl, and one without a care in the world. She stepped forward with a waft of cherry lip gloss and cocoa-butter hand cream, as if she had wandered in from a day on the beach and was about to get ready to go out for the evening. She was such a contrast to all the pale, angry, hideously depressed people Emma had spent the past five years with at Heathfield that Emma felt like she must be hallucinating. She immediately felt her shoulders relax; she had never met anyone with such magnetism.

'Hi, I'm Emma,' she managed, taking Amanda's hand.

'Welcome to your new home!' said Amanda, shaking her hand energetically as Emma looked around the room, which was still fairly uninspiring, but with one huge advantage over her cell at Heathfield: a large window overlooking grounds littered with white and purple flowers, and a woodland in the distance.

'Beautiful, aren't they?' Amanda said, picking up on Emma drinking in the view. 'Crocuses. And the room is east-facing so we get the sunrise!' she added, beaming.

'I told Emma you'd show her around, if that's OK?' Sam asked Amanda.

'Sure, I'd love to,' said Amanda. 'You good to go now, or did you want to unpack first?'

'I don't think unpacking will take me long,' Emma said, lifting up her black plastic bag of belongings.

'Yes, everyone always turns up with one of those from Heathfield. Sam makes a bit more of an effort to make us feel loved, don't you?' Amanda winked at Sam and let out an infectious giggle.

'I'll leave you two to get to know each other,' Sam said, as Amanda took Emma's bag and plonked it on the bottom bunk. She beamed at her, then took Emma's hand, pulling her into the corridor as if they were kids who had been friends all their lives.

Emma felt herself recoil at Amanda's forwardness. She had spent the last five years at Heathfield fearing for her safety and locking herself away to avoid the other prisoners, and it was too much too soon.

'Sorry, I'm not used to this,' said Emma, dropping her hand and pulling back. 'I think it might be better if I get settled in the room first.'

'Sure!' said Amanda, seeming not in the least bit offended. 'Whatever you like. I'll leave you to find your feet and come back in a bit with a cuppa for you. Don't worry, I know it's a huge adjustment, but you're safe now. See you in a bit,' she said, popping the multi coloured lolly in her mouth and skipping off down the corridor.

Emma stood watching Amanda go, feeling like she was in a dream. She could barely keep up with the events of the day. She had woken up in a Category A prison, and now she was here, which felt like the Little House on the Prairie in comparison. It was all too much.

She stood next to her bunk and listened to the sound of two of her fellow inmates chatting and laughing outside the open window. She went over, held her head up to the fresh air and gulped it in.

She hoped she hadn't offended Amanda – she didn't seem to have – but she just needed a bit of time to process all the changes. Maybe this was a new start. Maybe she needed to believe what Amanda had told her: that she really was safe.

She closed her eyes and drank in the sounds of the birds outside. Slowly she allowed herself a small, hopeful smile as she began to unpack her rather pitiful bag of belongings.

Chapter Eight

Rachel

Wednesday, 17 July 2024

Rachel looked up from the map of Greenham Common on the kitchen table as the front doorbell trilled into life. She had been lost in the memories of a nine-mile perimeter of land coming back to her, the days, weeks, months she had spent arresting the women there who had laid down their lives, mentally and physically, to try to stop the delivery of nuclear weapons onto the common. As the doorbell rang, she was sucked into the present, realising that as Adele was in her bedroom, and Alex was out searching for Sophia, she would need to answer it.

As she hurried down the hall, the front doorbell rang again. In all probability it was the press, trying their luck. Now an appeal had been released, the story would take off in earnest and journalists would be arriving in droves. She expected a tsunami of them in the next few hours, trying to get a quote or more photographs of Sophia from Alex and Adele.

Rachel opened the front door cautiously. On the doorstep stood a small, attractive woman Rachel guessed to be in her late fifties. Her hair was cut in a neat, grey bob and she wore a navy shirt, white jeans and loafers. The woman looked so like Adele – with her small frame and piercing blue eyes – that Rachel immediately knew she must be Adele's mother.

'Hello? Can I help you?' Rachel frowned into the sunshine.

'Yes, I'm here to see my daughter, Adele,' said the woman.

Rachel smiled warmly, looking up to the end of the drive, where a BBC news van was now parked, and an ITV van was pulling up. She guessed there must be a dozen reporters now waiting expectantly for their next move. 'Please come in,' said Rachel, stepping back.

The woman entered the house in a puff of lavender body spray as Rachel closed the door behind them. It struck Rachel as slightly odd that Adele's mother didn't have a key to her daughter's house, or maybe she did but hadn't wanted to let herself in under the circumstances.

'It's quite intimidating, walking through all those reporters. They are very aggressive,' Adele's mother said, her cheeks flushed.

'Yes, they keep us on our toes,' Rachel agreed. 'But they are a huge help in spreading the word. A necessary evil, I'd say.'

They stood slightly awkwardly in the hall for a moment, then Rachel reached out her hand. 'I'm Rachael Rees. I'm from Thames Valley Police. I've been assigned as the family liaison officer for Alex and Adele.'

'Hello, Rachel. I'm Felicity. I won't shake your hand; I've been painting all night, trying to keep myself busy, and I can never get it all off,' she said, moving towards the kitchen. Rachel stood for a moment, then followed her.

'Is there any news of Sophia?' Felicity asked hopefully. She looked very tired, Rachel thought, and had noticeable dark circles under her eyes. 'I don't want to keep bothering Adele, but it's hard.'

'Not yet. I believe Alex is out on the common and my superior officer is putting together a search plan now.'

'Is Adele here?' Felicity asked, glancing at the map on

the table. She was quiet but well spoken, possibly privately educated, Rachel guessed, with an air of confidence.

'Yes, she's resting upstairs,' Rachel said.

'I see.' Felicity frowned up at Rachel, clearly unsure of what to do with herself.

'Would you like a cup of tea, Felicity?' Rachel offered.

'I rather thought I'd be coming to help and join the search. Not sitting around drinking tea.'

'We are just in the process of setting the search up, so it will be great to have your help,' Rachel said reassuringly. 'And Ben James, the senior investigating officer, just sent out an appeal to the public, calling for assistance with witnesses, so we are hoping that will jog some people's memories on exactly where Sophia went missing from.'

'Witnesses to what?' Felicity looked at Rachel.

'Anyone who might have seen Sophia walking home from school, to help ascertain exactly from where and when she went missing,' Rachel said gently.

'I hear that the police haven't started searching yet,' Felicity said, putting her bag on the table.

'I know that Ben is planning for the search to start imminently now it's nearing twenty-four hours. Most missing children turn up within that time frame so we have to allow for that,' Rachel added.

'Alex tells me you think she's run away. Sophia wouldn't do that. She's a shy child and extremely close to her mother. They are inseparable,' Felicity said pointedly.

Rachel smiled gently at Felicity, whose arms were crossed. She had snapped the word 'inseparable' as if it irritated her slightly. 'I know that's how mothers and daughters can be,' Rachel offered.

'And what else have you been planning, now that you've realised she's not coming home of her own accord?' Felicity said, scanning the map on the table.

Rachel smiled warmly; people reacted differently to stress and it wasn't unusual for the family to be hostile when she first arrived. She needed to win their trust, and she had the experience not to take it personally. She couldn't help feeling, however, that winning Felicity over was going to be harder than most. 'We've been tracking down CCTV and doorbell cameras on her route home, and speaking to Sophia's friends and school staff during the evening and this morning.'

A slightly awkward silence fell between them, but Rachel let it be. It was her job to observe the family, and collect as much information as she possibly could from them in order to help find Sophia. She couldn't help noticing that when she'd arrived neither Alex nor Adele's family members had been in the house with them. Usually in her work as an FLO she found the house filled with family and friends within hours, wanting to comfort and support them. To the point that it sometimes resembled a house party and she had to ask people to leave. In fact she had never known for a home to be as empty as Alex and Adele's was in the wake of a family crisis. Felicity had mentioned painting all night to distract herself – had Adele asked her not to come, and if so, why? Wouldn't she desperately want her mother here?

Rachel looked around. 'Do you know where they keep the tea, Felicity?'

Rachel began opening the many cupboard doors, looking for mugs, until she finally found them. The kitchen was stunning and looked as if it was brand new and belonged in the pages of a magazine. There were no stains on the splashback, no watermarks in the sink, no food spatters on the hob. White granite worktops, pale grey cupboards and copper bar stools surrounded a large island with an induction hob at the centre.

The whole room was open plan, with a television and wood burner at one end, and a large corner sofa and dining table dividing the room up. Sliding doors opened up onto a large, neatly manicured garden, which backed onto Greenham Common. It was beautifully designed, with prints on the walls and fresh flowers on the table. But Rachel couldn't help but feel it lacked homeliness. There was no sense that a young family lived there, no children's drawings stuck to the fridge, shoes dotted around, general mess or chaos.

'I'm not sure it feels right drinking tea when Sophia is no doubt in a terrible state somewhere out there,' Felicity said quietly.

'Well, we will need it to keep our strength up to support Alex and Adele. We will get Sophia home, don't worry,' Rachel said, as Felicity nodded gently. 'Do you know where the kettle is?' Rachel added.

'It's a boiling tap. I've never known how to work it. Alex is very territorial about his kitchen. We might have to settle for water, which is that button there,' Felicity added, pointing to the door of the fridge.

Rachel nodded, clocking Felicity's comment about Alex being territorial.

She handed Felicity a glass, then helped herself and sat down at the dining table a few chairs away from her. 'I noticed the For Sale sign – have they had much interest?' Rachel asked. 'It's a beautiful house.'

'Yes, I believe they have a buyer and are about to exchange.

It's a very stressful process for them. I suppose that will all have to be put on hold now.' Felicity shook her head.

'Hopefully not for long,' Rachel added. 'Do you know where they are moving to?'

'No,' Felicity said, offering no more information. 'It's good Adele is resting,' she added, as if trying to convince herself. 'Although I'd be surprised if she is asleep. She has trouble sleeping, always did, even as a child. She won't be able to sleep with Sophia missing.' She stared into her glass of water, twisting it around so it scraped on the table.

'Alex said Adele couldn't stop shaking this morning,' Felicity continued. 'She got cold, searching the common all night. I can't bear to think that Sophia might be out there alone . . .' Felicity suddenly started to cry and brushed her tears away angrily. She stood, walked over to the kitchen and got herself a tissue. 'I know how cold it gets at night on that common, even in the summer. It's surprising.'

Rachel nodded. Felicity suddenly looked a lot frailer and more vulnerable than she had done a few minutes before. And she kept referencing conversations with Alex, as if Adele and her mother hadn't spoken.

'Yes. It does.' Rachel hesitated before continuing. 'I spent many nights there in the eighties, during the Greenham Common protests.'

Felicity's tired eyes darted up to Rachel. 'Me too,' she said quietly. 'Although I rather suspect you were making arrests rather than supporting the cause.'

An image flashed into Rachel's mind: a male colleague dragging a woman away from the entrance to Greenham, as the protestors tried to stop the delivery of the nuclear weapons. Bitterly cold, the puff of the woman's breath as she sang, a sea of tired, dirty, broken women behind her. The woman's hip was cut as she was pulled over the cold hard tarmac, a small trail of blood following her.

'I did have to make a lot of arrests. I was very young at the time, and had mixed feelings about it all. We got close to some of the women. I admired them all a great deal, but we were under a lot of pressure from our superiors to deal with the situation,' Rachel said.

Felicity pulled out another of the dining chairs and perched on the edge, as if not committing herself fully to their conversation. An awkward silence fell between them.

'So Alex is still out searching the common, is he?' Felicity asked, sipping her water.

'I'm not sure where he is searching now, to be honest,' said Rachel. 'Apparently a lot of his friends have been calling asking to help and he's keen to coordinate them.'

'I see. It's nice to know he cares,' Felicity said.

'I'm sure he does.' Rachel noted a hint of sarcasm in Felicity's comment. She already felt that Felicity wasn't crazy about her son-in-law, but decided not to query her on it – yet. She found that prying too much before building any rapport could make family members prickly.

'Were you a Greenham woman, Felicity?' Rachel asked.

'Well, for a bit . . . I always felt guilty I didn't do more and couldn't stay longer. But it was . . . impossible. Mostly because of you lot, and the bailiffs,' Felicity said, looking up.

'Yes, I'm sorry,' Rachel said, meaning it, and letting it hang in the air for a moment. 'I've noticed that many of the women I've spoken to over the years who were at

Greenham say that – that they wish they'd done more. You did a lot more than most. You should be very proud.'

Felicity glared at Rachel, let out an irritable huff and shook her head, signalling to her that the subject was now off limits. Suddenly the front doorbell rang, making Rachel jump.

She went to answer it and Ben James dashed in. As Rachel closed the door behind him she could see that in the short time since Felicity had arrived, the press at the end of the path had doubled. Her stomach flipped. The amount of press interest always correlated with the amount of pressure from the public on the police – and therefore on her. She realised, as she closed the front door, that her hands were shaking.

She followed Ben into the kitchen. He had recently been transferred from the Met and she hadn't had many dealings with him yet. She'd heard that he was very ambitious; indeed, he was the youngest senior investigating officer she had ever worked with. He had dark hair, a narrow face, olive skin and a clipped London accent. He had an air about him that made her feel he was always looking to get on to the next thing. When you were talking to him, he would look over your shoulder distractedly, as if checking whether there was anyone more important he could be spending his time with.

'Hi, Rachel, how's it going? Where are Alex and Adele?' he said, looking around the kitchen.

'Adele is upstairs resting and Alex is out searching the common. Ben, this is Adele's mother, Felicity,' Rachel said.

'Hello. Ben James, senior investigating officer. Nice to

100

meet you, Felicity.' Ben stepped forward and reached out his hand, which Felicity took, albeit reluctantly.

'How is the search going?' Felicity asked.

'Yes, so the search is now under way. We've got a team of fifty, with sniffer dogs, on the common, then another team of fifty going door to door in the area. We've got two hundred volunteers who we are coordinating from the sports hall at Sophia's school. So a good number.'

Felicity nodded. 'Presumably you have no updates on Sophia's whereabouts?'

'Not yet. Rachel, could I have a word, please?' Ben said, throwing an insincere smile at Felicity as he walked Rachel down the hall and into a study with floor-to-ceiling bookcases and a large desk in the window overlooking the journalists at the end of the drive. There were wires all over the desk from where Alex's computer had been taken away for investigation.

Ben closed the door behind Rachel and then shut the blinds.

'So we've got an update. Alex's email account makes reference to a large transfer of money – two hundred and fifty grand – which he has just paid to Adele's grandfather, Edward Mills. It seems it was originally a long-term loan to help bail Alex's consultancy firm out due to two clients suing him. Edward sent several emails about two months ago saying he urgently needed the two hundred and fifty grand back. It seems Alex didn't have it so he's borrowed it from a dodgy firm of moneylenders who Edward Mills put him in touch with.'

'Do we know why the clients are suing him?'

'Not yet. Looks like it might be a straightforward case

of overpromising and under-delivering, but I'll let you know when I've got more on that.'

'Quarter of a million.' Rachel shook her head. 'That's a serious amount of money to owe someone.'

'Yes, and it looks like these moneylenders have been hounding Alex as he's missed the first two repayments.'

Rachel nodded. 'So we potentially have a motive for someone taking Alex's child.' In moments like this, she remembered how she used to feel; a discovery or disclosure that made the hair on the back of her neck stand up as her adrenaline sparked.

'Well, yes and no. I mean, the maximum sentence for kidnapping in this country is life imprisonment,' said Ben, glancing at his phone as it started to ring. 'So it is a serious amount of money, but I'm not sure two hundred and fifty grand is enough to risk life imprisonment for someone running a moneylending firm. I'm not convinced we've got a motive yet, but potentially there's something in this.'

'Maybe they wanted to scare the kid to make her dad cough up – and it went wrong,' Rachel suggested. 'So what's the plan?'

'We are getting Alex in anyway this morning to take his statement, and we will ask him about it. I'm going to do some background on this firm of moneylenders and find out the link to Edward Mills. We need to know why he recommended them. Has he had dealings with them before? Obviously I'll have to do some digging before I speak with Edward Mills or he could just shut me down,' Ben added.

'Can we speak to other clients, see how heavy-handed these people get with clients that don't pay?'

'Yes, good idea, but we need to tread carefully. I don't want these guys knowing we are sniffing around. If they are involved they could go to ground,' Ben said. 'In the meantime, I want you to speak to Adele and find out how much she knows about all this, i.e. Alex's financial situation and the loan. Why did Edward Mills suddenly need that money back so badly that he forced Alex to use loan sharks? Has Alex been hiding it all from Adele or does she know what a mess they are in?'

'The house is up for sale so she possibly knows something,' Rachel offered.

'We can't take that for granted. He could have told her all manner of lies.'

'I don't get the impression Adele's mother is massively keen on Alex, so I could try and press her on that,' Rachel suggested.

'Yes, do that,' said Ben, glancing down at his phone.

'When's the press conference?' Rachel asked.

'This afternoon, at three. You'll need to brief Adele. I'll prep Alex while we are on the search and we will meet you at the station,' Ben said as his phone rang again. 'Adele can do her statement tomorrow morning if Sophia hasn't turned up by then. We are still not giving up on the idea that she's with a friend or boyfriend Alex and Adele don't know about, but it's looking increasingly unlikely.'

'Sure, and she's young for her year – only just turned twelve – so a boyfriend seems unlikely,' Rachel said.

Ben nodded. 'I still feel quite in the dark about Sophia. The family are being cagey because they are convinced she hasn't run away, but we don't know her at all. We need more on Sophia's likes and dislikes. What groups and clubs did she go to? Is there a youth club she attends? Does she have a crush on a boy there her parents don't know about? Is there any money missing from Alex or Adele's wallets? Or their bank cards. Or bank accounts. Is Sophia very sensitive? Would she have any fear of coming home if she had been naughty? Try not to make Adele feel that the questions about Alex's finances are that important. We don't want them to feel we are judging them. We need them on side right now. We know nothing about this family. We don't want them shutting down before we've even started.'

Rachel felt a ripple of irritation in her guts. She knew when she was being mansplained to and this felt very close. She didn't need Ben to tell her how to do her job. Far from the idea that an FLO goes and meets the family, has a nice cup of tea, then leaves, the role provided a vital bridge between the victim's family and the investigation. She knew it was her job to get to know Sophia and her family as well as she possibly could, in the hope that they would disclose a vital bit of information that was crucial to the investigation and bring Sophia home. She had thirty years' experience in CID – she knew what was required of her – she just needed a bit more time with Alex, Adele and Felicity.

Rachel watched Ben as he frantically replied to the texts coming in. He hadn't asked her opinion on anything she'd observed so far. What could she have to offer? The police force was so politically correct now – on the surface – compared to when she'd started in the early eighties. The lockers were pristine and absent of pictures of topless women, the coffee table empty of page-three girls, yet she still felt the undercurrent that she had when she'd started out.

An era when women on the force found it hard to be taken seriously – something she experienced first-hand when she'd tried to track down the mother of a tiny baby who had been handed to her in 1983. It had been very early on in her career when baby Emma had been found on the steps of St Phillip's, and her boss had been as patronising then about her chances of finding the baby's mother as Ben was being now. She didn't know if it was because she was junior, or a woman, or a combination of both, but she'd felt utterly powerless. She often thought of that baby, and its mother, and how much more she could have done to find her. But she was a baby herself: she had no experience, no support from anyone, no resources.

She wasn't going to be bulldozed this time and she felt a flutter of her old spirit rearing its head. 'Ben,' she said as he looked up from his phone and frowned, 'I've heard very good things about you, but we haven't worked together before. You may not have been told, but I've been working in CID for thirty years. If anyone can get this family to talk, I can. I know what I'm doing, and when I have something to say that I think is important and relevant, I hope you'll listen.'

Ben looked at Rachel a little startled. 'Of course,' he said, nodding. A frantic knocking on the door of the study broke their conversation and Rachel took control and walked over to open it.

'What's going on? Who are you? 'Have you found Sophia?' Adele said, glaring at Ben. She stood in the hallway in front of her mother. Her skin was grey, her eyes blood-shot, her arms were crossed and she was shaking.

'No, Adele, I'm sorry, we haven't yet. My name is Ben James. I'm heading up the search for Sophia.' Ben stepped forward to shake Adele's hand but she didn't take it.

'So you've accepted she hasn't run away now?' Adele snapped, as tears filled her eyes.

She looked exhausted, thought Rachel, broken.

'An extensive search of the area is now under way and we have two hundred volunteers at Sophia's school. Everyone wants to help. We will do everything we can to get your daughter home safe,' Ben said. 'In the meantime, we have a press conference organised for three this afternoon, but Rachel will talk you through that. I'm going to head back to the station now, Rachel. I'll call you in an hour.'

Ben opened the front door and disappeared as quickly as he'd arrived, all the journalists watching him as he dashed down the path, into a waiting squad car.

As Rachel closed the front door and turned back to Adele, she was startled to see her doubled over.

'Where is she? Where the fuck is she?' she shouted at her mother.

'I don't know, darling, but we will find her,' said Felicity, as Adele began gagging and retching up bile.

Rachel looked at Felicity as she dashed over to put her arms around Adele.

Adele began to stagger, reaching out for the banister to steady herself, and Rachel caught her just before she fell. She lowered her down onto the bottom step of the stairs, and Felicity enveloped Adele's tiny frame as she began to sob hysterically.

'It's OK, sweetheart, we will find her. Won't we, Rachel?' said Felicity, looking at Rachel with tears in her eyes.

'Yes, we will,' Rachel said firmly, looking down at Felicity, who clutched her daughter as she sobbed like a child in her mother's arms.

Chapter Nine

Adele

Wednesday, 17 July 2024

Adele Norton walked into her grandmother's old dressing room at Maberley Manor and ran her fingers along the rows of beautifully pressed silk shirts, linen trousers, cashmere jumpers and Chanel jackets. She had been awake all night, searching the common for Sophia and lack of sleep was starting to distort time, disorientating her so she felt like a child again herself, gazing at the sequinned evening dresses, diamond-encrusted jewellery and sparkling mules that her grandmother had collected over the course of a lifetime. The dressing room smelled of Chanel No. 5, Camilla's signature scent, bottles of which were lined up across the mirrored dressing-room table under the bay window overlooking the garden, along with an array of lipstick, mascara, eyeliner and hairspray.

She couldn't remember a time when her grandmother hadn't exuded glamour. From the days when they were invited around to Maberley Manor for 'casual brunch', when she would answer the door in pristine white jeans, a chiffon shirt and Chanel pumps, her chestnut bob blow-dried until it shone like glass, through to huge garden parties, attended by colleagues of her grandfather's and their wives, Members of Parliament, the press and public relations managers. Camilla would float around in head-to-toe linen, huge costume jewellery, her feet in high wedges. These were events that she would plan for months, making sure every single detail was perfect at the Georgian mansion, the home she had inherited from her father, as he had from his father before that. The jewel in their family crown.

Adele had spent a lot of time with her grandmother, Camilla, but she felt that until the day she died, she was a closed book. Even when cancer was ravaging her body, her mask never slipped.

Adele sat in front of the dressing-table mirror and stared at her pale, drawn reflection. She had lost the sensation of overwhelming panic and had now slipped into numbness. She felt as if she wasn't in her body, as though she was dying and was watching herself from above. The clock on the bedside table told her that it was 2 p.m. Sophia had been missing for nearly twenty-four hours. It had been the longest day of her life. Her home felt like a pressure cooker, police coming and going, constantly talking on their mobiles, journalists ringing on the doorbell. The smell of all the people overwhelmed her: their aftershave and perfume, the waft of the onions in the sandwiches they ate, their coffee breath. It all made her want to heave. It didn't smell like her home because she could no longer smell Sophia.

She had sat at the dining table in her kitchen, trying to suppress her panic and fear as a swarm of police dressed in black raided their home. Rachel had explained that, as a matter of procedure, a team would visit the house to complete a detailed search. It hadn't been enough to take all their devices and computers, and Sophia's bedding and blanket for the sniffer dogs. It also seemed necessary for a flock of eight police officers to rain down on them and examine every single item they owned. From the loft to the basement, every drawer opened, every personal artefact scrutinised, every piece of furniture lifted off the ground as if Sophia herself would miraculously appear from underneath it.

It wasn't hard for Adele to interpret that she and Alex were viewed as potential suspects. The list of pointless questions had continued. Over and over again, she had been asked what Sophia had been dressed in on her way home from school, what Alex and Adele had been wearing that day, all of the family's movements the day Sophia had gone missing, and the day before that. They wanted school photographs of her in her uniform, recent video footage of Sophia, all the family's phone numbers and previous addresses. Was there anyone they knew who might be involved in Sophia's disappearance, even someone who just made them feel slightly uncomfortable? If Sophia had been taken, they said, it would have been by someone she knew, otherwise she would have lashed out, screamed, or done something to attract attention to herself. It was hard, they said, to abduct a twelve-year-old girl off the street without anyone noticing.

Alex was being irritatingly proactive and the hypocrisy was making her skin crawl. He had always been hard on Sophia, impatient and neglectful. And yet now she was missing, he was suddenly Father – and Husband – of the Year. Adele could hardly bring herself to look at him, the memory of the silent phone call the night before Sophia went missing haunting her. And the second call, which Alex had answered when he got home, telling whoever was at the other end of the line that he couldn't talk and not to call him at home. She agonised about mentioning the calls to

Rachel, their FLO, but if her husband was screwing someone else was it really likely to have anything to do with
Sophia going missing? The minute she mentioned it, she
would not be able to take it back. No doubt it would leak to
the press and the journalists outside would have something
to write about. She didn't feel ready to throw that grenade
into their marriage just yet. If Sophia, wherever she was,
was able to access a newspaper or magazine, reading about
her father having an affair would break her heart.

Besides, she didn't feel like she could trust the police,
when they had done nothing but take from her. She waited
for news from Rachel, waited for any developments or
disclosures – nothing, no updates, just more questions,
questions, questions for them. But when she had a question
herself, it was met with silence or excuses.

She had been taken in a daze to the press conference
by Rachel. She had met Alex there, as he had been giving
his statement for five hours at the police station. He
looked deathly pale and wouldn't meet her eye, which
worried her.

Rachel had warned her the school gymnasium would be
full of media. But she was still stunned when they were
greeted by an explosion of camera flashes. Several rows of
reporters, photographers and TV cameras lay in wait for
them. And if she or Alex looked at each other, or showed
any emotion, the flashes turned into a firework display. She
had been unable to speak, and stared down at the microphone in front of her while Alex told the baying mob of his
desperation to get their daughter back, and begged for
anyone who saw Sophia walking home the previous day to
come forward.

Adele looked down onto the manicured lawn below her grandmother's dressing-room window at Maberley Manor. The garden was a work of art. Every time she had come over to the house as a child, her grandfather had been on his ride-on mower, and he would beckon her over so she could sit on it with him. The garden was his pride and joy, and his whole year revolved around planting bulbs, pruning roses, training wisteria over the oak pergolas, and perfecting the lawn for the annual Mills garden party that was the highlight of Camilla's year – and the day her mother, Felicity, dreaded the most.

By the time she was ten, Adele had known the signs that the garden party was imminent. In the weeks leading up to it, her mother would start referring to it irritably: 'I suppose we will need to go shopping and get you a new dress. You've outgrown your blue one and my mother will comment on it.' Snapping at her father that he would need to get his suit dry-cleaned and his hair cut. The invitation would sit on the breakfast table, like an undetonated bomb, propped against the salt shaker, covered in specks of butter and jam; the familiar quarrels commencing in their otherwise peaceful household.

In all her thirty-seven years, Adele had never seen her mother and grandmother having a meaningful conversation. On the rare occasions they visited her grandparents at Maberley, they would have tea in the stuffy conservatory, her mother sitting awkwardly as Mrs Owen shuffled in and out bearing trays of sandwiches and cakes which her mother rarely touched. Adele would then pick her moment, when she could escape the tension in the air and rush to the room where she sat now. Brushing her hair with her grandmother's Mason Pearson hairbrush, trying on her make-up and heavy costume jewellery.

Adele picked up Camilla's red Chanel lipstick and slowly pressed it onto her pale lips. Just like she had as a little girl. For as long as she could remember, her whole life had been overshadowed by a feeling of exclusion, like walking into a room when everyone stops talking. Adele had learned from a very early age not to ask any questions and she had the sense that her mother was always running on empty. Adele knew there were secrets in her family – and now it sounded as if Alex was a member of the club she had always been excluded from.

Rachel had sat her down at the kitchen table that afternoon and broken the news gently. 'Adele, Alex's email account makes reference to a large transaction of money, two hundred and fifty thousand pounds, which Alex has just paid to your grandfather, Edward Mills. It seems it was originally a long-term loan to help with cashflow as Alex was being sued by two clients. Edward sent several emails about two months ago saying he urgently needed the money back. It seems Alex didn't have it, so he's borrowed it from an illegal firm of moneylenders, who Edward Mills, your grandfather, put him in touch with.'

'He owes a quarter of a million pounds to loan sharks?' Adele had repeated back to Rachel.

'Yes, and they've been hounding Alex for the money as he's missed the first two repayments.'

Adele nodded. 'Have *they* taken Sophia? Because of the money?' she said, feeling vomit threatening to come up again.

'That's what we are trying to find out. Maybe they just wanted to scare you both to make Alex pay up and they weren't expecting this level of press interest.'

'What do you mean? Are you saying they are going to do something to Sophia because she's on the news?' Adele stared at Rachel, panicked.

'No,' Rachel had replied firmly. 'That would not be in their interest. We are questioning Alex about it now and doing some background research on this firm to find out why Edward Mills recommended them and whether he has dealt with them before. We will bring Edward in for questioning later.'

'I want to talk to my grandfather now,' Adele had said, shooting to her feet. 'I can't sit here doing nothing. I'm losing my mind.'

'Adele, how much did you know about Alex's financial situation and the loan? Do you have any idea why Edward suddenly needed that money back so urgently that he forced Alex to use loan sharks?'

She was embarrassed to tell Rachel that her husband had kept her completely in the dark. Her own husband, sneaking around with her grandfather behind her back, borrowing more money than he could ever pay back, lying to her face, making decisions without her that affected their home and security. She had known that he was stretched and that they had to downsize to help alleviate the pressure, but not that Alex had borrowed a quarter of a million pounds from criminals. She felt dizzy as Rachel looked at her inquisitively and it took a great deal of strength not to throw up.

She had said nothing, then walked out of the room, picked up her car keys and opened the front door. She could hear Rachel coming after her, asking her to stay, but all she could hear was the hissing of pressure in her ears, and the cacophony of the press as they ran towards her. She had fought past the journalists, climbed into her car, started the engine and tried to pull away. But as she revved the engine, the sea of reporters had surrounded the car and made it impossible to drive off.

Rachel had suddenly appeared beside her, shouting at the reporters to move away, opened the car door, helped Adele to her own car, and eased her in. Rachel had then climbed into the driver's seat, and sat on her horn until the press had finally moved back and made a path they could get through. Rachel had pulled out onto the main road, the route Sophia would have taken home from school, a route which was now littered with black-uniformed search teams.

'Where are we going?' Rachel had asked eventually.

'To my grandfather's house, Maberley Manor,' Adele had said, as Rachel typed it into the sat nav and pressed start. She drove in silence until they arrived at the Georgian mansion, where Adele had asked Rachel to wait in the car.

Now Adele ran her fingers over the jewellery box, which lay on top of the glass-covered antique dressing table where she sat. Slowly she opened it and began to pick out the Butler & Wilson brooches: chunky aquamarine, garnet and rose quartz costume jewellery, which, unlike Camilla's ruby and diamond engagement rings and Cartier watches, were not locked away in the safe her grandmother had once told her about.

She then pulled open the top drawer and – looking out to the grounds to check her grandfather wasn't yet returning from his walk with the dogs – began rummaging through them. She wasn't sure what she was looking for, but the news of Alex and her grandfather's subterfuge gave her the feeling she had carte blanche. It was an open house now. Sophia's life could depend on it.

Glancing up again, Adele could see her grandfather walking back towards the house, his beloved cocker spaniels jumping up at his legs. He was seventy-nine years old, and since Camilla's death the year before, Adele had noticed a change in him. He had aged noticeably. His once determined strides across their vast garden had turned into an apologetic dodder. His six-foot-one frame had shrunk, due to him stooping over the sandalwood walking stick that accompanied him everywhere. Added to which, he was a shadow of a man without his effervescent wife. Adele had grown up watching them together; it was obvious Edward was deeply in love with Camilla and missed her terribly.

His eyes would fix on her as she flirted, sparkle as she told anecdotes and dim when she left the room. Adele would often hear him asking guests at their parties if they had seen his wife, as she danced from room to room, charming everyone she met.

Everyone, it seemed, wanted to be in Camilla's company – except her own daughter.

Adele felt her guts twist as Edward neared the house

and she quickly focused on Camilla's dressing table. The top drawer was filled with various skincare products, cotton wool pads, lotions and nail varnish remover. The second one contained a hairdryer, curlers, hairspray and kirby grips. Conscious that Edward would soon be at the kitchen door, she ploughed on to a drawer filled with a blotting pad, invitations to various events, an address book, and headed notepaper with 'Maberley Manor' written in italics. Adele heard the back door open, and her grandfather shouting at the dogs. She pressed on, with only one drawer to go.

In it, Adele found a large navy diary, the year 2023 embossed in bold white letters. She opened it up, flicking through the pages. It was packed with doctor's appointments, X-rays, consultants, blood tests. Towards the end of her life, Camilla's handwriting had become almost illegible and it was hard to make out.

As she returned the diary to the drawer, a Basildon Bond envelope slid out, with one word in slanted black writing on the front: 'Emma'. She opened it, and found it contained two letters. The first was dated nearly a year before, and was from a solicitor, Caroline Thomas, of Knight Solicitors in Newbury, confirming an appointment the following week, and enclosing the address and telephone number of a woman called Hazel Evans. The second, which she turned to quickly, knowing her grandfather would soon be making his way upstairs, was from Hazel Evans. Adele's hands shook as she carefully unfolded it and began to read the letter.

Dear Camilla,

It was lovely to receive your letter. I am sorry to hear you have been so poorly. It has been a long time since our paths have crossed, and of course I understand that it was a difficult time. I accept your apology and appreciate you offering it. I would love to meet and discuss your daughter, Felicity, or Fliss, as I knew her when we were at Greenham together. It was a magical time in my life, we were soul sisters, and it broke my heart that she felt we couldn't be part of each other's lives any more.

I was sad to read that the two of you are also estranged. I think Fliss is perhaps right to feel that we let her down, and I think it would be a good idea to try and make amends. However, I think we should tread carefully. I know Fliss, and I don't think we should push her into a corner with any enquiries to the council regarding a reunion with Emma. However, there is no harm in us trying to plant the seed. I understand your desire to make amends and that time is not a luxury you have.

I would love to help in any way that I can. I respect your request for complete discretion and of course I will not discuss this with anyone else. Please contact me, on 07842 339746, or at my practice on 01639 842996. You are welcome to visit me at my home town of Port Talbot, or I would be happy to come to you.

With very best wishes,
Hazel x

Adele stared at the page in disbelief, reading the same line over and over. *I know Fliss, and I don't think we should push her into a corner with any enquiries to the council regarding a reunion with Emma.* A reunion, with Emma? Was this the baby her mother had given up when she was seventeen? Her half-sister, the elephant in the room between her mother and her grandparents all these years? And why was this stranger, Hazel Evans, party to secrets in her family that she wasn't? Adele suddenly felt her cheeks burn with frustration and humiliation.

'Adele?'

Adele turned to see her grandfather reaching the top of the stairs, and hurriedly pushed the letters and thick cream envelope into her coat pocket.

'Hello,' she said, standing up.

'What are you doing here?' her grandfather asked, clearly startled. 'Is there any news of Sophia?'

Adele felt her chest tightening with adrenaline. 'No.'

'I'm so sorry, darling. I can't imagine what you are going through. Can I do anything?' he said, shuffling towards her. 'I saw someone was waiting for you outside.'

'It's a family liaison officer. She's with the police.'

'I see,' he said. 'Have I missed something, Adele? I'm not sure why you are here.'

'I actually came to ask you something,' she said, hesitating before Sophia's face flashed into her mind.

'OK,' he said, the warmth in his voice slipping suddenly.

'Why did you pressure Alex to pay you back the money that you lent him?' Her voice trembled. She didn't know if it was the shock, or that she had never confronted her

119

grandfather about anything before. She felt five again, as if she were standing in one of her party dresses, looking up at him. 'It's an awful lot of money and it put him – put us, as a family – under terrible pressure.'

Edward's face fell. 'Darling, it's complicated. I don't feel comfortable discussing this with you. It's between me and Alex.'

'OK.' Adele stared at him in disbelief. 'That's all you've got to say? I should probably warn you, the police think that the loan sharks you pressured Alex to borrow a quarter of a million pounds from may have something to do with Sophia's disappearance.'

Edward stared at his granddaughter wide-eyed. 'What on earth . . .? No, that's impossible.'

'No, Edward, it's not,' she said, her voice breaking. 'Who are these people? The police said you recommended them.'

'I didn't personally. Anthony Hislop, who is an old friend of the family's, put Alex in touch with them. Darling, I think it's very unlikely this has anything to do with Sophia—'

'I don't really care what you think, Edward. All I know is, the police are about to pick all our lives apart and there aren't going to be any secrets any more, between any of us,' Adele snapped. 'They are going to get you in for questioning and I suggest you tell them everything you know, for Sophia's sake,' she added, before storming past him and making her way down the large staircase where Mrs Owen, the housekeeper, was waiting patiently for her by the front door.

Mrs Owen had worked for the family since her mother was a child – long before Adele was born. She was a small, buxom lady, who moved everywhere at bristling speed, despite now being in her early seventies. She was a woman of few words, and was ruthlessly efficient. Her long-suffering husband had died a decade before, but Mrs Owen still lived in the small gatekeeper's cottage at the entrance to Maberley Manor and had devoted herself to Edward and Camilla for as long as Adele could remember.

'Adele, I'm so glad to see you. Is there any news of Sophia?' Mrs Owen asked anxiously.

Adele ignored Mrs Owen. She felt crushed and desperately confused. Edward Mills owned Maberley Manor. Even if, for some reason, he had a cashflow problem and needed the money he had lent to Alex back urgently, he had a house crammed to the rafters with valuable paintings, antiques and artefacts he could sell.

Adele had now experienced her grandfather's cruelty first hand, and it hurt. She had come to him, cap in hand, asking for information potentially relating to her missing daughter, his own flesh and blood, and he had turned her away. Her heart ached at the thought of her mother growing up with Camilla and Edward as her parents.

Adele glanced up to see if her grandfather was following her. 'Mr Mills has been so worried,' Mrs Owen added.

'I doubt that,' Adele snapped, walking past the housekeeper. She knew her grandfather's behaviour wasn't the housekeeper's fault, but she was too stressed and overwhelmed to be diplomatic.

'Adele, he has. He is terribly stressed. He cares very deeply for Sophia and he is not in good health at the moment. I am worried about him,' she added.

'Well, I'm sorry to hear that, Mrs Owen, but I don't have the strength to worry about my grandfather today,' Adele said, hurrying towards the car where Rachel was standing. Rachel looked up as Adele walked towards her.

'Adele!' called Edward from behind her. 'Darling, don't leave like this.'

As Adele reached Rachel she turned back. 'Rachel, this is my grandfather, Edward Mills. Edward, this is our family liaison officer. She's been sent to make tea and spy on us.'

'I see,' he said, smiling nervously as Rachel frowned at Adele, then looked at Edward.

'Nice to meet you, Mr Mills.'

'Sorry, did you want to add anything?' Adele said, glaring at her grandfather.

Edward hesitated, glancing at Rachel. 'I can't believe any associate of Anthony Hislop's would have anything to do with this. I've known him for forty years.'

'Well, you can mention that later in your interview,' Adele said curtly.

'I really don't want us to part on bad terms. Things are troubling enough already,' Edward said.

'OK, well, that's very thoughtful of you,' Adele replied sarcastically. 'I guess the police will be in touch with you later on today. Hopefully you'll be willing to share more with them than you have done with me.'

Adele walked away, leaving her grandfather stunned. She had no one now. She couldn't trust Alex or Edward. And her mother had always been a closed book – there would be no comfort to be found there. She was on her own.

'Let's go,' said Adele, as she opened the car door and she and Rachel climbed in.

Rachel started the car as Edward and Mrs Owen watched

them in silence. '"Spy on us"?' Rachel questioned, smiling gently.

'Well, you are, aren't you?' Adele said bluntly.

'I'm here to support you and Alex, and help to get Sophia home safely,' Rachel said firmly.

'Yes, that's why you grill me constantly about every aspect of our lives, and don't tell me anything about the investigation. I'm sorry, I can't be doing with tiptoeing around everyone's bullshit any more. I've done it all my life and I've had enough. All I care about right now is getting Sophia back.'

'And we will. Am I taking you home?' Rachel asked.

'No. To Port Talbot, please,' Adele said, glaring at her grandfather's back as he walked away. Edward looked frail and Mrs Owen had her arm around him and was helping him back up the steps towards the house.

'Port Talbot, in Wales?' Rachel frowned.

'Is there another?' Adele pulled the thick Basildon Bond envelope from her pocket, with the word 'Emma', written in slanted writing on the front.

'Adele, I can't take you to Wales. Ben wants us in the house, in case there are any developments. He's already concerned that we've come here,' Rachel said gently.

'Right, so you aren't here to support me. I'm not going back to sit in the fucking house, and do nothing. Can you take me to Newbury station? I'll get there myself.'

Rachel glanced down at the letter in Adele's hand as she discarded the envelope on the floor of Rachel's car.

'I'll have to call Ben on the way to Port Talbot. He won't be happy,' Rachel said after a pause. 'We will have to come back tonight.'

'Fine.' Adele nodded. 'Thank you. That's the address.' She pointed to the top of the letter.

Rachel entered Hazel's address into her sat nav, then glanced in her rear-view mirror at Edward Mills, who had turned back to look at them as Mrs Owen closed the door to Maberley Manor.

Chapter Ten

Felicity

Wednesday, 1 December 1982

Felicity stood at the gates of Greenham Common and felt a flutter of unease through her whole body. It was only three in the afternoon, but it was already starting to get dark, and she was pregnant with no home and no more than a few pound notes in her purse. She looked up to the entrance of the common, where a large white sheet was embroidered with the words 'Green Gate'. None of the women had noticed her. They seemed completely focused on the warmth from a fire in a large steel barrel, the smoke thick and the blaze struggling to stay alight in the drizzling rain. They were engrossed in conversation, smiling and chatting, wrapped up in gloves and hats and coats, with so many layers on they looked like walking jumble sales. One of the women was sitting in a chair next to the main road, with a big sign that read 'Women's Peace Camp – Do you have time to stop and chat?'

Felicity suddenly felt shy and overcome with nerves, her feet rooted to the spot. She looked up as a helicopter roared over the site, its blades threatening to put out the women's fire completely. It hovered, the noise shredding the peaceful atmosphere. It seemed to be lingering over them with intent, threatening their tents, which were merely saplings bent over and pinned down with tarpaulins resting on top, which broke free and began to dance along the ground, gathering mud and rain on their way. The women all looked up, gesturing for the pilot to move away, as they scattered, trying to rescue what they could. Felicity gazed along the endless wire fence that surrounded the entire nine-mile perimeter of the base. Despite the peace signs and the ribbons and balloons tied to the fence, the helicopter made the atmosphere feel threatening and full of danger. Finally, after minutes that felt like hours, the helicopter moved away, and she began to walk towards the women who were now slowly putting back together their shelters and gathering their disrupted belongings. She felt silly and out of place, standing there watching them, clinging to her hold-all. They were all dressed in heavy boots and big coats. She looked down at her flimsy trainers and pulled her woollen duffel coat around her self-consciously.

'Hello,' said a young woman with a soft Welsh accent, short, unkempt, raven-black hair, weather-beaten cheeks and very large bosoms squashed into her dungarees and tight T-shirt. 'Welcome. Would you like to join us?' She pulled out a chair next to her.

Felicity looked at the girl's outstretched hand. It was only a few steps, but as she walked towards her, it felt like a journey into another world, another life. Eventually she found her voice and nodded. 'Thank you.'

'We're in a bit of a mess here,' the girl said, as Felicity approached. 'Sit, make yourself at home. Once we've got the fire restarted we can make a brew.' Every sentence she said went up at the end. The Welsh accent was such a happy one, she thought, and sounded to her like a song.

Felicity sat down, taking in the sounds and smells

surrounding her. She took a deep breath in through her nose, and out; everyone and everything around her seemed to smell of woodsmoke. A blonde woman with a warm smile, wearing a big black woollen jumper, thick gloves and her hair in dreadlocks, was tending to the fire, managing to get it started again. Taking her time, she filled a tin kettle from a water butt and proceeded to hang it over the flames. Felicity looked around. There were probably a total of twelve women at the Green Gate. Everyone seemed to have a purpose. A group of three were chatting and scribbling in a notebook; two were washing up; two others were trying to put the tents back together; another three were peeling vegetables. They were all ignoring Felicity but it didn't feel hostile. She didn't feel unwanted. She felt welcome, but it all felt very alien to her and she wasn't sure why. As she sat and watched, drinking in the atmosphere, she realised nobody was rushing, fussing, staring, sizing her up, asking her who she was, trying to figure her out, like all the girls at school and the adults in her parents' world; the endless questions: *So how's school? What A levels are you taking? Where are you planning to go to university? Do you have a boyfriend? What do you plan to do with your life?*

'Excuse the hair,' said the woman, ruffling at her messy barnet. 'Clara cut it last night. It was really long, but she can't cut hair. She just kept hacking away, one side, then the other side, trying to get it to balance, until I looked like this.' She giggled.

'Rude,' called out the blonde girl with dreadlocks, as her fire sprang into life again.

'Luckily nobody is looking at me.'

'You look beautiful, Hazel,' said another woman. 'The military look suits you.'

Felicity smiled. She looked again at the wire fence surrounding the base and her eyes drank in the work of art the women had turned it into. They had decorated the fence with flowers, photographs of their children, teddy bears, pictures of doves and CND symbols. Someone had even pinned up their wedding dress. There were scores of multi coloured ribbons tied to the fence as far as the eye could see.

'It's beautiful, isn't it?' said Hazel. 'Feel free to put anything up.'

Felicity hesitated, feeling self-conscious again. 'What sort of thing should I put up there?' she asked.

'Anything you feel like, anything real, that means something to you, something you want to protect, something worth fighting for.'

Felicity smiled, stood up and walked over to fence; it *was* beautiful. She read the messages of love and hope, stared into the pictures faded from the rain, and then went back to her holdall, which she had put down by the chair. She pulled out her pregnancy test as Hazel looked over at her. She found a piece of pink ribbon and tied it to the fence, then walked back and sat down. Hazel smiled, but said nothing, as if she knew Felicity would talk when she was ready.

The light was starting to go now, but the flames were strong. The two women who had been chopping vegetables put them in a pan over the fire with some garlic, beans and tinned tomatoes. It smelled amazing and Felicity suddenly realised she hadn't eaten all day.

'What's your name?' Hazel asked, her green eyes narrowing as she smiled.

'Felicity, but everyone calls me Fliss.'

'Well, you're very welcome. It's nice to have you here. Every woman who comes brings their power,' said Clara, sitting down next to them and handing Fliss a mug of tea.

Fliss felt comforted by the way they all huddled round, making her feel welcome.

'It must be tough living out here?' she asked, already finding it hard to handle the cold. Her bum felt numb after just a few minutes of sitting on the chair, outside in the bitter cold, the brutal wind from the common showing no mercy, a sea of frosty frozen mud already beginning to encase her feet.

'Most people don't stay long. They come and go at the weekends and when they can. It's incredibly hard-going, living here full-time, and most people who try to burn out. Winter is obviously the worst – the rain, the sleet, the snow; morale gets very low. The evictions are the hardest to bear. They are very difficult to recover from,' said Clara.

'Evictions?' Fliss asked.

'Yes, the council bailiffs come here regularly and take all our things, our tents and sleeping bags, benders, food, anything that helps us to survive. Which is upsetting because this is common land and they are very rough with us.'

'What's a bender?' Fliss frowned.

'A sapling, tied to the ground with a tarpaulin sheet over the top. They are our homes. It's why Green Gate is popular – because there are woods here, with lots of young trees and firewood.'

'God, it's brutal out here,' Fliss said, shocked by the conditions the women were living in.

'However hard it is, imagine how much harder a nuclear winter would be.' Hazel looked at the ground, drawing heart shapes with a stick in her hand.

Fliss nodded. She had heard the announcements on the radio, and read the 'protect and survive' leaflet pushed through the front door of Maberley Manor; that in the event of a nuclear missile attack, the government would give a four minute warning. Four minutes to say goodbye to loved ones. Four minutes to prop suitcases against the walls, stuffed with clothes, books or anything that might help to absorb the radiation.

'I've seen the protect and survive guidance,' she said.

'I'd never get to my kids in four minutes, if they were at school,' said one of the women, who was sitting on the other side of the fire. She had short brown curly hair, and a multi coloured scarf and gloves that reminded Fliss of *Doctor Who*.

'A lot of us are mothers who felt powerless, we had to do something,' Clara said.

'It's why most of us just come up at the weekends, or for a night or two, because we can't leave our kids for longer than that.'

'So how did it all start?' Fliss said, hugging her tea for warmth. 'Who were the first women here?'

'Five housewives from Wales just felt like they had to do something, but they didn't know what. They knew the government were planning to house the nuclear warheads at Greenham, so they walked here from Cardiff. But nobody was interested. They couldn't get one newspaper or magazine to write about it, and we still can't.'

'Why? It's incredible what you are doing here, standing up to the government. It's such a great David and Goliath story,' Fliss added.

Clara shrugged. 'It's just plain old misogyny: women need to know their place. The country is run by men: all the police here, the politicians, the soldiers on the other side of the fence – even Maggie is a man's woman. And the politicians own the press.'

'Why is it so important to get press coverage?' Fliss asked.

'Because it gives us credibility. Heseltine says we have no support, but if the press write about us it proves him wrong and more people will come here.'

'But how do you get the press's attention?' Fliss asked.

'Well, we haven't been able to yet. That's why we are pinning all our hopes on Embrace the Base this Sunday,' Clara added.

'What's Embrace the Base?' Fliss frowned, pulling her coat tighter around her as the wind howled.

Two women suddenly appeared next to their group, one holding a walkie-talkie, one holding a clipboard.

'Are any of you able to go into town in the morning and use the public pay phone? We've decided that if all of us call five women and ask them to call five women, we can spread the word about Sunday quicker.'

'Sure, no problem. Do you want us to hand them out as well?' said Hazel, standing and taking one of the photo-copied sheets from the girl.

'We don't have that many copies, and besides, we haven't

a great deal of support locally so they'll probably end up in the bin. Just call as many people as you can, and if you need change for the phone, come and get some from Yellow Gate.'

'Are you up for that?' said Hazel, smiling at Fliss.

'What?' asked Fliss.

'Coming into town with me in the morning and calling five women you know.'

Fliss felt her heart sink. She didn't really know five women, least of all anyone who would be sympathetic to this cause. 'My mother is a member of the Ratepayers Against Greenham Encampments . . .' Fliss flushed with embarrassment.

Hazel laughed. 'Love it! Good for you! Well, we've got a list of all the women who have ever visited Greenham here. You can call some of them instead of your mum's friends. I warn you, though, going into town isn't fun. The locals hate us.'

'Sounds like an adventure,' said Fliss, pulling a face, which made Hazel giggle. 'So what is Embrace the Base anyway?'

Hazel smiled. 'Well, Rebecca, who is a genius, had this amazing idea to get as many women as we can to encircle the entire nine-mile perimeter of the Greenham Common airbase. The press, the police and everyone who is against us keep saying we have no support, but if we can get sixteen thousand women here . . .'

'Sixteen thousand?!' Fliss exclaimed.

'That's how many women we need to link arms around the base. Everyone has told us we are insane, but we have to try.' Hazel beamed through the drizzling rain.

Fliss felt butterflies. The image in her mind of thousands of women surrounding the base, holding hands, was a beautiful – if far-fetched – one.

'Sex-starved bitches!' A Ford Escort roared past with its window down.

'Up yours, granddad!' Hazel called out in her strong Welsh accent, before letting out a hearty laugh, her green eyes sparkling.

It was incredible to Fliss that they stayed so cheerful, living in these horrendous conditions, caked in mud, soaking wet, with no home comforts. Her mother had a fit if she ran out of avocados.

Clara smiled. 'Some of the locals aren't too keen on us being here. They come at night, mostly, and throw cow slurry in the tents and set off fire crackers. But a few of them are very kind and bring blankets and food for us.'

'Here you go,' said another girl with dreadlocks, handing Fliss a steaming cup of vegetable stew in a tin mug.

'This is Hannah,' said Hazel.

'Thank you,' said Fliss. Despite the freezing wind, the warmth between the women was infectious. Fliss felt as if she could touch it. 'I'll do what I can to help, but I don't have any money, I'm sorry. I'm not sure I have much to offer.'

Clara nodded. 'You'll learn here that you have a great deal more to offer than you realise. Everyone who comes gives us strength and we sing a lot, to keep our spirits up.'

The seriousness of what the women were trying to do had grabbed Fliss straight away, but there was also a great

133

lightness and warmth to the feel of the place and she felt immediately accepted.

Hazel smiled at her and began to sing.

You can't kill the spirit,
She is like a mountain.
Old and strong, she goes on and on and on . . .

Hazel had a beautiful voice and the others joined in happily, harmoniously, repeating the verse.

Fliss looked down at the Embrace the Base letter she had in her hands and began to read.

On 12 December 1979, the decision was made by NATO to place American Cruise Missiles in Britain. In December 1983, the missiles are due to arrive at Greenham Common, Berkshire. This year, 12 Dec 1982, the women from the women's peace camp are calling on as many women from Britain, Europe and the world, to come together around the proposed Cruise Missile base, to show that these missiles are wrong and that the continued escalation is not the way.

Below the blurb was a beautiful sketch of Greenham Common and the words: 'An ocean of women encircle the base, 12 Dec 1982'.

You are a spring and if you send this to 10 other women, who then do the same, we will become rivers that will flow together on 12 Dec and become an ocean of women's energy. Believe it will work and it will work.

At some point in the day we will link up around the base – if not woman to woman then using scarves and wool to fill in the gaps, so bring scarves and wool if you can.

We can also weave webs on the fence, bring pictures to peg up – banners, posters, photos, women and children's clothes, nappies, etc., anything related to 'real' life as opposed to the unreal world that the military base represents. This is a chance for women of all ages, opinions, backgrounds to come together before it is too late.

Fliss smiled to herself. Despite the impression she had got from her mother that the Greenham Common women were chaotic drifters, the camp felt organised and full of optimism. It was a beautiful vision, to embrace the base, and the idea to bring scarves and wool was an inspired one. However many women turned up, it would surely be a beautiful sight. Staring at the leaflet, her eyes began to swim. It was getting late and she felt very tired. She had slept in the back of her car before, camping in Cornwall, and she decided that it would be the best thing for tonight.

'I have my car here, in the car park. I think I'm going to sleep there for the night,' Fliss said, yawning.

'OK, what car have you got?' asked Hazel.

'It's a red Mini.'

'I'll bring you a cuppa in the morning and then we can go into town together.'

'Great.' Fliss smiled.

Back at her car, she unlocked the boot and put down the seat. She laid out all her duvets and pillows, and clicked on the torch. She felt strangely content. The worst had happened. She had told her mother about the baby and Camilla had kicked her out.

But she was still alive, the world hadn't ended and she had made a new friend. She felt an urge to put pen to paper, and with the smell of woodsmoke all over her clothes, and the faint sound of the women singing round the campfire, she pulled out her diary from her holdall and began to write.

Chapter Eleven

Emma

Friday, 8 March 2024

Emma looked out of her cell window at the sun as it rose over the Bristol countryside surrounding Westwood Park open prison and listened to the sound of Amanda's soft snores.

It had been exactly a month since she had received the news of her reduced sentence from her solicitor, Michael Vincent. Thirty days since she had been moved from a high-security prison on the outskirts of Surrey to an Elizabethan mansion close to Bristol, with acres of land, manicured gardens, a working farm and a shop.

Amanda, her new cell mate, had immediately set about making her feel at home. Amanda was a petite, bubbly woman, who had such a positive and open manner it was hard to believe the card on their cell door – as every prisoner had for the purpose of transparency – saying that she was serving six years for attempted murder.

It was strange, sharing a cell with someone after being on her own for so long. Emma had become so introverted, so scared to make eye contact or share any personal information with another prisoner in case it was used against her, that she had completely forgotten how comforting it could be to just chat. The atmosphere at Westwood Park, or WWP, as everyone called it, was also completely different from Heathfield. People smiled at one another. Everyone was either working on the farm, on the acres of land, or in town, so the prisoners had a purpose. They weren't sitting in their cells eighteen hours a day with nowhere positive to channel their frustration.

Over time, Emma could feel her jaw softening and her shoulders relaxing. She woke when she had slept enough, not because she was disturbed by the shouting or screaming of a traumatised prisoner. And when she fell asleep it was because she was tired from all the fresh air and physical work, rather than because her brain finally crashed from the all-consuming, endless worry.

Sam, the governor, had encouraged her to leave Westwood and wander into town for an hour, but it still felt too much, too soon. If she had a relative she could meet up with – her adoptive mother, possibly – it would be worth dragging herself out of her comfort zone for. But she hadn't heard from Sally, and the thought of wandering around a strange town on her own – or asking Amanda to come with her for company because she had no one else – was too embarrassing and depressing to contemplate. She would get there, she told herself, in time.

After being given her options, and following a chat with Sam, Emma had decided to work in the farm shop. She had been tortured about what to do. She knew gardening would hurt her arm, and she couldn't bear to work on the farm with the pigs, knowing she would get attached to them before they ended up as sausages on the shelves in the farm shop. She wanted to start mixing with the general public again, if she had any hope of coping once she was released, and the farm shop felt like a compromise. It was open to the public two days a week, meaning she would be serving customers, but the rest of her time she would be by herself coordinating the day-to-day admin.

As she had worked in a pub for years, Emma was familiar with stocktaking, shelf-stacking, being in charge of tills and petty cash. It all came quite naturally to her, and she found her organisational skills returned fairly quickly. A month wasn't long enough to undo five years of trauma, however, and despite feeling the benefits of the fresh air and the relaxed atmosphere, the constant knot in her stomach didn't really abate. She felt surprisingly comforted, therefore, when Amanda warned her about being lulled into a false sense of security at WWP.

'Everyone looks very friendly, and the atmosphere is less rigid, but that isn't necessarily a good thing,' Amanda had said quietly in their cell during Emma's second week. 'Don't forget these are convicted criminals, and you shouldn't let your guard down, any more than you did at Heathfield. If anything, you need to be more careful: because it's not high security, the lines here are blurred.'

'In what way?' Emma had asked, trying and failing to get comfortable on her bunk.

'A lot of the girls come from disadvantaged backgrounds. Most grew up in care, and quite often they have no one. This place breeds jealously. If they see you have home visits, and people who love you visiting, they will start a rumour or plant drugs so you get sent back to Heathfield. They will even be jealous of our friendship.'

Emma had been shocked, but said nothing; she didn't

want to tell Amanda that she had no one, so it was unlikely anyone would feel jealous of her.

'I'm very close to my mum,' Amanda had continued. 'She comes to see me all the time, and the other girls notice and are very jealous of that, because they don't have anyone.'

Emma had laid in the dark, just listening to the sound of her own heart racing, not sure how to respond. Unlike Amanda, who was clearly counting down the days until she got out, Emma was trying not to think too much about her imminent release. Whenever her mind crept into the future, she envisaged climbing into a taxi on her own, and heading to some homeless hostel, which Sam, the governor, had arranged for her. The thought made her feel as though she were floating on a life raft in the middle of the ocean with no sign of land.

'My advice, if you want it, is to keep your circle small,' Amanda pressed on. 'Don't try and get on with everyone, just pick your person and stick with them. You let your guard down here because it feels friendly, but they will pull the rug from under you. People here lie; they aren't as nice as they seem. And just to warn you, they will tell you stuff about me that isn't true and vice versa. They will try and trick us to break us up, but we mustn't let them. We need to stick together.'

'Yeah, OK,' Emma said, grateful for the tip. She had kept herself to herself most of her life, and particularly at Heath-field, so she didn't have a problem doing the same here.

Soon after that, Emma had fallen asleep, unable to share how she was feeling about anything in those early days.

But Amanda had a very infectious, childlike way about

her, which quickly won Emma's trust. She seemed guarded with everyone else, but poured her heart out to Emma, which made her feel special; telling her every detail about her poverty-stricken upbringing, living on a council estate, with a string of abusive stepdads, after her father died from a drugs overdose when she was four.

'My parents were both drug addicts,' she had said cheerfully over dinner one night. 'But I forgive them. They turned to drugs to cope. Their childhoods were filled with abuse and violence. My mum has always done her best. I mean, there wasn't always food in the cupboards and she'd disappear for a few days sometimes when I was little, but she was ill. She'd never let me down now. She's clean and I trust her to stay that way.'

Amanda's mum had indeed visited several times in the few weeks Emma had been at WWP. Amanda chose to meet her in town rather than in the visitors centre because she hated the idea of the other inmates snooping on her private life. Amanda would book the time out with the governor, then walk into town, returning with bags of chocolates and biscuits her mum had bought, which she would happily share with Emma.

'She's been sober for eight years now. And she's sworn off men too, after I had to stab her last boyfriend,' Amanda added casually, as Emma struggled not to spit out her cornflakes at Amanda's throw-away comment.

For two years he had been great, Amanda had said, and he'd even asked for Amanda's permission to propose to her mother. Then it had started. He used to beat her mother up in front of her, she explained, and she was terrified to go to school and leave her.

'Eventually she kicked him out – she couldn't take it any more – but he kept coming back and threatening her. One day she was scared witless and phoned the coppers, but the bastards did nothing. He came round, found us in the kitchen and I watched him break her arm. She was screaming my name and I thought he was going to kill her, so I grabbed a kitchen knife and stabbed him. There was blood everywhere. It was crazy.' She had giggled, biting into a red farm-grown apple she'd picked that day.

'But why did you go to prison when you were protecting her?' Emma had asked, wide-eyed.

'Judge didn't like me,' Amanda said, shrugging. 'I don't care. I'd do it again. And he knows that. I told him in court, next time I'd finish the job. It's probably what fucked me,' she smirked.

Emma was getting used to the fact that Amanda's manner didn't always marry with what she was saying, giggling when she was talking about stabbing a man a case in point.

Emma felt her right arm throbbing with pain as it sometimes still did in the heat, and rolled over onto her back. She ran her fingers over the scar tissue. Moving to WWP had been like the early days at Heathfield all over again. She felt continually lost and unsettled, despite Amanda's best efforts to make her feel at home. The prospect of being released and having nowhere to go weighed heavily on her. Her letters to her adoptive mother still went unanswered, and her hopes of a reconciliation by the time she was released were now fading. She found it impossible to forgive herself – for the fire and her father's death – and her mother obviously hadn't either.

She had managed to keep her scars hidden in prison, being in a cell on her own and living in long-sleeved T-shirts, even in the shower. The laser treatment had helped enormously but her upper arm and neck were still covered in stretched, pale scar tissue. She had been terrified that the scars would affect the small heart-shaped birthmark just behind her ear, which she stupidly saw as something her birth mother had given her. But luckily it had remained intact. She had no idea how she would cope wearing a dress again, or a swimming costume. It was a permanent reminder of that night, and perhaps a consequence she deserved, a sentiment she had eventually shared with Amanda.

'That's bullshit, babe. Your solicitor was right. That fire was an accident, you are a good person who made a mistake, you have to forgive yourself,' Amanda had said, linking arms with Emma as they had walked to the dining room after doing the stocktake together in the shop one evening.

'I don't think my mother would agree with you.'

'Well, she sounds like a bitch. Jesus Christ, haven't you suffered enough?' Emma had found it strange how tactile Amanda was. She had grown up in a household where affection was rarely shown. Her adoptive parents almost recoiled if she ever tried to hug them, and she had never known them to hold hands or kiss in front of her. Amanda, on the other hand, was like a puppy. Always pawing at her, linking arms, hugging her, or jumping on her back. Emma had never been a touchy-feely person, but it was hard not to feel drawn to Amanda's ways after so much mental and physical isolation at Heathfield. She was like a breath of fresh air and it was hard to believe that she had been through so much pain in her life. She found joy in the smallest things. She would get fits of giggles about slipping over on the farm, or doing impressions of the pigs troughing their breakfast, and in her typical childlike way she would ask endless questions about Emma's life.

As the days drew on, Emma found her guard slipping. As they had got changed for bed one night, Amanda had asked her about the scar tissue on her right arm. Emma had found herself opening up about her long road to recovery. The months of pain, skin grafts, laser treatments, and all while she was on remand at Heathfield Prison, waiting for her sentence hearing. Amanda had been extremely interested in every detail: how often they changed the bandages, what they put on the burns, how long it took to recover. She had then gently moved on to the cause of the fire, easing out of Emma the lead-up to that night, why she was in the garage, her relationship with her adoptive parents. Emma had frequently felt uncomfortable during the conversation: that she was being disloyal to her adoptive parents, telling Amanda how she often felt unloved. But nobody had ever shown such a profound interest in her before. Amanda seemed to relish the tiny details about her life, as if she were putting together a jigsaw puzzle.

'What did you mean when you said my parents weren't blameless?' Emma asked.

'I meant what I said. The fire wasn't all your fault. Your parents had a part to play in what happened,' Amanda said, smiling, as they sat down to eat their dinner.

'How?' asked Emma, suddenly losing her appetite, despite the food at WWP being far superior to Heathfield's.

'Well, my guess is that the reason you were in that garage in the first place was because of the way they treated you and made you feel. No one who is happy in their own skin, and a loved member of any family, would be in a freezing-cold garage in the middle of winter, sleeping in a chair and smoking mind-altering drugs. You were there just to get through the night, because you felt desperately lonely but had nowhere else to go. They made you feel that way. They made you feel unwanted and unwelcome in your own home, for which the fault lay at their door entirely.'

Emma shook her head. 'I was hard work – I *am* hard work – I should have known better, I was thirty four at the time, I'd just split up with my boyfriend and I was in a bad place. They hated me smoking drugs in their house but I continued to do so.'

'We are all hard work, Emma. You are human. You were addicted to weed because you were in pain and needed to escape. They needed to help you deal with it: go to Narcotics Anonymous meetings, or family therapy.'

'For a bit of dope?' Emma frowned.

'It's not a bit of dope. I've dealt with drugs all my life. Drugs are a Band-Aid. They mask deep-rooted suffering. Happy people don't touch them. I've never touched them. They killed my dad and they nearly killed my mum.'

'My parents would rather die than go to a Narcotics Anonymous meeting with me . . .' Emma trailed off, realising what she'd just said.

'Exactly.'

Emma paused for a moment, picking at her food, then shook her head. 'No, really, they were very good to me.'

'Good to you? You're their daughter, not a stray dog,' Amanda said, wolfing down her dinner heartily.

'Well, actually, I kind of am,' said Emma, biting down on her lip. 'I'm adopted.'

Amanda frowned. 'You're adopted?'

Emma had never told any of her friends that she was adopted, she had never trusted anyone enough to share how she really felt about it.

Her social worker discussed it with her in their meetings after she was expelled from school, and she was offered some counselling sessions. They would try and discuss her feelings on the issue, but due to budget cuts it tended to be a different counsellor every week so by the time they'd introduced themselves, time was up and she never built up enough of a bond to trust them with her true feelings about being adopted – and how she had found out.

Two of the other prisoners suddenly appeared with trays full of food and plonked themselves down at their table.

'We're having a private conversation – can you sit somewhere else, please?' Amanda said, not taking her eyes off Emma.

'Fuck off, Amanda. We can sit here if we want,' one of the girls sighed.

'You fuck off,' snapped Amanda, slamming down her palm on the table and glaring at them until they stood up and scuttled off.

'Remind me never to get in a fight with you,' Emma said nervously. 'Sam will have words with you about that.'

Amanda laughed. 'I couldn't give a flying fuck about Sam. I cannot believe you're adopted. Well, I can actually, it explains a *lot*. Tell me. Everything. Now. And none of that coy shit, Emma – I want every detail, about all of it. What age were you adopted, who is your birth mother, why did she give you up, how did you find out you're adopted, why couldn't your parents have children of their own? Talk.'

'OK,' said Emma, deciding that if Amanda really cared and wanted to know, what harm could it do?

Chapter Twelve

Rachel

Wednesday, 17 July 2024

Rachel pulled over outside Hazel Evans' treatment rooms in Port Talbot and turned to Adele. She was asleep in the passenger seat, mumbling anxiously and clutching the letter from Hazel Evans to Adele's grandmother, Camilla, which Adele had read to her during the drive.

Adele had told Rachel that her mother, Felicity, gave a baby up for adoption when she was seventeen and that this child could be who Hazel was referring to in the letter when she mentioned a reunion. Adele knew nothing about the baby, she'd said, just that her mother couldn't cope when Adele was born, because of the trauma of having to give up her first child.

Rachel looked at her phone. It was five o'clock, two and a half hours since they'd left Maberley Manor in Kingsclere, and she had three missed calls from her boss, Ben James. She quietly opened the car door, keen not to wake Adele from her much-needed sleep, and closed it. She dialled Ben's number, and he answered immediately.

'Why are you in Port Talbot, Rachel?' Ben snapped, after picking up immediately.

'Adele wanted to come here,' Rachel said calmly.

'Why?'

'I don't fully understand that yet,' Rachel replied honestly.

'Meaning?'

'I will hopefully know more soon, which I will share with you as soon as I can. As requested, I told Adele about her grandfather lending her husband a quarter of a million pounds, then demanding it back, forcing Alex to use loan sharks. Adele knew Alex was worried about money, which is why they are selling the house, but clearly she had no idea about the sums involved. She was angry and wanted to speak to her grandfather about it in person.'

'I think it would have been a good idea to stop her,' Ben said.

'She walked out of her house and was mobbed by the press. I had to intervene and help. When she refused to go back in the house there was nothing I could do but take her to her grandfather. She's not under arrest,' Rachel said pointedly.

'I am aware of that, Rachel. That still doesn't answer my question as to why you are in Port Talbot. The number of reporters is mounting outside the house, and neither Alex nor Adele are here. It doesn't look great.'

'Adele found a letter at her grandparents' house that relates to her mother. It upset her and she wanted to pursue it,' Rachel said, looking over at Adele, who was stirring.

'Pursue what?'

'I don't know, Ben. That's what I don't fully understand. Adele read the letter to me on the way here. It is from a woman called Hazel Evans to her grandmother, Camilla, and it mentions Adele's mother, Felicity. And a reunion.'

'A reunion with who?' Ben pressed.

'That's what Adele wants to find out. She didn't say

much about it, but she knows her mother gave up a baby for adoption when she was only seventeen. She was institutionalised when Adele was born and it shaped her whole childhood, but her mother shut her down if Adele ever asked her about it.'

'What's this got to do with Sophia?' Ben asked.

'I don't know – possibly nothing – but what harm can it do if she wants to pursue it? My shift is over; I'm doing this on my own time, and I will have her back tonight. She was losing her mind at home. She wants to do this; I say we let her. So what if it doesn't lead anywhere? It will give us a chance to get to know each other a bit and build some trust.' Rachel watched Adele, who had opened her eyes and was looking around in a daze.

'OK,' Ben said, softening. 'You're right.'

'Thank you. Any news on the loan sharks?' Rachel enquired.

Ben paused, his temper settling. 'As you say, the Nortons are obviously selling the house for financial reasons, and Alex is desperate. Turns out the company who loaned Alex the money has a shareholder who is a contact of Edward Mills called Anthony Hislop. Fingers in lots of pies, apparently. Been investigated for tax evasion and fraud a couple of times, but we've never been able to get him. We are bringing him and Edward Mills in this evening.'

'Anthony Hislop? I'm sure Edward mentioned him,' Rachel said.

'What did he say?'

'That he's known him for forty years and he can't believe any associate of Anthony Hislop's would have anything to do with Sophia going missing.'

'OK, well, I'm going over there soon to pick him up,' Ben added. 'There's one other thing.'

'Go on,' Rachel said, still watching Adele.

'We've been told that a local school girl reported a man following her home recently.'

'Do they know who he is?' Rachel asked.

'No. She told her parents, who reported it to the school, but there wasn't much they could do. They asked female pupils not to walk home on their own. But it wasn't Sophia's school . . .'

'. . . So she didn't get the memo? I'm guessing there's no artist's impression?' Rachel asked.

'Nope, but we've asked the girl to do one now. It was over a month ago, though, so she's probably forgotten what he looks like. I wouldn't mention this to Adele until we have the sketch we can show her and release to the press.'

'OK, I've got to go,' Rachel said. 'I'll keep you updated when we're on our way back to Greenham. I'll be back for my shift at ten tomorrow morning. Do you want me at the station or Adele and Alex's house?'

'Adele's house. Call me later. Second press conference is scheduled for nine tomorrow morning. Can you try and get Adele to find something of Sophia's to bring with her, a teddy, or a picture?'

'Roger that. More soon.' Rachel hung up the phone, dashed over to the passenger side and opened the car door.

Adele was struggling to come round. She had been up all night and was absolutely exhausted. She looked at Rachel and started to cry. 'When I woke up I forgot for a split second where I was and that Sophia is missing. I thought it had all been a nightmare,' she said.

151

'It's OK, Adele, take your time.' Rachel took her hand. 'Do you want me to get you some water?'

Adele wiped her tears away. 'No. My brain just won't stop with these images of Sophia locked up somewhere, hurt and shouting for me.'

'I know. We will get her home, Adele. Are you sure you want to meet Hazel still, because we can just go home again if you'd rather?' Rachel pressed gently, handing Adele a tissue.

'No, I want to ask her about her letter. What time did we say we were meeting her again?' Adele asked, wiping her snotty tears away. It was a warm day but she was shivering.

Adele had phoned ahead and spoken to the receptionist at Hazel's practice, saying she was Felicity Mills's daughter and asking if it was possible to have a chat with Hazel Evans. After putting Adele on hold for quite a while, the receptionist had informed her that Hazel finished at five and was happy to meet in the café next door, if she could get there for then.

'You know this could potentially be a conversation where you learn things about your mother that you didn't know before? Do you feel OK with that, given your emotional state?'

'Yes,' Adele said decisively.

Rachel picked Hazel's letter up from Adele's lap and helped her out of the car. She opened the door of the café and the smell of frying bacon and sausages engulfed them. Rachel hadn't eaten all day and she decided that she needed something to keep her going.

152

'Good afternoon, what can I get you?' said the middle-aged woman behind the counter in a soft Welsh accent as Rachel approached.

'A bacon butty and a tea, please,' said Rachel, tugging at her bag for her wallet. 'Can I get you a sandwich, Adele?'

Adele shook her head.

'You should try and have something. How about a tea with some sugar?' To which Adele nodded. 'Two teas, please.'

Rachel paid, and as they waited at the counter, she looked around. The café was obviously popular, and lots of tables were filled with happily chatting patrons. The Welsh always made the English look so miserable, she thought to herself, as the doorbell chimed behind her and she turned to see who had walked in. It was a woman around her own age with dark greying hair, green eyes and a broad grin. She was wearing flared jeans and a hand-woven brightly coloured cardigan.

The woman stopped in her tracks as soon as she saw Adele. 'You must be Adele. You look so like your mum,' she said warmly, holding out her hand, which Adele took weakly.

'Rachel?' the woman enquired, turning to her.

'Yes, and you must be Hazel?' Rachel said, taking Hazel's hand.

'Pleased to meet you,' said Hazel, smiling as the woman behind the counter handed Rachel her sandwich and two teas. 'Oooh, bacon sarnie, good call. Can I have the same and a tea, Marge?'

'Sure thing, Hazel. I'll bring them over.'

'Shall we sit?' said Hazel, walking towards a table by a fogged-up window. She put her canvas bag on the floor and sat down with a groan. 'What a day! So how was your journey? Where have you come from?'

'Greenham Common,' said Rachel, conscious that Hazel's letter made mention of Greenham.

'Oh goodness, my old stomping ground,' said Hazel cheerfully.

'I really appreciate you meeting us,' said Rachel, slightly unnerved by the woman now sitting opposite her. She was very relaxed and friendly, but gave Rachel the impression she was a force of nature. Adele stared at Hazel intensely, as if she were looking for clues.

'It's lovely to meet you, Adele. Your mother and I were very close once upon a time.'

Adele nodded, saying nothing.

'So, is it OK, Adele, if I explain to Hazel who I am and why we are here?' Rachel asked Adele gently.

Adele finally took her eyes off Hazel, turned to Rachel and nodded.

'So, my name is Rachel Rees. I'm a detective constable with CID at Thames Valley Police.'

'Oh right, goodness. Did you ever work at Greenham Common? You might have arrested me if you did,' Hazel said, giggling as Marge brought over her tea. 'Thanks, babe.'

'I did, yes.' Rachel stared at Hazel as she took a sip. Rachel had made so many arrests of the Greenham women during that time, but she felt a ripple of recognition as Hazel looked up with her striking green eyes.

'So, we are here,' Rachel continued, pulling herself back to the present, 'as I've been assigned as the family liaison officer to Adele and her family, because her daughter, Sophia – Felicity's granddaughter – who is twelve, didn't come home from school yesterday. And she is now officially missing.'

Hazel's eyes widened. 'Oh dear, I'm sorry to hear that,' she said, putting her hand over Adele's. 'I heard a girl was missing on the radio coming into work this morning, but I had no idea it was Felicity's granddaughter.'

Adele nodded, pulling her hand away gently and putting it in her lap. Rachel had noticed, in the short time she had known Adele, that physical contact made her uncomfortable.

'So thank you for agreeing to meet us,' Rachel said, pulling out her notebook and the letter Hazel had written to Camilla. 'Adele found some correspondence this afternoon at her grandmother's house, which you wrote to Camilla a little over a year ago. It mentions a reunion with someone called Emma. And we were wondering if we could ask you about it.'

'Of course you can. I've been tearing my hair out for months not knowing what to do, and then out of the blue I get a call from Camilla's granddaughter. I thought finally there was some news,' Hazel said merrily.

Adele and Rachel frowned. 'News? Sorry – what have you been tearing your hair out about?' Rachel asked.

'The will, of course,' Hazel said, matter-of-factly. 'I can't believe it, to be honest, you coming all the way down here. I've never known a copper do anything other than make life more difficult,' she added, shaking her head at Adele.

'Well, I'm sorry to hear you feel that way. Hopefully I can change your mind about us.' Rachel felt a knot forming in her stomach. Hazel was smiling at her again, as she hugged her mug and took a sip. Perhaps it was the fact she

155

was Welsh and a Greenham woman, but Rachel couldn't help but feel disarmed by her.

'What will?' Adele asked.

'Your grandmother's, of course.'

'So Emma is the child that my mother gave up for adoption?' Adele clarified.

'Yes,' Hazel said, 'and Camilla wanted to leave her some money because she felt guilty about what happened.'

Rachel smiled reservedly and caught her breath. Hazel had the most piercing green eyes she had ever seen. She was sure she had seen them before. She had a singsong way of talking in her strong Welsh accent, which sounded very friendly, but if you took her words out of context they were actually quite confrontational. There were so many Greenham women, but Hazel's distinctive eyes, her Welsh accent and her character felt familiar.

'OK,' Rachel said gently. 'So can we back up a little bit? How do you know Adele's grandmother Camilla?' she asked, pen poised over her notebook.

'I don't really,' Hazel said simply. 'She contacted me about a year ago, when she found out she was dying. As you probably know,' she added, turning to Adele, 'she was pretty much estranged from Felicity, because of Emma.'

'I see,' said Rachel, writing down Hazel's thoughts and glancing over at Adele, who was staring at Hazel wide-eyed. She was nervous that Hazel was about to tear open wounds which would be impossible to stitch up, but Adele had assured her she wanted to have this conversation. She wanted to get to the truth about her family.

'And Emma is definitely the name of Felicity's daughter, who she gave up?'

'Yes, I'd say Felicity was forced to give her up, but I don't want to upset anyone,' Hazel said, looking at Adele.

'What do you mean, "forced"?' Adele asked.

'Well, they sent Felicity and Emma away, to a relative up north. And the baby was adopted there, according to Camilla.'

'Why would they send her away?' Adele asked quietly. 'That's so cruel.'

'They was furious with her, utterly humiliated.' Hazel looked at Adele. 'I mean, not only did Felicity get pregnant by a married man, she also ran off to live at Greenham Common with all of us hippies, and Edward worked for Heseltine, the man whose job it was to shut the Greenham protest down. How was he supposed to stop thirty-five thousand women protesting, when he couldn't even stop his own daughter?'

'When did you last see Felicity?' Rachel asked, looking up from her notebook.

'Night of 1 April 1983,' Hazel said decisively. 'The day of the Campaign for Nuclear Disarmament. Two hundred women entered the base to have a picnic dressed as animals. They sent the heavies in to evict us once and for all – the council, Ministry of Defence and the police. It was horrendous, like a battlefield. I was arrested, but I ran away.'

'I was there!' Rachel said, the memories rushing back to her. Rachel's heart skipped a beat. She did remember Hazel, the girl with the green eyes whom one of the male officers had arrested. 'I put you in my van. It was me you ran away from.'

'Well, there you go. I was trying to get back to Felicity

157

and the baby,' Hazel said, as the words hung in the air. 'She was hysterical, saying her parents were going to send her and the baby away. So I agreed to go with her to Port Talbot, get her and Emma settled and then come back to the camp. And then this big brute of a copper dragged me away from Emma and the baby and arrested me. We were both screaming and Emma was crying.'

'Yes, he was very heavy-handed with you,' Rachel said, 'so I took over.' That was the morning the baby was handed in. Hazel had got away because the man who found baby Emma had distracted her outside the police station. Rachel stared at Hazel, speechless.

'I ran all the way back to the camp, but Felicity was gone. I panicked. I knew she had mentioned her parents living at Maberley Manor. We'd bumped into Camilla a couple of times in town. Camilla hated me at the time; she thought I was the reason Felicity stayed at Greenham. But I had to risk it. I got a bus out to Kingsclere, but by the time I arrived Felicity and the baby were gone,' Hazel said, the memory clearly upsetting her as Rachel and Adele listened intently. 'I begged Camilla to tell me where they were, but she said she was staying with a relative. Maybe that's why you can't find any trace of Emma locally, because she was adopted elsewhere. I wrote a dozen letters but Fliss never replied.'

Rachel let Hazel's words sink in. So, by arresting Hazel she'd played a part in Emma and Felicity being separated. If the baby brought to the police station had been Felicity's baby, Hazel had missed seeing her – and potentially recognising her – by seconds. But if Camilla and Edward sent

Felicity and the baby away, how could Emma have been left on the steps of St Phillip's?

'Do you know for sure that baby Emma was sent away with Felicity?' Rachel asked.

'Well, I've never spoken to Felicity about it, but Camilla said so. Unless she lied. Why?' Hazel frowned.

'Just trying to get things straight in my mind.' Rachel didn't want to share her thoughts about the foundling just yet. 'Do you know Emma's surname, Hazel? In case we want to try to trace her?'

'No. Good luck finding out. Nobody knows her name, or where she is, except Edward. He refused to tell Camilla, which is why she came up with a plan to force Edward's hand. She wanted the help of somebody who already knew about Emma.'

'So Camilla wanted you to help with her plan to find Emma, did you say?' Rachel said, writing it down.

'Yes, she remembered me, and had my address from the letters I sent to Felicity. She wrote to me asking if I would visit her at Maberley Manor to discuss baby Emma, which I did. I don't think Port Talbot was really her thing.' She giggled.

'And did you let Fliss know her mother had been in touch with you?' Rachel asked.

'Me and Fliss don't speak either. I think I remind her of that difficult time. I still miss her. I was in love with her, but I knew Felicity didn't see me in that way. She's the bravest person I ever met,' she said, sipping her tea.

'Mum?' Adele asked.

'Yes! She's a warrior. I brought this. I thought you might like to see it. I have it up in my treatment room,' Hazel

159

said, handing her an A4 frame of the front cover of the *Guardian* from 13 December 1982. It looked like hundreds of women holding hands, facing out, surrounding a very high barbed-wire fence.

'You were there?' asked Adele as Hazel stirred some sugar in her tea.

'Yes, me and your mum. Embrace the Base, that was called.'

'Embrace the Base,' Adele repeated. 'What does it mean?'

'Thousands of women holding hands around the nine-mile perimeter of the base where they stored the nuclear weapons. We literally embraced the base,' Hazel said, holding her arms out in a circle. 'That was a brutal winter. The first weapons were due to arrive the following year and we were losing the fight. Until that day. It changed everything.'

Marge set Adele's sandwich down on the table as they all looked at the picture. Rachel felt uncomfortable, sitting with Hazel and Felicity's daughter as Hazel spoke of how the police tried to break them.

'The press, the police, the politicians, all the locals were against us. They kept spinning the narrative that we had no support, and we decided if we could prove that we did, it would silence them. And, my God, did we succeed!' said Hazel, beaming at the memory. 'There was no way we could have predicted that turnout, never in our wildest dreams.'

'How many women turned up?' Adele asked, taking a sip of her warm, sweet tea.

'The organisers worked out it would take sixteen thousand women to link hands round the whole base. Everyone told us we were insane, that there was no way we could get sixteen thousand women to the middle of nowhere, in the depths of winter. But thirty-five thousand women showed up in the end. And it was all word of mouth. We had no money, no internet. The first busloads arrived from Scotland at dawn and they just kept coming and coming. It was incredible, a heartbeat moment, like a storm brewing, from the first rain drops at dawn through to thunder and lightning when we all linked hands that night and this sort of primal whoop went up around the whole camp. We sang our hearts out. Your mum loved it.'

Adele smiled. 'How long did you live there?'

'It was very stressful to live there full-time. But your mum had a Mini. We used to sleep in there together every night. It was luxury. She was so childlike. We'd have done anything for each other. She actually got arrested trying to save me.'

'Mum got arrested?' Adele asked, eyes wide.

'Once.'

'Really? Did she go to prison?'

Hazel nodded. 'Holloway.'

'Holloway? Why has she never told me this?' asked Adele, sighing.

'She gave birth to Emma there,' Hazel said quietly. 'Her parents collected her, and I only saw her once again after that: the night I told you about, when she came to Greenham with baby Emma. So you didn't know about the money left to Emma in the will?' she asked Adele.

'No,' said Adele. 'Dad told me that Mum had had a baby before me, but she wouldn't talk about it. Nobody would. I've only found out her name today.'

'So what was this plan Camilla came to you with?' Rachel asked, trying to rein Hazel back in.

'Camilla and I went down to the solicitor, because she wanted to add something to her will – it's called a codicil – leaving Emma this money. But she had to do it without Edward knowing until after her death, or he would have made her take it out. The idea was that he would then be forced to contact Emma and give her this money.'

'And how much was it?'

'Quarter of a million, I think,' Hazel said, as Adele and Rachel looked at each other in astonishment. 'And a ruby ring that Camilla left to me so I'd know if he'd followed her wishes in the codicil. But the ring was actually for Fliss. Camilla made me promise to contact her solicitor if he didn't pay up. When I get the ring, I'll give it to Fliss. But we both wanted Emma to be found and be given her money.'

'But you never got the ring?' Adele asked.

'No, which means he hasn't actioned the codicil and given Emma the money. Camilla said he wasn't going to be happy; he was probably expecting to keep that money himself,' Hazel added with disdain.

'And did you contact the solicitor?' Rachel asked.

'Yes, a couple of times, but she wasn't very helpful. She said it wasn't her job to make sure the stipulations of the will were fulfilled and that I should get my own legal advice. Which, of course, I can't afford.'

'Do you have the name of the solicitor?' Rachel asked.

'Sure,' Hazel said, heaving her bag onto the table, and pulling out packets of chewing gum, a bottle of water, a few receipts and hair bands, and eventually a small address book.

162

'Caroline Thomas, Knight Solicitors, Newbury,' she said, reading out the number as Rachel jotted the details down.

'So you didn't try and find Emma yourselves?' Adele asked Hazel.

'Camilla had tried already. But the local authority had no record of her. They searched their historic records, all the children adopted at that time. Then they looked into the Care First System, where each local authority has their own database they use to log all the details of all the children in their area. No baby was adopted with their surname. There is no trace of an Emma Mills.'

'That doesn't make any sense,' said Rachel. 'Edward would have needed Emma's birth certificate to register her for adoption, so he couldn't have changed her name.'

'I know, right. So then Camilla started looking into Felicity's maternity records, to see if she had antenatal care and go from there. She found out Emma was born in the maternity hospital at Holloway, which Camilla knew about because she and Edward collected Felicity and Emma from there. After that, Felicity and Emma were turned over to the care of Newbury Council midwives, who came to visit at Maberley Manor. But that stopped after six weeks and there was no record of any follow-up visits. The trail stops then. There is no sign of baby Emma anywhere after that. Edward told Camilla that he had the baby adopted through an agency, but he refused to share any other details.'

'And do you know when this was, roughly? That baby Emma was adopted?' Rachel asked.

'Spring 1983, I think.'

Rachel paused for a while to take in what Hazel was

saying. 'So if Emma was adopted in the early eighties, they wouldn't have asked as many questions as they do now. She would have had an older-style midwife, and the baby's wellbeing wouldn't have been as scrutinised then as it would be now. If Edward told the midwife that the baby had gone to live with extended family because her mum was too young, got her future ahead of her, can't cope, etc., they wouldn't have questioned it. Especially from someone as well respected as Edward Mills.'

'But the local authority told Camilla that if it had all been done above board, through the official channels, there would be a record of Emma's adoption.' Hazel added. 'They called it "being relinquished", the woman at the council said. There is no record of a child of that name being relinquished by a family.'

'So what are you saying happened?' Rachel asked.

Hazel shrugged. 'I have no idea. That's your job, I guess.'

Rachel nodded, slightly taken aback again by Hazel's abruptness, then looked through her notes. 'So the plan with the will was to, what, call his bluff? Flush out the truth about baby Emma? Why didn't Camilla just go to the police?'

'She didn't want to. She was too unwell, and she loved Edward. She didn't want a scandal or any of her rich friends knowing and then going public. She just wanted Edward to pay Emma quietly. He obviously changed Emma's name, or the family name on the adoption paperwork, to hide her identity, or there would be some sort of record. I think he knows where she is. Emma deserves that money and Felicity and Emma deserve to find each other so they can have some peace. You don't give up a baby and forget about it. I should imagine it completely eats you up inside every day. It's ruined Fliss's life, and clearly deeply affected Camilla, Adele and, no doubt, Emma's too.'

Hazel looked at her watch. 'I'm really sorry, I've got to get back to my dog. He's been alone all afternoon.'

'Yes, of course. Thank you so much again for coming.' Rachel stood.

'No worries. Here's my number,' said Hazel, handing Adele a card. 'I'm here for you if you need me. I will be thinking of you and Sophia. I know she will find her way back to you, Adele.'

Adele took the card and pushed it into her back pocket.

Rachel saw Hazel to the door of the café.

'I'm pleased you're on to Edward. Don't let him get away with it again, will you?' Hazel said quietly, before darting out of the door.

Rachel looked back at Adele. Any colour remaining in her cheeks had completely drained away now as she, too, stood up and walked over to Rachel.

'We need to find Emma,' she said determinedly.

Chapter Thirteen

Adele

Wednesday, 17 July 2024

As Adele and Rachel walked out of the café towards the car, the light was starting to mellow. Rachel looked at her watch. It was nearly seven.

'There's a chance Emma could have Sophia, because my grandfather hasn't paid her the money my grandmother left her.'

'Adele, we need to proceed with caution,' Rachel said, as she got into the driver's seat and Adele climbed in beside her.

'Why? It's a life-changing amount of money – what if she is broke and bitter and furious Edward hasn't paid her?'

Rachel looked briefly at Adele before pulling out of their parking space and heading back in the direction of Berkshire. 'I need to speak to Camilla's solicitor and find out if what Hazel has told us is true.'

'Which bit? That he owes my half-sister a quarter of a million pounds, or that he took her away from my mother?'

Rachel's silence was infuriating her. Why had she brought her here if she wasn't going to act on what Hazel had said?

'I need to speak to my grandfather again,' Adele pressed.

'You can't at the moment. Ben James, the SIO, is taking him in for questioning this evening.'

'Well, this is more important. Emma could have Sophia! You need to speak to Ben and explain the situation.'

'I will update him as soon as we get back,' Rachel said firmly.

'No. We need to pull over and call him now!'

'Adele, I'm sorry, but Ben won't act tonight on the information we have from Hazel. She could be lying about all of this. I need to speak to Camilla's solicitor, and verify that what Hazel has told us is true. I also need to confirm with the council that there is no record of baby Emma. I will do everything I can to get Ben to move on this, but we only have one shot at it. Right now he's set on the idea that these loan sharks Alex hasn't paid have something to do with Sophia going missing, and if I take something to him that doesn't check out, we've blown it. I will do what I can, but it will take time to find Emma,' Rachel continued, 'and if she is unstable we need to find out as much as we possibly can about her before we approach her. If she has got Sophia and her motivation is the money, it's unlikely she will do anything to hurt Sophia. Because then she gets nothing.'

'Do you promise you will talk to my grandmother's solicitor today?' Adele said, relenting.

'I promise I will make contact today,' Rachel said firmly.

Adele stared out of the window as Rachel drove them back towards Newbury. The roundabouts out of Newbury were slow and they were stuck behind a lorry bellowing out diesel fumes, adding to Adele's constant state of nausea.

They were stuck, powerless; there was nothing she could do. She suddenly felt a desperate need to be back at home. She wished she'd never come here. This long-lost sister could be nothing to do with Sophia's disappearance – how would she know about the money, for a start? Adele hadn't even known about her grandmother's will – Edward hadn't told anyone – so how was this stranger supposed to have found out?

She was clutching at straws, using her dysfunctional family to try and create a reason for Sophia's disappearance. Anything rather than face up to the idea that Alex, her own husband, could be to blame. Trying desperately to find something to focus on rather than think about the fact that she had no idea where her daughter was, who she was with, or what was happening to her.

She wanted the police out of her house. She wanted her home and life back. She needed to lie on Sophia's bed, find something that smelled of her, her teddy, her blankie. The ache in her body to hold her daughter was all-consuming. She couldn't think of anything she wouldn't give to have her daughter back.

Adele started to feel very hot, her chest felt tight, and she began to breathe deeply to try to calm down.

'I don't feel too good,' she said, acid rising from her stomach and making her retch. 'I think I'm going to be sick.'

'OK, I'll pull over,' said Rachel. They were off the M4 now, and on the home stretch back to Greenham Common. Rachel pulled into the hard shoulder and put the hazards on.

'I'm going to be sick,' Adele said, leaning forward as her chest tightened again, pushing the air out of her lungs.

Suddenly a burning sensation started rushing up her arms and her legs, a tingling feeling that made her panic.

'I think I'm having a heart attack,' she said, her eyes wide as she bent double, trying to breathe.

'You're OK. Here, have some water,' said Rachel, rubbing her back. 'I think it's an anxiety attack. Just try and breathe. You're safe, Adele, you're OK.'

'I can't breathe,' Adele gasped as Rachel pulled her out of the car onto the bank by the road. The fresh air was comforting; she could hear the traffic rushing by. She sat on the grass, leaning forward, focusing everything she had on getting air into her lungs.

'In through your nose, out through your mouth, you're OK,' said Rachel calmly, continuing to rub her back as Adele slowly felt the oxygen getting into her system again. As her body began to relax, the pain in her chest started to pass. Rachel handed her the water and she took a sip, then slowly she sat back and looked at the sky, watching the clouds drift in front of the bright moon. Another day had passed, another day without her baby. Tears were rolling down her cheeks, which burned with adrenaline as the cars rushed past.

'Where is she, Rachel?'

'I don't know, but we will find her.'

'I can't do this,' said Adele. 'I can't live without Sophia.'

'We shouldn't stay by the main road. It's dangerous. Can you get back in the car OK now?' Rachel asked.

Adele nodded, and slowly climbed back in. Rachel waited for a gap in the traffic, then pulled out. Her phone started to ring.

'Do you want me to answer it?' Adele asked. 'It's Ben.'

'No, he probably just wants to know where we are. He'll text if it's urgent. We're nearly there. Not long now,' she said as they headed down the dual carriageway into Newbury.

'I have to go home now, Adele, but I will be back in the morning,' Rachel said as they neared Adele's house. 'I'm going to try to get hold of the solicitor Hazel mentioned, but if she's gone home I will speak to her first thing. And I'll also get up to speed with Ben about everything they have done today. He's planning another press conference first thing, but we can talk you through it.'

'Oh God, I can't face the press again,' Adele sighed.

'I know it's really hard, but it's very important to keep the press invested in Sophia. The more press interest there is, the more pressure it keeps on everyone – including the police. If you have any more photos or a cuddly toy of Sophia's you could take to the press conference – anything new you could share with the press about what Sophia is like – it will all help. It just takes one person to see the press conference on the news – who has maybe noticed someone acting strangely, or seen Sophia briefly somewhere – to call us.'

'OK,' Adele said quietly. 'Thank you, Rachel.'

'You're welcome.'

As they approached the house, Adele saw that in the time they had been gone, the police presence had doubled. The light was gone, and all along the A333, she could see people with head torches lining the road. She opened the window to get some much-needed air. 'Sophia!

Sophia! Sophia!' She could hear them all shouting for her daughter. She inhaled the night air. She felt empty; she couldn't remember the last time she had eaten anything.

As they turned into Greenham Park Road, she saw the pack of journalists had also swollen so that they were spilling onto the street, the lights from the TV camera crews turning night into day. As Rachel slowed and pulled up, journalists began to surround the car again, shouting questions and blocking Adele's door. Rachel pushed her way out and rushed around to the passenger side, letting Adele out.

Adele looked over to the front door of her house as it opened and Ben came out, bringing Leia, Sophia's dog, on a lead.

'Oh my God! It's Leia!' Adele said, running towards the white lurcher. As she reached Leia, she sunk onto the driveway and heard the clatter of camera shutters as the press surrounded her.

'Get back, please,' said Ben, pushing his way through the crowd.

Adele was sobbing, her tears soaking Leia's white shaggy coat as she clung to the dog for dear life. Finally Ben managed to get to her and pulled her up.

'Where was she?' Adele asked. Her legs were weak so Ben helped her inside, and the dog trotted after them loyally.

'They found her by the cycle path on the main road. She was just running around by herself; she nearly got hit by a car,' Ben said. 'There is a lot more CCTV around that area, and we have a blurred image of what appears

171

to be a turquoise Fiat 500 stopping at the side of the road. We don't have a registration, but now we have more to go on the teams are trawling CCTV footage from elsewhere. They think whoever has Sophia dropped the dog off.'

'Leia,' Adele said, as she sunk to the floor and clutched Leia, and Ben closed the door to the cacophony of journalists yelling their questions from the end of the driveway.

Felicity was standing in the hallway, watching Adele. Adele looked up at her and Felicity smiled weakly at her daughter. Ben's phone began to ring.

'Give me a minute,' he said, and dashed off into the kitchen.

'Is Alex not back yet?' Adele asked her mother.

'No, they are still questioning him at the police station. Adele, I need to talk to you. Upstairs, if possible,' Felicity said, looking up to check that Ben wasn't listening.

'What is it, Mum?' Adele asked, as Leia followed Ben into the kitchen. 'You're scaring me. Do you know something about Sophia?'

Felicity led the way silently up the stairs into Adele's bedroom and closed the door behind them.

'Mum, what is it?' Adele pleaded.

Felicity was very pale as she walked over to the window and closed the curtains. 'I recognise the car that Leia was in.'

'What do you mean? The turquoise Fiat?'

'Yes, the one in the CCTV footage. I've seen it before.'

'Where? Have you told Ben?' Adele asked.

'No, I wanted to tell you first,' Felicity said, her voice shaking. 'I saw Alex with a woman. They were walking

172

Leia on the common and then they got into that car. I'm sure of it.'

'Oh God,' Adele said. 'When? Why didn't you tell me?'

'About a fortnight ago. I'm sorry. I didn't know how to tell you. You are always so defensive when I talk about Alex,' Felicity said quietly.

'Because you've never liked him!' Adele snapped. 'And you were right. He's a liar and a cheat.' She was unable to hold back the tears. 'My own husband has been sneaking around behind my back, borrowing more money than he could ever pay back, lying to my face, making decisions that affect our home and security. I knew that we were stretched, but not that Alex had borrowed a quarter of a million pounds from loan sharks. Are you happy now?'

'Of course not. I do like him, Adele. That's not fair.' Felicity's face was flushed.

'Oh my God, I'm so sick of being fair. My whole life I've been fair and reasonable and understanding about the fact that you've never shown me any real fucking love.' Adele looked at her mother, a rage building inside her that she had never expressed before.

For as long as she could remember, she had felt powerless. As a child she had an overwhelming feeling that it was her job to save her mother. But however hard she tried, she couldn't fill the void. Adele would make it her job to be funny, positive, cheerful, just the three of them, out for meals, on Christmas Day, when the dreaded silence would invariably descend upon their little family. She felt a constant need for her mother's approval on all aspects of her life, before she was able to feel good about herself and her choices. She felt overwhelmed by her mother's moods, as if they were her fault. That if she could find the key to her mother's happiness, Felicity would turn into the mother she always craved: strong, unconditionally loving, happy.

Her childhood was long gone. Yet still the feeling of helplessness and powerlessness over her life lingered. It was why she had married Alex, with his overbearing personality. He told her what to do, what to think, how to feel. She had spent so long trying to please her mother, and now her husband, she had no idea who she was any more. Alex didn't care about how she really felt, who she really was, any more than her mother did.

'I'm sorry you feel that way, Adele,' Felicity said defensively. 'I've done the best I can.'

'Well, it wasn't good enough,' said Adele. 'There, I've said it. I feel angry with you all the time. All the time.'

Felicity stood in stunned silence.

'I could always sense you pulling away,' Adele continued. 'You didn't have the emotional strength to deal with me, and I felt it. I felt your pain. We've never talked about it, Mum, but I know you had another baby girl. I know you gave her up and it broke you. You don't get over having a baby taken away from you.'

Felicity fixed a cold stare on Adele, the one she always gave her when Adele veered into emotional territory.

'I don't think we should talk about this now, Adele. There are a lot more pressing things we need to focus on,' Felicity said firmly, heading for the bedroom door.

'Well, I want to. I need to talk about it now,' Adele pleaded. 'Mum, please. If we are going to go downstairs and tell Ben that my husband is having an affair, which I think he is, then the press will find out and my life as I know it is gone. I need you; I need us to be a team. Please. Don't walk out on me when I need you most,' Adele sobbed.

Felicity reached for the bedroom door handle, then stopped. Slowly she turned round and walked back across the bedroom and sat on Adele's dressing-table chair. 'OK, what do you want to know?' she said finally.

Adele wiped her tears and her nose with the sleeve of her jumper. She took a deep breath. 'Is her name Emma?'

'That is what I named her, but I don't know if that's still her name,' Felicity said, her eyes sparkling with tears.

'Do you know anything about her? Where she lives? What happened to her?'

'No. I asked my parents a lot in the first year, but they refused to talk about her, so in the end I gave up.'

'Have you ever tried to find her?' Adele asked gently.

Felicity looked down. 'Once. I tried the council, but they had no record of an Emma Mills being adopted in 1983. So I didn't know what to do after that. I know there are options now with DNA websites, but I'm frightened that too much time has passed and she will hate me. I think about her every day . . . every single day.'

Adele pressed on, not knowing if she would ever get the chance again. 'Dad told me that ten days after I was born, you were rushed to a psychiatric hospital. That he phoned the doctor as he was very worried about you, and a crisis team visited our house and confirmed that you were suffering from postpartum psychosis.'

'Yes, that's true,' Felicity said, closing her eyes and taking a deep breath. 'I couldn't sleep at all, and I sort of went beyond tiredness and started feeling elated. I believed that you and me had a divine purpose in the end of the world, which I thought was imminent. I had vivid hallucinations of angels, who threatened to take you away from me. In the end Dad was so worried I would harm you that he called our GP and I was taken to a local psychiatric hospital.'

'Did I go with you?' Adele asked, transfixed, afraid that her mother would stop talking if she so much as moved.

'No. I struggled to bond with you. I was terrified that if I did, you would be taken away too. Dad was your primary carer, really. When I came home from hospital, I didn't know what to do with you. I used to stare at you on the play mat, wondering how long I had you for. You looked so like her, just looking at you was extremely painful.'

'What do you mean, "taken away"?' Adele asked.

Felicity paused, then: 'Granddad took Emma while I was sleeping. Then he sent me away to finishing school in Switzerland.'

Adele stared at her mother. Hazel had told her and Rachel a different story: that Felicity and Emma had been sent away to relatives – together. She didn't feel it was the right time to talk to her mother about meeting Hazel. Or that Camilla had told Hazel a different story. She didn't know if Hazel was lying, or Camilla was, or who to believe.

'Oh, Mum, I'm so sorry that happened to you,' Adele said, going over to her mother and taking her hand. 'Mum, we have to tell them about this woman you saw Alex with.

Would you recognise her if you saw her again? Can you describe her to Ben?'

Felicity nodded. 'Yes, I think so.'

Adele took a deep breath. 'Mum, I think it could be Emma.'

'What do you mean? *My* Emma?' Felicity stared at Adele, wide-eyed.

'I don't know. Camilla left Emma a quarter of a million pounds in her will. But Granddad gave it to Alex instead. I can't help thinking the two are connected somehow.'

There was a knock on the door, making them both jump.

'Adele, it's Ben. I'm sorry to intrude – can we talk?'

'Yes,' said Adele. She turned back to Felicity and smiled warmly. 'Thanks, Mum.' The awkwardness that usually hung in the air between them was suddenly gone.

'You need to eat. You can't faint at the press conference. That won't help Sophia,' Felicity said, and Adele nodded.

Felicity helped Adele to the door of her bedroom and down to the kitchen where Ben was waiting. 'I'm sorry to have disturbed you, but I need to ask you a couple of questions.'

'OK,' said Adele as Felicity sat down next to her daughter.

'So it turns out that Anthony Hislop, who is the man that your grandfather referred Alex to for the loan, has been involved in some fraudulent activity. He has revealed to us that Alex isn't who people think he is. He owes a lot of money to the "wrong people". Including Anthony, who is extremely angry his name is being dragged through the press and he's ready to dish the dirt on Alex. This quarter of a million is the tip of the iceberg, it seems. Do you know that Alex has a bank account in Ireland? Looks like he's been trying to squirrel some rainy-day cash away.'

'Ireland? Alex has never been to Ireland, as far as I know,' Adele said.

'Well, he went to Galway twice last month, according to flights he booked. We are in the process of working out why he went and who he stayed with. He mentions visiting family in the email to the travel agent.'

'Alex doesn't have any family,' Adele said. 'His parents died when he was a teenager, and he has no siblings.'

'So, I wanted to let you know, Adele, we have been questioning your husband extensively,' Ben went on. 'We are keeping him in overnight and we will continue to question him in the morning.'

'Do you think he has anything to do with Sophia's disappearance?' Adele asked as tears stung her eyes again.

'I'm not sure. But obviously we aren't taking any risks. We are investigating all Alex's contacts, with Anthony Hislop's assistance, to see if we can find any connection with the owner of this turquoise Fiat, who we are closing in on.'

'Sorry, did you say Anthony Hislop?' Felicity clarified.

'Yes.'

'He's an acquaintance of Granddad's. Anthony put Alex in touch with the loan sharks who lent him the money,' Adele added.

The colour drained from Felicity's face. 'Anthony is not a nice man.'

'What do you mean? How do you know Anthony?' Adele looked at her mother.

'Has Alex introduced Anthony to Sophia?' Felicity asked urgently.

'We don't know that yet,' Ben said.

'Mum, what's going on?'

Felicity regarded her daughter with panic in her blue eyes. 'Anthony seduced me when I was fifteen. He got me pregnant and then abandoned me. Adele, Anthony Hislop is Emma's father.'

Chapter Fourteen

Felicity

Sunday, 12 December 1982

Fliss startled awake from a bad dream and looked at her watch. It was six o'clock in the morning on 12 December 1982, the day everyone at Greenham had been planning for, hoping that enough women would turn up to encircle the entire nine-mile perimeter, and earn some much-needed headlines.

She turned over slowly, not wanting to wake Hazel, who was asleep next to her. She was nearly seven months pregnant now. The kicks in her stomach were becoming a daily occurrence and her growing bump was making it harder to move around in the back of her car. Hazel turned over and let out a grumble in her sleep, telling whoever she was dreaming about to 'piss off' in her rich Welsh accent. Fliss smiled to herself. It was hard to comprehend that she had only known her eccentric green-eyed friend for twelve days. Fliss reached into her bag for her diary, and began to write. It would be the only chance she would have as, once Hazel woke, they would no doubt spend the rest of the day together. It was hard to find the words to express how much her world had changed in every way since she had arrived at Greenham, but she had to put something down so that she wouldn't forget, and could one day look back.

She and Hazel had immediately clicked, falling into a

routine of going everywhere and doing everything together during the day: washing pans, cooking food, walking into Newbury to sign on or get supplies, eating dinner and singing round the campfire until midnight, then climbing into the back of the Mini and cuddling up in Felicity's sleeping bag together, with five blankets on top of them. Fliss had never even shared a bed with a friend before, let alone a sleeping bag, but Hazel had invited herself in on the second night and never left. It was the only way to keep warm, snuggled up together, and it was surprisingly cosy. Fliss imagined in time her bump would get in the way, but for now, she and Hazel fitted as perfectly as a jigsaw puzzle. She loved pretty much everything about Hazel, but mostly her Welsh accent. She made everything sound like a song. Even the ugliest words sounded pretty.

She watched Hazel sleeping, smiled at her rosebud lips, light freckles and giraffe-like eyelashes. She had never had a real friend before. She had always felt comfortable with younger children, and with old people, but with her peers she felt self-conscious, awkward and left out. She thought people at school liked her – they were perfectly nice to her face – but then she'd hear about the girls at school meeting up in town without her, or at house parties that she was never invited to. She knew she wasn't the prettiest or the trendiest, but she was loyal and kind and she didn't know why nobody really liked her. Maybe they sensed she didn't really like herself. She was awkward, never knew what to say, and if she tried to be funny it always came out wrong and fell flat.

Her parents made her feel the same way. Busy with their dinner parties and events, they never seemed to want her around. The house was always buzzing with people, the sound of laughter, wine glasses clinking, cigarette smoke wafting up the stairs. They both seemed to thrive on the company of others, anyone except her. Her mother dripped charm, making people feel at ease with her questions and endless stories. Their lives were crammed with social engagements: trips up to London, shopping, entertaining. They had so much energy, but Fliss felt exhausted just watching them. Her mother had long given up trying to show her off after too many occasions of Fliss standing awkwardly as her mother chastised her for not 'making an effort'. When she wasn't away at boarding school, which she loathed with a passion, she spent most of her life locked in her bedroom. Finally, at the age of sixteen, she had refused to go back to school and told them that she would be going to the local sixth-form college, and if they tried to send her away to school again she would run away. Her parents had eventually agreed, but she had seen no more of them than when she was away.

As soon as she had arrived at the peace camp at Greenham, Felicity had immediately been infected with the place. People had the courage to be themselves. They were cold, tired, hungry, dirty and emotionally drained, so there was no energy to pretend. They dressed in the same clothes every day; there was no image to keep up, no make-up to put on, no trying to out-do one another. It was Dunkirk – sink or swim. Everyone was there for each other. People knitted jumpers and scarves to keep each other warm, they cuddled together, made each other food, shared what little they had between them. At night, people would come and drum around the fire, sing and dance, read books or poetry to one another, celebrate the moon and paint each other's faces. Felicity felt guilty that she was living in her car and not suffering as badly as the other women, living out in nature, enduring the worst of the weather, the bailiffs and abuse. She felt like a part-timer, that she wasn't a proper Greenham Common woman. But they never made her feel bad or any less.

What she loved most was the camaraderie; that the women refused to elect representatives or leaders. Everyone was responsible for themselves. She would often hear police officers asking who was in charge and it confused them to be told that the camp was leaderless. There was no one woman the authorities could target to make it stop, as if they were taking on the whole of womankind. Felicity felt loved and included at Greenham, in a way she never had before.

And it was mostly because of Hazel, who was her antidote. She was full of love for everyone because she was so loved. Every hair on her head was cherished by her parents, who visited regularly with armfuls of supplies: tins of soup, flasks of tea, chocolate and blankets. They lived in a small council house in the valleys of the South Wales coalfields, and they thought what Hazel was doing was wonderful. Hazel's family had very little, but they were a very happy threesome who clearly adored each other. Hazel's mother was a cleaner, her father was a miner and he spoke often of the threat of pit closures. He was a man who believed you should fight for what you thought was right, and they were proud that Hazel had stuck at school, done well in her O levels and was now making her mark on the world.

Felicity's parents, on the other hand, having heard that

she had made Greenham her home, had severed all ties with her. The first time her mother had seen her in town, she had read her the riot act, demanding to know why she was so determined to humiliate her father. She had tried to drag Fliss home with her, but Fliss had pulled away.

'You are making a complete fool of yourself, and us. If you don't come with me right now, you can forget about coming home ever again,' her mother had hissed, as Fliss had stood shaking from the fear and the cold, until Hazel had stepped in front of her and announced defiantly, 'She is home.'

Thereafter, if her mother saw her in town, she turned away from her, and her father made no attempt to come to see her at the camp. As a Conservative MP, having a pregnant unmarried daughter living at Greenham Common was an unspeakable embarrassment which he was no doubt terrified would end up in the newspapers. Felicity knew he couldn't risk coming to see her at Greenham. She was on her own, and yet she had never felt less so. She hadn't told Hazel that the father of her baby was a colleague of her father's. She was too scared Hazel would say something, and despite the way she had been treated, Fliss didn't want to humiliate her family. Besides, she was happy now she had Hazel. She just wanted to focus on the future – and her baby.

'My parents have said you and the baby can live with us,' Hazel had announced one day when, for once, it stopped raining. 'Until you get on your feet, you can sleep in my room and I'll take the sofa. Unless you need to rest and then I can take her – it's a girl, I'm sure of it.'

Fliss had smiled at her friend, so overwhelmed with

184

gratitude she had been unable to respond for fear she might cry. How could people who had nothing be so kind? Be so willing to open their home and take her in when her parents, who had more money and bedrooms than they knew what to do with, had turned their backs on her?

'Why are you so nice to me?' she had asked one evening by the fire, as they shared a can of cider together.

Hazel had laughed. 'Because I love you.'

Fliss felt shocked. Nobody had ever told her they loved her before. 'But why, why do you love me?'

'Because you're lush.'

Felicity had no idea what that meant, but in her lovely Welsh accent, it sounded like a compliment and so Fliss just laughed. Hazel wasn't scared of anyone – she hadn't a self-conscious bone in her body. She had no idea what it was like to exist in Fliss's world of self-doubt. She spent her days in the moment, chatting, relaxed, easy. People warmed to her; they wanted to do things for her, wanted to be with her. But for some reason Hazel wanted to be with Fliss, all the time, everywhere. It had only been ten days since she had arrived at Greenham, but she felt like a different person.

As Hazel slept on, Fliss heard the chatter of female voices outside her Mini. It was only six in the morning – people couldn't be arriving already, could they? She turned on her torch and shone it out of the car window. She could see a vehicle pulling up outside the entrance to Greenham Common, the hissing sound of coach doors opening.

Fliss opened the boot of her car and looked around, her eyes slow to focus in the cold misty morning. As they adjusted to the dawn she could scarcely believe what she

185

was seeing. Hundreds of cars filled the car park and coaches were backed up down the road, queuing to get onto the site.

'Hazel, wake up!' she said, shaking her gently.

Hazel stirred, then finally opened her emerald eyes.

'What?' she said grumpily.

'Look! Look! There are hundreds of women here!'

A huge smile broke on Hazel's lips, and she began to unzip the sleeping bag, rubbing her eyes and wiping away the condensation on the window. They climbed out of their cosy den and stepped into the rainy grey day.

'Oh my God!' she shrieked. 'They've done it!' Fliss smiled as they pulled on their wellington boots and began to join the throng of women walking towards the base. 'There are going to be enough women to encircle the whole base.'

'Come on. I need to pee,' said Hazel, taking Fliss's hand and ducking into the woods behind Yellow Gate, as Fliss followed her in. They were well hidden as the giggling, chatting, laughing crowds passed them by. Fliss watched the women in awe. Her insides felt like they would explode with love. She had never felt anything like it before.

Despite the drizzling rain and bitterly cold wind, the atmosphere was intensely warm as the women arrived in their droves. It felt to Hazel as if every women represented a rain drop and, as more and more arrived, a storm gathered. Morale had been low in the camp for the past few days. There had been a lot of bickering and the bailiffs' raids were getting increasingly hard to recover from as the women's supplies diminished and funds ran out. But now every woman was smiling, holding hands, comforted by one another's presence and the women from all over the country – the world – who kept coming and coming through the gates of Greenham.

Hazel and Fliss joined a queue under a large sheet of tarpaulin, where two women were sitting at a trestle table. The rain was dripping through onto their makeshift office, but their smiles were broad. The coaches couldn't unload the women fast enough, and they kept coming, from every direction, by foot, by car, joining the queue to sign up.

'Please make your way to Yellow Gate to register. We need to keep track of you all,' one woman bellowed over a Tannoy. It was a mud bath. As Hazel and Fliss giggled and slid around, someone lost her balance and took a tumble in front of them and Hazel tried to help her up until she too lost her balance and wiped out.

There were women with walkie-talkies everywhere, trestle tables covered with registration forms, and all sorts of wonderful leaflets and handmade posters. Over Tannoys safety instructions were bellowed out. As Hazel and Fliss stood in the long queue to register, one of the women started to sing and soon a dozen joined in, then a hundred. As far as the eye could see, the women sang, their voices ringing out through the unrelenting rain. Hazel took Fliss's hand and beamed at her.

We are women, we are women
We are strong, we are strong
We say no, we say no
To the bomb, to the bomb.

Sung to the tune of 'Frère Jacques', the repetitious song rang out against the harshness of the military base, the women's voices like a choir, preaching peace in the face of nuclear weapons. It was beyond beautiful.

Fliss thought fleetingly of Camilla and her friends, their utter disgust at the women camping out at the common, peacefully trying to convey their message whilst the leaders of the world prepared to put life-ending bombs on their doorstep. But there was never any mention of the bombs in their objections, only of the dirty, trouble-making hippies. The organisers had had no way of knowing how many women were going to show up, or how much support they had. They had nothing but their own blind optimism. Today they were part of a revolution and, to Fliss, it felt like a dream.

Once they were registered, Hazel and Fliss began to walk around the fence, trying to find a section that had no women holding hands in front of it. They had to walk for miles and they watched in awe as thousands upon thousands of women took their places around the base, each tying on a photograph or an item of clothing that meant something to her. Only the night before the fence had been sparsely decorated; now it was hard to find an exposed section. Eventually Fliss and Hazel found a space, and smiled at the women to either side of them. They began to sing again, in harmony with the hundreds of women surrounding them.

You can't kill the spirit,
She is like a mountain.
Old and strong, she goes on and on and on . . .

Fliss had read in one of the leaflets that the plan was to squeeze the hand of the woman next to you and she in turn would do the same until the circle around the entire nine-mile perimeter linked up. Suddenly, she felt Hazel squeeze her hand and she turned to the blonde lady beside her, who must have been in her sixties, and squeezed her hand tight. Fliss felt her heart soar, and tears filled her eyes. An enormous whoop went up around the circle. It felt primeval, with every woman shouting and hollering. Someone called out on the Tannoy that thirty thousand women had signed up to Embrace The Base, and on that news the whooping escalated until it was deafening.

An hour or two passed as press photographers arrived and rushed to take pictures of this once-in-a-lifetime event.

Finally a helicopter appeared overhead, and then the police began to arrive in their vans to break the spell. At first they were standing around in disbelief, not knowing what to do or where to start.

The lady holding her hand turned to Fliss. 'The police are scared, you can tell. Look at them. They weren't expecting this.'

Fliss smiled at her as the woman squeezed her hand defiantly.

Fliss felt the energy of the circle infecting her. She had been scared her whole life, but now, suddenly, her fear was gone. She was part of something that was saying no. She had found her people.

It was the most thrilling thing she had ever encountered. She felt as if electricity was passing through her, as the energy circle of thirty thousand women enveloped her.

It was only when Fliss looked at the faces of the police who had begun to approach that she started to feel nervous. The reporters were arriving in their droves now: news crews, journalists, people rushing around taking photographs, asking the women for interviews. Fliss felt pleased that Yellow Gate finally had the press coverage that they so desperately craved. There was no way that the world wouldn't hear about Greenham Common today. It had been a triumph.

But Fliss knew all too well that her father and his colleagues wouldn't take it lying down. When a photo journalist began snapping pictures of her and Hazel, she knew within hours her parents, and their friends, would find out that she was at the heart of today's event.

Fliss looked down into the barrel of the press camera pointing at her, and for the first time in her life she didn't care. Feeling her baby kick reassuringly, she gripped Hazel's hand, and smiled at her friend.

She had found her place in the world, and she was here to stay.

Chapter Fifteen

Emma

Saturday, 1 June 2024

'I've made a decision,' said Amanda one Saturday morning as she got ready to meet her mum in town. 'While I'm out, I'm gonna do some digging on your birth mother.'

Emma felt her tummy turn over. Ever since she had told Amanda about being adopted, Amanda had talked about little else. She had even taken to writing it all down in a notebook, recording every tiny detail, which she had painstakingly extracted from Emma.

At first she had just listened attentively to what Emma told her about how it really felt to be adopted. Emma had never had anyone listen to her before – really listen – without cutting her short or dismissing her feelings. It was a strange sensation. She kept apologising for talking about herself too much, and asking Amanda if she wanted to talk about something else. But Amanda seemed fascinated, and encouraged her to talk, endlessly, interpreting how she felt in ways that Emma hadn't considered before. They would go for walks in the grounds of Westwood after work, and sit in the shade on the warmest days, Emma lying on the grass, staring up at the sky, Amanda propped up on her elbows with a little notepad she would use to record what Emma was saying.

She had told Amanda that her adoptive parents did their

best. She had always been well fed and cared for, but she had felt something was amiss. Although it had been a terrible shock to find out she was adopted, when she had overheard them talking about it when she was fifteen, in a way it had also been a relief.

She had learned much later that there had been another baby, Anna, who had died before her parents adopted Emma. Anna had died suddenly at four months, from an undiagnosed heart condition. Her adoptive mother had a history of miscarriage and high blood pressure, which must have made the death of their first and only biological child all the more devastating.

Emma had found out quite by accident one day, as they attended St Phillip's Sunday service. Every week, after the service, Emma would be instructed to sit in the car while her parents took flowers and walked into the graveyard. They would appear sometime later, her mother's eyes red, her father looking pale. She never asked what they were doing and they never told her. But one morning, when she was around eleven, she decided to spy on them, and watched as her mother knelt down in front of a gravestone, laying down her bunch of daffodils picked from the garden, as her father rested his hand on her shoulder. As they chatted to the vicar the following week, Emma had run over to the grave, and read the inscription.

Anna Jane Blake
04.01.1980–16.05.1980
We held you in our arms for a little while
But we will hold you in our hearts forever

She never told them that she knew, but it explained why they felt unable to show her love and affection. They were heartbroken, as was she, thinking about Anna Jane Blake the older sister she could have had all those years.

She saw it as her role to be good. Not to cause them any more heartache. However, she told Amanda, that had all changed when she had overheard them talking about her being adopted. She felt catastrophically let down – that she had been lied to her whole life – and her world had come crashing down. She had been unable to keep the mask in place any more, and she began skipping school, and drinking in the local park with the wrong crowd, to escape her continuously looping thoughts about being given up.

Overnight, she had become obsessed about her birth mother, worried to the point of not being able to sleep. What could possibly have driven a mother to give up her baby? She didn't want to cause the woman any distress, but she became completely preoccupied with the idea of finding her. She finally plucked up the courage to talk to her adoptive mother, Sally, but Sally had strongly suggested she forget the idea.

'I knew this day would come, Emma,' Sally told her, 'but I think you are headed for a world of pain if you go down that road. She made it very clear she couldn't cope, and she will almost certainly be married now, perhaps to a man unaware of her past, and possibly have other children. I think it would be cruel to stir up the past.'

Emma began to do some research about women who had given up babies for adoption. They were supposed to have put past indiscretions and misfortunes behind them and started afresh, but instead she read countless stories of a lifetime of loss and regret.

'These women never, ever got over losing their babies. What if my birth mother still thinks about me?' she had asked Amanda. 'What if giving me up was a moment of madness? I would do anything to know that she was all right, and to tell her I was OK.'

'Are you OK, though?' Amanda asked, reaching for Emma's hand. 'Could you really tell her that?'

Emma had no reply. Nobody had ever asked her that question before.

'I could help you, if you like – do some digging, see where it leads,' Amanda suggested.

'What do you mean, "do some digging"?' Emma asked.

'I mean, try and find your birth mother,' Amanda said.

Emma bit down on her lip. She didn't know how to respond or what to say. Her head spun with the implications of what Amanda was suggesting, but she had no idea how to even begin to unpick what she was feeling.

Mostly she felt torn.

All her life she had believed that nobody was really interested in her or how she was feeling except in a very superficial way. Every time she had tried to express herself to her adoptive parents, she had felt dismissed, pushed away, and it broke her heart afresh. Now Amanda was doing the opposite and Emma almost didn't know how to deal with it. She didn't want to appear ungrateful, so she stayed silent and let Amanda take the lead. Still she couldn't help the feeling of unease growing in her stomach.

'Don't worry, Emma, it won't be long before you become eligible for short visits home and then we can join forces.'

'You won't approach her without me, if you find her?'

'What?' Amanda spun round. 'Of course not. She's your mother. I just want to help you find her. If you don't want to contact her after we do, that's totally up to you.'

Emma had let out a sigh of relief. She'd had the feeling that, since telling Amanda she was adopted, she was strapped into the carriage of a rollercoaster that was creeping up to the precipice, about to fall.

Emma had nodded.

'Did you want me to post that letter while I'm out?' Amanda said.

Emma looked down at the stamped envelope addressed to her adoptive mother, Sally, on her bedside table.

'Sure. Thank you.'

'Have you ever had a reply?'

Emma shook her head.

'Well, I think that's cruel,' said Amanda. 'The fire was an accident and you don't just give up on your kids like that.'

Emma looked down at her hands and began picking at the skin around her nails. 'We've never had a great relationship. She probably just thinks I'm after my trust fund.'

'What trust fund?' Amanda asked.

Emma sighed. 'It's just a bit of money they've put away for me every year.'

'But if it's a trust fund, that should have been yours when you turned eighteen.'

Emma shrugged. 'Who knows? I guess they can do what they want. It's their money. Maybe Sally decided to keep it because of what happened.'

Amanda frowned. 'How much is it?'

'No idea. A few grand, maybe,' Emma said sadly. 'Not a life-changing amount, but it might have helped.'

'I was thinking,' said Amanda. 'I know you're worrying about where you're gonna go when you get out of here. But maybe we could get a flat. We can get jobs and hang out together,' she said, beaming.

Emma said nothing and shifted awkwardly on her bunk. Amanda had become very possessive of her lately. She rarely let her talk to any of the other prisoners, scowling at her if she even said good morning to one of the other girls, and it was beginning to grate a bit. She had enjoyed her friendship with Amanda, but she was starting to entertain the idea of Amanda moving on when she left WWP and them both having some space.

'What do you think?' Amanda asked.

'I haven't really thought that far ahead,' said Emma.

'I know, but you can't put it off forever. I'm out of here in two weeks, and you'll only be a couple of months behind.'

'I'm kind of a loner. I've always liked being on my own,' Emma said.

'I know, but I don't want you to feel like that any more,' Amanda said. 'Anyway, gotta go. Wish me luck! Hopefully I'll have some news when I get back.'

Emma smiled as Amanda dashed out of the room, and she began to get dressed for the day. It would be nice to have a little bit of space. Maybe she would ask one of the other girls to go for a wander round the grounds. It was a beautiful June day, and it was important she started to reach out beyond Amanda's clutches. Maybe she would even be brave enough to venture into town.

Walking along the corridor towards the dining room, her tummy rumbling, she began to rehearse in her head how she would ask one of the girls, Jen, who she sometimes worked with in the shop, if she fancied a walk later. She didn't want to come across as needy or weird.

She got her breakfast and saw that Jen was sitting with a friend at one of the tables. Emma passed slowly with her tray, hoping that Jen would say something.

'Hi, Emma. Wanna sit here?'

'Oh. Hi, Jen,' Emma said, pretending she hadn't noticed her. 'Sure.' She tried to sound casual.

'Where's the old ball and chain then?' said Jen, smiling wryly as Emma sat down.

Emma felt her stomach jolt. 'Who?'

Jen smiled. 'Amanda.'

'Oh, she's meeting someone in town,' Emma said, emptying her tray onto the table.

'Nice for you to have some space.'

'She's OK, she's been a good friend.'

Emma saw Jen catch her mate's eye. The whole exchange was making her feel uncomfortable. She wished she had just sat on her own; she felt disloyal to Amanda. Amanda had told her not to trust anyone and she was right: WWP was making her think she was in some holiday camp when she was in prison. She needed to be cautious who she trusted.

'Who is Amanda meeting then?'

'Her mum, I think,' said Emma, starting to eat her porridge.

'Her mum?' said Jen, frowning. 'I doubt that.'

Her friend sniggered and Emma began to feel increasingly

197

ill at ease. She wanted to move, but knew it would be extremely rude to do so.

'I thought they were close,' said Emma, after a long uncomfortable silence. 'She meets her in town all the time.'

The two exchanged looks. 'Whatever. See you in the shop later,' Jen said, smiling, as they got up and walked away, whispering.

'Sure, see you later,' said Emma, trying to sound casual, her head spinning with panic.

She always got social situations wrong. What did they mean? What were they talking about? They were not to be trusted, as Amanda said, and were just trying to wind her up. How would they know how close Amanda was to her mum? Amanda was her friend. She was the only one who she should listen to. Wasn't she?

As the two girls walked out of the hall, Sam the governor walked in.

'Hi, Emma. How's things?'

'OK,' she said quietly.

'You should have gone with Amanda into town.'

'I don't want to intrude,' Emma said.

'Intrude? She's not meeting anyone today, is she?'

Amanda had lied to her and she felt herself flush. 'Um, no, probably not. I'm just making excuses. I will go, soon, I promise.'

Emma watched Sam go, feeling a flutter of unease at the amount of information she had shared about her life with Amanda. Amanda had her adoptive mother's address, Emma had told her about the trust fund, she knew her whole life story.

Emma looked down at her porridge, and suddenly felt

quite sick. She had come so far, got through the whole of her sentence in a high-security prison, and now with the end in sight she had trusted a woman she knew barely anything about – other than that she was convicted of stabbing a man, and the other inmates really didn't like her.

Just like Amanda had said, Westwood Park Prison had lulled her into a false sense of security, and now she had no idea what she had done or who she was really dealing with.

Chapter Sixteen

Rachel

Wednesday, 17 July 2024

Rachel pulled up in front of her house, and let out a weary sigh.

Since walking into Thames Valley Police station that morning, her day hadn't let up for a moment and her thoughts were a jumbled mess. She felt so exhausted, she didn't know how she was going to even muster the energy to get out of her car and walk up to her front door.

She looked at her watch, which told her it was eight o'clock, long past her dinner time, and she hadn't eaten since breakfast, having left the bacon sandwich she had ordered in the café in Port Talbot to go cold. Rachel climbed out of her car, retrieved her bag, coat and laptop from the back seat and walked up the path of the small, detached bungalow that she and David had bought when they had first received his diagnosis.

Her feet tapped quietly on the path and she could hear her heavy breathing as she approached her front door in the silent cul-de-sac. It seemed deathly quiet in comparison to the media circus she had just escaped from at Adele's house, and as she rummaged for her keys she felt a stab of loneliness at the thought of the dark, quiet house on the other side of her front door.

Finally, she found the key, and plunged it into the lock,

flicked on the lights and wandered into the kitchen to fill the kettle and examine the contents of the fridge.

Even when her husband was at his most unwell and she arrived home to a Macmillan nurse, a hissing oxygen machine or the sound of David struggling with his breathing, it was better than this silence. She had thought, towards the end, that she wanted his suffering to be over, that she would be relieved when he was finally at peace. But nothing could have prepared her for losing her husband of thirty years. The void was unfathomable, the silence overwhelming, the guilt never letting up. She was desperately lonely, but didn't want company; she was exhausted but couldn't sleep. She was endlessly troubled that she had given in too easily to David's desire not to pursue IVF and now it was too late to have a family. She was childless and all alone in the world.

She missed the Macmillan nurses terribly. They were so cheerful and positive, particularly on the most difficult days, acting as if it wasn't a job, but a privilege to share someone's last weeks on earth. Rachel had learned so much from them: about David's cancer, how to manage the pain, any financial support she should be getting. They helped her fill out forms, comforting her, making her giggle with inappropriate jokes about various bodily fluids. When she was with them, she felt part of something bigger than David's cancer. When they were in the house, she felt OK, and far from it, now that they were gone. One of the nurses she had bonded with in particular, Pippa, had been there at the end of David's life. She was a large woman, full of chatter and laughter, with three grown-up sons, eight grandchildren, and a life bursting with busyness and love.

She had told Rachel to call her any time she needed some support, and even now, Rachel often scrolled down to Pippa's number, sometimes composing a text, her finger lingering over the send button. But something always stopped her. Pippa was so busy, Rachel didn't want to bother her, and besides, what would she say?

Rachel took off her heels and slid her feet into her slippers. She grabbed some biscuits from the cupboard, made herself some tea, and stirred in a large spoon of sugar. She wanted a glass of wine but she felt that there might be developments at any time. Ben or Adele could call her, and she needed to have her wits about her. She blew into the mug to cool it down and took a sip, the sugar immediately comforting her and entering her bloodstream. She then pulled a cottage pie from the freezer, turned the oven on, and slid it in. Despite it being July, there was a chill in the air and the house felt cold. She walked into the lounge and flicked on the gas fire, put the TV on quietly in the background for company and sat in her large armchair, tucking her legs underneath her.

They had chosen the house for practical reasons rather than because they'd fallen in love with it. The door was wide enough for David's wheelchair, there were floorboards throughout, which helped for rolling trolleys of pills, oxygen and food around, and there was a downstairs study and bathroom they had knocked through and converted into David's bedroom so he wouldn't need to go to a hospice. She had never loved it, and as a result it didn't feel like home. No amount of cushions, or throws or pictures could make up for the fact that she didn't feel like she belonged there, but selling up would mean leaving David behind and she didn't feel strong enough yet. She wasn't sure what she was waiting for – a feeling or sign that it was time to move on perhaps – but right now her head hurt if she tried to think about it too much.

She cast her mind back to that morning, when Ben James had told her about the huge amount of money Alex had borrowed from moneylenders. The hair on the back of her neck had stood up, her adrenaline sparking into life. She was fifty-eight now – two years left to retirement – and she knew her days in Thames Valley Police were numbered. But despite the dreadful trauma Adele was going through, she had felt useful, in supporting her, and taking her to see Hazel. She had been assertive with Ben, so much so that she had even surprised herself. Talk of Greenham made her realise how far she had come since being a new woman police constable, how much she had learned, how much she still had to offer. It was so hard to carry on living without David, but she had to find a way. She and Adele had started the day on a hostile footing, in the most difficult of circumstances, but now they had some level of trust, and it felt good.

Rachel's thoughts turned back to the events of the day. With every hour that ticked by, experience told her, it became less and less likely they would find Sophia alive. Some cases she found easier to deal with than others. Adele's pain was getting to her because there was still a sense that it wasn't over, that Sophia's life was still in their hands. When she attended murders or car crashes, the loved one was already gone. This case could still go either way, and she felt unsettled that, following their chat with Hazel, she may have had a part to play in Felicity's baby being taken away.

But how much Camilla's will, Felicity's child, or Alex's debts had to do with Sophia's disappearance, was something that could take months or even years to unpick – and time was not a luxury they had.

Although she had promised Adele she would update Ben about their conversation with Hazel, she knew he wouldn't take her seriously until she had a solid motive for Emma to have taken Sophia. That would mean jumping through a lot of hoops: speaking to Edward's solicitor to confirm Camilla had indeed left Emma a quarter of a million pounds, confirming that Edward had knowledge of the codicil and hadn't made any attempt to find Emma and pay her the money Camilla wanted her to have. Proving that Emma also somehow knew about the money that was owed to her and was furious enough about Edward not giving it to her to take such drastic action as abducting Sophia. And to do that she would have to find Emma, which could take weeks. Particularly if there was no trace of her and she didn't want to be found.

Added to which, she had spoken to Ben about the development with Sophia's dog turning up and she knew he would be completely focused on two tasks: first, trawling all the CCTV in the area, shops, garages, home-security cameras, which may have picked up the registration of the turquoise Fiat containing Leia – and potentially Sophia – as it stopped to drop the dog off. Because if they could ascertain that car's number plate, they would have their first significant lead.

Secondly, interviewing Alex Norton. Rachel's instinct told her that Ben wasn't sure if Alex actually had anything to do with Sophia's disappearance, but that the financial mess he was in may well have set off a chain of events that had led to her abduction. Alex was clearly a dodgy character who lied for a living, and it was now Ben's job to unpick all that deception and try to find a path to Sophia. A huge task, which would occupy all his time and attention.

Precious time they didn't have.

So while Ben was focused elsewhere, she would do some digging around baby Emma; get her ducks in a row in case Alex or the turquoise Fiat turned out to be dead ends.

Rachel ate a biscuit hungrily, opened her notebook and fired up her laptop.

'Caroline Thomas, Knight Solicitors, Newbury,' she said out loud as she Googled their website. She found Caroline's email address and sent a message asking her to get in touch, urgently, regarding Camilla's will and the alleged codicil benefiting her estranged granddaughter.

She then turned her attention to baby Emma, who by now would be over forty years old. Although it was possible Hazel was lying to them about the will, and the part Edward played in forcing Fliss to give up her baby, her instinct told her that Hazel was being honest. However, the fact still remained that Hazel didn't know Camilla well and was taking Camilla's word for it that she had made a codicil and been unable to trace Emma herself.

Rachel rubbed her neck and settled into her task of finding baby Emma as the room began to warm up. She had various contacts in the council, but no one would be available at this time of night, and Edward Mills certainly wouldn't be willing – or available – to talk to her after a day of being questioned. She needed to plan her next move, but her brain was awash with the events of the day, and the meeting with Hazel. Talk of Greenham had shaken her up. She remembered vividly 2 April 1983, when she had been arresting women all night, and in the last vanload had been green-eyed Hazel Evans.

That long April night had had a profound and lasting effect on her. The world, at the time, had felt very unstable: two minutes to midnight, the doomsday clock had predicted. Standing around for hours in the rain and mud, she had spoken to many women there who had given their babies up to the care system, or had decided not to have children at all, feeling that their role as protestors against the nuclear might of the world had to take precedent over their desire to have children. Because if it didn't, there might be no world for those children to inherit.

It had a bearing on her and David's decision not to have IVF when children didn't come naturally. There were enough children in the world, they had decided. If it was meant to be, it would happen. But it wasn't, and they had been very happy together, just the two of them. Or rather, he'd convinced her that they were. But she always had a niggling feeling that she would regret giving up on having children too easily.

And she often thought about the baby that had been handed to her, at the end of a long night shift. She had suspected, at the time, that it was a Greenham woman who had given her baby up, and had she been a little older and more experienced, she might have been able to convince David that they should adopt the baby themselves.

Rachel paused for a moment, then put down her tea, and walked along the hallway to the hatch into the loft. She lowered down the ladder, and slowly climbed the steps on her exhausted legs. She turned on the light and began moving all her old work boxes around, scanning the dates, until she found the right one, labelled '1983–1984'. She pulled it out, and carried it back down the ladder into the living room. She began sifting through the old battered notebooks until she found April 1983, her scrawled hand-writing bringing back to life the Greenham Common protests, which had been in full swing at the time and dominated every page.

Finally she found it. *Howell Jenkins*, her notes read, in her scrawled handwriting, *caretaker St Phillip's church, Newbury. Found baby in cardboard box, on church steps, six a.m. 2 April. Driver, male, possibly green classic car, Jag E-Type? Wrapped in pink blanket, tiepin, initials EJM in box with baby. Baby warm and well, called ambulance immedi-ately. Envelope addressed to 'Emma' and cash inside. Baby taken away by paramedics. Will attend hospital later today and meet children's services.*

The following pages were filled with her attempts at trying to find the baby's mother. She had put flyers up, gone door to door in the vicinity of St Phillip's church, and written a press release with all the details apart from the cash and the car, which her boss said to leave out. Nobody had seen any-thing, responded to the press release or come forward.

Rachel's mind darted back to the conversation they'd had that day with Hazel in the café.

'Did my mum ever go to prison?' Adele had asked, wide eyed.

'Holloway. She gave birth there. Her parents took her home after she had the baby. I only saw her once after that . . . at Greenham. She was pleading for my help with the baby, but I got arrested. I did a runner when the police unloaded us but when I got back to Greenham she was gone. I never saw her again.'

Rachel looked back into the box containing all her old notebooks and pulled out the article from the *Newbury Times*, dated 3 April 1983, the day after baby Emma had been found. She peeled back the bent page and began to read.

Police are appealing for the mother of a baby girl found on the steps of a church in Newbury to come forward so that she can receive medical care and support.

The baby, named Emma, was discovered inside a cardboard box on the steps of St Phillip's church in Newbury just before 7 a.m. yesterday. Police discovered a tiepin with the initials EJM wrapped in her blanket. She has been discharged from hospital and is in the care of foster parents.

The little girl was found by church caretaker, Howell Jenkins, in sub-zero temperatures.

Emma's mother is yet to come forward, and Newbury police are deeply concerned for her wellbeing. WPC Rachel Rees said: 'Baby Emma is being well cared for by her foster parents and is a healthy, happy baby.

'We are appealing for any witnesses who may have been in the area of St Phillip's church in the early hours of 2 April to come forward. Emma was well dressed in a baby grow, a pink hand-knitted cardigan, mittens and she was wrapped in a thick woollen blanket. Hospital staff guess her age to be around six weeks and her mother must have cared for her during that time. Parenting can be overwhelming and we

want to assure Emma's mother that she is not in trouble. We can offer her help and support.

'The silver tiepin with the initials EJM is of particular importance. Please look closely at the attached photograph. To anyone who may recognise baby Emma, know a lady who was due to give birth but doesn't now have a baby, or who recognises the tiepin, I'd urge you to come forward and help us locate her. This can be done in confidence.'

It was too much of a coincidence for Rachel not to consider the fact that the baby she had thought of often over the past forty years could be Felicity's daughter of the same name. But if Edward Mills, or indeed Felicity, had anything to do with abandoning that little girl, they could be looking at a prison term of between ten and twenty-five years. It was not something she would be suggesting to Ben James before she had some proof to back it up, but she couldn't help sensing that this was a thought that was going to keep her awake that night.

She stared at the article again. They had known she was called Emma because that name was written on the front of the envelope. But there was no mention of it in the article. Rachel remembered that her boss at the time hadn't let her mention the money in the envelope because it was a large amount in 1983 – a thousand pounds, if she recalled correctly. He had argued that people might contact them about the baby for the wrong reasons, and it had frustrated her, mostly because of the distinctive tall, slanted handwriting on the front. Where had that envelope gone? Had she asked Bill Bailey to bag it up as evidence? She remembered they had photographed it for the newspaper but hadn't been allowed to use it. Was there any chance the police still had a record of that somewhere?

In the midst of her thoughts, her email pinged, and she turned back to her laptop and opened it up. It was a message from Caroline Thomas at Knight Solicitors in Newbury, suggesting a meeting at eight thirty the following morning. She fired back a reply, agreeing to the meeting, which would give her forty-five minutes before she would need to leave the solicitors in Newbury to get back to Adele's house for her shift to start at ten.

Suddenly her phone rang, making her jump. Ben's number came up on the screen. He would no doubt be irritated that she had taken Adele away for the day, and wanting a further explanation. She raced to gather her thoughts as she answered the call.

'Rachel, it's Ben,' he said curtly.

'Hi, Ben,' she said, waiting for the onslaught.

'There's been a development,' he said.

Rachel's heart sank, expecting the worst. 'Go on.'

'It looks like Adele's husband has been having an affair. Felicity, Adele's mother, saw them together. We're getting her to do an artist's sketch now. But she was seen walking the family dog with Alex, so the dog knows her. If this woman has anything to do with Sophia's disappearance, it would explain why the dog went with her. Felicity also says they got into a turquoise Fiat, same as the one we have on CCTV dumping Sophia's dog.'

'Any chance this woman could have met Sophia? It would explain why she went with her without a fuss.'

'We don't know that yet. But it's very sensitive,

obviously, as releasing this information, or the sketch, would be very difficult for Adele. Alex has been living a double life. It seems he's got some ties to Ireland, which we are trying to ascertain. And he owes a lot of money to a few unsavoury characters, according to Anthony Hislop.'

'Does Adele know anyone in Ireland?' Rachel asked.

'No, she had no idea Alex had been there. No luck with the car registration yet either, but we are working flat out.'

It was on the tip of Rachel's tongue to tell Ben about baby Emma but experience stopped her.

'Did you get anywhere with Edward Mills? I mean, did he say why he needed the quarter of a million back so urgently?' she asked instead.

'Yes, he said his wife left it to a family member whom he hadn't been able to trace, and that he had presumed it would be OK to loan it to his son-in-law in the meantime. But the solicitor got in touch and accused him of not fulfilling his role as trustee of his wife's will, so he panicked and decided to transfer the money to the solicitor to keep on hold until the beneficiary could be traced, so that he couldn't be accused of any wrongdoing.'

'Did he give you details about the family member, a name, or why he couldn't trace them?' Rachel probed.

'He said it was his granddaughter, who was adopted at birth. But he's found her in the last couple of days, apparently, via a DNA website. So they are transferring the money over to her tomorrow, I believe.'

'Right,' said Rachel, letting the news sink in. Edward had found Felicity's daughter, in order to pay her inheritance, before Sophia even went missing, so there was no reason for Emma to have taken her. She was almost embarrassed about her idea that a baby that had been handed to her in a cardboard box in 1983 could have anything to do with the disappearance of Sophia.

'Another thing,' Ben added. 'This Anthony Hislop, friend of Edward Mills, shareholder of the moneylenders who Alex is in the shit with, got Adele's mother pregnant when she was sixteen. He's the father of the baby she gave up, who Camilla left the money to. He's not a nice character, by all accounts. Felicity is concerned he may have had access to Sophia.'

'OK, thanks for the update. I'll see you in the morning,' Rachel said, as Ben ended the call.

Rachel went into the kitchen to serve up her cottage pie. She felt unsettled. Anthony Hislop, who was involved in getting Alex into financial difficulties, was baby Emma's father. Yet another link from the events of today to baby Emma. It seemed the past was trying to get her attention and wouldn't let her go. She looked at her watch. It was nearly 9 p.m., another night Adele had to get through without Sophia. Rachel looked at her old notebook again, reading her faded handwriting out loud.

'Envelope £1,000 cash, Basildon Bond, name Emma. Slanted handwriting.'

She frowned, thinking back to Adele climbing into her car earlier with Camilla's letters, a niggling memory grating at her frazzled brain. She picked up her car keys and went outside to her car. There on the floor on the passenger side was a Basildon Bond envelope with the name 'Emma' in the same tall, slanted handwriting on the front. Rachel's heart skipped a beat. Had it been Camilla's handwriting on the envelope left with the foundling that day?

There was only one way to find out.

Rachel walked back inside and picked up her mobile again. She couldn't bother Ben with this – he had too much on his plate – she needed the help of an old friend, someone who might have a vague memory of the day baby Emma had been found. Rachel scrolled down to Detective Inspector Bill Bailey's name, and pressed the green button.

'Hi, Rachel, you OK?' he said, answering after only one ring. She had never, ever called him out of hours before.

'Yes. I'm sorry to call you late. Have you got a minute?'

'No problem. Yes, of course, what's up?'

Rachel felt her body relax. Despite being promoted way above her over the years since they had started out as kids, he was a good guy who always acted as if they were still equal colleagues.

'Do you remember, when we were just starting out, that baby being brought into the police station?' Rachel asked. 'You were behind reception, I think. I was processing a vanload of Greenham women.'

'The foundling? Yeah, sure, I remember. Quite a rare event. Never had one since, to be honest.'

She could hear the sounds of his home life in the background, his wife calling out to their teenage sons to tidy up, the clattering of plates, the radio on. A busy, bustling household.

'This may sound strange, but there was an envelope with a load of cash in with the baby. About a thousand pounds, I think.'

'I don't remember that bit – sorry,' Bill said.

'That's OK, you don't need to. I'm pretty sure I asked you to bag it up and put it in the evidence book. My boss at the time wouldn't let me use it for the newspaper article, in case people came forward just for the money. My question is, how long do we keep evidence for? Like, how many years?'

'Indefinitely, if a case isn't solved,' Bill said promptly. 'Even if they don't have the envelope, they will have a record and a photograph of it at the Newbury Evidence Management Unit.'

Rachel's arms started to prickle again with adrenaline. 'Bill, can you use your clout to get me in there?'

'Sure, no problem. I'll call them in the morning,' he said cheerfully.

'No, Bill,' said Rachel. 'I need to go there now.'

Chapter Seventeen

Adele

'There has been a significant update. Who would you like to be in the room when I share it with you?'

Ben James, the senior investigating officer, had returned from taking a call in the study and was standing in the middle of the Nortons' kitchen, facing Adele. It was dark now, gone midnight, and Adele had no idea how she was going to make it through another night.

She looked over at her mother, who was poring over a map of the local area and littering it with Post-it notes. They had been out since Adele returned from Wales, showing support for the hundreds of locals who had turned up to help search for Sophia, until Adele had nearly fainted on the main road. Her mother had brought her back and insisted she eat some toast, which tasted like cardboard. She took to her bed then, staring at the ceiling, listening to the press outside chatting and exchanging gossip and hot drinks, until she had finally given in and walked downstairs to the kitchen where she sat now.

The shock was starting to morph into a terrifying numbness. She no longer shook or cried or felt nauseous. She just stared, motionless, unable to process what people were saying to her, as if they were talking from the end of a long tunnel, their voices muffled and distant. She was scared her body was sinking into an acceptance of the situation; as if it knew something she didn't.

Ben James didn't look as if he'd sat down all day. When he'd first arrived, he had been clean shaven, his shirt starched, his tie straight, his aftershave strong. Now, hours later, his sharpness was fading. In between dashing in and out of the kitchen to take phone calls, and talking Adele and her mother through various updates regarding press conferences and statements, he had been at the police station, trawling through hours and hours of CCTV of the area where Leia had been found wandering the streets.

Alex hadn't yet come home from the station. Adele had given up asking Ben what they had found out from him. Every time she did, he told her that he would update her as soon as he could. She felt embarrassed and humiliated that Ben now knew a great deal more about her husband than she did. She had been too naïve and trusting to go snooping into his personal information and find out whether what he was telling her about their financial situation was the truth. The fact was, she had checked out of this marriage months, maybe even years ago, and she didn't want to know how financially screwed he was. It was his problem, she concluded in her head, and when they got divorced she would get Sophia and he would have to sort out his own messes. It never occurred to her that things were so bad – that he was such a compulsive liar and gambler – that it would become a threat to Sophia's life. And for that she had to take some responsibility. She had buried her head in the sand, too absorbed with surviving his moods and anger to try and find a way out, blindly hoping that things would get better.

Until Ben James stood in front of her now.

This is it, thought Adele, this is the moment when nothing will ever be the same again. I have crossed over to another place, the land where no mother wants to live.

She sat frozen in her seat, and instinctively looked over at her mother, who had been pacing up and down the kitchen since their return, making endless cups of tea, and now stood motionless, staring back at her.

Adele couldn't answer Ben. The moment she said anything, she would be acknowledging this development of his and their lives would never be the same again.

'Can I suggest just you and your mother?' Ben said, immediately starting to herd his colleagues out of the room.

Adele focused on breathing. For the first time that she could remember, she reached out for her mother's hand. Felicity sat down in the chair next to her and took it.

Just say it, just say it . . . Adele chanted in her head, digging her nails into the table.

Adele wished Rachel was here. Another family liaison officer was on the night shift, a blonde middle-aged lady called Jane, who Adele hadn't taken to. Jane had spent her time so far trying to cheer them all up and saw it as her job to be positive. Adele just wished she would go. It was after midnight and everyone was exhausted.

Adele looked over at Leia asleep on the rug. She wanted to ask her where she'd been, what had happened to Sophia. She was the nearest thing to Sophia she had left in the world.

SIO Ben James looked at them all in turn, then took a breath. 'As you are aware, six months ago, Edward Mills lent Alex a quarter of a million pounds to help with cash flow problems in his consultancy practice. Three months ago, Edward needed that money back urgently, and so referred Alex to a colleague of his called Anthony Hislop who put Alex in touch with a money lending company – we have since discovered Anthony had shares in – so Alex could pay Edward back. However, Alex fell behind with the hefty repayments immediately and he was pressured with threatening phone calls and visits to his office, prompting him to put your home on the market.'

Adele looked at her mother. She didn't know how much of this Felicity knew, but the colour had drained from her face and her hands were shaking. Slowly she put them under the table.

'We interviewed Edward Mills to ask him why he needed the funds back urgently and he explained that his wife, Camilla, had left the money to a daughter Felicity had when she was seventeen years old, whom she gave up for adoption. He had been unable to find the child and, knowing Alex was in trouble financially, lent him the money instead. However, his solicitor chased him up in recent weeks and she said he was in breach of the terms of the will if he didn't find the child, and pay her. He consequently put his DNA on a reunion website and found his granddaughter. The funds are being paid to her tomorrow, I believe.'

'You've found my daughter?' Felicity asked.

'Your father, Edward Mills, has – yes.'

Adele turned to her mother and smiled gently, squeezing her hand. Nobody said a word. Adele could hear the rushing of blood in her ears as she stared at Ben. 'What has this got to do with Sophia?' she said finally.

Ben cleared his throat, and continued.

'I'm sorry to tell you that during the course of our investigation, we've found a lot of information on your husband's financial affairs. We are not at liberty to discuss those at the moment, but we will be charging him with several offences, including fraud and money laundering.'

Adele let out a whimper and covered her mouth. She stood and walked over to the sliding doors onto the garden. Felicity went to her. Adele turned her attention back to Ben James as the hissing in her ears intensified.

'Has one of these people Alex owes money to taken Sophia?'

'That's what we are trying to find out. Alex had a lot of money hidden in a bank account in Ireland, under the name of Conor Walsh. Who we have discovered is Alex's father.'

'Alex's father? But both Alex's parents are dead,' said Felicity, as Adele looked at her mother. 'They died when he was a teenager. He had to go into care.'

Ben opened up his laptop and slowly turned it so that Adele could see it. There was a photograph of Alex, taken a few years before, with two elderly people standing next to him smiling.

The older man was the image of Alex: dark eyes, Mediterranean skin tone. The woman was holding a child, a beautiful little girl, aged about three, who was beaming into the camera. Adele instantly recognised her as Sophia.

'That's my daughter. What's going on? Who are those people?'

'They are Alex's parents,' Ben said.

'What are you talking about?' Adele gasped. 'They can't be. Sophia would have said something to me.'

'She looks pretty young in the photograph, darling. Alex could have lied to her about who they were. Do the press know about this?' asked Felicity quietly.

'We are not discussing this matter with the press yet, but we felt you needed to know in case it is leaked due to the intense media interest in this case.'

'Does my grandfather know that Alex's parents are alive?' Adele asked.

'No, we've found nothing to suggest that. We haven't informed him of this development as we are trying to keep knowledge of it to a minimum. It seems Alex has kept his parents a secret from everyone in order to hide his money with them. They aren't aware they were being used, and they were told, by Alex, that you were estranged.'

Felicity gasped. 'Have they got Sophia?'

'No, we have an officer with them now, and they have no idea where Sophia is. However, as you know, Adele, your mother, Felicity, saw Alex with a woman, who she has given us an artist's impression of. Your mother also confirmed that she saw this woman and Alex in a turquoise Fiat. The same make and colour of car that Leia was dropped off in. Both of Alex's parents have said that they met a woman claiming to be Alex's girlfriend recently. And that Alex was having some problems with her. They have also done an artist's impression of the woman, and it matches very closely with your mother's.'

Ben clicked on the keys of his laptop and turned it back to Adele. On his screen was another picture: a sketch of a blonde woman, with blue staring eyes, hair in plaits, and a round, childlike face. 'We estimate her to be in her forties.'

Adele stared at the woman, looking for any family resemblance, but saw none.

'According to his parents, Alex had a brief liaison with the woman but she was struggling to accept it was over. They said she was very intense. "Threatening" was the word they used. Ideally we would wait to get the car registration and trace her that way, but that information is not forthcoming at the moment. Adele, as you know, today we will be into the third day of Sophia's disappearance.'

Adele nodded. 'I know.'

'We need to speed things up for Sophia's sake. With your permission, we would like to release this woman's picture to the press as a person of interest in the case. We don't need to mention a relationship. Alex has also done an artist's impression of her, but has no idea where she is, or even if the name he knows her by is her real name. We think there is a chance that she could have Sophia and we need to see if the public recognise her and know who – or where – she is.'

Adele looked around the room. Her mother's lips were moving, but she couldn't hear anything. She had nearly drowned once as a child. She and her mother had gone for an evening swim at Caswell Bay in the Gower. Felicity had quickly got cold and got out of the sea. Trips to the beach were rare and Adele had begged to stay in and laid on her back, the waves lapping at her face and ears. She hadn't heard her mother shouting until the rip tide had got her. It must have been less than five minutes of swimming hard against the current, but she was only eight, and her body had grown weak and started to give up. It was a strange sensation, begging her arms and legs to cooperate and keep her afloat as they had defied her and gone limp from the exhaustion. She had begun to swallow water, and tried to cry out, but it had proved impossible as the waves engulfed her.

The sensation she had at that moment, before the lifeguard pulled her out, was exactly the one she felt now. She was suffocating, convinced that someone was, at that very moment, hurting Sophia and she was feeling exactly what her daughter was feeling.

'Adele, breathe, breathe, breathe!' Felicity was saying to her as she slumped on the floor by the dining-room table.

Slowly she started to come round. Ben gave her a glass of water, then lifted her and carried her up the stairs. Her eyes fell on the coats on the hooks as they passed – Sophia's new bomber jacket hanging untouched. She had been asked so many times by the police what Sophia was wearing that day, and every time it triggered the painful memory of the last time she had spoken to her little girl. Sophia had begged her to let her wear her new jacket when she had left for school that day. She was in the senior school now and all her school friends were being allowed to wear their non-uniform coats. They had quarrelled, and Sophia had eventually given up and stormed off down the road on her own in her school coat. However much Adele tried to comfort herself, the fact remained that if that was the last time that she would have seen her daughter, they had parted on bad terms.

Ben pushed open the bedroom door with his hip, his hands were digging into her and hurting her as he walked her towards the bed. Her husband should be doing this, she thought. Her husband should be by her side, and yet he was the reason they were in this situation. And she would never forgive him.

She hadn't spoken a word to him since Sophia had gone missing. She had asked Alex to meet Sophia from school when she'd found out she was running late, he had refused despite the fact that he would be working from home in the afternoon, as he said he had an urgent Teams meeting. It had led to an argument about why Sophia couldn't walk to and from school on her own like so many other kids her age. Sophia was sad, Adele had told him. She had no friends at her new school, Ruby had abandoned her; it wasn't about whether she was safe or not.

He had refused, knowing a crazy ex was after him, knowing he owed hundreds of thousands of pounds to dodgy moneylenders. He had known all these things, and yet he didn't care about making sure his daughter got home safely. He had screwed a woman who had got obsessed with him and taken Sophia as revenge. Adele felt no sympathy for his plight. She hoped he rotted in prison.

Why did he tell her that his parents were dead? And take Sophia to Ireland to visit them? That meant that he had never gone into care. Why was he laundering money and committing fraud? Who was this woman who was obsessed with him? How did he meet her?

It was beyond humiliating, and now Ben was going to release a picture of this women to the world and everyone would know Adele's business and that Alex was a cheat, a criminal and a lying fucking asshole.

Her husband of twenty years. She had no idea who he even was any more.

Chapter Eighteen

Felicity

Monday, 13 December 1982

Fliss woke inside the warmth of the sleeping bag in the boot of her Mini and lay very still, staring out of the window, and wondering if the day before had been a dream. She turned and saw her diary lying open next to her, which she vaguely remembered writing in the night before. She began to read back the words she had scrawled at two in the morning, before finally falling asleep after the most beautiful day of her life; slipping around in the mud, singing, dancing, body painting, laughing and holding hands as one of thirty-five thousand women who turned up to Embrace the Base at Greenham Common. Fliss sat up to get herself comfortable, being careful not to wake Hazel, who was still asleep beside her. She was a week shy of seven months gone and starting to get uncomfortable.

12 December 1982

I'm very tired but I wanted to write a few words while the events of today are still fresh in my mind. I still can't believe I was part of a day which will stay with me forever. I felt the rising power of the women at 'Embrace the Base', as we held hands and sang and danced until my legs gave out. There was a lady from Northumberland called Ruby next to me, who was in her sixties, and next to her, a housewife in her thirties, who had come all the way from Ireland.

When I heard the whooping of the women, telling us that the circle had joined, Hazel turned to me and smiled. I felt like I was truly loved for the first time in my life. I have found my home and I am here to stay.

Fliss read on, conscious that it was early and she didn't want to wake Hazel yet. Her writing was scrawled, but it was clearly dripping with emotion. She had cried several times during the day, as had many of the women surrounding her, overwhelmed to be part of such an inspiring manifestation of power and creativity.

We sang until our voices were hoarse. As night fell the organisers handed out candles, and as far as the eye could see were the stubborn flames, representing the spirit of the women. It was bitterly cold, and raining, but nothing could have broken our resolve as we continued to burn brightly.

It was getting more difficult by the day as her bump grew and her energy shrank, but until her baby was born she was determined to stay. Hazel's parents had offered to put her and the baby up, until she figured out where she was going to live and work. Really she had never felt so adrift, so unsure of where her life was going, and yet for the first time she was happy.

She could hear the sound of one of the organisers speaking on the Tannoy outside the gates, and she opened the window so that she could work out what was being said. A girl in her twenties, wearing dungarees and a thick grey hand-knitted jumper, was sitting in the middle of a large circle of women, reading from the *Guardian*, to great whoops and cheers from those surrounding her. Fliss smiled to herself as she listened to the journalist's take on Embrace the Base the day before.

'*It was a remarkable show of strength of the antinuclear lobby,*' the girl read as another loud cheer went up. '*Men were excluded from the demonstrations*' – a further huge cheer – '*and told to run the crèche, prepare the food and keep out of the way!*' A loud round of applause went up, which suddenly came to an abrupt halt as a police truck roared past. Then another, then another.

Fliss felt a flicker of panic and she twisted her body round to try to get a better view, as the vehicles stopped in front of their camp and uniformed policemen began pouring out.

'What is it? What's wrong?' said Hazel, stirring.

'I'm not sure,' said Fliss, leaning into the front seat and turning on the radio. She changed stations a couple of times until she heard the familiar sound of Michael Heseltine's dulcet tones.

'*We are having to face a range of new approaches, towards civil disobedience, towards public protest. Towards the attitudes of groups of people, who are prepared to involve in trespass, to cause disruption to the normal peaceful process of society.*'

'Why are there so many police vans?' said Hazel, frowning up at Fliss.

'*Thank you, Mr Heseltine,*' said the interviewer. '*Well, it is certainly a striking image, the sight of thirty thousand women encircling the RAF base at Greenham Common, and I believe that every national newspaper has printed a photograph of Embrace the Base this morning. The women of Greenham Common have achieved national and, I believe, global publicity, with their event yesterday. But it seems, according to you, the state is set to strike back.'*

Fliss turned off the radio. 'We have to go out there and help,' she said.

Hazel nodded her agreement and the two of them wriggled out of their sleeping bag and opened the boot of the car.

'We shouldn't have slept in the car last night. We should have stayed with the women,' said Hazel, jumping out and running towards the circle of women outside the gate.

The scene that met them was one that Fliss had not been prepared for. Gone was the goodwill, the candles and the happiness. Instead, police who had clearly been shipped in to deal with them were violently dragging the women away. The women were staying calm, not fighting back, their bodies limp, their mood peaceful. They were trying to sing their way through it – 'We are women . . . We are strong' – but the optimism from the previous day had suddenly evaporated.

Fliss watched as another group of policemen began tearing the women's tents down, dragging them across the muddy ground and throwing them in the back of the police vans. Fliss didn't recognise a lot of the women – many had stayed on from the protest the day before – but she spotted her friend Clara rushing after a policeman, pulling her sleeping bag and blankets back, until she was wrenched away and pushed to the ground. Fliss hurried over to her, and carefully helped her to the wooded area away from the mayhem. The skin on Clara's right arm was torn and blood was oozing from the gravel-filled wound. Carefully, Fliss pulled the bandanna from her hair and wrapped it round Clara's forearm. As Clara started to cry, shaking her head at the depressing scene unfolding, they watched in bewilderment as the policemen seemed to be enjoying their chance to exert their power over the women.

Fliss sat Clara down by the side of the road, and felt a sharp stab in her stomach. The baby clearly wasn't impressed by the demonstration, and Fliss forced herself to sit for a moment, looking around frantically for Hazel, who was now sitting in the middle of the women's circle. Fliss watched the men and tried to stay composed. They had a fire extinguisher and they were putting all the fires out, whilst kicking away stones that the women had hand-painted the day before at Embrace the Base. She had no idea why these men disliked them so much, felt such satisfaction creating devastation when just hours before there had been nothing but love and togetherness here.

As she watched and the singing got louder, Fliss felt her old self returning and a familiar cloud of depression began to descend. The establishment would never let the women win. There was too much at stake, too much money, an entire government's reputation. She knew from her father's work how politicians' minds worked, how they would stop at nothing.

How could a group of women with nothing but saplings, tarpaulin and lentil stew take on the nuclear might of the world? They were living in a dream world. Fliss watched as the police began forcing the women into the back of their vans. She had never been in trouble with the police before – what if she got arrested and her father found out? She was pregnant, without a home. If she ended up with a criminal record it could affect her chances of getting a job.

At that moment, when fear was close to consuming her, she caught Hazel's eye – she was sitting in the circle of women, smiling and singing her heart out. The women around her were being dragged away but she didn't care. She looked as if she were on a picnic in a park; she didn't think about how weak she was, she didn't focus on what she didn't have. She focused on her power, her strength. It was infectious and she was beckoning Fliss over. It was then that Fliss made the most important decision of her life.

She could always sit in her little box and do as she was told, and never question or try to change anything. And she would be perfectly safe. Or she could say no and take the consequences. How could she just sit there, watching, and let these women she had grown so close to, and who had made her happier than she'd ever been, be violently manhandled, and do nothing? If she didn't join them now, when it really mattered, then she was just a bystander. She would be no better than her parents. In fact she would be worse because she was a hypocrite.

Fliss slowly walked through the circle of women, trying not to fall, until she reached Hazel's outstretched hand and sat down. Hazel gripped her hand tightly and Fliss gripped the hand of the girl next to her. Fliss had never seen so many police before. More and more seemed to be appearing. It was as if the success of Embrace the Base and the publicity it had generated had ignited a fury within the government. The police had clearly been instructed to do whatever it took to get the women out.

'Oww, you're hurting my arm,' one woman cried, as a policeman dragged her towards the police van. She managed to break free from him and ran to the fence, rocking it backwards and forwards as if in a fit of rage. Another woman stood at the fence and joined her in pulling it back and forth, back and forth. Soon another joined, and another and another, until there were a hundred women, pushing and pulling at the wire fence surrounding the base. The fence began to buckle and bow, and the cement pillars holding it up started to falter. The police tried to pull the women back, but more came to help and soon the entire fence began to give way. The women continued to sing louder and stronger.

We are women, we are women
We are strong, we are strong,
We say no, we say no
To the bomb, to the bomb.

One policeman marched up to the fire that had been keeping them all warm and blasted it with a fire extinguisher. Fliss had tears in her eyes. The flames from the candles and the fires the women had lit the night before represented their spirit. But it could not be snuffed out for good. They would relight it, again and again. As many times as it took to get their message heard.

Suddenly she felt someone tugging hard at her arm and she remembered what they had been told: don't fight back, let your body go limp. But it hurt, it bloody hurt as the policeman dragged her along the hard concrete ground. She felt her skin tear at her hip, and she let out a cry of pain.

'Let go of her,' shouted Hazel. 'You're hurting her! She's pregnant.' She began trying to pull Fliss away from the officer.

'Don't think that just because you're pregnant we are going to treat you any different.' He sounded to Fliss like he had a northern accent. They had obviously shipped in as many policemen as they could from every corner of the country.

The pain soared through her, but she managed to let her body hang and focused on the women in the background shaking the fence so hard that it was starting to fall. Suddenly it gave way and, to a massive cheer, the women began running onto the air base, stepping over the fence which was now on the ground, with the police and American soldiers in pursuit.

You can't kill the spirit,
She is like a mountain.
Old and strong, she goes on and on and on . . .

Fliss lay by the road, singing as loud as she could to keep her spirits up, but before long she began to feel sick and dizzy. She needed to lie down before she threw up everywhere. Slowly she pulled her aching body up, staggering through the gate and towards the car park. She desperately needed her car, she needed to rest, she had stabbing pains in her stomach where she'd been dragged across the road. As soon as she saw it, her heart plummeted: on the windscreen of her Mini, a bright red notice with the word 'SEIZED' shouted out to her. And to her horror she realised that the large low-loader, beeping and reversing towards her, was backing up to her car.

Fliss stumbled towards her car, close to collapsing, opened the door and climbed in.

A policeman tried to pull her out, but she pushed him away with the pitiful remains of her strength, and slammed the door. This car was her home; it was everything she had in the world.

'Get off!' Fliss shouted.

'My name is Davis and on behalf of the High Court, we have seized this car,' said a man in a cheap-looking beige suit, who appeared next to her clutching a clip-board.

'You are not taking my car!' Fliss had never raised her voice to anyone before, let alone someone in authority. The car was parked on public land, in the car park next to the common. She was sure they had no right to take it.

She leaned forward, hugging the steering wheel. She heard Hazel shouting for her in the background.

The man pressed on. 'You are part of the Women's Peace Movement here on the common. Our instructions are to remove you and your assets, and this car is part of your assets.'

'You are not taking my car.' Fliss felt a rage building she had never experienced before. She gripped the steering wheel tightly, as if her life depended on it. She was pregnant, it was her shelter, she had nothing else.

'We have seized the car. It is now our property,' the man said, pulling at her to get her out.

'You are not taking my car,' she shouted again.

233

'So what are you going to do? Sit in it?' he snapped.

'Yes,' she spat.

'Then we will have to remove you.'

'Why can't she drive her own car?' said Hazel, suddenly appearing.

'Because we have seized it on behalf of the High Court,' Davis said, turning to Hazel.

'For what reason?'

'To repay the costs of removing the Peace Movement from Greenham.'

'Have you got a notice?' Hazel asked.

'Oh, yes, we have a High Court notice. The officer of the High Court will show it to you both. You will get in a lot of trouble if you drive away right now, young lady. You are taking Crown property.'

'I'm not taking Crown property. This is my car. It's all I have.' Fliss started to cry.

'Remove your personal belongings and get out of the car.' Davis smiled smugly. He was upbeat, as if he were enjoying her suffering.

Without warning, he and his gruff-looking colleague, who had by now climbed out of the low-loader, started forcefully to pull Fliss out of the car. Fliss tried to cling on to the steering wheel but they were too strong for her. She let out a cry of pain as they yanked at her arms until she felt her wrists would snap.

'Be careful, you're hurting her. Leave her alone!' Hazel cried.

The police officer pulled Hazel away, and she thrashed and kicked, trying to break free. Finally the two men managed to drag Fliss out of her car and pulled her to the side of the road as the driver hooked chains around the wheels of the Mini.

'Stand back, please,' the driver said, jumping back in the low-loader.

Hazel finally broke free and climbed onto the roof of Fliss's car. Fliss stood watching, one of the policemen holding her arms behind her back. She was helpless, unable to stop the tears as another policeman tried to pull Hazel off the roof by her legs but she held on tight to the car. Another man joined in, and together they pulled each of Hazel's legs until she cried out in pain.

Clara stepped in, and began yanking one of the policemen away by his jacket. 'Stop that. You are hurting her!' she shouted desperately.

The second policeman yanked Hazel so violently she lost her grip on Felicity's car and fell to the ground, whereupon the policeman signalled and the chains snapped taught, dragging the car onto the low-loader.

Slowly but surely, the women kept coming, standing in front of the truck, pushing the men back, but there were too many police surrounding them, and they dragged the women away one by one, locking them in the back of the police vans. Fliss's car was secured to the truck within minutes and it began to drive away as the women lay in the road and sang in protest. More police came, dragging them from the path of the truck and arresting them, until finally the vehicle moved and hurtled along the main road.

Fliss watched it go in disbelief and started to cry, as Hazel put her arms around her.

The women stood in stunned silence, staring at the

police officers, all linking arms and bearing down on all the Greenham women.

One voice rose clearly above the crowd. Then another joined in, then another. All the women stared at the police, and linked arms as if mirroring their behaviour.

> *Which side are you on?*
> *Which side are you on?*
> *Are you on the other side from me?*
> *Which side are you on?*
>
> *Are you on the side of atrocity?*
> *Are you on the side of perjury?*
> *Are you on the side of misery?*
> *Which side are you on?*

Soon, it sounded like a hundred women were singing, as the police stood staring at the women lined up in front of them. Fliss watched her car disappear into the distance, then sat on the road, put her head on her knees and sobbed.

Chapter Nineteen

Emma

Monday, 3 June 2024

'Emma, Emma, wake up!'

Emma stirred and opened her eyes to see Amanda staring down at her.

'I've found out who you are.' She was beaming from ear to ear. 'You're not going to believe it.'

As Emma slowly came round, Amanda was pacing the room as if she was high on amphetamines.

'What are you talking about?' said Emma, sitting up in her bunk bed and trying to prise herself from her deep sleep. 'What time is it?'

She looked at the clock by her bed. It was seven in the morning. Amanda was fully made up with red lipstick and heavy eye make-up. She looked as though she'd been up for hours.

'When did you get back? I thought you were coming back last night?' Emma asked.

'I needed another day, and Sam let me come back early this morning. I spent the weekend in Newbury, where you grew up,' Amanda said, pulling a chair up next to Emma's bed, 'and I've found out why you were adopted.' She put down her rucksack on the floor of their cell and rummaged around in it frantically.

Emma tried to shake herself awake, she wasn't sure if she

was dreaming. 'I don't understand. I thought you were going home to London to see your mum.'

'Never mind that. I explained to her. She knows we've got very close and that I want to help you,' Amanda said, pulling out a notebook from her bag, and flicking through the endless pages of scrawled handwriting. 'Get dressed. I've told Sam we're going for a walk. We haven't got long before work starts, but I don't want anyone else to hear this,' she said, looking at the door again as Jen passed by in her pyjamas.

Emma got herself out of bed, quickly pulled on her jeans, T-shirt and trainers, then walked into the bathroom, crossing paths with Jen, who she hadn't spoken to since their awkward encounter in the dining room.

'Come on, hurry up,' said Amanda, hovering at the bathroom door.

'Yeah, hurry up, Emma,' Jen echoed, sniggering. 'Is she not allowed to take a piss without you standing over her?' she said to Amanda, walking out of the toilet.

'Fuck off, Jen,' said Amanda, as Emma flushed the toilet, then washed her hands and face in cold water and pulled her hair back into a scruffy ponytail.

'Do you want to hear this or not?' Amanda said despondently as Emma walked back into the corridor. 'Because you don't seem very interested. We can forget the whole thing if you like.'

'Of course I want to hear it. Sorry, I'm just a bit taken aback. I didn't realise you were actually going to Newbury this weekend,' Emma said, her heart racing as they began walking towards the entrance of the former stately home that was the main prison building and out into the bright summer sunshine. It was so early that there was no one about, and the morning dew was still hanging in the air.

Amanda was crossing her arms defensively as they began to walk towards the surrounding fields side by side. It was a beautiful day already, with a light mist sitting over the perfectly cut grass. As they passed the farm, they could hear the pigs squealing and the hens clucking happily. Amanda had become very quiet, and suddenly Emma felt a surge of guilt. The conversation with Jen in the dining room on the Saturday – along with Amanda's possessive behaviour – had started to make her nervous, but the fact was that Jen hadn't actually given her any information that contradicted Amanda's version of events. She knew no more about Jen than she did Amanda. Amanda could be right to be possessive; perhaps she was also right about the others wanting to come between them. Emma was finding Westwood Park a huge adjustment. She was being allowed a great deal more freedom, but she was finding that disorientating and debilitating after so long at Heathfield. She had kept herself to herself entirely there and this close friendship with Amanda was new territory that she was finding hard to navigate.

The fact was that nobody else had ever shown the slightest bit of interest in helping her trace her birth parents, and in the space of one weekend, Amanda was claiming to have made some real progress. Emma linked her arm through Amanda's and smiled warmly.

'I'm sorry, this is all just so raw. You trying to find out who my birth mother is. I'm really grateful, but I don't know how to feel about any of it. Normally, I guess, I'd have a social worker or someone, guiding me every step of the way.'

'A social worker?' Amanda scoffed, softening. 'You'll be lucky. They'd never commit themselves to something like this. You'd have a different one every week. There's no way any social worker would have been able to find out what I did this weekend,' she said, stopping at a bench at the edge of a field full of wild flowers.

'You're right. So tell me!' said Emma, sitting down next to Amanda and smiling nervously. 'Every detail, I want to know where you started, who you spoke to and how it all played out. It's your turn not to skip anything now.'

'OK,' said Amanda. 'I'll need my trusty notebook.' She retrieved it from her rucksack and licked her finger enthusiastically to help her flip through the pages. Emma giggled at her studious pose. 'So I didn't speak to anyone, I just walked in the back door of your mother's house while she was having a bath and went through her filing cabinet until I found this.'

Amanda held out a newspaper cutting, and smiled broadly again as Emma laughed nervously.

'You are joking?' Emma's eyes were wide.

'No,' Amanda said. 'Look!'

'Hang on a second,' Emma said, not registering the newspaper article. 'You broke into my adoptive mother's house and went through my parents' filing cabinet?'

'Yes – do you want to know who you are or not?' Amanda said, waving the cutting.

'Well, yes, I want to know, but not by breaking the law.'

'Oh, get over yourself – you're a convict. Anyway, you haven't broken the law, I have.'

'But that filing cabinet is always locked. I tried to open

240

it myself a couple of times.' Emma shook her head incredulously.

'I found the key in the top drawer of the dressing table in your mother's bedroom.'

Emma's mouth dropped open. 'The bedroom next to the bathroom where she was having a bath?'

'Yup.' Amanda giggled again. 'Look, we can talk about this later. Read it, will you! It explains why your adoptive parents didn't want to fucking tell you anything.'

Emma looked down at the cutting, then slowly took it from Amanda's hand. The newspaper article was from the *Newbury Times*, dated 3 April 1983. She looked at Amanda, then back to the crinkled page and began to read.

Police are appealing for the mother of a baby girl found on the steps of a church in Newbury to come forward so that she can receive medical care and support.

The baby, named Emma, was discovered inside a cardboard box on the steps of St Phillip's church in Newbury just before 7 a.m. yesterday. Police discovered a tiepin with the initials EJM wrapped in her blanket. She has been discharged from hospital and is in the care of foster parents.

The little girl is believed to be about six weeks old and was found by church caretaker, Howell Jenkins, in sub-zero temperatures.

Emma's mother is yet to come forward, and Newbury police are deeply concerned for her wellbeing. WPC Rachel Rees said: Baby Emma is being well cared for by her foster parents and is a healthy, happy baby.

'We are appealing for any witnesses who may have been in the area of St Phillip's church in the early hours of 2 April to come forward. Emma was well dressed in a baby grow, a pink hand-knitted cardigan, mittens and she was wrapped in a thick woollen blanket. Hospital staff guess her age to be around six weeks and her mother must have cared for her during that time. Parenting can be overwhelming and we want to assure Emma's mother that she is not in trouble. We can offer her help and support.

'The silver tiepin with the initials EJM is of particular importance. Please look closely at the attached photograph. To anyone who may recognise baby Emma, know a lady who was due to give birth but doesn't now have a baby, or who recognises the tiepin, I'd urge you to come forward and help us locate her. This can be done in confidence.'

'Ladies!' Sam the governor said, standing over them. 'I've been looking for you. You should be getting ready for work.'

Emma looked at her watch and jumped up. 'Shit! Sorry, Sam.'

'Emma, I need to talk to you in my office now, please,' Sam said.

Amanda looked at Emma. 'Sounds important. You can fill me in when you get back.'

'If she chooses to, Amanda,' Sam said curtly. 'Now get to breakfast, please. You're already late.'

Amanda and Emma followed Sam back in silence.

Emma couldn't react to what she had just read without Sam overhearing. She didn't even know if the article was about her. How could she be a foundling? All her life she'd

242

had an image in her head of her birth mother as a young girl, unable to cope, and having her adopted by a loving family. Saying goodbye properly, going through all the official channels.

Now, if this was really her story, in actual fact she'd been dumped on church steps in the middle of winter in a cardboard box. What if she hadn't been discovered? She could have died. Did her birth mother really care that little about her?

Emma followed Sam into her small, tidy office, feeling a pain in her tummy. She needed to be alone to digest this news. She desperately wanted it not to be true, but she had a niggling feeling that it was.

'Emma, please take a seat. I have some good news. Well, I hope you will think it's good news. Your mother, Sally Blake, has been in touch this morning. She's going to travel up from Newbury to come and visit you.'

Emma's stomach lurched and she put her hand over her mouth. 'You're kidding. Really?'

'I wouldn't joke about something like that, Emma. Yes, really,' said Sam gently.

'Do you think she knows I'm being released soon?' Emma couldn't help the elation she felt reaching her smile.

'I suppose it's possible. Your solicitor will be keeping Sally informed if you've asked him to, but I wouldn't want to jump to any conclusions about her motives. I suspect she would just like to chat with you and see how you both feel. Do you feel up to that?' Sam said.

'Yes, definitely. I'd love that,' said Emma.

'Good. I'll accept the request. It will most likely be next

weekend now. You can have the visits room to yourself, for privacy.'

Emma nodded, tears suddenly stinging her eyes.

'Good, OK, I'll arrange it and confirm the time next week – probably Sunday afternoon,' Sam said, standing to signify the end of their conversation.

Emma stood to go.

'One other thing,' Sam added. 'Are things OK with you and Amanda?'

'Yes, fine. Why?'

'I'm glad you're making friends, but it can be hard coming to the relative freedom of WWP, learning to manage your own boundaries, and if you want to talk to anyone, I'm here. Or you can always ask to talk to our prison chaplain.'

'Thank you, Sam.' Emma nodded and went back to her room, where Amanda was waiting.

'Well?'

'I thought you'd have gone to work by now. Won't you get in trouble?' Emma said, quickly changing into her shop uniform.

'No, it's fine. What did Sam say?' Amanda pressed.

Emma paused, wanting to keep the information to herself so she could digest it.

'Spit it out,' Amanda said irritably.

'My adoptive mother, Sally, wants to see me,' Emma said quietly.

'Why?' Amanda frowned.

'Um, maybe she's finally forgiven me,' Emma said, taken aback by Amanda's open hostility.

'About time. Well, I hope you haven't forgiven her,' Amanda snapped.

'What for?' Emma said quietly.

'What for? For leaving you to rot in prison for five years without so much as a letter or phone call?' Amanda scoffed. 'You need to start holding her to account, Emma, if you are ever going to heal.'

'She lost her husband, in a fire that I started,' Emma said, tears spiking her eyes. 'Please don't spoil this for me. I'm really happy she wants to see me. Maybe we can start to build some bridges now.'

'I don't know why you'd want to, but that's your business, I guess. I just think if you're going to build some bridges, as you put it, she needs to accept some responsibility. When is she coming?'

'Next weekend,' Emma said, wishing Amanda would go and leave her in peace.

'That's a shame, I'll be in Newbury. I would have liked to meet her. Plenty of time for that, I guess.' Amanda shrugged.

'Newbury? What do you mean?' Emma frowned.

'I'm going back to do some more digging next weekend.' Amanda was putting her notebook back in her rucksack.

'More digging? On what?' Emma felt her tummy turn over.

'You, of course. Find out who dumped you on the church steps.'

'I think that will take a bit more than one weekend,' Emma said quietly.

'Yeah, you don't know me very well yet, do you? And I guess it's easier if your mother isn't at home,' Amanda said.

'Amanda, please don't go back to my parent's house.

245

You could get us both in a lot of trouble.' Emma was shaking.

'I won't get caught. I took a spare key.' Amanda giggled. 'Anyway, I really don't care. I'm getting out in ten days, and there is no bloody way I'm ever coming back to this shit hole,' she added cheerfully.

'Ten days?' Emma shrieked, as Amanda looked at her disapprovingly. 'Oh my God! I can't believe it. You must be so happy.' Emma smiled, surprised at the wave of relief she felt.

'Don't worry, we'll be seeing plenty of each other when you get out,' Amanda said, as if reading her mind.

Emma nodded, overwhelmed with the developments of her morning. Five years of nothing, and now, in the space of one weekend, Sally wanted to see her and Amanda was threatening to find out who her birth mother was. It was too much to take in. She felt the long-lost feeling of hope returning to her body, like a warm blanket.

'Right, I'm off. See you at lunch,' Amanda said finally.

Emma nodded. 'Thank you for everything you've done, Amanda. You're a good friend.'

Emma knew she only had roughly a month left at WWP and she was determined to use the time wisely. Amanda had become so all-consuming that it was hard to find any headspace to think about life beyond the here and now. Maybe, in Amanda's absence, she could befriend some of the other prisoners, get some guidance from Sam and work out what she was going to do with herself when she got out. She was excited at the thought of talking to her mother after all this time. She had missed her.

Maybe they could start afresh and Sally could help

Emma find her birth mother – now that Amanda had got the ball rolling. It was possible Sally hadn't wanted to tell her the truth about being a foundling because she didn't want to hurt her. If Emma could tell her that she knew, maybe when they saw each other at the weekend, it might open the floodgates.

Surely if she was coming to visit her it meant that Sally had finally forgiven her.

Emma was happy for Amanda that she was getting out and would be reunited with her mother. She had probably become so focused on Emma's life out of boredom.

It had been an education to meet Amanda, and Emma would be forever grateful about what she had discovered, but she felt that perhaps once Amanda left, their relationship would naturally come to an end.

And in time Amanda would probably forget all about her.

Chapter Twenty

Rachel

Thursday, 18 July 2024

Detective Constable Rachel Rees crawled along Newbury High Street, straining to see the shop numbers and a sign for Knights Solicitors. Finally, a navy-blue door with gold embossed numbers caught her eye, and a placard confirmed to her she was in the right place. She pulled into a parking space a few doors down, reached for her bag and notebook and climbed out. Her watch told her it was exactly eight thirty.

'DS Rachel Rees, to see Caroline Thomas,' she said, after a female voice answered the intercom.

'Come in, we're on the first floor,' the woman said, as Rachel stepped inside the Victorian terrace and began to climb the carpeted stairs.

They were into the third day of Sophia's disappearance, and Rachel's eyes fizzed from lack of sleep. After her call to DI Bill Bailey the night before, Bill had managed to get hold of the Evidence Management Officer, Richard Tanner. He had reluctantly agreed to meet her at the Evidence Management Unit in Newbury, where they held all the evidence for Thames Valley Police, later that evening.

Richard, a middle-aged, clean-shaven, athletic man, had arrived in a red Ford Ka slightly after Rachel, and taken her to the bowels of the Evidence Management Unit.

Though he had started off a little frostily, grumbling about the amount of out-of-hours work he had been expected to do lately, he was grateful for the biscuits and coffee she brought with her and soon warmed to the task of finding the Evidence Storage Box for April 1983.

Richard had been in his role for twenty-eight years, he told her as they searched, and was coming up for retirement. Rachel felt she had got lucky, as she often found with grumpy people, they were grumpy for a reason; because they were good at their jobs and were often taken for granted. Overly cheerful people, she had concluded over the years, tended to be rather flaky. Richard was a case in point, grouchy and meticulous about his evidence-keeping skills and in under an hour she was staring at a photograph of a cream envelope with the word 'Emma' – in Camilla's distinctive, slanted hand writing – on the front.

'Detective Constable Rees? I'm Caroline Thomas,' said the woman who was already waiting for her in the smart, white-washed reception, its large sash windows overlooking the High Street. She was small, dark and perfectly turned out.

'Hello,' Rachel said, holding out her hand. 'Nice to meet you.'

'Do come through,' said Caroline, leading her down the corridor.

The middle-aged receptionist peered at Rachel over her glasses. Rachel always felt she was nothing special to look at. She made the best of her willowy frame, wavy chestnut hair, fair complexion and grey eyes, but she rarely turned heads. That was until she was in uniform, or once people knew she was a police officer. Then their curious stare would linger or they would listen in when she spoke, in the hope they would catch a bit of gossip.

Caroline stood at the threshold of her neatly furnished office and gestured for Rachel to go in, then closed the door behind them. She then led Rachel to a coffee table by the window, and they sat down opposite one another. Caroline rearranged herself a couple of times, then cleared her throat self-consciously.

'Thank you so much for fitting me in this morning,' Rachel said.

'No problem. How can I help?'

Rachel opened her notebook and pulled her pen from her bag.

'So, as I mentioned in my email, I am looking into the will of Camilla Mills, and specifically a codicil leaving a quarter of a million pounds to her estranged granddaughter, Emma.'

'Yes. I've actually been with Knights for fifteen years and I've never come across this issue before.'

'What issue is that?' Rachel enquired.

'Non-payment of a codicil. I presumed that's why you are here?'

'Well, partly,' said Rachel. 'I'm hoping you can talk me through what happened with your client, Camilla Mills, and how the codicil came about in the first place.'

'It's been a long process. Trying to reach a resolution with Mr Mills has been tricky,' Caroline said.

'I see,' said Rachel.

'My boss actually told me to contact the SRA . . . That's the Solicitors Regulation Authority,' Caroline clarified, noting Rachel's frown, 'to check with them. One of my main concerns was breaking client confidentiality.'

Rachel looked up from her notebook. 'If you are worried about client confidentiality you needn't be. Your client, Camilla Mills, has passed away so that no longer applies.'

'But her husband, Edward Mills, is still alive.'

'OK, so let's just focus on Camilla. I understand from a woman named Hazel Evans that Camilla wanted to leave a large sum of money to Emma in her will, but needed to do it without her husband, Edward, knowing until after her death. Is that correct?'

Rachel's head was still spinning from finding the envelope in Camilla's distinctive writing, proving, along with Hazel's account of the timings of Felicity's baby's birth, that the baby she was handed in a cardboard box in April 1983 was Emma Mills – Felicity's daughter and Adele's half-sister. She now needed to find out why Camilla, on her deathbed, had been determined to paint Edward as the villain of the piece, essentially framing her husband for Emma's abandonment. Her handwriting on the envelope of cash found with baby Emma proved that, at the very least, Camilla knew that Emma was about to be left. And possibly, even, that she had been the one to leave her there.

'That's right,' Caroline said. 'The last time I saw Camilla was about a year ago. She called me to say that she had terminal cancer, and wanted to add a codicil to her and her husband's mirror will.'

'And a codicil is?' Rachel scribbled the word down.

'It's like a caveat, an add-on. She mentioned that her

husband wouldn't be happy she was adding one, so she didn't want him to know about it until after she died. I made an appointment for her to come down here. Sorry, would you like a coffee?' Caroline added, seemingly starting to relax.

'Yes, please. White, no sugar,' Rachel said, as Caroline walked over to a smart-looking coffee machine on a sideboard at the end of the room.

'I read through the notes again this morning to jog my memory,' Caroline said, picking up a file as she passed her desk with Rachel's coffee, before handing it over. 'So when I make a will I make contemporaneous attendance notes, confirming the client has capacity, and anything else that is discussed or takes place during the meeting. I tend to write everything down. I draw up so many wills, it would be impossible to remember otherwise.'

'I'm the same,' said Rachel warmly.

Caroline opened the file, and took a sip of water from the glass on the coffee table. 'Just stop me if any of this doesn't make sense,' she said, looking up at Rachel. 'So Camilla Mills came in with a friend, called Hazel Evans, for moral support as she was concerned about her husband's reaction to the codicil. I asked Hazel to wait outside while I had the meeting with Camilla.' Caroline looked down at her file. 'So I've written here: "Client attended Newbury office on 5 July 2023, at 10 a.m., in order to provide the instructions to add a clause to her original will and testimony. The client instructed me that she wished to now add the following gifts . . ."'

Caroline sat back in her seat, crossed her legs, and continued to read as Rachel scribbled her notes.

'"One – a gift in the sum of two hundred and fifty thousand pounds tax free to my granddaughter Emma who was adopted at six weeks of age in 1983. Emma was my daughter Felicity's first child. Felicity was very young at the time, and she was unable to look after the baby. My husband is fully aware of the details of who Emma was adopted by, and will know how to contact her. He sorted it all out. I had an emotional breakdown and couldn't deal with it.

'"Two – I also give my good friend Hazel Evans my single garnet platinum ring. It was a gift from my mother. She has been a true friend and it is a token to remember me by."'

'"Good friend"?' Rachel queried, looking up from her notes. 'I understood from Hazel that they barely knew each other.'

'Well, it's Hazel who has been in touch to say that she never received the ring, and suspects that Edward, Camilla's husband, also hasn't fulfilled Camilla's wish for Emma to have the two hundred and fifty thousand pounds,' Caroline said, fixing her gaze on Rachel.

'I see,' said Rachel. 'And this codicil, it definitely happened, it wasn't just a meeting?'

'Definitely. Camilla wanted to wait outside with Hazel while I wrote it up. She came back in and signed it, then I put it in the file.' Caroline frowned. 'I remember now she was very keen to get it done there and then. She really didn't look well. She had lost a lot of weight.'

'Am I able to have a copy of the codicil?' asked Rachel.

'Yes, of course,' Caroline said. 'I've made you one already, along with the original will.' She pulled them out of the file and handed them over.

'Thank you. Did Camilla say why her husband would be so against the codicil?' Rachel asked, pen poised.

'Yes, I asked her. She said when she knew she was dying, she had an overwhelming desire to see that Emma, her granddaughter, was financially looked after, but that her husband was always reluctant to talk about the little girl. Camilla had some family money, which was ring-fenced in her name as her parents were wary of Edward's motives when they married,' Caroline said.

'What do you think they meant by "Edward's motives"?' Rachel said, stopping her mid-flow.

'I don't know, but I got the impression Camilla was the one with the family money. I believe Maberley Manor was inherited from her parents.'

'And it now belongs to Edward?'

'Yes, and then it will go to their granddaughter, Adele, as they disinherited their daughter Felicity,' Caroline clarified.

'Because she got pregnant?' Rachel said, eyes wide.

'I don't know why, I only know they were estranged,' Caroline said simply.

'I see. Would Emma be entitled to half of Maberley?'

'No, Adele is named as the sole beneficiary. Which is why I think Camilla was particularly keen to leave Emma this money.'

'Possibly so Emma wouldn't contest the will?' Rachel suggested.

'Maybe, but I think it was more because she said she worried about Emma a lot, whether she was happy and had a good life. She said Adele, her other granddaughter, would inherit the house, Maberley Manor, so she didn't think

Adele would be upset if she found out Emma had been left this money.'

Rachel wrote down everything as quickly as she could. 'Interesting that Felicity, her own daughter, didn't seem to enter into Camilla's conscience – or the codicil – at all,' Rachel offered, to which Caroline shrugged.

'So what happened then, when Camilla Mills passed away? I presume her husband, Edward, contacted you?' Rachel asked.

'Yes, I told him to come down to the office with his ID and the death certificate and I'd release the will,' Caroline said, setting the file back on the table.

'So is there not a second executor on the will? I thought there had to be two?' Rachel frowned.

'No, we advise for there to be two, but there's no legal requirement. With a mirror will, it tends to be that husband and wife are each other's executor as the estate automatically goes to the other spouse.'

'Unless there's a codicil,' Rachel added. 'So were you worried about his reaction?'

'Not really. Our role was done, and it was now over to him. As executor he'd have a legal obligation to administer the estate, which means collecting in the assets, discharging the liabilities, distributing the gifts, liaising with third parties such as HMRC, filling out forms to deal with inheritance tax, organising valuations for properties, writing to the banks to get date-of-death valuations, paying for the funeral. And applying for probate. So I presumed he'd just take it on board with everything else. It's not really any of my business.'

'And do you remember his reaction?' Rachel asked.

'No, I remember giving the will to him, and specifically pointing out the codicil. He didn't say anything at that time.'

'Did he ask if anyone else knew about it?'

Caroline shook her head. 'No, and I didn't tell him Hazel came with his wife. So this is normally where my role ends. The solicitor has no legal obligation to make sure that the wishes of the testator are carried out – we aren't the executor. So I forgot about it, to be honest, until Hazel got in touch a few months later to say she hadn't received her ring.'

'And how would you describe Edward Mills?' said Rachel, thinking back to the frail-looking man she had met at Maberley the previous day.

'I don't know really. An old-fashioned gentleman, I suppose: well-spoken, old money, pillar of the community . . .'

'Old money?' Rachel queried.

'Yes, sorry, it's a term we use. Family money is old money, low-key, never openly discussed, rather than self-made and brash. Living in a mansion, driving a beaten-up old Volvo, that sort of thing.'

'So tell me what the Solicitors Regulation Authority said when you contacted them about Edward Mills?'

'They asked about the probate, and whether he'd attached the codicil. Obviously the probate is a public document,' Caroline added.

'Did he have to apply for probate?'

'Yes. If there is an estate of over seventy-five thousand pounds, which there was, you have to submit the last will and the codicil to the probate registry as part of the probate application. The banks require probate to give the trustees control of the funds. And he did submit the original will. But I checked, and the codicil wasn't with it.'

'So he's definitely been dishonest?' Rachel said, noting it down.

'Well, yes, but my impression is that he didn't want this issue with his estranged granddaughter to be public knowledge, rather than there being any intentional wrongdoing. As soon as I put him under pressure, he paid up. I think he had every intention of fulfilling the codicil, he is just . . .'

'What?' Rachel pressed.

'I don't know. He seemed rather shell-shocked.' Caroline hesitated. 'Off the record, I felt a bit sorry for him. Camilla was always the driving force when they came in together. He never said much. The whole thing just seemed odd. She almost implied he was abusive. That she wanted to leave this money to Emma, and he wouldn't let her. But I'm not so sure. I guess marriage is complicated,' Caroline said, shaking her head. 'Again, not my business.'

'OK, so how did you leave it with Edward?'

'I told him he's under a legal obligation to carry out the obligations of the estate as per the wishes of the testator, his wife, Camilla.'

'And what did he say?'

'He said it was an oversight and that he'd correct it. I wrote to him immediately saying that he had seven days to make the payment as per the codicil, and grant me a copy of the transfer, or I was under duty to notify the police. That was a few months ago and he made a request to transfer the funds to our client account until he found Emma, which he has now done. We have it in a holding account and it is due to be transferred to Emma shortly.'

Rachel felt her heart lurch and she looked up at Caroline. 'So, he's definitely found Emma?'

'Yes.'

'Right,' said Rachel, writing that down. 'Did Edward say how he'd found her?'

'Yes, he decided to do a DNA test to speed things up once I put the pressure on, and they are a match according to the ancestry website he used. I've had the paperwork through and it all checks out. I'm glad we got there in the end.'

'Yes. Could you possibly email me a copy of that paperwork?' Rachel said, holding her breath. If Caroline said no, she would need a search warrant to get the ancestry website to release the information to her, which would take too long.

'Of course, it's just an email, and I'll have to delete names, but I'm happy to forward it so you have the proof.'

'Many thanks,' said Rachel, letting out a silent sigh of relief. 'When are you planning to transfer the funds to Emma?'

'Tomorrow morning, hopefully,' Caroline said.

'So you have the contact details of Edward's estranged granddaughter?' Rachel asked.

'Yes, but unfortunately I can't give out personal information.'

'Of course. I understand, thank you,' Rachel said, standing up.

'Give me a call if there's anything else I can help you with. I'll forward the email now from the ancestry website.'

Rachel thanked Caroline for her time, and made her way outside.

She climbed into her car and sat back in her seat. Superficially, it had been a very conclusive conversation.

It was obvious that Edward had decided to ignore the codicil and lend the two hundred and fifty thousand pounds to Alex to help with his business – until his solicitor threatened him with contacting the police.

It wasn't beyond the realms of possibility that Emma would put her DNA details on a website in the hope of finding her birth family. But it still bothered her that Edward had dragged his feet for a year, then managed to find his long-lost granddaughter, and coughed up the money, the day after Sophia went missing.

Rachel's email pinged into life, and she opened the solicitor's email from the ancestry website. She scrolled down and looked at the dates. The DNA sample had been submitted in early July, less than three weeks ago. Why? Had Emma found out about the money? She needed to find her and speak to her, and although the solicitor wouldn't give her the details, she knew now that the foundling she had been handed – who she was now sure was Felicity's daughter – would be fairly easy to trace. She knew baby Emma had been adopted locally, and by a couple affiliated to the church where Emma was found.

Rachel looked at her watch. It was now nine o'clock. Her shift was starting at ten and she needed to get to Adele's house to update her on her meeting with the solicitor. As she scrolled down Caroline's email again, she saw at the bottom of it that the solicitor had cc'd two people: Edward Mills and Amanda Harris.

No contact details or address, but a name – Amanda Harris. She was tempted to ask Caroline who this Amanda

Harris was, but it had probably been a mistake on Caroline's part and if Rachel flagged it, she might let Amanda know that the police had her name. Better to keep it to herself, in case it was useful. It might even be Emma's name today, Rachel reflected.

Rachel was due at Adele's at ten, but first she needed to make a pit stop. To unravel the truth, she had to find Emma. And her instinct was telling her to go back to the place where Felicity's baby had been left on that stormy night in April 1983. On the steps of St Phillip's church in Newbury.

Chapter Twenty-One

Adele

Thursday, 18 July 2024

Adele clutched the cup of black coffee her mother handed her and walked over to the newspapers scattered over her kitchen table. It was now nine o'clock on Thursday morning, she reflected, and she hadn't slept since Monday night.

'DOES THIS WOMAN HAVE SOPHIA?' the headlines of the national press hollered.

Ben James was poring over the first editions of the newspapers, which had just been delivered, commenting to Jane – the FLO who had spent the night at the house – on how well the artist's impressions had come out. The majority of the country was just waking up, he'd said, so their designated helpline hadn't started getting calls yet, but Ben had told Adele he hoped they would have some leads by lunchtime.

The night had been extremely long and painful. The thought of Sophia out there alone, possibly cold and terrified, plagued Adele. She had lain in her bed, staring at the ceiling, willing the sun to come up, while her mother slept in the armchair next to her bed.

Adele started pacing the kitchen. She found it impossible to sit still and her skin felt as if spiders were crawling all over her. She started to feel dizzy again and tried to take some deep breaths as her chest tightened.

'Mum, do you mind if we go for a walk? I can't stand it in here any more,' Adele asked, turning to Felicity.

'I'm not sure that's a good idea.' Ben's eyes darted over to Adele. 'The press might follow you.'

'Why don't we sneak out the side gate?' said Felicity assertively, standing up. 'We can access the common from the alley. I'm sure no one will see us.'

'OK,' Ben conceded, 'but I think Jane should go with you.'

'I think we will be OK, but thank you for the thought,' Felicity said firmly.

Adele smiled gratefully at her mother. She didn't think Felicity had it in her to defy a police officer, but since meeting Hazel, she had discovered a lot about her mother that she'd no idea about before now.

Felicity fetched her and Adele's coats, as Jane and Ben exchanged bemused looks. Felicity helped her daughter up, fed her arms into her coat as if she were a small child and zipped it up for her. It occurred to Adele that she couldn't ever remember a time when she had let her mother zip up her coat – or do anything for her, in fact. And it dawned on her in that moment that maybe their distant relationship wasn't all Felicity's fault. Maybe she had been difficult herself at times.

Felicity slid open the door, helped her daughter through and closed it again, as Ben and Jane watched them go. Adele inhaled the morning air, and looked up at the sun gratefully, as Felicity opened the gate at the end of their garden and peered down at the cluster of press standing at the mouth of their driveway.

Nobody was watching them as Felicity pulled up Adele's

hood and they turned left, down the alleyway, towards Greenham Common. As they walked side by side, Adele weakly linked her arm through her mother's. She found comfort in her mother's stride and fell into step with her, letting the fresh air flood through her body.

'Mum, I went to see a woman yesterday who you were at Greenham with. Someone called Hazel Evans.'

'Why?' Felicity looked over at her.

'Because I found a letter from your mother to her in Camilla's dressing table. She was asking for Hazel's help in reuniting you and Emma.'

'That's rich,' Felicity sighed, letting Adele's words sink in for a minute. 'I don't understand why my mother would go to Hazel Evans. I haven't seen her in nearly forty years. Mother couldn't stand her at the time. She blamed Hazel for corrupting me and making me stay at Greenham.'

'Were you happy there, Mum? At Greenham,' Adele asked.

Felicity nodded. 'Happier than I've ever been – for a while, anyway. But it was incredibly tough. I stayed for three months, and that was long enough for me. After I had my baby, I just couldn't take the cold any more. I was scared for her safety. The bailiffs would come back night after night and take all our shelter and food, and the police were getting increasingly heavy-handed. I went back just after Emma was born and begged Hazel to come away with me, to her parents' house in Port Talbot like she promised, but she was arrested. I had to go home again. I had nowhere else to go. And that was the night they took Emma away from me.'

'I'm so sorry, Mum. Taking your baby away from you in

your sleep is barbaric.' Adele squeezed her mother's arm. 'I'm horrified your parents did that to you. I never understood why you were so hard on them. I wish I'd known.' Adele looked at her mother and started to cry.

Felicity stopped walking and held her daughter. 'It's OK, sweetheart. Don't upset yourself thinking about the past. We need to stay focused on you and Sophia.'

'I can't believe Alex kept so many secrets from me. Why would he tell me that his parents were dead? Then take Sophia to meet them?'

'I don't know, darling. There's so much we need to unpick, but you mustn't blame yourself. None of this is your fault.'

'But what if it is? What if I'm partly to blame for burying my head in the sand? You never liked him. I wish you and I had been closer; I might have listened to you. If anything, the fact that you didn't like him made me want him more. Just to prove you wrong,' Adele confessed.

'Well, I'm glad, because if you hadn't married Alex, we wouldn't have Sophia.' Felicity started to cry then, too, and the two women held each other on Greenham Common.

'I can't live without her, Mum,' Adele sobbed.

'You won't have to. They will find her. I know they will. I have every faith in Ben, and Rachel,' Felicity said firmly.

'Why would Alex do this to me – put our baby at risk like that? I feel so alone.'

'You're not alone, darling,' Felicity said, holding her daughter tighter.

Slowly the two of them started to walk again. Felicity still had her arm around Adele. It was strange for them both, being so physically close, but they found it hard to let each other go.

'Hazel told me about your friendship and how hard things were at Greenham. You should be very proud of yourself,' Adele said.

'Well, to be honest, when I think about that time now, all I remember is the pain. I lost everyone I loved – my parents, Hazel, Emma.' Felicity's voice was faint.

'But you met Dad,' Adele said, pulling a tissue from her pocket and blowing her nose.

'Yes, I did,' Felicity said, smiling weakly.

'Do you miss him? We never really talk about him any more,' Adele said sadly.

'Of course I do, very much. You know me: I handle these things by myself. Maybe selfishly, but it's how I've always coped.'

Adele nodded, welling up again. The two of them walked along in silence for a little while. 'You've never told me how you met,' Adele said. 'I mean, I know it was at Greenham, but you've always been rather coy about it.'

'No, well, I'm slightly ashamed.' Felicity looked at her daughter and smiled. The sound of the traffic had faded as they disappeared into the heart of the common. There wasn't another soul around.

'What do you mean? Why ashamed?' Adele asked.

'It was the night all the women broke into the military base where they kept the nuclear weapons, and danced on the silos.' Felicity grinned at the memory.

'Well, that sounds pretty magical – and dangerous. What are silos?' Adele asked.

'They are underground structures that store the guided missiles – nuclear weapons,' Felicity explained.

'Wow, OK, and you danced on them?' Adele was wide eyed.

'Well, after Embrace the Base we had to keep the media interested. The women running the Greenham peace camp knew the government's main argument for having weapons in the UK was that they kept us safe. It was someone's idea to break into the base and prove it wasn't secure. So we did. Some of the women cut the fences and climbed through, Hazel and I climbed over it.'

'And danced?' Adele laughed gently.

'It was the most amazing night. I was actually terrified to go in. Fearless Hazel went in straight away, of course. It was dreamlike, watching the women holding hands, singing their hearts out on these weapons of mass destruction. So I decided to join them.'

'You were in the nuclear base?'

'Yes, but unfortunately I got caught rather quickly. Because of my big bump, I couldn't run. The police were pretty rough with me, but luckily Dad stepped in.'

Adele put her arm around Felicity. 'Mum!'

'I still ended up in Holloway though,' Felicity said, her smile fading.

'Hazel said that was where you gave birth.'

'It was. I think the stress of going to prison made the baby come early.'

Adele's mobile phone started to ring, and she scrambled in her pocket, pulling it out. Ben's number was flashing on the screen.

'Hi, Ben, any news?' she said, as Felicity took her hand. 'OK, we will come back now.'

'Is everything OK?' Felicity asked.

Adele ended the call and starting walking back towards the house. 'Yes, apparently they are already getting a few calls about the artist's impression of this woman you saw Alex with. Ben wants me back at the house in case there are any developments.'

'Well, that's really positive news,' Felicity said, matching her daughter's stride.

'How do you feel about Edward tracking Emma down?' Adele asked.

'I don't know really.'

'I bet she wants to meet you, Mum. You can tell her what happened, and that you never would have given her up. I can come with you if you want me to. I'd like to meet her.'

Adele paused, knowing the conversation was extremely painful for her mother and not wanting to press her further.

'Let's not worry about that now. They seem to be closing in on this woman, whoever she is, and that's all that matters,' Felicity said.

'I hope so, Mum. I really hope you're right,' said Adele, picking up the pace, as they walked away from Greenham Common towards home.

Chapter Twenty-Two

Felicity

New Year's Day, 1983

'Fliss, wake up. We're going in now. Are you coming?' said Hazel in her soft Welsh accent. She had turned on her torch and was rolling up her sleeping bag and blankets. Sleeping under the bender was bitterly cold. It only kept the snow and rain off their heads, and didn't provide any real warmth, so they slept in their clothes, hats, gloves and any blankets they could get their hands on. The nights at Greenham, during the winter, were something they just had to survive. There was no real rest or comfort to be had.

Fliss looked up at Hazel, who was smiling widely, and yawned. She glanced at her watch. 'It's only four a.m. . . .'

Hazel laughed. Getting up didn't take long, aside from putting on their boots and peeing in the woods behind Green Gate, but Hazel was frantically tying her laces. 'They want to go now, while the soldiers are still asleep. They were partying last night, so we're hoping they are sleeping it off, which will give us a chance to get to the silos.'

Fliss's heart sank. Today was the day they had been talk-ing about for a week now: the plan to use ladders and fling pieces of carpet over the barbed wire to enable them to climb over the fence. To get into the base, and dance on the bunkers, made of solid concrete and sealed with steel doors, which had been built over the past weeks in order to house the American nuclear weapons.

Fliss struggled to move. She was exhausted, and for the past week she had really been starting to suffer. Since her car had been seized, she'd felt lost and rootless, vulnerable in a way she hadn't before. She was seven and a half months pregnant now, sleeping on the ground, under benders. Her bump was so large it was difficult to get comfortable, however many blankets she lay on. The baby was also moving a lot, making the impending reality hard to ignore. The baby had gone from feeling like gentle butterflies and a distant dream to a person kicking and punching her for most of the day and night. She couldn't give birth at Greenham, in the mud and the cold – it would be far too dangerous – but if she went into the hospital the social services would discover she was homeless and contact her parents. She'd heard stories at Greenham about women having their children taken away, into the care system, or their husbands getting full custody. She knew that if her parents got hold of her baby it would be given up for adoption within days.

'Come on, we have to go now. I don't want to miss this,' Hazel said excitedly.

'I'm worried it's dangerous,' Fliss said quietly. 'I mean, it's an American military base we're breaking into.'

'That's exactly why we have to do it. Michael Heseltine claims that the silos are the most secure structures on earth, in one of the most secret and well-guarded bases in Europe,' said Hazel enthusiastically. 'We just need to make it onto the silos and we will definitely get some press coverage. It will make him look like a fool.'

Despite Fliss's concerns, the plan had obviously taken shape in Hazel's mind. She had signed up to be one of the women to climb over the fence and she couldn't wait. Hazel was now smiling and chatting with the other women, an excitement ignited inside her. They had got hold of some thick carpet, she understood, to throw over the barbed wire. Using ladders to climb up the fence, they would then just jump down the other side.

Fliss felt sick. She knew there were American soldiers, with guns, inside the base. Her huge baby bump would make it nearly impossible to climb the fence and run to the silos with the other women.

'Don't worry, we will need people this side, Fliss, to help us get over the fence. Besides, it will be very hard for you to climb over with your bump,' said Hazel, as if reading her mind. 'I'm going to go over to Yellow Gate and see if it's time to go. Do you want to come?'

Fliss wiggled out of her sleeping bag and used a tree root to push herself up. It was impossible for her to move at all now without letting out a heavy groan.

'I'm worried that I won't be able to stay here for much longer. It can't be good for the baby,' Fliss said as they walked towards Yellow Gate. 'It's different now I don't have my car. I just can't get warm.'

'Don't worry. I told you, we can stay with my parents. You can sleep in my room,' she said cheerfully.

'But won't you mind sleeping on the sofa?' Fliss said, trying to keep up with Hazel's stride.

'Of course not. Anything for you. Anyway, I might not even be there at first,' Hazel said casually.

Fliss felt her heart plummet. 'What do you mean, you won't be there?'

'Well, they might need me to stay on here. It's selfish of me to leave now. I mean, maybe you should have the baby here after all. Another woman has done it, hasn't she?' Hazel said cheerfully.

Fliss tried not to say anything she'd regret, but the idea of being in a virtual stranger's house, with her newborn baby crying all night, was growing more absurd by the day. And now it sounded like Hazel was planning to abandon her. Absurd, too, was the idea of giving birth in a bender, with no sanitation. She was in awe of the mother who had done it, but Fliss herself could barely get through the night. She was a walking wreck. Throwing childbirth and then a newborn into the equation would break her entirely.

'Wouldn't your parents resent the baby? I mean, they barely know me,' she said weakly. Her depression was starting to return. She had been living in a dream world, and it felt like it was all about to come crashing down. She didn't know how much longer she could take living at the base. Hazel was so committed – she was there for the long haul – but Fliss was feeling her strength fading by the day. She was beginning to think she should never have come here. She should have stayed at home until she worked out a plan. Now she had nothing but the baby kicking inside her and the growing realisation that there was no way she would be able to keep it.

Every time she felt that she had made their shelter comfortable enough to cope, the bailiffs would return and tear it all apart, confiscating every blanket and sleeping bag that she had managed to get hold of in the only charity shop in Newbury that would serve the Greenham women. The bailiffs' visits were becoming more and more regular – almost daily now – and although she had only been camping at Greenham for three months, the bitter cold, the endless rain, the lack of food or any kind of sanitation was starting to feel too much as her baby's birth loomed.

'I would just feel dreadful leaving now,' said Hazel. 'Our numbers have increased ten times since Embrace the Base, the tide has finally turned and our power is peaking.'

Fliss was about to protest but stopped herself. She didn't want to sound needy and clingy. Hazel loved her because she thought she was brave and bold, neither of which was true. Hazel was so infectious, her energy all-consuming, her love for life pulled Fliss in and moulded her from a nobody into a somebody. Without Hazel she would wither back into the pathetic person she had been before.

'Are you scared of dying?' asked Hazel cheerfully.

'Um, I'm not sure,' said Fliss, slightly taken aback.

Fliss had never been scared of dying. She had only ever been scared of living. At boarding school she often fantasised at night of falling asleep and not waking up. She didn't want to die, as such, suffer a painful death, but wishing she had never existed was a regular dream. Being with Hazel was the first time she could ever remember being happy, and wanting to live. But she didn't want to say any of that, so she said what she thought normal people would say as she and Hazel fell into step together.

'A bit, I suppose. I try not to think about it. Hopefully it's a long way off. Why do you ask?'

'I just think, as long as you're old and you've lived life and embraced your fears, it would feel OK.'

'And are you saying climbing over that fence where there are armed soldiers waiting for you is OK because you're embracing your fears? You know they're allowed to shoot you, because you're trespassing.'

'They won't!' Hazel just smiled, as Clara ran over and grabbed her by the arm. 'We're going in, now!' she whispered excitedly.

Fliss watched as Clara held the ladder, and the first woman began climbing up it with a roll of carpet over her shoulder. When she reached the top, she unravelled it, forming a barrier over the barbed wire.

'What is the plan when we get in there?' Hazel asked Clara.

'Just run fast towards the silos, and if you can climb up on them, then do. We are going to hold hands if we can and dance on the silos. I've organised a press photographer to come down in case we manage to make it onto the before we get arrested.'

Fliss watched as the first woman made it over and a queue of women behind her lined up at the bottom of the ladder. They were all quiet, not wanting to draw attention to themselves, but she could feel their excitement and energy radiating. Fliss's whole body was shaking as she watched Hazel moving towards the fence.

The atmosphere was electric, sparking from one woman to the next. She looked at her friend, beaming in the moonlight as she got ready to step onto the bottom rung. Fliss held her breath. There was no way of knowing how the military was going to react to the women running across the base. Within seconds Hazel was jumping down the other side and, taking Clara's hand, she began to run into the blackness.

Another woman began to climb the ladder, then another and another. There must have been twenty, thirty, forty, Fliss counted. They kept going, running into the darkness towards the silos.

In the eerie silence, Fliss felt as if she was going to be sick. She had no way of knowing if Hazel was OK. The sun was beginning to rise, and she could just about make out the faint sound of the women singing in the distance. Then the photographer who Clara had organised appeared next to her and began snapping away. Fliss could see the women forming a circle of sisterhood, silhouetted against the cold, winter sky. She looked up at the barbed-wire fences, which had been unable to keep them out, and felt a desperate urge to join them.

Suddenly she heard the sound of the soldiers shouting, and panic like she'd never experienced before bolted through her. She rushed towards the ladder, and put one foot on, then another, just wanting to raise herself up so she had a better view. She kept climbing, until she had nearly reached the top. All she had to do was put one leg over, then lower herself down on the other side. She had to join them, she had to help. She would never forgive herself if something happened to Hazel. This was her chance to prove how much the cause meant to her. She couldn't just stand by and watch.

When she reached the top, she found it surprisingly easy to swing her leg over and then clamber down on the other side. She looked around – she couldn't see anyone coming towards her – and, taking a deep breath, she began to walk as quickly as she could towards the silos. It was very strange being inside the base, and she couldn't help feeling both thrilled and terrified. They could have been anybody, and it was shocking that a bunch of women were able to break into the base and stroll around. If this was the level of security that they were planning to have for the nuclear weapons, it was terrifying. As she got nearer, she could see the women now, on the silos. They were in a huge circle, dancing round and singing at the top of their lungs.

It was an incredible sight, their silhouette against the rising dawn.

We don't want your wars
We don't like your cause
We won't fight your wars
At Greenham . . .

The women were singing loudly and repeatedly. It was the most exciting thing Fliss had ever witnessed. She suddenly saw Hazel and began to shout her name. Hazel turned and beamed at her, beckoning for her to come up onto the silos. It was surprisingly easy to climb up on to the concrete mound with a little help, and before long, she was one of the women, holding hands, singing her heart out. Time froze; it was like a dream. The light was hazy and the wind cold, but Fliss had never felt more alive.

The day was fully light now, and Fliss could see two photographers at the fence taking pictures of them. Then her heart skipped a beat as she saw in the distance a military Jeep ploughing towards them. Two, three, then four soldiers, carrying guns, suddenly appeared, and started climbing up onto the silos. Within seconds the women had started to scatter.

'Run, Fliss, run,' Hazel shouted, as one of the soldiers grabbed on to her and dragged her towards his vehicle. Hazel managed to break away but Fliss couldn't. Her bump was too large, and the same man gripped her arms from behind as he walked her towards his Jeep.

Quickly he put her in the passenger seat and then left her there to go after Hazel.

'Leave her alone!' Fliss shouted.

She looked around. The soldier had left his vehicle running. Fliss began to form a plan. This was her chance to help Hazel and the others get away.

The driver's seat in the Jeep was pushed right back, so she managed to manoeuvre herself into it, pushed the clutch in and then the gear stick into first. After taking a deep breath, she slowly pressed down on the accelerator and began driving in the opposite direction to the women.

The engine was loud, and she pressed down on the horn in the centre of the steering wheel in order to get the attention of the soldier pursuing Hazel. It worked. Soon she had the soldier running after her, then another, then another, as Fliss drove around the base in a circle.

She could see the women running towards the fence, climbing back over to safety, but she kept driving. Policemen had entered the base now and were also chasing after her, shouting at her to stop. She felt strangely fearless, as if the rushing wind in her ears had blown her terror away.

Soon, however, her confidence started to fade and she

began to slow. One of the soldiers threw himself on the bonnet and shouted at her furiously, 'Stop!' His face was contorted with rage and all the adrenaline from the past minute left her body with a violent jolt as she pushed her foot on the brake.

'Get out of the vehicle and put your hands where I can see them. You're lucky we didn't shoot you,' he said, aggressively pulling her from the Jeep, snapping handcuffs on her trembling wrists and pushing her to her knees before kicking her in the back until she was on the ground.

'She's pregnant, be careful with her!' Hazel cried out from the other side of the fence. 'Help her, please, someone help her!'

As she lay on the ground, her stomach throbbing, Fliss heard footsteps rushing towards her. The soldier's foot was still on her back, she couldn't move her head and her baby was kicking her hard. Stabbing pains shot up her back and across her middle and she cried out in pain.

'This is one of my citizens. Let her go,' said a male voice above her with a thick British accent.

'Who are you?' the American asked dismissively.

'James Stanton, British Ministry of Defence police.'

Fliss tried to look up at him but the American still had his boot in her back. She looked around desperately. There were several police cars at the entrance to the base now, and dozens of policemen were running towards them.

'Let her go,' the Englishman said again firmly, and finally the man took his foot off Fliss's back and moved away. Slowly James helped Fliss up. 'Take her handcuffs off, now,' he barked, and after a prolonged stand-off the soldier eventually did as he was told.

'Are you OK?' he said, as Fliss stood trembling next to him.

The man was older than the soldiers – in his forties, Fliss guessed – with kind eyes that crinkled at the edges and a warm smile that showed his slightly crooked teeth.

'I think so. My baby isn't very happy,' she said, rubbing her belly and fighting back tears.

'Here, let me help you,' he said, leading her over to a tree stump near the entrance.

'Thank you. I'm very grateful to you . . .'

'James, James Stanton. You've got some guts, girl,' he said, holding out his hand to shake hers.

'Felicity. I'm not sure what came over me.' Fliss examined her knees, which were cut and covered in blood from being pushed to the ground by the American soldier.

'Oh dear, we're in trouble now, Felicity,' James added, watching a group of policemen heading towards them at full pelt. James had piercing blue eyes, and was calm as a spring stream whilst everyone around him was losing their heads.

As soon as the first policeman reached her, he put his hand on her shoulder. 'Well, young lady, that wasn't very clever, was it, stealing an American Jeep? I suspect you'll be off to Holloway after your day in court. Come on, let's go.'

He snapped handcuffs on her and Fliss immediately felt the weight of the world on her shoulders.

'Thank you again, James,' she said quietly, her voice trembling, as the police led her to their vehicle and slammed the door behind her. From her cell in the back of the van, she could hear Hazel and Clara calling her name as she passed them at the entrance to Greenham.

Then the van turned onto the main road in the direction of Newbury police station and their voices faded into the distance.

Felicity sat down in her cell, cradled her bump and stared out of the tiny barred window, as the enormity of what she had done slowly began to hit home.

Chapter Twenty-Three

Emma

Sunday, 9 June 2024

Emma lay on her bunk staring at the faded cutting that Amanda had given her the week before. She read it again, as she had done a thousand times since.

> Police are appealing for the mother of a baby girl found on the steps of a church in Newbury to come forward so that she can receive medical care and support.
>
> The baby, named Emma, was discovered inside a cardboard box on the steps of St Phillip's church in Newbury just before 7 a.m. yesterday. Police discovered a tiepin with the initials EJM wrapped in her blanket. She has been discharged from hospital and is in the care of foster parents.

She still didn't know whether to believe it. She had absolutely no proof that Amanda had found the article in her adoptive mother's house or whether she was trying to trick her, for some reason. It all seemed rather unreal, yet the churning in the pit of her stomach told her it was true.

It made sense of why her parents had always been so secretive, and had never told her she was adopted. They knew that one day it would inevitably lead to questions about her birth mother, and that Emma would want to trace her. Perhaps they had hoped to spare her the pain of finding out that she had been dumped in a cardboard box on the coldest night of the year and would have absolutely no chance of ever finding her real mother.

But that was not their decision to make. If it was her in the article, then she had a right to know.

She looked back down at the newsprint. There was a small black-and-white picture of her as a baby, and next to her the silver tiepin, with the engraved initials enlarged. EJM. Where was that tiepin, she wondered. Had Sally kept it? If so, why? If she was the baby in the photograph and the tiepin had been found with her, it belonged to her and she should have it. It was the only thing that her mother had given her, she thought sadly, apart from the heart-shaped birthmark behind her ear.

Emma looked at her watch. It wasn't long before her adoptive mother, Sally, was due at the prison. Emma usually loved having some space from Amanda, but she knew Amanda had spent the day in Newbury 'doing some more digging', as she put it. It made her extremely anxious to know that while Sally was on her way to see Emma, Amanda would have probably been in Sally's house, rooting through all her things, looking for clues and goodness knows what else. Emma felt a mixture of horror and fascination as Amanda had explained her plan to her.

'I'm going to go back to where you were found, on the church steps at St Phillip's, and see if there is anyone still living or working there, who saw anything. This Howell Jenkins, who found you, might still be the caretaker, for all we know.'

Emma stared at the photograph of herself in the newspaper and listened to the sound of shoes clicking on the floor outside her room. Was that Sam coming to get her to tell her Sally was in the visits room? She had no idea what time her mother was coming, or when Amanda was coming back. She'd felt on edge all day.

The footsteps reached her door and it burst open. Amanda walked in, flustered and red in the face.

'God, it's too hot out there,' she said, pulling off her layers frantically until she was down to a tiny vest top.

Emma watched her unloading the contents of her bag onto the table.

'I thought you weren't due back until tonight,' Emma said.

'Well, I got what I needed, so I didn't need to stay any longer. I know everything about the guy who dumped you when you were a baby, and he's fucking loaded.'

Emma stood up from the bunk and stared at Amanda with bated breath.

'Guy? What do you mean? Didn't my mother leave me there?' Emma said, staring open-mouthed at Amanda.

'Come on, let's go for a walk. I don't want anyone listening in,' Amanda said, pulling a bottle of water from her bag, and grabbing Emma's arm.

It had begun, Amanda said, with a train from Bristol Temple Meads to Newbury, where Amanda had got a taxi straight to St Phillip's, the church where Emma had been found as a baby, over forty years earlier.

'I stood there for a while,' Amanda said, 'and just looked around, trying to put myself in the mindset of whoever had left you there. I mean, it's quite a risky thing to do with a six-week-old baby, and it was cold – really cold – that day, so I came to the conclusion that it must have been someone who knew the church, went there regularly, perhaps, and would be quite sure that you would be found quickly. So I just sat on a bench a little way up the road, and watched.'

'Watched what?' Emma asked.

'The people coming and going into the church. It's a weekend, so there was a lot of coming and going. People tend to stick with one church all their lives, and a tiny baby being left on the steps would have been talked about for months, years afterwards by the regulars,' Amanda said. 'So I just sat and waited.'

'For?' Emma pressed.

'Someone elderly. Who looked like they knew their way around,' Amanda went on confidently, as if this kind of behaviour were second nature to her.

'And how long did you have to wait?'

'About two hours. A few people came and went, but they were all a bit too bustling, moving too fast. I needed someone who wasn't in a rush. And I couldn't be seen talking to more than one. I had to get the right person first time so as not to make anyone suspicious I was up to something.'

'Blimey. Two hours!' said Emma.

'An elderly gentleman in a wheelchair arrived with what looked like his carer, or daughter maybe. I could tell by the way they opened the gate, and navigated the steps – all of it really – that they knew the place. They went into the graveyard, and so after a while I followed them in.'

Amanda had wandered around, she said, watching the couple who laid flowers on one of the graves and then sat on a bench in the graveyard for a while. She had taken her time, and then slowly approached them and asked if she could sit down at the other end of the bench. They had exchanged pleasantries and told Amanda they were there

283

to visit his wife's grave – the girl's mother – and that the family had been coming to St Phillip's for nearly fifty years. Amanda had then told them that she was looking for Howell Jenkins, who used to be the caretaker at the church.

'Ah, Howell, yes, he's retired now. Lives in a bungalow just up the road, I believe. He still comes to the Sunday service every week. It's at nine, if you wanted to come tomorrow. He will definitely be there. He is hard to miss,' they said, 'tall, with a head of thick white hair, always dressed in his shirt and braces, with a warm smile.'

Amanda had asked for any tips for a present for him, and they had suggested sherry. She'd gone into Newbury to buy a cheap suit from Next, and that night she had stayed at a local Travelodge, before rising bright and early to make sure she was back at the church on time. She had spotted Howell easily, she said, and when the service was over she'd waited while he spoke to a number of people. Finally he had walked towards his bungalow, with the support of his walking stick, and she had followed, stopping him as he walked up his driveway.

'Excuse me, Howell?' she had said. 'I'm sorry to bother you, but I was wondering if you could help me. My friend Emma Blake was found as a baby, by you I believe, on the steps of St Phillip's church.'

He had invited her in for a cup of tea, after some heavy hints from Amanda, and they had chatted. He was in his early eighties and living alone with his cat, Spider. The house was clean enough, she said, but had all the hallmarks of a lonely man: discarded newspapers, a TV tray for his lap, well-thumbed copies of the *Radio Times*. They had moved on to the subject of Emma after some time, as Amanda hadn't wanted to appear pushy.

'I'm sorry, Amanda, I really know very little about who left Emma that day. I do know she was adopted by a couple from the church, Sally and Jim Blake – we were all devastated to hear about Jim's passing.'

She had noticed a slight shift, she said, in his persona whenever the subject of Emma came up. He had gone from seeming relaxed and happy to talk, to edgy. She had suggested, then, that they have a sherry.

'The article mentions a tiepin wrapped up in the baby's blanket,' she had said. 'Do you think it maybe fell in there by mistake? Not sure why a baby would have a man's tiepin.'

'Yes,' he'd said, 'she was warmly dressed, and her clothes were very pretty. They looked expensive. I think she'd come from a good home. And then there was the cash.'

'Cash?'

'Yes, a fair amount, in an envelope, but obviously they didn't mention that in the article.'

Amanda had written down the word 'cash' in her notebook, immediately convinced this related to the trust fund that Emma had mentioned. She had sensed Howell Jenkins wanted to say more and suggested a second sherry outside in his well-tended garden. It was then, after much admiration of his bedding plants, that he had opened up a little bit.

'You know, there was something else they didn't mention in the article.'

'Oh, yes?' Amanda had said, as casually as she could muster.

'The make of the car that the man who left her there was driving.' He had taken another sip of his sherry and smiled at her. 'I can't be sure, of course, but I am a fan of classic cars. I was pretty sure it was a classic E-Type Jag, a green one, and I doubt there are many of them locally. I was surprised the police didn't pursue that any further.'

'Man? You think a man left her?' Amanda had asked.

'Yes. He was wearing a cap, like a shooting cap. I could make out his silhouette. Perhaps it was his tiepin in the box,' he said, his words slurring slightly. 'How is she doing now, Emma? Is she out of prison?'

'Very soon. She's looking forward to starting over. The fire was an accident and Sally has forgiven her. She wanted me to thank you, again, for saving her life.'

'Really no need, I didn't do much. I think of her often, we miss them at church. We don't see much of Sally either, since Jim died,' he added.

He had offered Amanda some lunch but she had politely declined, keen to get back to Sally's house and see what else she could find. She had made him a cup of tea but by the time she left he was asleep in his reclining chair.

Then Amanda had sat on a bench at the bus stop outside Sally's house, and waited. Watching her get ready in her bedroom which faced the road, before leaving in a taxi.

'I made sure there weren't any nosy neighbours with eyes on me, and then I snuck round the back and let myself in.'

'So how did you find him, the man who left me?' Emma asked eagerly.

'It didn't take long. It was in the same filing cabinet, different file. Four deposits, every five years, into an account in your name. From someone called Edward James Mills. EJM, just like the tiepin.'

'Four deposits?' Emma echoed. 'How much for?'

'Just a few hundred quid,' said Amanda, shiftily.

'So my parents knew this guy, Edward James Mills, left me on the steps?' Emma said, shocked.

'Looks that way. And he's absolutely loaded – lives in a mansion just outside Newbury.'

Emma looked out to the woods beyond the grounds of the prison, and suddenly felt the urge to run. She was finding it very hard to think about anything other than the fact that her adoptive mother, Sally, was coming to see her for the first time since she had been incarcerated over five years ago.

She had wanted it to be a happy reunion. They had much to discuss, a lot of wounds to heal, and a great deal of ground to make up. Once she was released, Emma wanted to get a job, rent a place, find her feet. Now, with all this new information from Amanda, she was filled with such anger and confusion towards Sally, she didn't know how she was going to keep a lid on it.

'You've been a good friend, Amanda,' Emma said, meaning it. 'Thank you for everything you've done for me.'

Emma was beginning to feel quite overwhelmed by Amanda's obsession with her life, and a knot had permanently formed in her stomach over the past few days. The thought of Amanda leaving Westwood Park was a relief, and she felt sure that now she was leaving, Amanda would find another passion project, and their friendship would naturally fade away.

'Are you still seeing your adoptive mother today?' Amanda asked, pulling her rucksack onto her shoulder.

Emma paused, not wanting to talk to Amanda about Sally. 'Yes,' she said finally. 'I don't know what to say to her about all this.'

Amanda looked at her intently. 'You have the right to ask for some answers,' she said.

Emma laughed nervously at Amanda's stern tone. They stood awkwardly for a moment, before Amanda stepped in closer. 'If you let her walk all over you today, you will be walked all over for the rest of your life.'

'Amanda,' Emma said defensively.

'No, it's not OK. That woman, your mother, has treated you very badly. She has lied to you and caused you pain when she should have been protecting you. Your desires and needs are just as important as hers. They might not have been recognised when you were younger but you have the power to make sure that they are now. Try fighting your corner, and you'll find that things start to shift in your favour.'

'OK,' said Emma, 'I'll try.'

'Do more than try. You know, I was going to tell you this when you got out but I think you should know now. Howell Jenkins told me that there was an envelope in the box you were found in, containing a large amount of cash.'

'What?'

'He didn't say how much, but I presume that's the trust fund you mentioned. It's not your adoptive parents' money, it's your money. It was meant for you. Forty-one years they've kept that, or spent it, who knows? As well as the money this guy Edward has deposited. If that had been invested properly, you could have used that to set yourself up in a home or a business. If I hadn't broken into Sally's house, you might never have known.'

Emma stood staring at Amanda, speechless.

'You need to get angry, Emma. What your parents did to you is wrong.'

'Emma! There you are. I've been looking for you. Sally Blake is here,' said Sam, approaching.

'I'll call you later and see how it went with your mum,' said Amanda walking away.

Emma followed Sam back inside, through the prison and on to the reception wing. By the time she reached the entrance to the visits room her pulse was racing. Apart from her solicitor, no one had come to visit her the entire time she had been locked up.

'Blake, Emma Blake,' shouted the lady in charge of prison visits, before leaving her standing alone at the door of the large room overlooking the prison farm. Emma pressed her thumb nails into her palms, desperate for the wait to be over. She felt as if she was going to be sick waiting to be called through.

Given the nod, she finally walked into the visits room, where she was led to an empty table. Above the door was a notice that stated visitors found with drugs were liable to prosecution and that the penalty would be six months in prison. After a long wait, a door opened and Sally walked in. At first she couldn't see Emma and for a few seconds Emma watched her, trying to read her body language to detect her mood. Then Sally spotted her.

Sally frowned as she walked towards her, and Emma felt her bottom lip start to tremble. They both stood, Emma desperate for a hug but not wanting to initiate it. It had been five years since she had seen her in court, but Sally looked twenty years older. Her mousy hair was thinner and had been cut into a wispy bob, her face was plagued with lines, and she had dark circles under her eyes. Emma couldn't help thinking Sally looked very unhappy.

When it was obvious there wasn't going to be a hug or kiss from her mother, they sat at the table, in pained silence, as Sally scanned the environment with a scowl. Emma had tried hard to make herself presentable but, without any financial means to do so she had found it difficult. She could tell her mother was shocked by her appearance. Emma had always been curvy, but during the last five years she must have lost over three stone.

'How are you?' Sally asked, without any warmth in her voice.

'I'm fine, Mum, really,' she forced out. 'It's great to see you. Thank you for coming.'

'You look like you've lost a lot of weight,' Sally said finally.

'It's only because my clothes are big,' Emma lied, with no idea why.

Despite everything, Emma still yearned for a reassuring hug, or smile, but she could tell her mother wasn't prepared to give her one. She could feel a frostiness coming from her. Her lips were pursed and she clung to her handbag, which was in her lap, as if Emma might snatch it from her. Emma felt like a teenager again. As if no time had passed at all.

The visit room had a snack bar and her mother looked at the other family members buying treats, but she stayed seated. Emma couldn't help the tears that were escaping. She hadn't known what to expect, but she had assumed her mother wanted to see her in order for the two of them to reconcile, yet Emma could have reached out and touched the hostility coming from Sally.

'How are you, Mum?' Emma asked.

Sally glared at her and said nothing.

'Did you have to wait long to come in?' Emma added desperately. Her guts were doing somersaults. She didn't know why Sally was being so cold towards her. If she still resented her as much as she seemed to, why had she come? Couldn't she just have written? Had she come to tell Emma that just because her prison sentence was nearly done, it didn't mean Sally would ever forgive her. Her thoughts raced as she dug her fingernails into her leg. How long did her mother want her to suffer? Did Sally not hold one ounce of sympathy for the five years of hell she'd been through? Amanda's talk came racing back to her, and she had a fleeting wish for Amanda to walk in and defend her.

'No. I must say, it's very smart here. Not what I expected at all.' Sally sniffed, looking out of the window.

'The last place I was in wasn't like this at all. It was horrible, a Category A prison.'

'Good,' said Sally.

Emma caught her breath, feeling like she'd been punched in the guts at Sally's desire for her to suffer. A strained silence fell between them. Emma felt like throwing up.

'Is everything OK, Mum?'

Sally glared at her. 'I don't know how you can sit there and act so innocent.'

Emma felt her heart shatter, as the tears poured out uncontrollably now. 'I have accepted responsibility for what happened, Mum. And I will never forgive myself, as I've written in countless letters to you, which you never replied to. But it was an accident. Surely I've been punished enough?'

Sally scoffed as tears stung her eyes. She reached into her bag and pulled out a tissue as she shook her head disapprovingly.

'If you have something to say, Mum, please say it,' Emma said gently.

'I don't know how you did it from here, but I presume you put someone up to it.'

Emma stared at Sally, racking her brains for clues as to what she was talking about.

'Finish your visit,' the guard said, as Sally looked up at her.

'Did what from here? What are you talking about?'

'Broke into my house and stole my notebook, so you could empty your trust fund.'

'What?' Emma said as the room started to spin.

'Finish up now, ladies, please.'

Sally nodded and stood up. 'I'm not going to press charges, but I want to make it clear that I never want to see or hear from you again. And if I do, I will make sure the police know about this.'

Sally started to put her coat on. Emma's head pounded. There was only one person who could have done this: Amanda. Emma looked up as Sally went to walk away, Amanda's words ringing in her ears: *Stick up for yourself.*

'Mum,' Emma called out, her voice shaky.

Sally sighed and spun round.

'Were you ever planning on giving me my money?'

Sally charged back. 'Your father invested that money,

which is why it has done so well. If we'd have given it to you, it would be long gone by now.'

'Maybe, maybe not,' said Emma, fighting to maintain her composure. 'I know it's only a couple of grand, but it was mine.'

Sally glared at Emma. 'A couple of grand? Who told you that?'

'My friend. Why?'

'What friend? How on earth does she know about your trust fund? Is she the one who broke in?'

'She knows a lot! She knows I'm a foundling, Mum. That I was left out in the cold when I was only six weeks old. And, do you know what, it makes perfect sense. I've felt that way all my life.'

'How dare you? We did everything we could. We took you in, we clothed you, fed you. And look what you did in return. You murdered my husband.'

'It was an accident! And I want you to know that even though you will never forgive me, I have forgiven myself.'

Sally continued to glare at Emma, then turned and stormed out, as Emma sank back into her chair and wept.

Chapter Twenty-Four

Rachel

Thursday, 18 July 2024

Rachel pulled onto the A339 from Newbury to Greenham Common and let out a heavy sigh as the BBC news on the radio jumped into life. *'Police have released an artist's impression of a woman they are keen to talk to in connection with the disappearance of missing schoolgirl Sophia Norton. Senior Investigating Officer Ben James has appealed for the public's help in the search for the twelve-year-old, who hasn't been seen since leaving school on Tuesday afternoon. He said, "If you recognise this woman, please call 0842 799426, which will go straight through to our investigations team. We have reason to believe this woman may know Sophia's whereabouts. We are now into the third day and are very concerned for Sophia's wellbeing. Any sightings or CCTV, doorbell or dash-cam footage of Sophia or a turquoise Fiat around four p.m. on Tuesday in the Sandleford Lodge Park area could help us hugely in our investigation so please contact us."'*

As Rachel passed a sign informing her that Greenham Common was only five miles away, her eyes fell on the landmark she was looking for: a placard saying St Phillip's church, Newbury, which she recognised immediately. Rachel pulled over and gazed at the stone steps leading up to the large Roman Catholic church and the wooden door at its entrance, which was slightly ajar. She looked at the clock on her dash. It was still only nine fifteen and she didn't need to be at Adele's until ten.

She opened the door and stepped out, walking slowly up to the top step where Howell Jenkins had found baby Emma forty-one years ago.

She looked around. There was no sign of anyone, but she felt the presence of someone, or something – the past weighing down on her perhaps. She pulled her coat tightly around her, imagining baby Emma lying in a cardboard box on that bitterly cold night, waiting to be found.

Had they come back, whoever left her that morning? Did they pass the steps often and think of the baby they had left that day?

She could still hear Howell's voice as she unloaded the Greenham women from the back of her van that frosty morning in April 1983.

'Can I help you?' came a male voice from the church doorway.

Rachel spun round to see a tall, elderly gentleman with a warm smile, holding two full black bin bags.

Rachel knew those eyes. It had been over forty years, but he still looked the same.

'Howell Jenkins?' she said, returning his smile.

'Yes?'

'I was just thinking about you,' said Rachel, warmly.

Howell walked away from the church door, down to a Transit van in front of which Rachel had parked, and opened the boot. He threw the black bags in then slammed it shut. Then he turned back to her, frowning.

'Do we know each other?'

Rachel walked towards him, and held out her hand. 'We have met, yes. My name is Detective Constable Rachel Rees. I work for the Criminal Investigations Department at Thames Valley Police. I doubt you remember – it was over forty years ago now.'

'My goodness, of course I remember,' said Howell. 'It's not every day you find a baby. I don't suppose my memory of that morning will ever leave me.'

'No, me neither,' Rachel agreed. 'I often think of her, and wonder how she is.'

Howell nodded, pulling closed the church door and locking it.

'I was tempted to adopt the baby myself,' Rachel added, 'but my husband didn't want to have children.'

Howell smiled. 'I don't blame you. She was a beautiful child.'

'Do you know what became of her?' Rachel remembered Howell's warm manner, his kind eyes. They had more lines around them now, but otherwise they were exactly the same.

'Of course. She was adopted by a couple from the church. Jim and Sally Blake.'

'Really? Does she still live with them?' Rachel asked.

'Sadly not. Do you not know?'

'Know what?'

'Emma, the child – well, she's in her forties now – she set fire to the house. It was an accident but Jim Blake was killed in the blaze so she went to prison for manslaughter. She got a long sentence, but I believe she is due to come out soon.'

Rachel felt her stomach drop. 'Oh, that's tragic. I had no idea.'

'It was devastating. We are a very close-knit community here,' Howell stated.

'How dreadful for the family. Is her adoptive mother, Sally Blake, still alive?' Rachel asked.

'Yes, she lives just up the road there,' Howell said. 'She doesn't come to church as much now, but her and Jim used to be regulars. That's how they had the opportunity to adopt Emma. They were patrons of the church for years. Jim is buried here.'

'Do you know Sally Blake's address, Howell? I'd like to pop in and see her, and pay my respects.'

Howell nodded and pointed down the road. 'It's the bungalow just on the corner of Lemming Crescent, number eighteen, I think; white fence. Look out for the pink roses. She's a keen gardener like me.'

'Thank you, Howell. Well, it was nice to see you again,' said Rachel, turning to go.

'It's funny, I haven't spoken to anyone about baby Emma for years, and now two people within weeks of each other,' Howell added as an afterthought.

Rachel paused and turned back. 'Sorry, two people what?' She winced as a motorbike roared past.

'Coming to see me about baby Emma,' Howell said.

'Really? Who was the other person?' Rachel frowned.

'I think she said her name was Amanda,' he said absentmindedly.

Rachel stared at Howell, desperately racking her brain for the name that Camilla's solicitor had given her. 'Was it Amanda Harris?'

'Yes, yes, that sounds right,' Howell said, as Rachel's heart quickened.

'Thanks, Howell,' Rachel said, trying to keep the tension out of her voice. 'And why did she come to see you about the baby?'

'She wanted to ask me some questions about the morning baby Emma was left. She said she and Emma were friends and she was doing some research into her birth family.'

Rachel paused, trying to unpick Howell's statement. 'So Amanda is Emma's friend. Are you sure it wasn't Emma herself?'

'No, no. I knew Emma well before she went away,' Howell confirmed. 'She said Emma is finding it all rather difficult to deal with herself, but she is actively looking for her family now and Amanda is helping her. I told Amanda everything I could remember. I think I was helpful. I hope I was.'

Rachel caught her breath. 'I'm sure you were, Howell. Did Amanda leave a contact number or forwarding address?'

'No, I don't think so . . . no. Did I do something wrong? She was very nice.'

'No, not at all.' Rachel smiled at Howell Jenkins, who was now frowning at her.

Rachel's head started to spin. Was it possible that this Amanda Harris wasn't baby Emma at all and was posing as her in order to get Edward's money? But then how would she have got hold of Emma's DNA? What if her instincts were right, and this woman that Alex had been seen with had something to do with all this? It seemed too much of a coincidence.

Instinctively she reached for her bag, pulled out her phone and logged into the Thames Valley Police website.

Quickly she scrolled down to the artist's impression of the woman Felicity had seen Alex with. She walked back over to Howell and showed him her phone.

'One more thing, if you don't mind, Howell?'

'Of course,' he said, turning back.

'Can you tell me if this looks like the woman who came to ask you about baby Emma?'

Howell reached into his pocket and pulled out some reading glasses. Slowly he pushed them onto his nose and peered at the picture. It felt like forever to Rachel before he spoke.

'Why yes, that looks a lot like her,' he said. 'She had her hair in plaits, just like that.'

'Thank you, Howell, you've been very helpful,' Rachel said, as he nodded and turned to go.

Rachel felt her heart thudding in her chest as she made her way along the main road, and turned into Lemming Crescent.

Her head was spinning from the conversation with Howell Jenkins. The baby who had been left on the steps of St Phillip's church was adopted by Sally and Jim Blake, and was called Emma Blake. And she was currently in prison. So she couldn't have had anything to do with Sophia's disappearance. But perhaps this friend of hers, Amanda Harris, did. Had they cooked up a plan together, or was Amanda posing as Emma?

She needed to speak to Ben James urgently and tell him what she had found out, but first she needed to confirm with Emma's mother that Emma wasn't the girl in the picture. It would be the first question Ben would ask her. Howell could be wrong that they weren't the same person, or just confused. She couldn't take an old man's word for it.

She immediately saw the bungalow with the white fence, pink roses lining the border of a neatly kept garden, and lace blinds lowered despite the sunny day. She opened the gate and made her way down. There wasn't a blade of grass out of place, and a sign saying 'No cold callers' was fastened to the letter box.

Rachel took a breath and knocked on the door of Emma's adoptive mother's house. After a while, she heard footsteps slowly making their way along the hall, and the tinkling of the safety lock being secured. Finally the door opened a fraction, and a pale woman with short grey hair and a full face of make-up peered out. 'Yes?'

'Mrs Blake? Mrs Sally Blake?' Rachel asked, holding up her badge.

'Yes?' The woman frowned.

'My name is Detective Constable Rachel Rees. I work for the Criminal Investigations Department at Thames Valley Police.'

'Oh dear, what's she done now?' Sally flushed with embarrassment.

'Who?' Rachel asked.

'Emma, I presume that's what you are here about?' Sally sneered.

'Well, yes,' said Rachel as the woman tutted and shook her head.

'Could I come in, please?' Rachel asked, as Sally peered at her badge.

Sally stepped back, closed the door, took off the security chain and opened it again. 'Come in.'

Rachel stepped into the narrow hall of the bungalow. It smelled of bleach and was sparsely decorated, with a vase of fake tulips on a small table and abstract pictures of city-scapes on the wall. There were no photographs of Emma anywhere to be seen.

'Come through,' Sally said. She was a slim woman, and she was wearing neatly pressed beige trousers and a plain white T-shirt. She led Rachel through to the kitchen, but didn't offer her a seat or a cup of tea.

Rachel smiled gently. 'I was wondering if I could ask you a few questions about your daughter, Emma?'

'Yes, of course,' Sally said curtly, folding her arms.

'I understand you adopted her when she was a baby?' Rachel opened her notebook and stood slightly awkwardly at the door of the kitchen.

'Yes, she was left on the steps of St Phillip's church. Howell Jenkins found her. The vicar at the time knew that we wanted children and couldn't have a family of our own. Had I known then what I know now, I would certainly have reconsidered.'

'I'm sorry to hear that,' said Rachel sadly, the image of the beautiful baby that had been handed to her flashing into her mind. 'I was actually just talking with Howell at the church. I'm sorry to hear about your husband.'

'That girl has brought us a great deal of sadness and pain. Did Howell tell you that Emma is in prison for set-ting fire to our home?'

Rachel nodded.

'Is that why you are here? To warn me that she is due out soon?' Sally asked.

Rachel frowned, slightly taken aback. 'I'm actually

interested in an acquaintance of your daughter's, someone named Amanda Harris. I was wondering if your daughter has ever mentioned her?'

Sally stared at Rachel, a look of complete bemusement on her face. 'I beg your pardon? You do know that my daughter is in prison?'

'Yes.'

'How on earth would I know about her acquaintances then?' Sally snapped.

'So you don't have a relationship with Emma any more?'

'She killed my husband,' Sally said coldly.

'I see. I thought Howell said she was charged with man-slaughter? Was it not an accident?'

'How on earth would you know? Were you at the trial?' Sally said curtly.

'Well, no. But I was actually the police constable who Howell Jenkins handed Emma in to that morning. I took her to the hospital and turned her over to social services, so I guess, strictly speaking, I have met Emma. She was a beautiful baby.'

Rachel watched Sally as her lip twitched, and her face flushed with anger. 'Well, looks can be deceiving.'

'So you don't speak to her?' Rachel asked.

Sally glared at her. 'I went to see her in prison, for the first time, about a month ago.'

'OK, was there a reason for that?'

Sally sighed. 'Well, yes. I haven't reported this to the police, because frankly I saw little point, but I'm not going to lie to you. Somebody broke into the house. I don't know who, but it must have been when I was here because there was no damage, and they stole a notebook

302

of mine with the passwords for my bank accounts. There was one account in Emma's name, and it was emptied shortly afterwards. Emma couldn't have done it because she's locked up, but I presume she paid someone else to. Perhaps it was this acquaintance of hers – Amanda, did you say?'

'So, why was the account in Emma's name?' Rachel asked.

'There was an envelope with a thousand pounds in it when Emma was found as a baby. If you found her you might know that, I guess. My husband invested it, in an account in Emma's name, and it was emptied.'

'How much was in the account, may I ask?' Rachel pressed, staring at her. She had no way of making Sally tell her. She could only hope she would offer the information voluntarily.

Sally paused. 'It was several thousand pounds.'

'Several?' Rachel pressed.

'I think thirty in total,' she said quietly, not meeting Rachel's eye.

'But you said there was a thousand in the envelope she was left with. Where did the other twenty-nine thousand come from?'

'Yes, well, it obviously accrued interest.'

Rachel frowned.

'My husband was good with money, and he topped it up over the years,' Sally said shiftily. 'We could have spent it on her upkeep, but we didn't. My husband was very good with money,' she repeated nervously. 'He was putting it away until she was ready.'

'I see. Ready for what?' Rachel asked.

'To be responsible, of course. Not blow it on drugs and alcohol.'

'But it's her money. Wouldn't that be her choice?' Rachel said.

Sally stared at her, horrified. 'This is why I didn't report the burglary. I knew you would take the side of the person breaking into my house.'

Rachel smiled weakly, sadness sweeping through her that the baby she had handed over to social services all those years ago had ended up in the hands of this woman. 'Do you have any idea who baby Emma's parents are?' she asked.

Sally flushed red, looked away for a moment, then back at Rachel. 'No.'

Rachel nodded. Her job was as much about dealing with people as it was about crime. Studying the details of their lives, whether the actions they were accused of were out of character or part of a pattern of chaos and turmoil. Criminals usually took very little responsibility for their own lives, blaming others or some external reason for their situation. She read people so well after thirty years that she knew instantly if someone was lying to her. It wasn't even something she could articulate; it wasn't eye contact or lack of it, shiftiness, talking too much or too little. She just instinctively knew, and it was from spending so much of her career being lied to. And Sally Blake was lying to her now.

A thousand pounds in 1983, even if invested wisely, wouldn't be worth thirty thousand today. It seemed quite obvious to her that Emma's bank account had been topped up over the years by someone outside the family. Someone who felt guilty for leaving a baby on the steps of a church in sub-zero temperatures. Rachel guessed that this person had also made contributions to Sally's bank account over the years to make life a little easier. But Rachel had no way of proving any of it, and it was obvious that Sally wasn't going to offer anything up.

'One more question, if you don't mind, Mrs Blake. Then I'll leave you in peace.' Rachel pulled her mobile phone from her pocket. 'Can I ask you if you recognise this woman?' Rachel said, holding out the artist's impression of the woman Felicity had seen Alex with.

Slowly Sally looked from Rachel to the phone. 'No,' she said. 'No, I don't.'

'I see. Can I possibly get a photograph of Emma, if you have one?'

Sally let out a sigh. 'Well, it will be about ten years old. I haven't taken one since a while before she went to prison.'

'That'll be fine,' said Rachel.

Sally disappeared down the hallway, then after a while returned holding a single photograph, which she handed to Rachel.

Rachel looked down at it, and her heart skipped a beat. The girl in the picture was blonde and blue-eyed, just like Adele. She was curvy, with a pretty face and a shy smile. The blue eyes were very familiar, the exact ones she had stared into on the morning of 2 April 1983.

'Do you mind if I keep this photograph, please, Mrs Blake?' Rachel asked.

'Of course not. I don't want it,' she said sternly.

Rachel closed her notebook, thanked her, and left. She walked back along the rose-bordered pathway, and climbed into her car, pulled out her mobile phone from her bag and dialled Ben's number.

'Ben, it's Rachel. We need to talk.'

Chapter Twenty-Five

Adele

Adele watched from the window of her bedroom as her mother pushed her way past the throng of press waiting at the end of the driveway, pulled her coat tightly around her, and walked off in the direction of Greenham Common.

Adele knew Felicity was exhausted, she had barely slept for two nights, and the stress was taking its toll on her too. Ben had just told Adele that Alex was coming home. After being detained for thirty-six hours he had been released on bail pending further enquiries.

As the police car containing Alex had pulled up outside the house, Felicity had told Adele that she would give her some space to talk to her husband and had left, but Adele knew Felicity just didn't want to see her son-in-law. And she understood and sympathised. She didn't really want to see Alex herself.

The press went nuts as Alex climbed out of the car, hanging his head, and she watched him walk up the path, accompanied by Ben James.

She had been scared of his temper for longer than she could remember, but in the last forty-eight hours everything had changed. There was no going back: she wanted a divorce, whatever he said to her.

Her head spun round as she heard a knock on the door,

and slowly Alex opened it, his olive skin so pale that he looked a shade of green. And he appeared to have lost a stone in weight since Tuesday night.

'Can I come in?' he said sheepishly.

Adele nodded. She moved away from the window so as not to give the press an opportunity to see her and Alex together. Then she sat down in the armchair in the corner of the room and crossed her arms, waiting.

'I didn't sleep with that woman,' Alex offered.

'I really don't care, Alex,' Adele snapped.

'OK, but I just want you to know, I think she planned this all along. I met her in a bar, and I think she knew exactly who I was. She made a beeline for me and we had a few drinks, and one kiss. That was it. Before I know it, she's calling our house, turning up at work, at the gym.'

'At your parents' house in Ireland?' Adele spat.

'I can explain that, Adele. I never wanted to lie to you about them. Our relationship has always been difficult and . . .'

'Stop, Alex, just stop. You took my daughter to meet them! I put up with so much of your temper and moods and delusions of grandeur, quite frankly, because I felt sorry for you that your parents had died. That you went into care.'

'I did. I did go into care for a bit – well, not care exactly, supported accommodation – but we've put all that behind us now. I just never knew how to talk to you about it all. You never seemed very interested.'

'Don't you fucking dare!' Adele shouted. 'Don't you fucking dare turn this on me. You are a liar, a sick, twisted liar.'

'OK, I haven't been entirely honest, but I would never do anything to hurt Sophia, and I have never been unfaithful to you.'

Adele laughed. 'Yes, Alex, you have. You lie and cheat and take from me every day. You have taken my confidence and my self-esteem and my joy. And I want a divorce.'

'I knew you'd say that, but I know we can work through this now. I agree I need help and I need to go to counselling.'

'Yes, Alex, you do. I really think that would be great, for you as Sophia's father, and my ex-husband. But it's over between us. I will never ever trust you or be able to forgive you, and there is nothing you can say to change my mind.'

Adele's mobile started to ring, interrupting them. She looked over, checking as she always did that it wasn't Sophia, and was surprised to see 'Edward Home' flashing on the screen. She frowned and went to answer it.

'Hello? Edward?' She looked over to Alex, who was watching her.

'Adele, it isn't Edward. It's Mrs Owen. I'm so sorry to call you but it's important.' In all the years that Adele had known her, Mrs Owen had never called her on her mobile.

'Mrs Owen, are you OK? What's happened?' Alex moved nearer to Adele so that he could listen in to the call.

'It's Mr Mills. I called an ambulance – he's had a stroke.'

'No! When?'

'About an hour ago, he's in hospital now. Adele, he has been so stressed, about Sophia . . .' Mrs Owen started to cry. 'And this woman.'

'What woman?' Adele said.

308

'Oh, Adele, she came to the house on Tuesday morning. She said she was Emma, the baby Miss Felicity gave up when she was a teenager. Mr Edward set up the meeting.'

'What? Why?'

'Because they were a match on the DNA website, but he said he wanted to meet her before he gave her the money Camilla had left her. He was so nervous about meeting her, but when she came here he knew it wasn't her.'

'How?'

'Because Emma had a birthmark behind her ear, a little heart. And this woman didn't. Her hair was in bunches, and there was no birthmark there. She didn't look like Felicity at all. He knew she wasn't Felicity's baby.'

'Oh my goodness, Mrs Owen, what happened?'

'They were in the library. I didn't hear what they said, but she was raising her voice and Mr Edward was very upset when she left. He wouldn't tell me what they discussed, but I knew something was very wrong. Adele, when we were waiting for the ambulance he told me that this woman has Sophia. And that I must make sure the money the solicitor has goes through, or we will never see Miss Sophia again. He made me promise not to tell the police, but I can't stand it, Adele. I didn't know what to do.'

There was a sharp knock at the bedroom door, as Adele stood in stunned silence, clutching her mobile to her ear.

'Can we come in? I need to update you both.' Ben was at the door.

'Mrs Owen, I need to call you back. Thank you for phoning. You've done the right thing telling me,' Adele added, ending the call.

'Detective Constable Rees just called me to tell me that

309

she has reason to believe that a woman called Amanda Harris is posing as your half-sister, Emma Blake, in order to obtain the money left to her by your grandmother Camilla Mills.'

'I know,' said Adele. 'My grandfather's housekeeper just called. A woman came to see him claiming to be Emma and told him that if he didn't transfer the money by tomorrow, we'd never see Sophia again. Who is this Amanda Harris?'

'Until just a few weeks ago, Amanda Harris and Emma were both doing prison time in a facility called Westwood Park. But Amanda was recently released.'

'Well, according to Edward she has Sophia, so where is she now?'

'We have a squad car at Amanda's home address in Bristol. Neither Amanda nor Sophia are there, but there is evidence that they were.'

'What evidence?' Adele barked.

'Sophia's school jumper, her bag and also several sketches of Leia, which we suspect were drawn by her. Also we have finally got some dash-cam footage from a taxi on the main road where Leia was found. The woman letting Leia out of the car appears to be Amanda Harris. The prison governor at Westwood Park has also confirmed that the sketch photofit from your mother's description strongly resembles Amanda Harris.'

'Can you see Sophia in the car?' Adele asked desperately.

'There looks to be a child in the back of the vehicle, yes, but we can't identify her as Sophia at this point.'

'Where is the vehicle registered to?' Alex asked.

'It's registered in Emma Blake's name, to the flat in Bristol, which is also in Emma's name. We've got sniffer dogs on our way there to help with identifying the clothing as Sophia's and to try and pick up any trace of her outside the flats. I'm planning to go there now with Rachel, and I was hoping you would accompany us.'

'Of course,' said Alex.

'So does Emma have any idea where Amanda is?'

'As I said, Amanda was released at the end of June, but Emma is still there and, according to Sam, the governor at the prison, she hasn't heard from her. However, Rachel is planning to speak with Emma, to try and get some more information from her about Amanda, if possible. We need to work out where she might have taken Sophia. Apparently, Emma has taken the news very badly, and feels responsible for Sophia. She keeps asking if her birth mother knows and blames her.'

'Mum doesn't know any of this yet, she's gone for a walk.'

'I think it would help if Felicity went and put Emma's mind at ease. We need her as relaxed as possible to try and help us with our enquiries.'

'Do you want me to ask Mum?' Adele offered.

'Yes. We think it might be best coming from you,' Ben said, nodding.

'OK, that's fine, but I don't know exactly where she is. I saw her walking towards the common.'

'I'll get her,' said Alex, turning to leave.

'No, I'll go,' said Adele. 'We always do the same loop. Besides, she doesn't want to see you.'

'Aren't we wasting time?' Alex pleaded. 'I mean, shouldn't we go to the flat in Bristol now, in case they come back?'

'Emma is actually our best bet,' said Ben, firmly. 'Amanda and Sophia aren't at the flat, which means they are vulnerable right now. We can't just stake out the flat, we desperately need to speak to someone who might know where they have gone. Amanda won't hurt Sophia because essentially Sophia is the only collateral she has. I have told the solicitor not to transfer the money yet because it's the only control we have over her – but not to notify Amanda that there are any issues. I don't want her to suspect we are on to her. This also mustn't leave this room. Do you understand? If this leaks, and Amanda finds out she isn't getting the money, it will put Sophia's life in danger.'

'Of course, we understand,' said Alex.

'We will take two cars. An officer will drive you to the common, to collect your mother, Adele. Alex, maybe you and I can go in the second car,' said Ben, picking up Adele's discomfort at her proximity to her husband. 'Rachel will meet your mother at Westwood Park Prison to manage the interview with Emma. And the three of us will go to the flat in Bristol to identify Sophia's belongings.'

'Thank you,' said Adele. 'So where does all this leave Anthony Hislop?'

'We have found no evidence that Anthony Hislop or any of his associates have had contact with Sophia, and he is no longer our prime suspect. Amanda Harris is.'

Adele left through the back door, stepped out into the alleyway and hurried down the path as the throng of reporters, sensing a development, rushed towards Alex and Ben at the front door. Alex and Ben pushed their way towards one of two waiting squad cars and then drove, at speed, towards the common where Adele was headed.

The light was fading now, and Adele felt constant nausea at the thought of trying to get through another night without Sophia. Within minutes she saw her mother walking towards her, her head lowered against the evening chill.

'Hi, Mum,' said Adele gently.

'Adele, is there some news?'

'Sort of. Shall we sit?' Adele said, gesturing to a bench a few feet from where they stood.

'What's happened? Have you heard from Sophia?'

'There's been some developments. It turns out that the baby you gave up – Emma Blake, her name is now – is in prison for manslaughter.'

'Manslaughter, why? Oh, no, please don't say Emma had something to do with Sophia's disappearance?' Felicity asked anxiously.

'We don't have all the answers yet, but what we do know is that Emma made an acquaintance in prison called Amanda Harris, and the police think that Amanda has Sophia.'

'Why do they think that?'

'Amanda found out that Emma was owed a quarter of a million pounds, and tried to pose as her by using Emma's DNA. However, Edward asked to meet her before he paid up, and he knew immediately that she wasn't Emma. Amanda said that if he didn't transfer the money within forty-eight hours, we'd never see Sophia again, and that he wasn't to tell a soul. He hasn't paid her, but the stress has really taken its toll. Mum, I'm so sorry, but Granddad has had a stroke. He's in hospital. Mrs Owen called me and told me everything.'

Felicity stared at her daughter. 'Does Edward know where Amanda is?'

'No, but staff at the prison have identified her from your sketch. She's recently made parole, they've traced her to an address in Bristol, but she and Sophia aren't there. However, there is evidence they have been there recently.'

'If Emma knows Amanda from prison, does Emma know where they might be?' Felicity asked.

'That's what we need to try and find out. And I was wondering if you would go with us and talk to Emma.'

'Me?' Felicity said, surprised. She looked out over the common thoughtfully. 'Does Emma want to talk to me? It might upset her.'

'According to Ben James she's very distressed and worried that we are all blaming her. She keeps asking if you know. I think she would take great comfort in you going to see her and reassuring her.'

'OK, of course, whatever I can do to help,' Felicity said calmly.

'Thank you, Mum.' Adele took her hand.

'Is Dad OK?' Felicity asked.

'Honestly, I don't know. But if you want to go to him, I understand.'

'No, he would want me to help you and Sophia first,' she said. 'I wish I'd never left Greenham,' she added, as they walked quickly towards the police car waiting for them. 'This is the gate we lived at, Hazel and I. We slept in the Mini, in that car park. When they took my car, it sealed my fate. I just couldn't protect my baby.'

'It's OK, Mum. You were a child yourself,' Adele said, taking her hand. 'You have to forgive yourself.'

'I should never have gone home. I'm so scared to face

Emma. What kind of life has she had if she's ended up in prison?' Felicity said, starting to cry.

Adele stopped and held her mother. 'Mum, if she wants to see you, then it'll be OK. That's wonderful, isn't it? You can't change the past, it's what you do now that matters. And I'm here for you. I'm happy I have a sister. We can make a fresh start, all of us, when Sophia is home safe. Emma's always been with us really. I've always felt like someone was missing.'

Felicity nodded, wiping her tears away with the back of her hand. 'I'm afraid.'

'Mum, remember you are a warrior. If you can sleep out here, in the wind and the snow, and the sleet, with no shelter, stand up to all those police, dance on those silos at dawn while armed soldiers chase you; if you can give birth alone in Holloway, you can do this. You can meet your daughter again. Yes?'

'Yes,' said Felicity firmly, as they walked towards Ben standing by the two squad cars at the entrance to Greenham Common. 'Let's go and get Sophia,' he said, as the two of them climbed into the back, clinging to each other for dear life.

Chapter Twenty-Six

Felicity

Tuesday, 15 February 1983

'Hold out your wrists,' the officer said to Fliss, before she snapped the handcuffs into place.

Fliss shakily lowered her hands on top of her bump, which her largest pair of leggings and baggiest lumberjack shirt were straining to cover now that she was eight and a half months gone. The cuffs felt cold and alien against her skin, and as she caught sight of herself in the revolving glass door she barely recognised herself: pregnant, penniless, and a convicted criminal on her way to Holloway Prison. It was unimaginable how much her life had changed in the two years since her father's colleague had walked into the pub where she worked, seduced her, got her pregnant, then turned his back on her. Greenham had wanted her when no one else had, but now she was paying the price for the fleeting happiness she had felt in its arms.

Eight weeks in custody for taking a vehicle without consent. She still couldn't believe the judge had been so hard on her. She was offered a fine but she hadn't a penny to her name, so she would be spending the next eight weeks in Holloway Prison. She had contemplated calling her parents and asking them for the money, but they already knew about the case. There had been reporters at her hearing, the word was out in no time that an MP's daughter was being charged with stealing an army vehicle and driving it around the American military base at Greenham Common. If they cared at all they could have found out where she was and helped her. Their silence told her everything she needed to know, and she didn't have the strength to call them and beg.

Eight weeks – she was still reeling. That would take her over her due date. She had no idea what that meant for her and the baby. Would it be taken away from her? Would she have to give birth in prison, alone? She had asked the prison guard who had taken her down to the holding cell, but she hadn't answered her. She wasn't a human being now.

'The van's here, Mills. This way.' She was Mills now, not Fliss. Soon she would be just a prisoner number. Eight weeks in Holloway – it was a waking nightmare. She felt dizzy with panic and had no idea how she was going to cope when they closed and locked the cell door for the first time. What the other women would be like, how the guards would treat her, how often she would be allowed to wash, whether she would be bullied. Her legs were shaking so much she could hardly walk. For once she was glad she had two prison guards by her side, to catch her if she fell.

Fliss stepped outside the Newbury court building and saw the large prison vehicle with blacked-out windows. One of the prison officers stepped in front of her and into the back of the van as the other officer ushered Fliss in and closed the van doors behind them. Handcuffed, she got in awkwardly, her bump making it impossible to see her feet now. Her vision began to spin, her heart pounded, she hadn't felt her baby kick her for hours now and she was utterly terrified.

Fliss eased herself down onto a ripped and dirty seat, the floor was littered with cigarette butts, and with the windows firmly shut, the smell of stale nicotine and sweat was overpowering. She feared the fresh air, which had been so abundant at Greenham, was about to become scarce.

She knew they couldn't see in, but within seconds of pulling away from the court, a press photographer pushed his camera up to the window and set the flash off. She recoiled at the bright light, knowing that it belonged to the reporter she had seen in court, scribbling notes, words that her father would read over the breakfast table the following morning. Accompanied by a photograph of his daughter, inside the van, bound for Holloway Women's Prison.

Someone must have realised who she was, the daughter of an MP, a member of the Conservative Party, whose job it was to support his government's stance on nuclear weapons. Her fate was now sealed, her disloyalty laid bare: her father would never speak to her again. If her family hadn't written her off already, they would now. There would probably be reporters and journalists at Maberley Manor already, ringing on the bell, hassling Mr and Mrs Owen. She felt sick, and it took all her strength not to throw up on the floor of the police van.

Fliss felt the meek, submissive girl she was before she went to Greenham slowly creeping back in. How could she get through this without Hazel or Clara? If she had just danced on the silos, like the other women, she would be fine. Why had she got so swept up in the moment, wanting to be the hero? They hadn't asked her to do it; she had brought this upon herself. She was showing off, a stupid child. She had wanted Hazel to love her and respect her and think of her as one of them.

She watched the world outside rushing by, longing to be one of the people going about their day, wishing she was the girl she had been before. The girl who thought she had problems, crying herself to sleep at boarding school. Greenham hadn't changed her at all. She was still a coward, too scared to call her parents, face the music, and ask them for the money to pay her fine. She pitied the baby growing inside her. How did she think she was going to support it? She had nothing, no home, no money. They were going to take her child away and she deserved it; her baby was better off without her.

The police van pulled to a stop at the gates of the prison, vivid red-brick walls and a large black gate looming over her. As the gate began to slide open, Fliss felt her whole body start to shake, her teeth chattering in her head, a rush of cold blood through her veins. She was desperate to feel the comforting familiar movements of her baby's feet and hands, which were terrifyingly absent. She had never felt all-consuming panic like this. She would wake up soon, in her car boot at Greenham, and tell Hazel about her dream, make tea over the fire as they cuddled up together under a blanket they had bought in a charity shop. But as the van pulled through another gate and the engine was turned off, a side door in the prison opened and the guard eased her up onto her feet.

Women around the fire at Greenham had talked about Holloway, being put in a cell with prisoners who were mentally unstable, sometimes women who were a real threat, who were violent, and screamed and hit their heads against the wall until they bled. Some of the prison guards had even confessed that they had put new prisoners with unstable women deliberately to break them in their first few days. A few of them spoke of the fear of the first time, the sense of isolation, the terror of the realisation they were under the control of others.

Clara, who had been incarcerated in Holloway for a month, remembered the lack of oxygen the most; windows being only two inches wide meant she spent much of her time with her lips pressed up against the glass, desperate for fresh air. There were days and days and days when you didn't get out at all.

As she walked towards the entrance, Fliss could hear the women's voices around the fire, talking about Holloway. *The first time is the worst. If you can get through that, you can get through anything.* On shaky legs, Fliss shuffled inside the stark reception area. The exposed-brick walls and concrete floor were unwelcoming, much like the female officers sitting at the desk.

'Sit down,' one of them barked. 'Name, date of birth?'

'Felicity Mills, 8 June 1965.'

'What's your sentence?'

'Eight weeks.'

The woman continued to bark questions, scribbling on a card in front of her before handing it to Fliss: *N72436 MILLS.*

'That's your prison number,' the officer next to her said. 'Now you need to go over to that cubicle and take your clothes off.'

'What for?'

'You have to be strip-searched,' she said matter-of-factly.

Felicity felt like she'd been punched. 'But I'm pregnant.'

'That don't mean you ain't hiding nothing. Come on,

sooner you get on with it, sooner it's over,' the woman said, gesturing to a small changing room with a thin curtain.

Slowly, under the fierce strip light, Fliss removed her jeans, jumper, vest, underwear, bra, socks and shoes before the prison guards examined every stitch of her clothing. Fliss stood on the cold concrete floor, naked and humiliated. She wrapped her arms around herself, trying to cover up her breasts and bump, as her teeth chattered frantically. Her baby kicked her hard on her bladder and she let out a gasp of discomfort.

'You can get dressed again,' said the guard, as Fliss swallowed her tears. She barely had time to pull her knickers back on before the woman stepped forward and handed her a bed pack: two starched white sheets, a starched pillowcase, an itchy brown blanket and a thin towel stamped with the initials HMP.

'Hurry up, we need to get you to your cell,' said the guard, as the baby kicked her hard again, sending a shard of pain rippling through her pelvis.

Fliss followed the woman to a white door, where she took a ring full of keys from her belt and pushed one into the lock, then slid the door open. Immediately the noise hit her. A corridor of shrieking and wailing, like a walkway through a monkey sanctuary. The women prisoners could obviously hear them through the closed hatches of their locked cell doors, and began banging as they passed, shouting to be let out. Fliss's baby kicked again. Every one of these women had started out as innocent babies, Fliss thought. What had happened to them to end up in this hellhole? What had gone so wrong for her to end up in here with them?

Finally they reached the end of the corridor where an open cell door waited. The guard gestured for Fliss to go in.

Fliss hesitated, looking back in the direction that she had come, feeling like the outside world was now just a figment of her imagination. She gathered all her strength and stepped over the threshold, and before she had time to reach the end of the tiny space the door slammed shut.

She spun round, startled, as the guard locked the door behind her. She walked back over to the door, and put her palms up against it, pressing as hard as she could. The baby kicked hard again as she started to cry. Eight weeks? She couldn't get through the next eight hours. Her cell was so hot, she struggled to breathe. It stank of vomit and bleach. She craved the bitter cold of Greenham; she craved the fire, and Hazel and the family she had made there. She had never felt so alone. She went to the tiny window, but it was shut tight. She stared out onto a wall with barbed wire running the length of it, then behind it another wall with more barbed wire, and another. The outside world felt a thousand miles away.

She turned and scanned the room. Inside the tiny cell was a metal bed with a stained mattress, and on it she placed the sheet, pillowcase, towel and blanket. There was a small table, a single chair, and a toilet behind a waist-high screen. Outside, along the wing corridor, a woman screamed, another shouted obscenities, some banged on their cell doors. It sounded like a madhouse.

'All right, Mills, we'll check on ya during the night. Try and get some sleep.'

Shaking, paralysed with fear, she lay down on the thin mattress, knowing she wouldn't sleep a wink as the bed creaked loudly underneath her. The baby kicked again and again, and the soaring pain accompanying the kicks began to spread into one giant contraction. She tried to turn over

322

and block out the torture and the screams outside her cell, but panic overwhelmed her. Felicity attempted to breathe through it, tried to pull the scratchy blanket over her to get some comfort, but it felt like being stabbed with tiny needles in the baking-hot sun. Fliss tried to close her eyes. She was exhausted, but her adrenaline made it impossible for her to rest. She tried to breathe through the pains in her stomach again, tried to calm herself, but the woman next door was trying to kick her cell door open, and another was threatening to kill herself. Fliss heard running footsteps, followed by the noise of jangling keys opposite her cell.

As the hours went on the stabbing pains increased, soaring through her insides like a red-hot poker. As the screams started to fade, and the darkness of the night took over, a woman in the next cell began to sing and Felicity tried to take herself out of her body, back to Greenham and to Hazel.

If we're attacked we bear the blame
They say that we began the game
And though you prove your injury
The judge may set the rapist free

Fliss was in so much pain, and so terrified, she began to scream for her mother. She couldn't help herself. She wanted to be at home, in her bedroom. She wished she had never left. Regret coursed through her veins, as if they had already taken away her baby. She cried out for help, screaming like the women on the wing, the women trying to kill themselves.

She heard the running of footsteps again, but this time they were for her. She heard the keys opening her door.

'What is it, Mills?'

'It's my baby. I think my baby is coming,' she gasped.

'How pregnant are you?'

'Eight and a half months.'

Another soaring pain, and then a flood of liquid between her legs. It was too painful to lie down any longer, so she sat up, and saw a puddle of red liquid under the bed.

'I'm bleeding,' she said, feeling the life draining out of her. She was going to pass out, and there was nothing she could do to stop herself.

'OK, we're transferring you to the maternity wing. Can you walk?'

Fliss stood for a moment before her legs went from under her and she fell back onto the bed. 'I want my mother,' she cried.

'We will contact her.'

'I want her here.'

'She won't be able to come to the hospital, but we will contact her.'

'Please don't take my baby away.'

The pain was too much now. Fliss couldn't talk any more. Every time she went to speak, the stabbing sensations took her breath away.

'Please, I want my mother.'

The pain took her out of her body, through the gates of Maberley, across the gravel drive, through the front door, the smells of the kitchen, the venison, the gravy, the red wine stains on her mother's lips, the Chanel No. 5, the fireplace ablaze. The guests, sitting around the table, laughing and pointing at her, as she stood bleeding in the doorway.

She was on a trolley now, being wheeled through the prison. She heard someone scream and this time it was her.

The strip lights along the corridor flashed above as the guards ran alongside her.

'Please don't take my baby away,' she cried out, taking the woman's hand.

But the guard didn't answer her. Soon another officer joined her, talking over her head, using her prison number, not her name.

She was no longer a person; her baby wasn't a person. They had no rights.

She had gone to Greenham to find freedom, and now they were at the mercy of the State.

'Help me!' she cried, as they lifted her onto a bed, and began to examine her. The pain was like nothing she had ever experienced before.

The guards and doctors moved around her, in a blur: 'we need to transfer her', 'the baby's heartbeat is faint . . .' She felt a needle in her arm, then the sound of an ambulance siren in the distance as she begged for her mother. Over and over and over again.

But she never came.

Chapter Twenty-Seven

Emma

Saturday, 22 June 2024

'Amanda, your taxi is here, if you want to say your good-byes,' Sam, the governor, said, as she stood at the doorway of Amanda and Emma's cell at Westwood Park Prison.

Emma looked up at Amanda as she put the last of her belongings into her holdall and zipped it up.

'Is your mum not coming to get you?' Emma asked.

'No, she's meeting me at the station,' Amanda said curtly.

Emma nodded, fearful that Amanda was lying to her about her relationship with her mum, and had been for some time. Why would a mother who had missed her daughter so desperately, and apparently visited her every week, wait at the station down the road on such a momentous day as her only daughter being released from a lengthy prison sentence?

She had no issue with Amanda being estranged from her mum – she herself was estranged from her adoptive mother, Sally – but it made her question why Amanda would want to go to such elaborate lengths to hide the fact. It also begged the question of what else Amanda was hiding.

She still hadn't confronted Amanda about what her adoptive mother had told her about the trust fund. The fact was, she was starting to feel pretty scared of Amanda and what she was capable of, and she was nervous to bring it up. The trust fund Amanda now had access to was money she desperately needed once she was back out in the world, but if it meant Amanda disappeared from her life, she figured it might be worth it.

Since Emma's brief, awkward conversation with Jen in the lunch hall, Amanda had been watching Emma even more closely and so she hadn't had the opportunity to probe Jen any further about Amanda. But she had got the distinct impression Jen felt Amanda was not who she made herself out to be. And once her suspicions were ignited, Emma started to notice little things that didn't marry with what Amanda had told her: a bag of chocolates or baked goodies, which were supposedly gifts from her mother, with a receipt and Amanda's bank card in the bottom. Or Amanda disappearing to make long phone calls to her mother (which she would then relay at length to Emma), with no phone card to pay for them.

Emma smiled, not wanting to give away the awkwardness and paranoia she now felt in Amanda's company. Despite stealing from her, she harboured no ill feelings towards Amanda. In some ways she had been a good friend and helped Emma to see her world in a different light; most significantly by planting the seed in Emma's head that the fire that had killed her father wasn't all her fault, and that her adoptive parents hadn't been entirely blameless.

Indeed, Amanda had listened to Emma in a way nobody ever had done before. They had spent hours walking and talking in the woods surrounding Westwood Park Open Prison and Amanda had pushed her to share her feelings about being adopted. Things she had never talked about with anyone: her low self-esteem, anxiety, depression, a deep-rooted fear of abandonment and an all-consuming grief for the person she should have, would have been, had she been raised by her birth mother, whose name – according to Amanda – was Felicity Stanton.

It was Edward Mills, a retired Conservative MP, living in a Georgian mansion on the outskirts of Newbury, who had put her into a cardboard box on the passenger seat of his vintage E-Type Jaguar – accidentally dropping his initialled tiepin into the makeshift crib in the process – then left her to her fate on the steps of St Phillip's.

And once Amanda had decided Sir Edward James Mills, as he was now known, was the culprit, there had been no stopping her. Amanda had spent every waking minute researching Edward and finding out as much as she possibly could about him. She even persuaded Emma to send off for a DNA kit, which she did, before Amanda posted it off on her next trip into town to meet her mother.

'If any of your birth family are looking for you, they will be on one of those DNA sites,' Amanda had said excitedly.

'I'm not sure I'm ready for all this,' Emma had replied rather feebly.

'Look, it says here if you take a DNA test and then change your mind, each of the companies will, at your request, delete your account and data and destroy your DNA sample. OK? Come on, it's worth a shot. What if your birth mother has been searching for you all these years?'

Every day Amanda would disappear off into town and spend hours at an internet café, then come back, flicking through her trusty notebook and announce various facts she had discovered about Edward James Mills and his prominent place in the world, which she read out to Emma as she lay on her bunk bed in their cell.

'When I get out, I'm going to follow him and see what dirt I can find out about him.'

'Why?' Emma had asked.

'Because he lives in a massive mansion and you're rotting in prison. He owes you, but no doubt he'll deny all of it. So it will be handy to have some leverage,' she had smiled.

Emma was pretty sure that this important-sounding person couldn't be the man who had left her and was slightly taken aback by the lengths Amanda was willing to go to in order to prove it. She had no idea how to react, or to know if Amanda was actually being serious. Half of her was slightly alarmed, and the other half flattered.

One thing she did know was that it had made her want to go and meet Howell Jenkins herself, to thank him for speaking with Amanda, and for saving her all those years ago.

'So I guess this is goodbye,' said Emma.

'Not for long. You're out in a month,' Amanda said cheerfully, as Emma's heart sank. 'We'll go straight to your grandfather's house. It was easy to get in – the back door was open. I managed to get some good stuff from his email. His password was sellotaped to a Post-it in the top drawer,' Amanda said, throwing her eyes to heaven. 'I can't wait to tell you about it. We are gonna be rich, girl.'

'Amanda, this needs to stop.'

'What are you talking about?'

'I never asked you to do any of this.'

Amanda frowned. 'Yes, Emma, you did. Don't start losing your nerve now. They owe you, big time, and we are going to make them pay.'

'Amanda, it's my family. I want to find out about them in my own way.'

'No, Emma, because that won't happen, will it? You'll talk yourself out of it, which is why you need me. This is why people are walking all over you, because you're so fucking weak.'

'Stay out of my life, Amanda, and stay away from my birth family, or I'll tell Sam what you've been doing.'

'No, I don't think you will. It will play havoc with your release, trust me. I'll see you in a few weeks,' she said cheerfully.

Emma watched Amanda go, feeling gripped with a panic she hadn't felt since her first night at Heathfield. She was getting out, she knew who her birth family was, she should be happy . . . but she felt utterly terrified of what Amanda was capable of.

'Emma. Emma? Are you OK?' Sam was walking towards her.

'Yes,' she mumbled, unconvincingly. She knew Amanda was right, and that saying anything to Sam would mean all hell broke loose and it would delay her release date. Amanda would claim Emma knew about everything they were doing, she would say they had decided to do it together. She was up to her neck and she needed to stay quiet.

She had only a month left to go, and she couldn't bear to be accused of being in on it. She couldn't tell her solicitor either. It would be his job to tell her to report Amanda. Then who would believe her? Her heart and thoughts raced as she walked back to her quiet cell, sitting down on the bottom bunk to read the article, as she had so many times before.

The little girl is believed to be about six weeks old and was found by church caretaker, Howell Jenkins, in sub-zero temperatures.

Emma's mother is yet to come forward, and Newbury police are deeply concerned for her wellbeing. Women's Police Constable Rachel Rees said: 'Baby Emma is being well cared for by her foster parents and is a healthy, happy baby.'

'Women's Police Constable Rachel Rees,' Emma said out loud, running her fingers over the name.

WPC Rachel Rees, the policewoman who had tried to find out who she really belonged to.

She was so close to getting out, but Amanda potentially knew who her birth family were, and they needed to be warned about her – even if it meant repercussions for Emma. She curled up in a ball on her bunk, tears stinging her eyes.

Maybe if she could get a message to this Rachel Rees, if she was still in the force, she could warn her. But how was she supposed to do that? Contact the police anonymously from her prison cell? The idea was ridiculous. And they probably wouldn't do anything to intervene anyway.

No. She had no choice. She would have to wait the four weeks until Friday, 19 July, when she was due to be released.

Amanda wasn't a bad person, she was just trying to help. She already had the money, chances are she'd just disappear.

And, even if she didn't, Emma pondered, how much harm could one woman really do in four short weeks?

Chapter Twenty-Eight

Rachel

Thursday, 18 July 2024

Felicity Stanton sat in the private visits room at Westwood Park Prison waiting for Emma, her daughter who she hadn't seen for forty-one years, to walk through the door.

'Emma won't be long. How are you feeling?' asked Rachel, putting her hand over Felicity's.

'Nervous. Very nervous,' said Felicity, her voice trembling. 'Are you sure Emma didn't have anything to do with Amanda trying to steal this money?' she asked, looking at the door for the hundredth time.

'Well, it would make no sense. The money is Emma's, so there is no need for her to be deceptive and try to steal it. It was obvious to Sam, the governor here, when she told Emma about Sophia, that Emma had no idea what Amanda had done,' Rachel said.

'How did Amanda find out about the will then?'

'We don't know, but we suspect she broke into Edward's house, Maberley Manor, and went through his study. She did the same in Emma's adoptive mother's house.'

'Does Emma know how much money my mother left to her?'

'No, not yet. I thought you'd like to tell her,' Rachel said. 'It's a pretty life-changing thing for Camilla to do.'

Felicity shook her head. 'I've never told anyone this

before, but I think it was my mother that took Emma from me. I think she tried to frame my father as a bully by adding the codicil to the will, and saying that my father couldn't find out about it until after her death. I think she felt guilty and wanted me to believe it was all his fault. I heard them arguing one night, soon after she took Emma away. It was obvious he was horrified. But the damage was done by then. It would have destroyed his career and family if he had gone to the police. I heard her laughing at his coward-ice as she called it. She could be very cruel, my mother.'

'It was Camilla's handwriting on the envelope that I found next to baby Emma.' Rachel added, 'I knew she was your baby because Adele had an identical envelope with Camilla's distinctive, curved writing. Howell Jenkins was convinced it was a man who left the baby, because of the cap they were wearing.'

'My mum always wore a peaked cap when she was driv-ing, because it was a convertible, and she didn't want her perfect bob spoiling. She drove that Jag more than he did. She loved fast cars – and men. It used to upset him terribly. She bullied him, really. And she was always sneaking out to see Anthony Hislop. He was her friend more than my father's. She adored him. She was absolutely furious when Anthony started showing an interest in me, her chubby little girl . . . Mother was too old for him by then, I guess he liked the younger ones.' Felicity shook her head at the memory.

'Anyway, we mustn't let the past consume us. We are here to ask Emma about Amanda, in case she can think of any-thing that might lead us to Sophia, is that right?' said Felicity, changing the subject. 'What did Amanda do anyway? Why is she in prison with Emma, I mean?'

'She stabbed her ex-boyfriend in the stomach because he finished the relationship,' Rachel said matter-of-factly.

'How terrifying.'

'Yes, she has a long track record of harassment and stalking in relationships. According to Sam, she is attractive and very charming,' Rachel said.

'And this is the woman who you think has Sophia?' Felicity clarified nervously.

'Yes, but she gets nothing if Sophia is harmed, so we are hopeful,' Rachel said.

Felicity looked up at the clock. It was ticking loudly. Every second that Sophia was missing felt like an hour. She hadn't left Adele's side for two days, and their relationship had transformed in that time; she wished Adele was there with her – to meet her half-sister.

'Where is Adele now?' Felicity asked.

'She's at the flat where we believe Amanda has been keeping Sophia. She rented it out in Emma's name, presumably with some of the money she took from Emma's trust fund. We needed Adele and Alex to ID Sophia's clothing and school bag.'

'Poor Adele,' said Felicity quietly. 'I'll never forgive myself if anything happens to Sophia. Adele told me that Emma is in prison for manslaughter – do you know what she did exactly?' Felicity asked nervously.

Rachel noticed how pale Felicity was. It had been two very long days since Sophia had gone missing, and Felicity looked as if she had hardly slept. And now, on top of this, she was about to meet her long-lost daughter who had been stolen from her as a baby.

'I'm not an expert on her case, but from what I know, she was convicted of arson,' Rachel said gently.

'Arson?' Felicity let out a heavy sigh. 'Why? What did she set fire to?'

'Her adoptive parents' house. She pleaded not guilty, and claims it was an accident. She lit a fire pit in the garage to keep warm, and then fell asleep, but the fire resulted in the death of her adoptive father so the judge came down on her pretty hard.'

'Oh dear God, the poor child,' said Felicity instinctively.

'Obviously you will have to get her side of the story, but I think she has had quite a rough time.'

Felicity started to cry. 'How long has she been here?'

'Well, she's only been at Westwood Park for six months. But she was in a high-security prison for five years, I believe. I think she got ten years for manslaughter. And she was due to be released tomorrow. But I have no idea what will happen now. There will have to be a full investigation into how this situation with Amanda came about.'

'But she shouldn't be punished for Amanda stealing from her and taking Sophia. Poor Emma. This is all my fault,' Felicity said as Rachel put her arm around her.

'It's not. You were so young. You were in an impossible situation,' Rachel said.

'I should have fought harder. I should never have given her up,' said Felicity, as they heard footsteps coming down the corridor. 'How am I going to tell her what happened to her?'

'From what Sam has told me, she knows she is a found-ling, and very much still wants to be in your life. She is terrified you blame her for what's happened with Amanda and Sophia.'

Felicity's hands were shaking. Rachel stood and got her some water, which she drank gratefully.

'I think they're coming,' said Rachel, as Felicity rose on shaking legs and Rachel took her hand.

Slowly the door opened, and two women appeared, one with a lanyard hanging from her neck and holding a set of keys. The other, lagging behind, was a pale blonde woman with piercing blue eyes, just like Felicity's.

'Hi, Felicity. I'm Sam, the governor here. And this is Emma.' Sam smiled warmly, urging Emma to step forward.

Felicity stood for a moment, rooted to the spot, then Rachel nodded to Felicity, and gestured for her to go over to her daughter, which she did.

The two women stood looking at each other for several seconds. Then Emma started crying, and Felicity smiled gently at her. The similarity was undeniable: the way they stood, their body shape, their hair colour, the tone of their skin. Emma was an echo of Felicity.

'Hello, darling,' said Felicity. 'It's lovely to see you again.'

All the tension fell from Felicity's body as Emma launched herself at her mother and the two of them held each other and cried.

Rachel grinned at Sam and walked over to her.

'Thank you, again, for arranging the visit at such short notice, Sam,' Rachel said.

'No problem, Emma was so happy to hear that her mum was on her way. She's been very upset about what's happened with Amanda and Adele's daughter,' Sam said.

'I feel terrible about Sophia. I'm so sorry, this is all my

fault,' Emma said, pulling back from her mother and wiping her eyes with her sleeve.

'How is this your fault?' asked Felicity, frowning.

'If I hadn't trusted her, she would never have come looking for you all. I still don't know how she managed it. I've been wanting to find you for over forty years, and she does it within a month.'

'I was so sorry to hear about the fire, Emma. How horrifying for you to lose your father like that,' Felicity said.

'It was an accident,' Emma said. 'I fell asleep. I loved my dad – I never would have done anything to hurt him.' Emma started to cry again.

'I'm sure you wouldn't. We have a lot to catch up on, sweetheart,' said Felicity, kindly.

'Have they found Sophia?' Emma asked anxiously.

Felicity shook her head and turned to Rachel. 'No, but I understand they think she's in Bristol. But they don't know where. Amanda has rented a flat out in your name.'

Emma nodded, taking in Rachel's words. 'But they aren't there?'

'No, but there are signs they've been there: Sophia's school jumper and school bag,' Rachel said.

'I apologise, but I've got to go and dig out Amanda's file, see if I can find anything that helps,' said Sam.

'Of course,' said Rachel. 'Thank you.'

Rachel turned to Emma. 'Hi, Emma, I'm Detective Constable Rachel Rees. Thank you for meeting with us today. We're very grateful. I was actually the police constable who you were handed in to when you were left on the steps of St Phillip's as a baby.'

'Rachel Rees? Oh my goodness, I was only rereading the

article they wrote about me the other day. Thank you for taking care of me,' Emma said.

'You're welcome. I've thought of you often over the years. I hope you don't mind me getting straight to the point here, Emma, but we don't have a lot of time. Do you know how Amanda managed to find out Edward Mills was involved in abandoning you?' Rachel pulled her pad from her bag and opened it as Emma nodded.

'She broke into my adoptive mother's house, Sally Blake, and stole the notebook with her computer passwords. She logged into Sally's bank accounts and found an account in my name with several deposits from an Edward James Mills. Obviously that matched with the tiepin mentioned in the newspaper article and so she started doing some research on him. After she'd emptied my trust fund, of course,' Emma added.

'How much do you think she took – did she tell you?' Rachel asked, opening her notebook.

'I don't know. I was a bit scared of her so I didn't want to antagonise her. I think there was a thousand pounds in an envelope in the cardboard box I was found in, plus the deposits Edward Mills made, which Amanda said were a few hundred. So I guess there was a couple of grand in there.'

Rachel looked at Emma. 'Thirty thousand, actually.'

'What? Thirty thousand pounds? Sally kept thirty thousand pounds hidden from me? But that's a huge amount of money,' she gasped, her voice shaking as Rachel and Felicity exchanged looks, both mindful of the quarter of a million pounds from Camilla that lay in wait for her. 'I suppose that's all gone now?' Emma asked.

'We suspect so,' Rachel said.

338

'Well, I've found you,' said Emma, squeezing her mother's hand, 'so I don't care about the money.'

Felicity looked at Rachel, who nodded at her. 'Emma, actually . . . Amanda discovered that you stand to inherit a lot more than that,' said Rachel. 'Your grandmother, Camilla Mills, Felicity's mother, left you two hundred and fifty thousand pounds in her will.'

'What?' said Emma again, tears immediately stinging her eyes. 'Why?'

'Because she wanted you to be taken care of,' said Felicity.

'But I can't accept that!' Emma said, shocked. 'I don't deserve that sort of money.'

'Yes,' said Felicity, 'you really do.'

Rachel's revelation hung in the air for a moment, as Emma stared at her mother incredulously. Felicity took Emma's hands in hers and smiled gently.

'I don't know if you remember doing a swab, Emma, but Amanda stole your DNA and claimed to be you,' Rachel continued. 'But your grandfather didn't pay her the money because he knew it wasn't you. Apparently she didn't have the birthmark behind her ear that he remembered you have.'

Emma nodded. 'I always saw that birthmark as a present from my birth mother. A sign that she would be able to find me,' she said gazing at Felicity. 'I knew you wouldn't have abandoned me, in a cardboard box, and I was right.'

'What do you mean?' Felicity said, leaning in.

'I know it was Edward who left me on the steps of St Phillip's church in Newbury, when I was a baby,' Emma said, looking at her mother. 'Not you.'

Felicity's chest tightened and she focused on the cup of water on the table, which she slowly picked up and drank from.

'I'm sorry to put you in this situation, Emma, when you have so much to catch up on with your mother,' Rachel said anxiously, 'but I was wondering if Amanda told you anything that might help us in our search for Sophia.'

'I don't know. We had so many conversations about a lot of things. She mostly asked about me, though, and she didn't share a lot. Now I know why.'

'As I said, we think they may be in Bristol, but it's a huge city, and we don't know where to start.'

'What sort of things might be helpful?'

'Maybe a place that meant something to her. Do you know why she might have moved to Bristol?'

'She never mentioned Bristol. She was very close to her mother, I know that much. She used to talk about her a lot, she would come and visit her all the time and bring lots of gifts.'

'OK, we will try and find her,' said Rachel, scribbling in her notebook as Sam came bustling back into the room holding an A4 file.

'I'm not sure if Amanda was telling the truth about her, though,' Emma added as an afterthought.

'What makes you say that?' Rachel asked.

'Well, I don't know, I used to be quite jealous of her relationship with her mother. Amanda made it sound like she worshipped the ground Amanda walked on. She was even in prison because of her. She said her mother had a violent and abusive boyfriend who Amanda stabbed in order to protect her mother.'

'It wasn't her mother's boyfriend,' Sam interjected, as all eyes fell on her, 'it was Amanda's boyfriend – well, her ex-boyfriend, who had broken up with her. She followed him into his apartment and stabbed him when she found out he was seeing someone else.'

'What? But why would she lie to me about that?'

'I guess the story about her mum is a lot more heroic,' Felicity offered. 'Are you not told what your fellow prisoners are in for?'

'I knew it was manslaughter – that she'd stabbed a bloke – but I never doubted her story. Why would I? She adores her mum, so it made sense.'

'What was her mum like? Do we have any details about her mother on file, Sam?' Rachel asked, as Sam flicked through the file.

'It's strange. I never saw her mum, Amanda always met her in town,' Emma said. 'On the day Amanda was released, her mother didn't come and get her. Which I found strange. And there was something else.'

'What?' Rachel asked.

'I felt mean thinking it, but there was a receipt at the bottom of the bag of goodies she brought back here once. It was supposed to be from her mother, but I got the impression Amanda had bought them herself,' Emma added, shaking her head.

'Amanda's mother's dead,' Sam said. They all turned and stared at her. 'According to her file, she threw herself off Clifton Suspension Bridge when Amanda was six. Amanda was there.'

'Oh my God!' Emma said, and the colour drained from Felicity's face.

'Emma, I think you need to come to Bristol with us now,' said Rachel. 'If she is there, Amanda might find it comforting to see a friend.'

Emma looked at Rachel with surprise. 'You want me to leave Westwood Park Prison with you now?'

'Yes, if you would be happy to come with us? I'm authorised to escort prisoners,' Rachel said, looking over at Sam, 'but we need to move quickly.'

'Of course, I'll do anything I can to help,' said Emma. 'Are you coming, Mum?' she asked, turning to Felicity.

'You know where to find Sophia?' Felicity clarified, her voice shaking.

'Possibly,' said Rachel, 'but we don't have her . . . yet.'

'I think I will go and see my father in hospital, if I'm not needed here,' Felicity said, her hands shaking as Emma leaned down and kissed her. 'Bring Sophia back to us, please.'

'I'll try,' said Emma, as she and Rachel dashed out of the room, and towards the exit of Westwood Park Prison.

Chapter Twenty-Nine

Rachel

Thursday, 18 July 2024

Rachel saw the Clifton Suspension Bridge lit up in the night sky and turned off her blues and twos.

'There it is,' she said to Emma, who had been very quiet in the seat next to her on their drive from Westwood Park Prison.

Emma looked like a rabbit caught in the headlights, Rachel thought to herself as they pulled over, and it wasn't surprising. It had been one hell of a rollercoaster ride for her. She had gone from the living hell of a secure prison for five long years, to being transferred to Westwood Park where, in the space of five months, she had met Amanda Harris, a force of nature by all accounts, who had won Emma's hard-earned trust and then broken her heart.

Now, the poor girl had been taken out of prison with no warning in order to comfort the girl who had turned her life upside down – and was expected to save the day. No wonder she had turned a pale shade of grey.

Rachel's boss had called her on the speaker phone en route and filled them in on Amanda Harris's background, and her mother, Katherine, who had jumped from the infamous bridge in 1989, when Amanda was just six years old.

It was reported in the newspapers at the time, he'd told them, that Katherine, an office secretary, was a local mother of one, who was suffering from depression following the unexpected death of her husband – Amanda's father – following a heart attack. Katherine Harris had taken Amanda with her to the bridge but one of the bridge staff had managed to grab the little girl before her mother jumped.

Amanda had been passed from pillar to post in the care system, being fostered by six families before ending up in a correctional facility for wayward teenagers. Since then she had been in and out of prison, for various harassment offences against ex-partners when they tried to end their relationship with her. The attempted manslaughter charge she had been in prison for when she met Emma had been her most serious offence. And it had been her boyfriend – not her mother's, as she had claimed to Emma – who had been her victim. He had not been abusive, and they had only dated for a short time, but he had tried to end the relationship after becoming spooked by her intensity, whereupon she had stabbed him.

Rachel parked and turned off her engine, texting her boss to tell him that she had arrived. It looked as if she and Emma were the first on the scene, and for a moment everything was silent apart from the traffic making its way over the bridge. After the events of the day, and the adrenaline rushing around her bloodstream, it felt to Rachel like the calm before the storm.

'So they think Amanda is here with Sophia?' Emma asked nervously.

'Possibly. I think we should go and take a look. Stay close, OK?' Rachel said.

'I'm nervous. I haven't been outside a prison in five and a half years,' Emma said.

344

'You'll be fine. I'll look after you,' Rachel assured her, as Emma stayed firmly in her seat.

'I'm scared I'll do or say something that will affect Sophia. I feel like I've done enough damage already.'

'Your mother is right, none of this is your fault. We want you here, Emma. It was our idea, not yours. If we find Amanda, and you feel comfortable talking to her, then I think you should. But please don't feel you have to. OK?'

'OK,' Emma said, nodding.

Walking towards the bridge, Emma stayed right beside Rachel, just as she'd asked. Rachel looked around for any signs of life but couldn't see any of the bridge staff who she knew had been notified. Or any of the other officers she was aware were en route here.

Where was everyone? Could she have got it wrong? Maybe Amanda and Sophia weren't here at all. Or maybe it was already too late, she thought, her heart sinking. The bridge – one of the oldest iron suspension bridges in the world – was stunningly beautiful, lit up, as it was, at night.

Rachel and Emma walked to the entrance of the bridge in silence, the small office next to them was unmanned, and the wind pushed them back, as Rachel glanced down at the vast hundred-metre drop to the River Avon below. Cars, bicycles and motorbikes rushed by, commuters on their way home from work, listening to their music, oblivious to Sophia's plight. The young girl was possibly out there in the darkness, alone and terrified, just as Amanda had been the night her mother jumped all those years ago.

Rachel and Emma began walking over the bridge, as Rachel strained to see any sign of Amanda and Sophia. The cars and lorries rattled Rachel's nervous system as she tried to stay calm and hoped for back-up to appear soon. A runner dashed past them, then a couple holding hands walked towards her, blocking her view of the bridge, until suddenly they passed and she saw a gathering at the far end of the bridge. A male figure, which she recognised as Alex, was talking to a woman, who sat on the ledge at the end of the bridge. A young girl was sitting next to her. They were facing outwards – towards the drop.

It would only take a second for Amanda to lean forward and they would both fall to their deaths.

Rachel's heart stopped as she pointed them out to Emma, who covered her mouth in shock.

Slowly they made their way towards them, as Emma continued to stay close. The wind was whipping up a frenzy now, whistling in Rachel's ears as Sophia's voice became audible. Adele was standing slightly back, leaning forward, her right foot out, as if she were ready to pounce at any moment. She was visibly shaking – from the biting wind, or shock or both. Ben was standing next to Adele and Alex, and he nodded as Rachel approached.

'Mummy,' Rachel could hear the girl saying. 'I'm worried about Leia.'

'It's OK, sweetheart,' said Adele, as Rachel and Emma stood back and took in the scene. 'She's safe at home.'

'Don't come any nearer,' Amanda snapped.

'We won't,' said Alex, as Adele looked at him nervously. Rachel didn't know Alex well, but sensed he was unpredictable. She knew that Alex had caused his wife a great deal of anguish and was a law unto himself. As she watched his wild eyes staring at his daughter's back, she was almost as nervous of what Alex would do as she was of Amanda.

Rachel knew from her forty years of experience that staying calm was paramount. She had broken up countless fights and arguments, just by lightening the mood, being the female in a room of men, making a joke, smiling, dispersing the tension. She refrained from shouting, calling out or even trying to make contact with Alex and Adele. As she approached them, she slowed to a walking pace and noticed that beyond them was a man in a high-vis jacket.

'Please don't hurt her, Amanda, please,' said Adele. 'I've spoken to my grandfather, he's doing everything he can to get the money to you, but he's in the hospital. He's had a stroke, so it's just going to take a little bit more time.'

Rachel edged forward until she was in the line of sight of Adele and Alex, but not Amanda and Sophia. It was completely dark now and easy to hide in the shadows. Everyone was so focused on Amanda and Sophia that they hadn't noticed her. Ben was just behind Adele and Alex, watching Rachel and Emma approach.

The man in the high-vis jacket, who Rachel guessed to be part of the bridge team, stepped forward. 'Amanda, why don't you come down and we can talk about this? You're scaring Sophia, and I'm sure you don't want to do that,' he said.

Suddenly Alex caught sight of her. Rachel signalled for him to move back but he ignored her. He just kept staring intensely at Sophia, as if taking his eyes off her for a second would send her plummeting to her death. Rachel signalled for Ben to get Alex to move back and Ben reached out for

Alex's arm, but Alex pulled away irritably. Ben and Rachel exchanged looks. Rachel knew what he was thinking: there was nothing they could do. Any altercation between Ben and Alex could put Sophia's life in jeopardy.

'Amanda, my name is Detective Constable Rachel Rees. I believe you've been speaking to Edward Mills about your money.'

'This is his fault. If he hadn't stopped that money going through, this would all be over.'

'Amanda, he hasn't stopped anything. It is very hard to get hold of that sort of money at such short notice, on top of which Edward is very seriously ill,' said Rachel.

'That's bullshit. I know the solicitor has it,' Amanda snapped.

'Yes, she does now, and we are ready to release it to you,' Rachel said calmly.

'Stop lying to me,' Amanda said, edging forward.

'Amanda, I know about your mother. I know why you've come here. And I want to help you.'

'No you don't. Nobody has ever wanted to help me. Why should Emma get the perfect family when she gets out, and I have no one? I deserve that money.'

Amanda inched forward again. Sophia let out a cry of panic. Adele screamed.

'Amanda, please.' Emma's voice came from behind Rachel. 'You can have my inheritance. I don't want it, truly. All I want is for you to hand over Sophia. You're so near the edge, I'm scared you're going to fall,' said Emma.

Rachel was impressed with how calm Emma sounded. She suddenly felt her confidence fail her. She had never handled a potential suicide before. She was used to people's

348

lives being in her hands, but she had support systems, protocols, paramedics and firefighters. In that moment, her years of experience seemed to melt away. She was terrified at how out of control it felt and the speed with which the situation was unravelling.

'Amanda, talk to me. Why are you doing this?' Emma asked. 'You don't want to hurt Sophia, I know you don't. You know how it feels to be in her situation. Look at her little hands, look at her face – she's terrified. I can only imagine how hard it must have been here with your mother that night.'

'Leave me alone. You don't know anything about my mother,' said Amanda, starting to cry.

'No, I don't, but I want to,' Emma said. 'You've done so much for me. You've found my family. I want to share them with you. You didn't have to lie to me about your mum. I wanted to know you better. I care about you.'

As Emma spoke, Rachel was watching Alex inch closer to Amanda. In turn, she signalled for Emma to keep going.

'Please, Amanda, come down, and we can talk about this. It's not too late to do the right thing. None of this can't be undone,' said Emma. 'You have a good heart, I know you do. You just need to have more faith in people. In me.'

'Stop pretending you care. You don't care about me. I've been on my own all my life, ever since she left me. I wish that man hadn't grabbed me. I had to watch her fall.'

'I'm so sorry, Amanda. That must have been horrific for you,' said Emma gently, as the wind howled around them all, biting at their skin, pushing them further towards the edge.

'I went from having the best mother in the world to having no one. All alone in the world. Do you know how that feels? Being passed around like you're nothing, nobody caring if you're part of their family one day and gone the next. Everything I owned was in a bin bag. I had no one.'

Rachel looked around at the yellow hue of the bridge lights, the look of anguish and pain on Adele's face, the focus in Alex's eyes as he glared at Sophia's back.

Alex was still inching forward. Rachel knew he was close to grabbing Sophia, and it would be up to her then, or Ben, to grab Amanda. The whole thing felt horrendously risky, Rachel thought. Back-up had arrived and had stopped the traffic now, and all was silent, as several police cars were parked at both the entrance and the exit to the bridge. All eyes were on Rachel, as she carefully inched forward.

'Amanda, let me help you,' said Emma as it started to rain. The wind was picking up, and Rachel was terrified the ledge that Sophia and Amanda were sitting on was going to become slippery. She could see scars on Amanda's arms, which were wrapped around Sophia.

'Tell me about your mother, Amanda,' said Emma, inching further forward. 'I want to know about her.' Rachel was cold, Sophia was shaking and calling out for her mother, their clothes soaked through, Sophia's hair was dripping wet and she was crying harder now, a primal, desperate cry. 'Mummy.'

'She was funny,' Amanda said quietly. 'She used to make me laugh with silly voices and hand puppets. She baked cakes for the neighbours and invited the old lady next door in for tea. She loved babies and hugs. Nobody really hugs you when you're a kid, except your mother. She used to wrap a towel around me when I was cold and tired and made everything better.'

Rachel began counting down from five, holding her fingers out clearly so that Ben could see. Tears were pouring down Adele's face and her whole body was shaking violently in the rain.

'The only person who loves you more than anyone in the world is your mother. Without her, you have no one. You know that Emma, don't you?' Amanda said slowly as Emma nodded her head and started to cry.

Rachel reached two and, before Ben could act, Alex lurched forward. He moved in under a second, wrapping his arm around his daughter's waist, and pulling her back off the ledge. A second too late, Rachel grabbed for Amanda's arm, and as she did, Amanda turned and looked at her with a strange mixture of surprise and acceptance. She looked over at Sophia, who was now wrapped in a cocoon of love with her parents, and she realised that Alex and Adele had their daughter, and the game was up.

She turned to Emma. 'Don't do it, Amanda, please. You're my friend – let me help you,' Emma said.

Amanda then slowly leaned forward, smiling, as if she were diving into a crystal-blue sea. 'I'm going to see her again,' she said quietly, before Adele let out a piercing scream and Amanda disappeared out of sight.

Chapter Thirty

Felicity

January 2025

Felicity took one last look at Maberley Manor before climbing into her father's Volvo, the vintage green Jaguar that Camilla had used to take Emma away from her still parked in the garage. She had no desire to ever return to this house, she thought to herself, as her father slowly lowered himself into the driver's seat next to her. He was recovering well from his stroke, but the long-term effects still lingered. Maberley Manor was sold, and Edward was moving into an assisted-living apartment, with a carer visiting every afternoon, and a porter at reception he could call on in an emergency.

Although Felicity had offered to drive, Edward reminded her he had permission from his consultant and started up the engine. They made their way down the long, gravelled driveway in silence, passing the 'Sold' sign at the entrance to the gates.

'Rachel tells me that Anthony Hislop has been convicted of money laundering,' Edward said, as they pulled onto the country lanes surrounding Kingsclere.

'So he got his just desserts eventually,' Felicity said after a long pause.

'I had no idea he was the man who got you pregnant, Felicity. I didn't even know there was anything between you.'

'Mother did,' said Felicity. 'I think it was part of the

reason she was so furious about my pregnancy. He'd moved on to a younger model. A younger, fatter model.'

'Yes, I never really liked the man, but Camilla was rather obsessed with him and insisted we work together. He always had something of a hold on me, financially. I could never manage the estate very well. He was more a friend of your mother's, going back to their childhood. He and your mother just told me what to do, and I foolishly went along with it. I will admit I was very weak when it came to Camilla. She had rather a hold over me – over most men, actually.'

They drove along. It was easier to talk side by side, Felicity thought; less confrontational. They had never really been honest with one another before, but since the episode with Sophia, all bets were off. It had changed her as a person. She didn't put up with silence any more.

'Emma told me that she thought you had left her on the steps, but I told her I thought it was Mother. It was, wasn't it?'

Edward let the words hang in the air for a while, then eventually nodded.

'Why didn't you do something when you found out that she had taken Emma away from me and left her on the church steps that night?' Felicity's stomach churned, she felt seventeen again, confronting her father about a subject that had been taboo for forty years.

'I'm sorry, Felicity, I should have gone to the police station to claim her, but Camilla said she'd say it was me who abandoned Emma if I did, and I was a coward,' he said, his voice shaking.

Felicity felt her guts twist. She wasn't sure she was ready to forgive him, but she wanted to hear him out, at least.

'I didn't know she'd taken Emma until the morning, by

353

which time the police had placed her with a foster family. You were understandably hysterical, and I kept asking Camilla what she'd done with Emma. She assured me the baby was fine, that she was in good hands. Then when I saw in the newspaper about the tiepin, I knew. But by then it was too late. She told me I couldn't go to the police, my career would be over, and that it was for the best. You weren't ready to be a mother. I think she planted the tiepin on purpose to make it look like it was me in case I did betray her.'

'She could be very cruel,' Felicity said, staring out of the window. 'Why do you think she wanted to leave Emma the money?'

'I don't know. Perhaps her illness softened her, but I think it was much more likely she wanted to exonerate herself once and for all. She knew that with these DNA websites Emma was much more likely to come looking for us. And she didn't want anyone finding out the truth and trampling on her grave.'

'Is that why you sent me away to finishing school so suddenly? So I wouldn't see the newspapers?' Felicity asked.

'Yes, it was your mother's idea. But again, I should have said no,' he said.

Felicity looked out of the window, and brushed away a tear with the back of her hand. The thought of that morning was still too much to bear: the pain of realising Emma was gone. Begging and pleading with her parents to tell her where her baby was. She felt as if her heart had been ripped out, and it had never really recovered.

They were on the main road now, the traffic rushing by sending Felicity into a hypnotic trance.

'I should have stood up to her over Emma and about a

great many things,' Edward continued. 'I am a weak man really, particularly when it came to your mother. This house was your mother's legacy. I could never manage it. Her family never thought I was good enough for her, and she reminded me of that daily. I've failed you, Felicity. I'm so sorry.' Edward fell silent and she turned to see that he was crying. 'I never wanted to send you away to finishing school. I knew how unhappy you were there. I thought that when Adele was born you would forget about Emma, but if anything, another baby made it worse. I hated Camilla for what she had done with Emma and I told her so. She said that no one would ever believe she could do such a thing, and sure enough, she had the last word in her will. Making out that she was the victim, that I had instigated the adoption and refused to tell either of you anything.'

'Why didn't you just give Emma the money anonymously, Dad?' Felicity asked.

'Because I didn't know where she was. And then Alex came to me. He was utterly desperate. He said they would kill him if he didn't find the money. But then I panicked when the solicitor threatened to go to the police and I had to ask for it back. He said no one would lend it to him, so I introduced him to Anthony.'

'Why didn't you borrow the money from Anthony's contact, rather than making Alex overstretch himself?'

'I sort of did, the loan was in Alex's name but I acted as guarantor as they wouldn't have proceeded otherwise. I signed no end of documents, but all my worth was in the house. All these antiques and paintings, they are worthless. When Alex missed the first two payments, they started threatening to take the house. I was almost relieved that my hand was forced, Maberley Manor has been a noose around my neck for so long. I was resigned to having to sell. Then Sophia went missing.'

'It will be good for us to be free of Maberley. It's a huge burden, Dad, and I hate it there. It holds nothing but bad memories for me. It's a beautiful house that's going to someone who will love it.'

'Yes, and I can help you and Adele – and Emma – in a way I haven't been able to before.' They were driving towards Greenham now, and Felicity spotted Adele and Sophia linking arms and standing on the kerb, waiting for her. It was a crisp day and the sun had made an appearance, but the two of them still looked frozen.

Since Sophia's abduction, Felicity and Adele's relationship had developed unrecognisably. They had no time for prickliness, hard feelings and unspoken words any more. They chatted honestly, and often, and sometimes it hurt, but most of the time it was a relief, and a huge weight off both their shoulders, an unburdening of nearly forty years of pent-up emotion.

And Emma had been a huge part of that. She was so childlike, Adele often said you would never know that she had spent five years in a high-security prison. She had an openness that rubbed off on them, and an innocence that was infectious. Her blonde hair and blue eyes made her the spitting image of Adele, but there the resemblance stopped. At first Emma had clearly been terrified to be back out in the real world. The more she told them, the more it seemed that her life, even before prison, hadn't held much happiness. But over time she seemed to grow relaxed in their company, and the three of them had an ease with one another they couldn't explain. It was like a conversation that they started halfway through, no beginning, no end. Emma was the jigsaw piece Felicity and Adele had been missing all their lives.

Where Adele and Felicity had always been picky eaters, Emma loved her food and would try anything new. While the two of them were wary of alcohol and hangovers, Emma could sample the whole cocktail menu and still be the last woman standing. And whereas Adele and Felicity preferred to visit places that were familiar in an organised manner, Emma pushed them to explore the world in a spontaneous and chaotic fashion. Emma brought them out of their shells and she wasn't afraid to make mistakes, look foolish, or laugh raucously at herself. And they loved her for it.

Edward pulled up in front of St Phillip's church and turned off the engine. Adele walked towards the car, smiling broadly, as Sophia, beaming, pulled open the car door. She was in white jeans, trainers and a black leather jacket. 'You are looking scarily grown up, Miss Sophia,' said Felicity, climbing out and hugging her granddaughter.

'Hi, Mum,' said Adele, kissing her mother on both cheeks, as Felicity's eyes fell on the beautiful black-and-white portrait of Amanda on the order of service in Adele's hand.

'Hi, darling, how are you?' Felicity asked.

'We're good, aren't we, poppet?' Adele said, looking down at Sophia.

'Dad's got a new flat, overlooking the river,' Sophia announced. 'And I've got my own room.'

'Wow, that's very exciting,' said Felicity, catching her daughter's eye as Sophia skipped on ahead.

'The divorce came through,' Adele said, linking her arm through her mother's, 'which I'm very grateful for, as his trial for fraud and tax evasion starts next month. Alex's parents have actually been over from Ireland to support him. It was strange meeting them at first, but they are lovely people. I think I might actually let Sophia spend some time with them.'

'Good. It sounds like they didn't know what Alex was up to.'

'No, and Alex is Sophia's dad. I want them to see each other, and to have a good relationship. Otherwise she will grow up with tons of issues and marry an asshole like her father,' she whispered to her mother, who giggled knowingly.

'And how are you feeling?' Felicity asked gently.

'Good, actually. I'm taking one day at a time. I've got Sophia back, and we've found Emma, so nothing else matters,' Adele said, squeezing her mother's arm and smiling. 'Just looking to the future, spending time with my half-sister.'

'And my auntie!' Sophia chimed in.

'And your auntie, that's right,' Felicity smiled, looking over at Emma, who was standing at the entrance gate to the church with Rachel.

Felicity walked over to Emma, who handed her a copy of the order of service. 'You OK, sweetheart?' Felicity asked.

'I'm good, thanks, Mum. How are you?'

'Fine, thank you. Hello, Rachel, nice to see you. Thank you for coming,' Felicity said as Rachel smiled back at her. 'How are things at Thames Valley Police?'

'Well, Ben offered me a promotion. Said he could learn a thing or two from my experience,' Rachel said, smiling.

'Congratulations,' Felicity said, beaming.

'Well, I've actually turned him down. And I'm signed up

to retrain as a Macmillan nurse. I spent a lot of time with them when my husband was dying and they made a huge impression on me. I feel like I want to give something back.'

'That's wonderful, Rachel, really,' Felicity said. 'I'm sure your husband would be very proud of you.'

'Thank you, Felicity. Yes, I think he would be,' Rachel said as the three of them walked towards the church.

'That's a lovely picture of Amanda, Emma,' Felicity noted, looking down at the photograph of Amanda smiling into the camera, with her signature blonde plaits and fixed gaze.

'I thought it captured her spirit,' Emma said. 'I found it in the flat when I was going through her things.'

Emma paused before going on. 'I have such mixed feelings about Amanda. She put you all through so much anguish, but for that period of time in prison, she was the best friend I ever had, and gave me the confidence to stand up for myself. There but for the grace of God go I. Like Amanda, I would be totally alone in the world, if not for you.'

'You do have us, and you will never be alone in the world again,' Felicity said.

As they approached the door of the church, Emma stopped suddenly and turned to her mother. 'We are standing on the steps where I was left, Mum,' said Emma, her eyes glistening with tears.

Felicity looked at her daughter, and then put her arms around her. 'So we are, my darling. And just look how far we've come,' she said, linking her arms through Emma and Rachel's as they walked into St Phillip's, passing the portrait of Amanda at the entrance, her eyes dancing mischievously in the bright winter sunshine.

Author's Note

When my agent, Rowan Lawton, suggested Greenham Common as the backdrop for my fifth novel, I had little idea about the incredible legacy of the women who campaigned there for eighteen years. According to the *Guardian*, Greenham was the largest female-led protest since the woman's suffrage movement in the 1900s, yet you're unlikely to find anyone under fifty who knows much about it.

In 1981 a small group of women, with no political experience, angered by the decision to site America's guided nuclear missiles in the UK, organised a one-hundred-and-twenty-mile protest march from Cardiff to Greenham Common Air Base in Berkshire. They were mothers, who had heard on the radio that, in the event of a nuclear attack, they would have just four minutes to find their children and say goodbye.

Although they tried to garner some press interest along the way, nobody was interested. When the group of thirty-six women finally arrived at the base, the security guards thought they were the cleaners. The women, at a loss, decided to set up camp and 'do a suffragette', chaining themselves to the fence. And so what started at a kitchen table in Wales, inspired a global movement. The Greenham women, and hundreds and thousands of protestors, gave us back our future.

Life at the camp was very tough, so numbers ebbed and flowed. Winter was torture: the rain and snow, alongside locals throwing slurry and pig's blood at them, and the council raiding the camps and confiscating any shelter or food they had on an almost daily basis meant morale got low.

'However hard it was, imagine how much harder a nuclear winter would be,' was the basis of their resolve.

The narrative given by Michael Heseltine was that without nuclear weapons we were vulnerable and open to attack; a popular stance amongst the British people. But it was the Greenham women's belief that the country was dangerously close to the threat of nuclear war and that, contrary to the belief that we needed to be armed to the teeth to combat the threat from Russia (with American weapons, under America's control, on British soil), if they could sway public opinion both in the UK and Russia, it would serve to calm the situation down on both sides.

And so, as part of their campaign, they did just that and travelled to Russia to speak with their Russian counterparts: women and men in Moscow who felt just as passionately as they did.

Nobody, in Russia or in the UK, wanted nuclear war. It was up to the Greenham women to convince the British public, and our leaders, of that. But none of the press were prepared to listen. It is fair to say the British media was predominantly misogynistic, created by men, for men.

Although we had our first female prime minister at the time, to call Margaret Thatcher a feminist would be to discredit the whole movement. As Zac Denman stated, 'Thatcher pulled the ladder up and blocked the entrance. She actively removed herself from women's causes, and she made no secret of her disdain for the feminist movement. She famously told Paul Johnson, the editor of the *New Statesman*, 'I hate feminism. It is a poison.'

According to the *Guardian*, 'Much of the tabloid media was prejudicial and referred to Greenham inhabitants as "dirty, filthy lesbians" . . . This was also a time when homophobia was rampant, ahead of section 28, and lesbians were losing custody of their children to violent spouses.' The camp provided a lot of women with a safe space from male violence. Greenham women made connections between policing, militarism, war and everyday male violence towards women. The Greenham camp and its slogans 'Arms are for linking' and 'Fight war, not wars', became an embarrassment to the British and US governments as the *Guardian* points out. So the Greenham women were silenced. It stands to reason perhaps that Greenham represented women saying no more to male oppression. But rather than explore this in the press, it was easier to condemn leftwing feminists and anti-war activists with one toxic slur, according to the *Guardian*.

When asked why men weren't allowed to join the camp, the women very openly said that any men who came changed the feel of the camps: they wanted to take over, organise and dominate. But Rebecca Johnson remains very grateful for the role that the men played to support the women. Greenham's success, she argues, 'includes a whole lot of men and a whole lot of boys growing up who were connected to every single woman who ever went to Greenham, whether she went for a day or she lived there for several years. Greenham had an impact on how we live our lives.' However, it still doesn't explain why the Greenham women haven't made it into school classrooms. Perhaps it is due to the fact that some people I spoke to still don't accept that the Greenham women had any part to play in helping to end the Cold War. But there is no doubt that the women had a huge role in waking up ordinary people, by making headlines, something that nearly broke them. After two years, the camp was dying out. They had no supplies, no press coverage, and they were quite literally freezing to death. They badly needed a PR stunt to jump-start their campaign. Then someone had the crazy idea to get as many women as they could to encircle the entire nine-mile perimeter of the Greenham Common airbase. It would prove they had support and give them a voice in the press. They estimated it would take 16,000 women to surround the base. Everyone told them they were insane. But they had to try.

With no mobile phones, social media or media support, each woman at the camp phoned five women and asked them to come to Embrace the Base. Then those five women phoned five women. And so on. They had no idea if anyone would come, but they knew it was their last hope.

At five o'clock in the morning of Embrace the Base, the first coachloads of women started to arrive at Greenham, and by the end of the day 35,000 women surrounded it. Organisers had feared that they would have to use lengths of string and material to help make up the circle, but the reality was that the women who turned up struggled to find a space in the circle.

When the women held hands, and joined the circle, there was an eruption of joy – and at last they had the press coverage they so desperately needed. Embrace the Base made the front-page headlines in every national newspaper in the country. The tide started to turn and as the protests grew in strength and numbers, there was a feeling in the UK and Russia that sense was beginning to prevail.

In September 2004 Mikhail Gorbachev came to London,

after signing the INF treaty with Ronald Reagan banning mid-range nuclear missiles, in 1987, something that had taken everybody by surprise.

He was asked at a press conference what it was that made him think he could trust Ronald Reagan, after Reagan had called the Soviet Union 'the evil empire'.

His answer gave the Greenham women all the vindication that they needed. 'I didn't think I could trust Reagan. But I knew I could trust the Greenham Common women not to let Reagan use it against me.' It wasn't Reagan that Gorbachev trusted, it was the Greenham women.

It was the Greenham Common women that helped the INF treaty become possible, and this led to the end of the Cold War.

As Catherine Fitzpatrick, Russian translator and Research Director pointed out, 'You don't get an INF treaty just by focusing on the missiles themselves. You get treaties when the nature of the regime changes. This inspires more trust. The belief that they are not capable of firing these weapons.' Nobody told the Greenham women anything about the INF treaty. When the army went in to fly the weapons out, the women actually thought they were flying more weapons in, and they stormed the runway. A local policeman well known to them stopped them and exclaimed, 'They are taking the missiles away, isn't that what you wanted?'

In 2000, the women reached their final goal. Eighteen years after the camp was formed, the common was returned to the people.

What started at a kitchen table in Wales inspired a global movement. One that deserves to be part of every school curriculum across the country.

Acknowledgements

I'm very grateful to a number of people who gave me hours of their precious time, providing research material, moral support, and tea, when I needed it most.

I always feel I have a guardian angel when I first start to pull together a plot. People who know about the topic I'm investigating seem to appear from nowhere. This time when I was giving a talk at the Women's Institute in Llanedi – the small village in South Wales where we live – they asked about the new book and I told them the subject was Greenham. 'Oh, you must talk to Pat. She was part of the initial march from Cardiff to Greenham in 1981!'

I did indeed talk to Patricia Rudland-Gill and her friend Sue Davies, who I would like to thank from the bottom of my heart for sharing many precious and emotional memories from their time at Greenham – as did Diana Clarke, who was introduced to me by my lovely friend Avrina Eggleston. Thank you also to former Royal Marine Al Floyd for his wonderful insights into his work at Greenham Common and other military bases in the late eighties.

Thank you, as always, to my mother-in-law Sue Kerry, for thrashing out the plot with me, patiently answering my never ending questions about her time at Sussex Police, and also for her brainwave about the wills. Thank you also to Michelle Bowen FCILEx for her invaluable legal input. Thanks also go to Jeremy Pendlebury (7BR Chambers) who is always incredibly generous with his time regarding any court queries I have.

Thank you to Sarah Marshall, for talking to me about how she juggles her work as a successful estate agent with being a mum of two. And thanks also to Jo Bish for sharing her knowledge of all things adoption, and also for her love and support as a friend. Thanks to Matthew Taylor, commercial diver, who gave up a whole afternoon discussing a plot strand that didn't make the final cut – it was still a huge contributing factor in honing and polishing my plot. Thank you also to Howell Jenkins for lending me his name.

Heartfelt thanks to my wonderful editor, Sherise Hobbs, who never fails to bring/drag out the best in me. And I feel very indebted also to my kind, talented and effervescent agent, Rowan Lawton, and her wonderful assistant, Eleanor Lawlor, for whom nothing is too much trouble.

Thank you to my Ya Ya Sisterhood: Clodagh Hartley, Claire Quy, Safaloy Lamond, Rebecca Cootes, Claire Perry-Riquet, Lisa Jenkins, Kate Osbaldeston, Josie Aggett, Hazel John, Harriet De Bene and Suzanne Lindfors for your unwavering friendship.

Last but not least, thank you to Steve Gunnis for your unwavering support and faith in me. And to my beautiful daughters Grace and Eleanor for showing me what love is.

Useful Sources

Documentaries

'Carry Greenham Home' – a 1983 documentary about the Greenham Common Women's Peace Camp created by Amanda Richardson and Beeban Kidron.

'Greenham' – a documentary film with archive from the period and new interviews combined to tell the story of Greenham Common (S4C).

'Mothers of the Revolution' – a feature-length documentary directed by Briar March.

Podcasts

The Greenham Common Women's Peace Camp – The History Hour, BBC.

Greenham Uncommon – a podcast by Greenham Women Everywhere, a partnership project between Scary Little Girls and The Heroine Collective.

Books and online articles

Out of the Darkness: Greenham Voices 1981–2000 by Kate Kerrow and Rebecca Mordan (The History Press).

'The Greenham Factor' by Rebecca Johnson – a booklet published in 1983–84 to raise funds for the Peace Camp at Greenham Common. It contains photos and quotes from many women who lived at the Camp in 1982–83, including the famous photo of women dancing on the cruise missile silo.

'Greenham Common – A Chronology', *Guardian* Newsroom.

Julie Bindel, 'Greenham Common at 40: We came to fight war and stayed for the feminism', *Guardian* – 29 August 2021.

Alex Meakin, 'Remembering RAF Greenham Common 25 years on', *BBC News*, 8 April 2025.

Jane Powell, 'Greenham Common Peace Camp Changed the World and my life', *pen Democracy*, 8 November 2021.

Rebecca Johnson, 'Date with History: What we Greenham Common women achieved', *Chatham House*, 28 July 2023.

Suzanne Moore et al., 'How the Greenham Common protests changed lives: We danced on top of the nuclear silos"', *Guardian*, 20th March 2017.

Neil Prior, 'From Rhondda to Greenham and the US Supreme Court', *BBC News*, 25 August 2021.

Celia Oultram-Turner, 'The Sound of Greenham Common Women's Peace Camp', Imperial War Museums website, 13 May 2021.

'The Speech We Ignored: Lord Louis Mountbatten on Nuclear War, May 11, 1979, Bible Student Archive

'The Defence of Britain | Michael Heseltine interview – Greenham Common', *TV Eye*, 31 March 1983.

Zac Denman, 'To Call Margaret Thatcher a Feminist is to Discredit the Whole Movement', *The Egalitarian*, 18 January 2024.

Various contributors, *Greenham Common Women's Peace Camp Songbook*

THE GIRL IN THE LETTER

Emily Gunnis

A heartbreaking letter. A girl locked away.
A mystery to be solved.

1956. When Ivy Jenkins falls pregnant
she is sent in disgrace to St Margaret's, a dark,
brooding house for unmarried mothers. Her baby
is adopted against her will. Ivy will never leave.

Present day. Samantha Harper is a journalist
desperate for a break. When she stumbles on a letter
from the past, the contents shock and move her.
The letter is from a young mother, begging to be
rescued from St Margaret's. Before it is too late.

Sam is pulled into the tragic story and discovers
a spate of unexplained deaths surrounding the
woman and her child. With St Margaret's set for
demolition, Sam has only hours to piece together
a sixty-year-old mystery before the truth, which lies
disturbingly close to home, is lost for ever. . .

Available to order now

H
REVIEW

THE MISSING DAUGHTER

Emily Gunnis

Some secrets are locked away for years . . .

Rebecca Waterhouse is just thirteen when
she witnesses her mother's death at the hand
of her father in Seaview Cottage.
But what else did she see?

Years later, Rebecca's daughters Iris and Jessie know
their mother will never speak of that terrible night.
But when Jessie goes missing, with her gravely
ill newborn, Iris realises the past may hold
the key to her sister's disappearance.

With Jessie in trouble, Iris must unravel
a twisting story of love and betrayal in
her mother's family history.

Only then will Seaview Cottage give up
its dark and tragic secret. . .

Available to order now

H
REVIEW

THE MIDWIFE'S SECRET

Emily Gunnis

It all began with a midwife's secret, long buried but if uncovered could save two families from the bitter tragedy that binds them. And prove the key that will free them all...

1969 On New Year's Eve, while the Hiltons of Yew Tree Manor prepare to host the party of the season, their little girl disappears. Suspicion falls on Bobby James, a young farmhand and the last person to see Alice before she vanished. Bobby protests his innocence, but he is sent away. Alice is never found.

Present day Architect Willow James is working on a development at Yew Tree when she discovers the land holds a secret. As she begins to dig deep into the past, she uncovers a web of injustice. And when another child goes missing, Willow knows the only way to stop history repeating itself is to right a terrible wrong...

Available to order now

H

REVIEW

THE GIRLS LEFT BEHIND

Emily Gunnis

No one wanted to end up at Morgate House,
but the girls had nowhere else to go. . .

1985. Separated from her little sister at the
children's home where they are taken as orphans,
Holly Moore is a troubled teenager in need of love.
When she meets a man who promises to take care
of her, she hopes her luck has finally changed.

2015. The clock is ticking for Superintendent Jo
Hamilton when the discovery of a young woman's
remains takes her back to an unsolved case from
the past. As a constable, Jo was often called out
to deal with runaways from Morgate House, but
when Holly Moore disappeared – after another
female resident fell from the cliffs – Jo was
convinced the home was hiding something. Now,
with only days before her forced retirement,
Jo decides to track down Holly's sister
and re-open the case. But will the trail
lead her disturbingly close to home?

Available to order now

REVIEW

Dear Reader,

We'd love your attention for one more page to tell you about the crisis in children's reading, and what we can all do.

Studies have shown that reading for fun is the **single biggest predictor of a child's future success** – more than family circumstance, parents' educational background or income. It improves academic results, mental health, wealth, communication skills and ambition.

The number of children reading for fun is in rapid decline. Young people have a lot of competition for their time, and a worryingly high number do not have a single book at home.

Our business works extensively with schools, libraries and literacy charities, but here are some ways we can all raise more readers:

- Reading to children for just 10 minutes a day makes a difference
- Don't give up if your children aren't regular readers – there will be books for them!
- Visit bookshops and libraries to get recommendations
- Encourage them to listen to audiobooks
- Support school libraries
- Give books as gifts

Thank you for reading.
www.JoinRaisingReaders.com